smile :)

Replacement
Copy — Give
to ROHN !

strong

D0381999

ALSO BY LAUREN KATE

FALLEN

TORMENT

LAUREN KATE

PASSION

A FALLEN NOVEL

DELACORTE PRESS

Text copyright © 2011 by Tinderbox Books, LLC and Lauren Kate

TINDERBOX

Jacket illustrations © 2011 by Fernanda Brussi Gonçalves with Rebecca Roeske

All rights reserved. Published in the United States by Delacorte Press,
an imprint of Random House Children's Books,
a division of Random House, Inc., New York.

Delacorte Press is a registered trademark and the colophon is a trademark of
Random House, Inc.

WWW.RANDOMHOUSE.COM/TEENS
WWW.FALLENBOOKS.COM

Library of Congress Cataloging-in-Publication Data is available upon request.
ISBN: 978-0-385-73916-0 (trade)
ISBN: 978-0-385-90774-3 (lib. bdg.)
ISBN: 978-0-375-89718-4 (ebook)

The text of this book is set in 12-point Classical Garamond BT.

Book design by Angela Carlino

Printed in the United States of America

10 9 8 7 6 5 4 3 2 1

First Edition

FOR M AND T,
HEAVEN-SENT MESSENGERS

ACKNOWLEDGMENTS

Impassioned thanks to Wendy Loggia, who envisioned this crazy book and whose sane support carries the series. To Beverly Horowitz, for her wisdom and style. To Michael Stearns and Ted Malawer, for making things soar. To Noreen Herits and Roshan Nozari: my gratitude for all you do deepens with each book. Special thanks to Krista Vitola, Barbara Perris, Angela Carlino, Judith Haut (I'll meet you at the Cheese Dip Festival in Little Rock)—and to Chip Gibson, whose trickle-down Chipenomics explains why everyone at Random House is so damn cool.

To the friends I've made around the world: Becky Stradwick and Lauren Bennett (fellow Lauren Kate!) in the UK, to Rino Balatbat and the folks at National Book Store in the Philippines, to the whole enthusiastic team at Random House Australia, to bloggers near and far. I'm honored to work with every one of you.

To my tremendous, loving family, with a special materteral shout-out to Jordan, Hailey, and David Franklin. To Anna Carey for the hikes and more. To the OBLC, whoop. And to Jason, my muse, my world, it just gets better all the time.

Failing to catch me at first keep encouraged,

Missing me one place search another,

I stop somewhere waiting for you.

⚜

—WALT WHITMAN, *Song of Myself*

PROLOGUE

❧ ✦ ☙

DARK HORSE

A shot rang out. A broad gate banged open. A pounding of horses' hooves echoed around the track like a massive clap of thunder.

"And they're off!"

Sophia Bliss adjusted the wide brim of her feathered hat. It was a muted shade of mauve, twenty-seven inches in diameter, with a drop-down chiffon veil. Large enough to make her look like a proper horseracing enthusiast, not so gaudy as to attract undue attention.

Three hats had been special-ordered from the same milliner in Hilton Head for the race that day. One—a butter-yellow bonnet—capped the snow-white head of Lyrica Crisp, who was sitting to the left of Miss Sophia, enjoying a corned beef sandwich. The other—a sea-foam-green felt hat with a fat polka-dotted satin ribbon—crowned the jet-black mane of Vivina Sole, who sat looking deceptively demure with her white-gloved hands crossed over her lap to Miss Sophia's right.

"Glorious day for a race," Lyrica said. At 136 years old, she was the youngest of the Elders of Zhsmaelim. She wiped a dot of mustard from the corner of her mouth. "Can you believe it's my first time at the tracks?"

"Shhh," Sophia hissed. Lyrica was such a twit. Today was not about horses at all, but rather a clandestine meeting of great minds. So what if the other great minds didn't happen to have shown up yet? They would be here. At this perfectly neutral location set forth in the gold letterpress invitation Sophia had received from an unknown sender. The others would be here to reveal themselves and come up with a plan of attack together. Any minute now. She hoped.

"Lovely day, lovely sport," Vivina said dryly. "Pity *our* horse in this race doesn't run in easy circles like these fillies. Isn't it, Sophia? Tough to wager where the thoroughbred Lucinda will finish."

"I said *shhh*," Sophia whispered. "Bite your cavalier tongue. There are spies everywhere."

"You're paranoid," Vivina said, drawing a high giggle from Lyrica.

"I'm what's left," Sophia said.

There used to be so many more—twenty-four Elders at the peak of the Zhsmaelim. A cluster of mortals, immortals, and a few transeternals, like Sophia herself. An axis of knowledge and passion and faith with a single uniting goal: to restore the world to its prelapsarian state, that brief, glorious moment before the angels' Fall. For better or for worse.

It was written, plain as day, in the code they'd drawn up together and had each signed: *For better or for worse.*

Because really, it could go either way.

Every coin had two sides. Heads and tails. Light and dark. Good and—

Well, the fact that the other Elders hadn't prepared themselves for both options was not Sophia's fault. It was, however, her cross to bear when one by one they sent in notices of their withdrawal. *Your purposes grow too dark.* Or: *The organization's standards have fallen.* Or: *The Elders have strayed too far from the original code.* The first flurry of letters arrived, predictably, within a week after the incident with the girl Pennyweather. They couldn't abide it, they'd claimed, the death of one small insignificant child. One careless moment with a dagger and suddenly the Elders were running scared, all of them fearing the wrath of the Scale.

Cowards.

Sophia did not fear the Scale. Their charge was to parole the fallen, not the righteous. Groundling angels such as Roland Sparks and Arriane Alter. As long as one did not defect from Heaven, one was free to sway a little. Desperate times practically begged for it. Sophia had nearly gone cross-eyed reading the spongy-hearted excuses of the other Elders. But even if she *had* wanted the defectors back—which she had not—there was nothing to be done.

Sophia Bliss—the school librarian who had only ever served as secretary on the Zhsmaelim board—was now the highest-ranking official among the Elders. There were just twelve of them left. And nine could not be trusted.

So that left the three of them here today in their enormous pastel hats, placing phony bets at the track. And waiting. It was pathetic, the depths to which they'd sunk.

A race came to its end. A staticky loudspeaker announced the winners and the odds for the next race. Well-heeled people and drunks all around them cheered or slumped lower in their seats.

And a girl, about nineteen, with a white-blond ponytail, brown trench coat, and thick, dark sunglasses, walked slowly up the aluminum steps toward the Elders.

Sophia stiffened. Why would *she* be here?

It was next to impossible to tell which direction the girl was looking in, and Sophia was trying hard not to stare. Not that it would matter; the girl wouldn't be able to see her. She was blind. But then—

The Outcast nodded once at Sophia. Oh yes—these fools could see the burning of a person's soul. It was dim, but Sophia's life force must still have been visible.

The girl took a seat in the empty row in front of the Elders, facing the track and flipping though a five-dollar tip sheet her blind eyes wouldn't be able to read.

"Hello." The Outcast's voice was a monotone. She didn't turn around.

"I really don't know why you're here," Miss Sophia said. It was a damp November day in Kentucky, but a sheen of sweat had broken out across her forehead. "Our collaboration ended when your cohorts failed to retrieve the girl. No amount of bitter blabber from the one who calls himself Phillip will change our minds." Sophia leaned forward, closer to the girl, and wrinkled her nose. "Everyone knows the Outcasts aren't to be trusted—"

"We are not here on business with you," the Outcast said, staring straight ahead. "You were but a vessel to get us closer to Lucinda. We remain uninterested in 'collaborating' with you."

"No one cares about your organization these days." Footsteps on the bleachers.

The boy was tall and slender, with a shaven head and a trench coat to match the girl's. His sunglasses were the cheap plastic variety found near the batteries at the drugstore.

Phillip slid onto the bleacher right next to Lyrica

Crisp. Like the Outcast girl, he didn't turn to face them when he spoke.

"I'm not surprised to find you here, Sophia." He lowered his sunglasses on his nose, revealing two empty white eyes. "Just disappointed that you didn't feel you could tell me that you'd been invited as well."

Lyrica gasped at the horrible white expanses behind his glasses. Even Vivina lost her cool and reared back. Sophia boiled inside.

The Outcast girl raised a golden card—the same invitation Sophia had received—scissored between her fingers. "We received this." Only, this one looked like it had been written in Braille. Sophia reached for it to make sure, but with a quick movement, the invitation disappeared back inside the girl's trench coat.

"Look, you little punks. I branded your starshots with the emblem of the Elders. You work for *me*—"

"Correction," Phillip said. "The Outcasts work for no one but themselves."

Sophia watched him crane his neck slightly, pretending to follow a horse around the track. She'd always thought it was eerie, the way they gave off the impression that they could see. When everyone knew *he'd* struck the lot of them blind with the flick of a finger.

"Shame you did such a poor job capturing her." Sophia felt her voice rise higher than she knew it should, drawing the eyes of an older couple crossing the grandstand. "We were supposed to work together," she hissed, "to hunt her down, and—and you failed."

"It would not have mattered one way or another."

"Come again?"

"She would still be lost in time. It was always her destiny. And the Elders would still be hanging on by a thread. That is yours."

She wanted to lunge at him, wanted to strangle him until those great white eyes bulged from their sockets. Her dagger felt like it was burning a hole through the calfskin handbag on her lap. If only it had been a star-shot. Sophia was rising from the bleacher when the voice came from behind them.

"Please be seated," it boomed. "This meeting is now called to order."

The voice. She knew at once whose it was. Calm and authoritative. Utterly humbling. It made the bleachers quake.

The nearby mortals noticed nothing, but a flush of heat rose on the back of Sophia's neck. It trickled through her body, numbing her. This was no ordinary fear. This was a crippling, stomach-souring terror. Did she dare to turn around?

The subtlest peek from the corner of her eye revealed a man in a tailored black suit. His dark hair was clipped short under his black hat. The face, kind and attractive, was not particularly memorable. Clean-shaven, straight-nosed, with brown eyes that felt familiar. Yet Miss Sophia had never seen him before. And still she knew who he was, knew it in the marrow of her bones.

"Where is Cam?" the voice behind them asked. "He was sent an invitation."

"Probably playing God inside the Announcers. Like the rest of them," Lyrica blurted out. Sophia swatted her.

"Playing *God*, did you say?"

Sophia searched for the words that would fix a gaffe like that. "Several of the others followed Lucinda backward into time," she said eventually. "Including two Nephilim. We aren't sure how many others."

"Dare I ask," the voice said, suddenly ice-cold, "why none of *you* elected to go after her?"

Sophia fought to swallow, to breathe. Her most intuitive movements were stunted by panic. "We can't exactly, well . . . We don't yet have the capabilities to—"

The Outcast girl cut her off. "The Outcasts are in the process of—"

"Silence," the voice commanded. "Spare me your excuses. They no longer matter, as you no longer matter."

For a long time, their group was quiet. It was terrifying not to know how to please him. When he finally spoke, his voice was softer, but no less lethal. "Too much at stake. I can't leave anything else to chance."

A pause.

Then, softly, he said, "The time has come for me to take matters into my own hands."

Sophia bit her gasp in two to hide her horror. But she could not stop her body's tremors. His direct involvement? Truly, it was the most terrifying prospect. She could not imagine working *with* him to—

"The rest of you will stay out of this," he said. "That is all."

"But—" It was an accident, but the word escaped Sophia's lips. She could not take it back. But all her decades of labor. All her plans. Her plans!

What came next was a long, earth-shattering roar.

It reverberated up through the bleachers, seeming to travel around the entire racetrack in a splinter of a second.

Sophia cringed. The noise seemed almost to crash *into* her, through her skin and down to her deepest core. She felt as if her heart was being drummed to pieces.

Lyrica and Vivina both pressed against her, eyes clamped shut. Even the Outcasts trembled.

Just when Sophia thought the sound of it would never cease, that it would be the death of her at last, his roar gave way to absolute pin-drop silence.

For a moment.

Enough time to look around and see that the other people at the racetrack had not heard anything at all.

In her ear he whispered, "Your time on this endeavor is up. Do not dare to get in my way."

Down below, another shot rang out. The broad gate banged open once again. Only this time, the pounding of horses' hooves against the dirt sounded like practically nothing, like the lightest rainfall falling on a canopy of trees.

Before the racehorses had crossed the starting line, the figure behind them had vanished, leaving only the mark of coal-black hoofprints singed into the planks of the grandstand.

ONE

UNDER FIRE

Moscow · October 15, 1941

Lucinda!

The voices reached her in the murky darkness.

Come back!

Wait!

She ignored them, pressing further. Echoes of her name bounced off the shadowy walls of the Announcer, sending licks of heat rippling across her skin. Was that Daniel's voice or Cam's? Arriane's or Gabbe's? Was it Roland pleading that she come back now, or was that Miles?

The calls grew harder to discern, until Luce couldn't tell them apart at all: good or evil. Enemy or friend. They should have been easier to separate, but nothing was easy anymore. Everything that had once been black and white now blended into gray.

Of course, both sides agreed on one thing: Everyone wanted to pull her out of the Announcer. For her *protection,* they would claim.

No, thanks.

Not now.

Not after they'd wrecked her parents' backyard, made it into another one of their dusty battlefields. She couldn't think about her parents' faces without wanting to turn back—not like she'd even know how to turn back inside an Announcer, anyway. Besides, it was too late. Cam had tried to *kill* her. Or what he thought was her. And Miles had saved her, but even that wasn't simple. He'd only been able to throw her reflection because he cared about her *too* much.

And Daniel? Did he care enough? She couldn't tell.

In the end, when the Outcast had approached her, Daniel and the others had stared at Luce like *she* was the one who owed *them* something.

You are our entrance into Heaven, the Outcast had told her. *The price.* What had that meant? Until a couple of weeks ago she hadn't even known the Outcasts existed. And yet, they wanted something from her—badly enough to battle Daniel for it. It must have had to do with the curse, the one that kept Luce reincarnated lifetime after lifetime. But what did they think Luce could do?

Was the answer buried somewhere here?

Her stomach lurched as she tumbled senselessly through the cold shadow, deep inside the chasm of the dark Announcer.

Luce—

The voices began to fade and grow dimmer. Soon they were barely whispers. Almost like they had given up. Until—

They started to grow louder again. Louder and clearer.

Luce—

No. She clamped her eyes shut to try to block them out.

Lucinda—

Lucy—

Lucia—

Luschka—

She was cold and she was tired and she didn't want to hear them. For once, she wanted to be left alone.

Luschka! Luschka! Luschka!

Her feet hit something with a *thwump.*

Something very, very cold.

She was standing on solid ground. She knew she wasn't tumbling anymore, though she couldn't see anything in front of her except for the blanket of blackness. Then she looked down at her Converse sneakers.

And gulped.

They were planted in a blanket of snow that reached midway up her calves. The dank coolness that she was used to—the shadowy tunnel she'd been traveling through, out of her backyard, into the past—was giving way to something else. Something blustery and absolutely frigid.

The first time Luce had stepped through an Announcer—from her Shoreline dorm room to Las Vegas—she'd been with her friends Shelby and Miles. At the end of the passage they'd met a barrier: a dark, shadowy curtain between them and the city. Because Miles was the only one who'd read the texts on stepping through, he'd started swiping the Announcer with a circular motion until the murky black shadow flaked away. Luce hadn't known until now that he'd been trouble-shooting.

This time, there was no barrier. Maybe because she was traveling alone, through an Announcer summoned of her own fierce will. But the way out was so easy. Almost too easy. The veil of blackness simply parted.

A blast of cold tore into her, making her knees lock with the chill. Her ribs stiffened and her eyes teared in the sharp, sudden wind.

Where was she?

Luce already regretted her panicked jump through time. Yes, she needed an escape, and yes, she wanted to trace her past, to save her former selves from all the pain, to understand what kind of love she'd had with Daniel all those other times. To *feel* it instead of being told about it. To understand—and then fix—whatever curse had been inflicted on Daniel and her.

But not like this. Frozen, alone, and completely unprepared for wherever, whenever she was.

She could see a snowy street in front of her, a steel-gray sky above white buildings. She could hear something rumbling in the distance. But she didn't want to think about what any of it meant.

"Wait," she whispered to the Announcer.

The shadow drifted hazily a foot or so beyond her fingertips. She tried to grasp it, but the Announcer eluded her, flicking farther away. She leaped for it, and caught a tiny damp piece of it between her fingers—

But then, in an instant, the Announcer shattered into soft black fragments on the snow. They faded, then were gone.

"Great," she muttered. "Now what?"

In the distance, the narrow road curved left to meet a shadowy intersection. The sidewalks were piled high with shoveled snow, which had been packed against two long banks of white stone buildings. They were striking, unlike anything Luce had ever seen, a few stories tall, with their entire façades carved into rows of bright white arches and elaborate columns.

All the windows were dark. Luce got the sense that the whole city might be dark. The only light came from a single gas streetlamp. If there was any moon, it was hidden by a thick blanket of cloud. Again something rumbled in the sky. Thunder?

Luce hugged her arms around her chest. She was freezing.

"Luschka!"

A woman's voice. Hoarse and raspy, like someone who'd spent her whole life barking orders. But the voice was trembling, too.

"Luschka, you idiot. Where are you?"

She sounded closer now. Was she talking to Luce? There was something else about that voice, something strange that Luce couldn't quite put into words.

When a figure came hobbling around the snowy street corner, Luce stared at the woman, trying to place her. She was very short and a little hunched over, maybe in her late sixties. Her bulky clothes seemed too big for her body. Her hair was tucked under a thick black scarf. When she saw Luce, her face scrunched into a complicated grimace.

"Where have you been?"

Luce looked around. She was the only other person on the street. The old woman was speaking to her.

"Right here," she heard herself say.

In Russian.

She clapped a hand over her mouth. So *that* was what had seemed so bizarre about the old woman's voice: She was speaking a language Luce had never learned. And yet, not only did Luce understand every word, but she could speak it back.

"I could kill you," the woman said, breathing heavily as she rushed toward Luce and threw her arms around her.

For such a frail-looking woman, her embrace was strong. The warmth of another body pressing into Luce after so much intense cold made her almost want to cry. She hugged back hard.

"Grandma?" she whispered, her lips close to the woman's ear, somehow knowing that was who the woman was.

"Of all the nights I get off work to find you gone," the woman said. "Now you're skipping around in the middle of the street like a lunatic? Did you even go to work today? Where is your sister?"

There was the rumbling in the sky again. It sounded like a bad storm moving closer. Moving fast. Luce shivered and shook her head. She didn't know.

"Aha," the woman said. "Not so carefree now." She squinted at Luce, then pushed her away to get a closer look. "My God, what are you wearing?"

Luce fidgeted as her past life's grandmother gaped at her jeans and ran her knobby fingers over the buttons of Luce's flannel shirt. She grabbed Luce's short, tangled ponytail. "Sometimes I think you are as crazy as your father, may he rest in peace."

"I just—" Luce's teeth were chattering. "I didn't know it was going to be so cold."

The woman spat on the snow to show her disapproval. She peeled off her overcoat. "Take this before you catch your death." She bundled the coat roughly around Luce, whose fingers were half frozen as she struggled to button it. Then her grandmother untied the scarf from her neck and wrapped it around Luce's head.

A great boom in the sky startled both of them. Now Luce knew it wasn't thunder. "What is that?" she whispered.

The old woman stared at her. "The war," she muttered. "Did you lose your wits along with your clothes? Come now. We must go."

As they waded down the snowy street, over the rough cobbles and the tram tracks set into them, Luce realized that the city wasn't empty after all. Few cars were parked along the road, but occasionally, down the darkened side streets, she heard the whinnies of carriage horses waiting for orders, their frosty breaths clotting the air. Silhouetted bodies scampered across rooftops. Down an alley, a man in a torn overcoat helped three small children through the hatched doors of a basement.

At the end of the narrow street, the road opened onto a broad, tree-lined avenue with a wide view of the city. The only cars parked here were military vehicles. They looked old-fashioned, almost absurd, like relics in a war museum: soft-top jeeps with giant fenders, bone-thin steering wheels, and the Soviet hammer and sickle painted onto the doors. But aside from Luce and her grandmother, there were no people on this street. Everything—except for the awful rumbling in the sky—was ghostly, eerily quiet.

In the distance, she could see a river, and far across it, a great building. Even in the darkness, she could make out its elaborate tiered spires and ornate onion-shaped domes, which seemed familiar and mythic at the same time. It took a moment to sink in—and then fear shot through Luce.

She was in Moscow.

And the city was a war zone.

Black smoke rose in the gray sky, marking the pockets of the city that had already been hit: to the left of the vast Kremlin, and just behind it, and again in the distance to the far right. There was no combat on the streets, no sign that enemy soldiers had crossed into the city yet on foot. But the flames licking the charred buildings, the incendiary smell of war everywhere, and the threat of more to come were somehow even worse.

This was by far the most messed-up thing Luce had ever done in her life—probably in *any* of her lives. Her parents would *kill* her if they knew where she was. Daniel might never speak to her again.

But then: What if they didn't even have the chance to be furious with her? She could die, right here in this war zone.

Why had she done this?

Because she'd *had* to. It was hard to unearth that small hint of pride in the midst of her panic. But it must have been there somewhere.

She'd *stepped through*. On her own. Into a distant place and a faraway time, into the past she needed to understand. This was what she'd wanted. She'd been pushed around like a chess piece long enough.

But what was she supposed to do now?

She picked up her pace and held tight to her grandmother's hand. Strange, this woman had no real sense of what Luce was going through, no real idea of who she even was, and yet the tug of her dry grip was the only thing keeping Luce moving.

"Where are we going?" Luce asked as her grandmother yanked her down another darkened street. The cobblestones tapered off and the road became unpaved and slippery. The snow had soaked through the canvas of Luce's tennis shoes, and her toes were starting to burn with the cold.

"To collect your sister, Kristina." The old woman scowled. "The one who works nights digging army trenches with her bare hands so you can get your beauty rest. Remember her?"

Where they stopped, there was no streetlamp to light the road. Luce blinked a few times to help her eyes adjust. They were standing in front of what looked like a very long ditch, right in the middle of the city.

There must have been a hundred people there. All of them bundled up to their ears. Some were down on their knees, digging with shovels. Some were digging with their hands. Some stood as if frozen, watching the sky. A few soldiers carted off heavy loads of earth and rock in splintery wheelbarrows and farm carts to add to the rubble barricade at the end of the street. Their bodies were hidden under thick army-issue wool coats that billowed out around their knees, but beneath their steel hats, their faces were as gaunt as any of the civilians'. Lucinda understood that they were all working together, the men in uniform and the women and children, turning their city into a fortress, doing anything they could, down to the very last minute, to keep the enemy tanks out.

"Kristina," her grandmother called, the same notes of panic-washed love in her voice as when she'd been looking for Luce.

A girl appeared at their side almost instantly. "What took you so long?"

Tall and thin, with dark strands of hair escaping from under the porkpie hat on her head, Kristina was so beautiful, Luce had to swallow a lump in her throat. She recognized the girl as family right away.

Seeing Kristina reminded Luce of Vera, another past life's sister. Luce must have had a hundred sisters across time. A thousand. All of them would have gone through something similar. Sisters and brothers and parents and friends whom Luce must have loved, then lost. None of them had known what was coming. All of them had been left behind to grieve.

Maybe there was a way to change that, to make it easier on the people who'd loved her. Maybe that was part of what Luce could do in her past lives.

The great boom of something exploding sounded across town. Close enough that the ground rocked under Luce's feet and her right eardrum felt like it was splitting. On the corner, air-raid sirens started going off.

"Baba." Kristina took hold of her grandmother's arm. She was near tears. "The Nazis—they're here, aren't they?"

The Germans. Luce's first time stepping through time on her own and she'd landed smack in World War II. "They're attacking Moscow?" Her voice wobbled. "Tonight?"

"We should have left town with the others," Kristina said bitterly. "Now it is too late."

"And abandoned your mother and your father and your grandfather, too?" Baba shook her head. "Left them alone in their graves?"

"Better we should join them in the c Kristina spat back. She reached for Luce, sque arm. "Did you know about the raid? You and y friend? Is that why you didn't come to work th ing? You were with him, weren't you?"

What did her sister think Luce could possit known? Who would she have been with?

Who but Daniel?

Of course. Luschka must be with him right no if her own family members were confusing *that* L with Luce . . .

Her chest constricted. How much time did she left before she died? What if Luce could find Lus before it happened?

"Luschka."

Her sister and grandmother were staring at her.

"What's wrong with her tonight?" Kristina asked.

"Let's go." Baba scowled. "You think the Mosc vitches are going to hold open their basement forever

The long drone of a fighter plane's propelle sounded over them in the sky. Close enough that whe Luce looked up, the dark swastika painted on the under side of its wings was clear. It sent a shiver through her Then another boom rocked the city, and the air grew caustic with dark smoke. They'd hit something nearby. Two more massive explosions made the ground shudder beneath her feet.

It was chaos on the street. The crowd at the trenches

was disappearing, everyone scattering up a dozen narrow streets. Some hustled down the stairs of the metro station on the corner to wait out the bombs underground; others disappeared into dark doorways.

A block away, Luce caught a glimpse of someone running: a girl, about her age, in a red hat and a long wool coat. She turned her head for just a second before she sprinted on. But it was long enough for Luce to know.

There she was.

Luschka.

She wrestled free of Baba's arm. "I'm sorry. I have to go."

Luce took a deep breath and ran down the street, straight into the roiling smoke, toward the heaviest bombing.

"Are you crazy?" Kristina yelled. But they didn't follow her. They would have had to be crazy themselves.

Luce's feet were numb as she tried to run through the calf-high snow on the sidewalk. When she reached the corner where she'd seen her red-hatted past self dash by, she slowed. Then she sucked in her breath.

A building that took up half of the city block directly in front of her had caved in. White stone was streaked with black ash. A fire churned deep inside the crater in the building's side.

The explosion had spat out heaps of unrecognizable debris from inside the building. The snow was streaked with red. Luce recoiled until she realized that the red

streaks were not blood but shreds of red silk. It must have been a tailor's shop. Several badly singed racks of clothes were scattered in the street. A mannequin lay on its side in a ditch. It was on fire. Luce had to cover her mouth with her grandmother's scarf to keep from choking on the fumes. Everywhere she stepped, shattered glass and stone cut into the snow.

She should turn back, find the grandmother and sister who would help her get to shelter, but she couldn't. She had to find Luschka. She'd never been so close to one of her past selves before. Luschka might be able to help her understand why Luce's own lifetime was different. Why Cam had shot a starshot into her reflection, thinking it was her, and told Daniel, "It was a better end for her." A better end than what?

She slowly turned around, trying to spot the flash of the red hat in the night.

There.

The girl was running downhill toward the river. Luce started running, too.

They ran at precisely the same pace. When Luce ducked at the sound of an explosion, Luschka ducked, too—in a weird echo of Luce's own movement. And when they reached the riverbank, and the city came into view, Luschka froze into the exact same rigid stance as Luce herself.

Fifty yards in front of Luce, her mirror image began to sob.

So much of Moscow was burning. So many homes were being leveled. Luce tried to fathom the other lives being destroyed across the city tonight, but they felt distant and unreachable, like something she'd read about in a history book.

The girl was on the move again. Running so fast Luce couldn't have caught her if she'd wanted to. They ran around giant craters cut into the cobblestone road. They ran past burning buildings, crackling with the awful racket a fire makes when it spreads to a new target. They ran past smashed, overturned military trucks, blackened arms hanging out at the sides.

Then Luschka hooked left down a street and Luce couldn't see her anymore.

Adrenaline kicked in. Luce pressed forward, her feet pounding harder, faster on the snowy street. People only ran this fast when they were desperate. When something bigger than them spurred them on.

Luschka could only be running toward one thing.

"Luschka—"

His voice.

Where was he? For a moment, Luce forgot her past self, forgot the Russian girl whose life was in danger of ending at any moment, forgot that this Daniel wasn't *her* Daniel, but then—

Of course he was.

He never died. He had always been there. He was always hers and she was always his. All she wanted was to find his arms, to bury herself in their grasp. He would know what she should be doing; he would be able to help her. Why had she doubted him before?

She ran, pulled in the direction of his voice. But she couldn't see Daniel anywhere. Nor Luschka. A block away from the river, Luce stopped short in a barren intersection.

Her breath felt strangled in her frozen lungs. A cold, throbbing pain tunneled deep inside her ears, and the icy pinpricks stabbing her feet made standing still unbearable.

But which way should she go?

Before her was a vast and empty lot, filled with rubble and cordoned off from the street by scaffolding and an iron fence. But even in the darkness, Luce could tell that this was an older demolition, not something destroyed by a bomb in the air raids.

It didn't look like much, just an ugly, abandoned sinkhole. She didn't know why she was still standing in front of it. Why she'd stopped running after Daniel's voice—

Until she gripped the fence, blinked, and saw a flash of something brilliant.

A church. A majestic white church filling this gaping hole. A huge triptych of marble arches on the front façade. Five golden spires extending high into the sky. And inside:

rows of waxed wooden pews as far as the eye could see. An altar at the top of a white flight of stairs. And all the walls and high arched ceilings covered with gorgeously ornate frescoes. Angels everywhere.

The Church of Christ the Savior.

How did Luce know that? Why would she feel with every fiber of her being that this nothingness had once been a formidable white church?

Because she had been there moments before. She saw someone else's handprints in the ash on the metal: Luschka had stopped here, too, had gazed at the ruins of the church and felt something.

Luce gripped the railing and blinked again and saw herself—or Luschka—as a girl.

She was seated inside on one of the pews in a white lace dress. An organ played as people filed in before a service. The handsome man to her left must have been her father, and the woman next to him, her mother. There was the grandmother Luce had just met, and Kristina. Both of them looked younger, better fed. Luce remembered her grandmother saying that both her parents were dead. But here they looked so alive. They seemed to know everyone, greeting each family passing their pew. Luce studied her past self watching her father as he shook hands with a good-looking young blond man. The young man leaned down over the pew and smiled at her. He had the most beautiful violet eyes.

She blinked again and the vision disappeared. The lot was once again little more than rubble. She was freezing. And alone. Another bomb went off across the river, and the shock of it dropped Luce to her knees. She covered her face with her hands—

Until she heard someone softly crying. She lifted her head and squinted into the deeper darkness of the ruins, and she saw him.

"Daniel," she whispered. He looked just the same. Almost radiating light, even in the freezing darkness. The blond hair she never wanted to stop running her fingers through, the violet-gray eyes that seemed to have been made to lock with hers. That formidable face, the high cheekbones, those lips. Her heart pounded and she had to tighten her grip on the iron fence to keep from running to him.

Because he wasn't alone.

He was with Luschka. Consoling her, stroking her cheek and kissing her tears away. Their arms were wrapped around one another, their heads tipped forward in a never-ending kiss. They were so lost in their embrace they didn't seem to feel the street rolling and quaking with another explosion. They looked like all there was in the world was just the two of them.

There was no space between their bodies. It was too dim to see where one of them ended and the other one began.

Lucinda got to her feet and crept forward, moving from one pile of rubble in the dark to the next, just longing to be closer to him.

"I thought I'd never find you," Luce heard her past self say.

"We will always find each other," Daniel answered, lifting her off the ground and squeezing her closer. "Always."

"Hey, you two!" A voice shouted from a doorway in a neighboring building. "Are you coming?"

Across the square from the empty lot, a small group of people were being herded into a solid stone building by a guy whose face Luce couldn't make out. That was where Luschka and Daniel were headed. It must have been their plan all along, to take shelter from the bombs together.

"Yes," Luschka called to the others. She looked at Daniel. "Let's go with them."

"No." His voice was curt. Nervous. Luce knew that tone all too well.

"We'll be safer off the street. Isn't this why we agreed to meet here?"

Daniel turned to look back behind them, his eyes sweeping right past the place where Luce was hiding. When the sky lit up with another round of golden-red explosions, Luschka screamed and buried her face in Daniel's chest. So Luce was the only one who saw his expression.

Something was weighing on him. Something greater than fear of the bombs.

Oh no.

"Daniil!" A boy near the building was still holding open the door to the shelter. "Luschka! Daniil!"

Everyone else was already inside.

That was when Daniil spun Luschka around, pulled her ear close to his lips. In her shadowy hiding place, Luce ached to know what he was whispering. If he was saying any of the things Daniel ever told *her* when she was upset or overwhelmed. She wanted to run to them, to pull Luschka away—but she couldn't. Something deep inside her would not budge.

She fixed on Luschka's expression as if her whole life depended on it.

Maybe it did.

Luschka nodded as Daniil spoke, and her face changed from terrified to calm, almost peaceful. She closed her eyes. She nodded one more time. Then she tipped back her head, and a smile spread slowly across her lips.

A smile?

But why? How? It was almost like she knew what was about to happen.

Daniil held her in his arms and dipped her low. He leaned in for another kiss, pressing his lips firmly against hers, running his hands through her hair, then down her sides, across every inch of her.

It was so passionate that Luce blushed, so intimate

she couldn't breathe, so gorgeous that she couldn't tear her eyes away. Not for a second.

Not even when Luschka screamed.

And burst into a column of searing white flame.

The cyclone of flames was otherworldly, fluid and almost elegant in a ghastly way, like a long silk scarf twisting around her pale body. It engulfed Luschka, flowed out of her and all around her, lighting up the spectacle of her burning limbs flailing, and flailing—and then not flailing anymore. Daniil didn't let go, not when the fire singed his clothes, not when he had to support the full weight of her slack, unconscious body, not when the flames burned away her flesh with an ugly, acrid hiss, not when her skin began to char and blacken.

Only when the blaze fizzled out—so fast, in the end, like the snuffing of a single candle—and there was nothing left to hold on to, nothing left but ashes, did Daniil drop his arms to his sides.

In all of Luce's wildest daydreams about going back and revisiting her past lives, she'd never once imagined this: her own death. The reality was more horrible than her darkest nightmares could ever have concocted. She stood in the cold snow, paralyzed by the vision, her body bereft of the capacity to move.

Daniil staggered back from the charred mass on the snow and began to weep. The tears streaming down his cheeks made clean tracks through the black soot that was all that was left of her. His face contorted. His hands shook. They looked bare and big and empty to Luce, as if—even though the thought made her oddly jealous—his hands belonged around Luschka's waist, in her hair, cupping her cheeks. What on earth did you do with your hands when the one thing they wanted to hold was suddenly, gruesomely gone? A whole girl, an entire life—gone.

The pain on his face took hold of Luce's heart and squeezed, wringing her out completely. On top of all the pain and confusion she felt, seeing his agony was worse.

This was how he felt every life.

Every death.

Over and over and over again.

Luce had been wrong to imagine that Daniel was selfish. It wasn't that he didn't care. It was that he cared so much, it wrecked him. She still hated it, but she suddenly understood his bitterness, his reservations about everything. Miles might very well love her, but his love was nothing like Daniel's.

It never could be.

"Daniel!" she cried, and left the shadows, racing toward him.

She wanted to return all the kisses and embraces she'd just witnessed him giving to her past self. She knew it was wrong, that everything was wrong.

Daniil's eyes widened. A look of abject horror crossed his face.

"What is this?" he said slowly. Accusingly. As if he

hadn't just let his Luschka die. As if Luce's being there was worse than watching Luschka die. He raised his hand, painted black with ash, and pointed at her. "What's going on?"

It was agony to have him look at her this way. She stopped in her tracks and blinked a tear away.

"Answer him," someone said, a voice from the shadows. "How did you get here?"

Luce would have recognized the haughty voice anywhere. She didn't need to see Cam step out of the doorway of the bomb shelter.

With a soft snap and rumble like an enormous flag being unfurled, he extended his great wings. They stretched out behind him, making him even more magnificent and intimidating than usual. Luce couldn't keep herself from staring. They cast a gold-hued glow on the dark street.

Luce squinted, trying to make sense of the scene in front of her. There were more of them, more figures lurking in the shadows. Now they all stepped forward.

Gabbe. Roland. Molly. Arriane.

All of them were there. All with their wings arched tightly forward. A shimmering sea of gold and silver, blindingly bright on the dark street. They looked tense. Their wing tips quivered, as if ready to spring into battle.

For once, Luce didn't feel intimidated by the glory of

their wings or the weight of their gazes. She felt disgusted.

"Do you all watch it *every* time?" she asked.

"Luschka," Gabbe said in an even voice. "Just tell us what's going on."

And then Daniil was there, gripping her shoulders. Shaking her.

"Luschka!"

"I'm not Luschka!" Luce shouted, breaking away from him and backing up a half dozen steps.

She was horrified. How they could live with themselves? How they could all just sit back and watch her die?

It was all too much. She wasn't ready to see this.

"Why are you looking at me like that?" Daniil asked.

"She's not who you think she is, Daniil," Gabbe said. "Luschka's dead. This is . . . this is—"

"*What is she?*" Daniil asked. "How is she standing here? When—"

"Look at her clothes. She's clearly—"

"Shut up, Cam, she might not be," Arriane said, but she looked fearful, too, that Luce might be whatever Cam was about to say she was. Another shrieking from the air, and then a blast of artillery shells raining down on the buildings across the street, deafening Luce, igniting a wooden warehouse. The angels had no concern for the war going on around them, only for her. There were twenty feet now between Luce and the angels, and they looked as wary of her as she felt of them. None of them drew closer.

In the light from the smoldering building, Daniil's shadow was thrown far ahead of his body. She focused on summoning it to her. Would it work? Her eyes narrowed, and every muscle in her body tensed. She was still so clumsy at this, never knowing what it took to get the shadow into her hands.

When the dark lines began to quiver, she pounced. She gripped the shadow with both hands and started twirling the dark mass into a ball, just as she'd seen her teachers, Steven and Francesca, do on one of her first days at Shoreline. Just-summoned Announcers were always messy and amorphous. They needed first to be spun into a distinct contour. Only then could they be pulled and stretched into a larger flat surface. Then the Announcer would transform: into a screen through which to glimpse the past—or into a portal through which to step.

This Announcer was sticky, but she soon pulled it apart, guided it into shape. She reached inside and opened the portal.

She couldn't stay here any longer. She had a mission now: to find herself alive in another time and learn what price the Outcasts had referred to, and eventually, to trace the origin of the curse between Daniel and her.

Then to break it.

The others gasped as she manipulated the Announcer.

"When did you learn how to do that?" Daniil whispered.

Luce shook her head. Her explanation would only baffle Daniil.

"Lucinda!" The last thing she heard was his voice calling out her true name.

Strange, she'd been looking right at his stricken face but hadn't seen his lips move. Her mind was playing tricks.

"Lucinda!" he shouted once more, his voice rising in panic, just before Luce dove headfirst into the beckoning darkness.

TWO

HEAVEN SENT

Moscow · October 15, 1941

"Lucinda!" Daniel shouted again, but too late: In that instant she was gone. He had only just emerged into the bleak, snow-swept landscape. He'd felt a flash of light behind him and the heat of a blaze nearby, but all he could see was Luce. He rushed toward her on the darkened street corner. She looked tiny in someone else's threadbare coat. She looked scared. He'd watched her open up a shadow and then—

"No!"

A rocket smashed into a building behind him. The

ground quaked, the street bucked and split, and a shower of glass and steel and concrete gathered up in the air and then rained down.

After that, the street went deadly quiet. But Daniel barely noticed. He just stood in disbelief among the debris.

"She's going further back," he muttered, brushing the dust from his shoulders.

"She's going further back," someone said.

That voice. *His* voice. An echo?

No, too close for an echo. Too clear to have come from inside his head.

"Who said that?" He dashed past a tangled mess of scaffolding to where Luce had been.

Two gasps.

Daniel was facing himself. Only not quite himself— an earlier version of himself, a slightly less cynical version of himself. But from when? Where was he?

"Don't touch!" Cam shouted at both of them. He was dressed in an officer's fatigues, combat boots, and a bulky black coat. At the sight of Daniel, his eyes blazed.

Unwittingly, both Daniels had drawn closer, stepping around one another in a cautious circle in the snow. Now they reared back.

"Stay away from me," the older one warned the newer. "It's dangerous."

"I know that," Daniel barked. "Don't you think I

know that?" Just being this close made his stomach lurch. "I was here before. I am *you.*"

"What do you want?"

"I'm—" Daniel looked around, trying to get his bearings. After thousands of years of living, of loving Luce and losing her, the tissue of his memories had grown ragged. Repetition made the past hard to recall. But this place wasn't so long ago, this place he remembered—

Desolate city. Snow on the streets. Fire in the sky.

It could have been one of a hundred wars.

But there—

The place on the street where the snow had melted. The dark crater in the sea of white. Daniel sank to his knees and reached for the ring of black ash stained on the ground. He closed his eyes. And he remembered the precise way she had died in his arms.

Moscow. 1941.

So this was what she was doing—tunneling into her past lives. Hoping to understand.

The thing was, there was no rhyme or reason to her deaths. More than anyone, Daniel knew *that.*

But there *were* certain lifetimes when he'd tried to shed some light for her, hoping it would change things. Sometimes he'd hoped to keep her alive longer, though that never really worked. Sometimes—like this time during the siege of Moscow—he'd chosen to send her on her way more quickly. To spare her. So that his kiss could be the last thing she felt in that lifetime.

And those were the lifetimes that cast the longest shadows across the eons. Those were the lifetimes that stood out and drew Luce like filings to a magnet as she stumbled through the Announcers. Those lives when he'd revealed to her what she needed to know, even though knowing it would destroy her.

Like her death in Moscow. He remembered it keenly and felt foolish. The daring words he'd whispered, the deep kiss he'd given her. The blissful realization on her face as she died. It had changed nothing. Her end was exactly the same as always.

And Daniel was exactly the same afterward, too: Bleak. Black. Empty. Gutted. Inconsolable.

Gabbe stepped forward to kick snow over the ring of ash where Luschka had died. Her featherlight wings glowed in the night and a shimmering aura surrounded her body as she hunched over in the snow. She was crying.

The rest of them came closer, too: Cam. Roland. Molly. Arriane.

And Daniil, long-ago Daniel, rounded out their motley group.

"If you're here to warn us about something," Arriane called, "then say your piece and go." Her iridescent wings folded forward, almost protectively. She stepped in front of Daniil, who looked a little green.

It was unlawful and unnatural for the angels to interact with their earlier selves. Daniel felt clammy and faint—whether that was because he was having to relive Luce's death or because he was so close to his previous self, he couldn't say.

"Warn us?" Molly sneered, walking in a circle around Daniel. "Why would Daniel Grigori go out of his way to warn us about anything?" She got in his face, taunting him with her copper-colored wings. "No, I remember what he's up to—this one has been skipping through the past for centuries. Always searching, always late."

"No," Daniel whispered. That couldn't be. He'd set out to catch her and he would.

"What she means to ask," Roland said to Daniel, "is what transpired to bring you here? From whenever you're coming from?"

"I'd almost forgotten," Cam said, massaging his temples. "He is after Lucinda. She has fallen out of time." He turned to Daniel and raised an eyebrow. "Maybe now you'll forsake your pride and ask for our help?"

"I don't need help."

"Seems as if you do," Cam jeered.

"Stay out of it," Daniel spat. "You're enough trouble to us later."

"Oh, how fun." Cam clapped. "You've given me something to look forward to."

"This is a dangerous game you're playing, Daniel," Roland said.

"*I know that.*"

Cam laughed a dark, sinister laugh. "So. We've finally reached the endgame, haven't we?"

Gabbe swallowed. "So . . . something's changed?"

"She's figuring it out!" Arriane said. "She's opening up Announcers and stepping through and she's *still alive!*"

Daniel's eyes blazed violet. He turned away from all of them, looking back at the ruins of the church, the first place where he'd laid eyes on Luschka. "I can't stay. I have to catch her."

"Well, from what I remember," Cam said softly, "you never will. The past is already written, brother."

"Your past, maybe. But not my future." Daniel couldn't think straight. His wings burned inside his body, aching to be released. She was gone. The street was empty. No one else to worry about.

He threw his shoulders back and let them out with a whoosh. There. That lightness. That deepest freedom. He could think more clearly now. What he needed was a moment alone. With himself. He shot the other Daniel a look and took off into the sky.

Moments later, he heard the sound again: the same whoosh of wings unfurling—the sound of another pair of wings, younger wings, taking flight from the ground below.

Daniel's earlier self caught up with him in the sky. "Where to?"

Wordlessly they settled on a third-story ledge near Patriarch's Pond, on the roof across from Luce's window, where they used to watch her sleep. The memory would be fresher in Daniil's mind, but the faint recollection of Luce lying dreaming under the covers still sent a warm rush across Daniel's wings.

Both were somber. In the bombed-out city, it was sad and ironic that her building had been spared when she hadn't. They stood in silence in the cold night, both carefully tucking back their wings so that they wouldn't accidentally touch.

"How are things for her in the future?"

Daniel sighed. "The good news is that something is different in this lifetime. Somehow the curse has been . . . altered."

"How?" Daniil looked up, and the hope that shone bright in his eyes darkened. "You mean to say, in her current lifetime she has not yet made a covenant?"

"We think not. That's part of it. It seems a loophole has opened up and allowed her to live beyond her usual time—"

"But it's so dangerous." Daniil spoke quickly, frantically, spewing out the same discourse that had been running through Daniel's mind ever since the last night at Sword & Cross, when he'd realized that this time was different: "She could die and not come back. That could be *the* end. Every single thing is on the line now."

"*I know.*"

Daniil stopped, composed himself. "I'm sorry. Of course you know. But . . . the question is, does *she* understand why this life is different?"

Daniel looked at his empty hands. "One of the Elders of Zhsmaelim got to her, interrogated her before Luce knew anything about her past. Lucinda recognizes that everyone is focused on the fact that she has not been baptized . . . but there is so much she doesn't know."

Daniil stepped to the edge of the roof and gazed at her dark window. "Then what's the bad news?"

"I fear there is also much that I don't know. I cannot predict the consequences of her fleeing backward into time if I don't find her, and stop her, before it's too late."

Down on the street, a siren blared. The air raid was over. Soon the Russians would be out combing the city, looking for survivors.

Daniel sifted through the shreds of his memory. *She was going further back—but to which lifetime?* He turned to look hard at his earlier self. "You recall it, too, don't you?"

"That . . . she is going back?"

"Yes. But how far back?" They spoke simultaneously, staring at the dark street.

"And where will she stop?" Daniel said abruptly,

backing away from the edge. He closed his eyes, took a breath. "Luce is different now. She's—" He could almost smell her. Clean, pure light, like sunshine. "Something fundamental has shifted. We finally have a real chance. And I—I have never been more elated . . . nor more sick with terror." He opened his eyes and was surprised to see Daniil nod.

"Daniel?"

"Yes?"

"What are you waiting for?" Daniil asked with a smile. "Go get her."

And with that, Daniel teased open a shadow along the roof ledge—an Announcer—and stepped inside.

THREE

FOOLS RUSH IN

MILAN, ITALY · MAY 25, 1918

Luce staggered out of the Announcer to the sound of explosions. She ducked and covered her ears.

Violent bursts rocked the ground. One heavy boom after another, each more spectacular and paralyzing than the one before, until the sound and the tremors reverberated so that there seemed to be no break in the assault. No way to escape the din, and no end.

Luce stumbled in the earsplitting darkness, curling into herself, trying to shield her body. The blasts thrummed in her chest, spat dirt into her eyes and mouth.

All this before she'd even had a chance to see where she'd ended up. With each bright explosion, she caught glimpses of rolling fields, crisscrossed with culverts and tumbledown fences. But then the flash would vanish and she'd be blind again.

Bombs. They were still going off.

Something was wrong. Luce had meant to step through time, to get away from Moscow and the war. But she must have ended up right back where she'd started. Roland had warned her about this—about the dangers of Announcer travel. But she'd been too stubborn to listen.

In the pitch-dark, Luce tripped over something and landed hard, facedown in the dirt.

Someone grunted. Someone Luce had landed on top of.

She gasped and squirmed away, feeling a sharp stab in her hip from where she'd fallen. But when she saw the man lying on the ground, she forgot her own pain.

He was young, about her age. Small, with delicate features and timid brown eyes. His face was pale. His breath came in shallow gasps. The hand cupped over his stomach was caked with black grime. And beneath that hand, his fatigues were soaked with dark red blood.

Luce couldn't look away from the wound. "I'm not supposed to be here," she whispered to herself.

The boy's lips trembled. His bloody hand shook when he made the sign of the cross over his chest. "Oh, I've died," he said, staring at her wide-eyed. "You are an angel. I've died and gone to— Am I in Heaven?"

He reached for her, his hand quaking. She wanted to scream or vomit, but all she could do was cover his hands and press them back over the gaping hole in his gut. Another boom rattled the ground and the boy lying on it. Fresh blood seeped through the web of Luce's fingers.

"I am Giovanni," he whispered, closing his eyes. "Please. Help me. Please."

Only then did Luce realize she wasn't in Moscow anymore. The ground below her was warmer. Not snow-covered, but a grassy plain that was torn up in places, exposing rich black soil. The air was dry and dusty. This boy had spoken to her in Italian, and just as she had in Moscow, she understood.

Her eyes had adjusted. She could see searchlights in the distance, roaming over purple-hued hills. And beyond the hills, an evening sky was flecked with bright white stars. Luce turned away. She couldn't see stars without thinking of Daniel, and she couldn't think about Daniel right now. Not with her hands pressed into this boy's belly, not with him about to die.

At least he hadn't died *yet*.

He only thought he had.

She couldn't blame him. After he'd been hit, he'd

probably gone into shock. And then maybe he'd seen her come through the Announcer, a black tunnel appearing out of thin air. He must have been terrified.

"You're going to be fine," she said, using the perfect Italian she'd always wanted to learn. It felt astonishingly natural on her tongue. Her voice, too, came out softer and smoother than she expected; it made her wonder what she'd been like in this lifetime.

A barrage of deafening shots made her jump. Gunfire. Endless, in quick succession, bright zipping tracers arcing through the sky, burning lines of white into her vision, followed by a lot of shouting in Italian. Then the thump of footsteps in the dirt. Coming closer.

"We're retreating," the boy mumbled. "That's not good."

Luce looked toward the sound of soldiers running in their direction and noticed for the first time that she and the injured soldier were not alone. At least ten other men lay wounded around them, moaning and trembling and bleeding into the black earth. Their clothes were singed and shredded from the land mine that must have taken them by surprise. The rich stink of rot and sweat and blood sat heavy in the air, coating everything. It was so horrific—Luce had to bite down on her lip to keep from screaming.

A man in an officer's uniform ran past her, then stopped. "What's *she* doing here? This is a war zone, not a place for nurses. You'll be no help to us dead, girl. At least make yourself useful. We need the casualties loaded up."

He stormed off before Luce could respond. Below her, the boy's eyes were beginning to droop and his whole body was shaking. She looked around desperately for help.

About a half mile away was a narrow dirt road with two ancient-looking trucks and two small, squat ambulances parked at its side.

"I'll be right back," Luce told the boy, pressing his hands more firmly against his stomach to control the bleeding. He whimpered when she pulled away.

She ran toward the trucks, stumbling over her feet when another shell came down behind her, making the earth buck.

A cluster of women in white uniforms stood gathered around the back of one of the trucks. Nurses. They would know what to do, how to help. But when Luce got close enough to see their faces, her heart sank. They were girls. Some of them couldn't have been older than fourteen. Their uniforms looked like costumes.

She scanned their faces, looking for herself in one of them. There must have been a reason why she'd stepped into this Hell. But no one looked familiar. It was hard to fathom the girls' calm, clear expressions. Not one of them showed the terror that Luce knew was clear on her own face. Maybe they had already seen enough of the war to grow used to what it did.

"Water." An older woman's voice came from inside the truck. "Bandages. Gauze."

She was distributing supplies to the girls, who loaded up, then set to work putting together a makeshift clinic on the side of the road. A row of injured men had already been moved behind the truck for treatment. More were on the way. Luce joined the line for supplies. It was dark and no one said a word to her. She could feel it now—the stress of the young nurses. They must have been trained to keep a poised, calm façade for the soldiers, but when the girl in front of Luce reached up to take her ration of supplies, her hands were shaking.

Around them, soldiers moved quickly in pairs, carrying the wounded under the arms and by the feet. Some of the men being carried mumbled questions about the battle, asking how badly they'd been hit. Then there were the ones more seriously injured, whose lips could form no questions because they were too busy biting off screams, who had to be hoisted by the waist because one or both of their legs had been blown off by a land mine.

"Water." A jug landed in Luce's arms. "Bandages. Gauze." The head nurse dumped the ration of supplies mechanically, ready to move on to the next girl, but then she didn't. She fixed her gaze on Luce. Her eyes traveled downward, and Luce realized she was still wearing the heavy wool coat from Luschka's grandmother in Moscow. Which was a good thing, because underneath the coat were her jeans and button-down shirt from her current life.

"Uniform," the woman finally said in the same monotone, tossing down a white dress and a nurse's cap like the other girls were wearing.

Luce nodded gratefully, then ducked behind a truck to change. It was a billowing white gown that reached her ankles and smelled strongly of bleach. She tried to wipe the soldier's blood off her hands, using the wool coat, then tossed it behind a tree. But by the time she'd buttoned the nurse's uniform, rolled up the sleeves, and tied the belt around her waist, it was completely covered with rusty red streaks.

She grabbed the supplies and ran back across the road. The scene before her was gruesome. The officer hadn't been lying. There were at least a hundred men who needed help. She looked at the bandages in her arms and wondered what it was she should be doing.

"Nurse!" a man called out. He was sliding a stretcher into the back of an ambulance. "Nurse! This one needs a nurse."

Luce realized that he was talking to her. "Oh," she said faintly. "Me?" She peered into the ambulance. It was cramped and dark inside. A space that looked like it had been made for two people now held six. The wounded soldiers were laid out on stretchers slid into three-tiered slings on either side. There was no place for Luce except on the floor.

Someone was shoving her to the side: a man, sliding another stretcher onto the small empty space on the floor. The soldier laid out on it was unconscious, his black hair plastered across his face.

"Go on," the soldier said to Luce. "It's leaving now."

When she didn't move, he pointed to a wooden stool affixed to the inside of the ambulance's back door with a crisscrossed rope. He bent down and made a stirrup with his hands to help Luce up onto the stool. Another shell shook the ground, and Luce couldn't hold back the scream that escaped her lips.

She glanced apologetically at the soldier, took a deep breath, and hopped up.

When she was seated on the tiny stool, he handed up the jug of water and the box of gauze and bandages. He started to shut the door.

"Wait," Luce whispered. "What do I do?"

The man paused. "You know how long the ride to Milan is. Dress their wounds and keep them comfortable. Do the best you can."

The door slammed with Luce on it. She had to grip the stool to keep from falling off and landing on the soldier at her feet. The ambulance was stifling hot. It smelled terrible. The only light came from a small lantern hanging from a nail in the corner. The only window was directly behind her head on the inside of the door. She didn't know what had happened to Giovanni, the boy with the bullet in his stomach. Whether she'd ever see him again. Whether he'd live through the night.

The engine started up. The ambulance shifted into gear and lurched forward. The soldier on one of the top slings began to moan.

After they'd reached a steady speed, Luce heard the pattering sound of a leak. Something was dripping. She leaned forward on the stool, squinting in the dim lantern light.

It was the blood of the soldier on the top bunk dripping through the woven sling onto the soldier in the middle bunk. The middle soldier's eyes were open. He was watching the blood fall on his chest, but he was injured so badly that he couldn't move away. He didn't make a sound. Not until the trickle of blood turned into a stream.

Luce whimpered along with the soldier. She started to rise from her stool, but there was no place for her to stand unless she straddled the soldier on the floor. Carefully, she wedged her feet around his chest. As the ambulance shuddered along the bumpy dirt road, she gripped the taut canvas of the top sling and held a fistful of gauze against its bottom. The blood soaked through onto her fingers within seconds.

"Help!" she called to the ambulance driver. She didn't know if he'd even be able to hear her.

"What is it?" The driver had a thick regional accent.

"This man back here—he's hemorrhaging. I think he's dying."

"We're all dying, gorgeous," the driver said. Really, he was flirting with her *now*? A second later, he turned around, glancing at her through the opening behind the driver's seat. "Look, I'm sorry. But there's nothing to do. I've gotta get the rest of these guys to the hospital."

He was right. It was already too late. When Luce took her hand away from under the stretcher, the blood began to gush again. So heavily it didn't seem possible.

Luce had no words of comfort for the boy in the middle sling, whose eyes were wide and petrified and whose lips whispered a furious Ave Maria. The stream of the other boy's blood dripped down his sides, pooling in the space where his hips met the sling.

Luce wanted to close her eyes and disappear. She wanted to sift through the shadows cast by the lantern, to find an Announcer that would take her somewhere else. Anywhere else.

Like the beach on the rocks below Shoreline's campus. Where Daniel had taken her dancing on the ocean, under the stars. Or the pristine swimming hole she'd glimpsed the two of them diving into, when she'd worn the yellow bathing suit. She would have taken Sword &

Cross over this ambulance, even the roughest moments, like the night she'd gone to meet Cam at that bar. Like when she'd kissed him. She would even have taken Moscow. This was worse. She'd never faced anything like this before.

Except—

Of course she had. She must already have lived through something almost exactly like this. It was why she'd ended up here. Somewhere in this war-torn world was the girl who died and came back to life and went on to become her. She was certain of it. She must have dressed wounds and carried water and suppressed the urge to vomit. It gave Luce strength to think about the girl who'd lived through this before.

The stream of blood began to trickle, then became a very slow drip. The boy beneath had fainted, so Luce watched silently by herself for a long time. Until the dripping stopped completely.

Then she reached for a towel and the water and began to wash the soldier in the middle bunk. It had been a while since he'd had a bath. Luce washed him gently and changed the bandage around his head. When he came to, she gave him sips of water. His breathing evened, and he stopped staring up at the sling above him in terror. He seemed to grow more comfortable.

All of the soldiers seemed to find some comfort as she tended to them, even the one in the middle of the floor, who never opened his eyes. She cleaned the face of the boy in the top bunk who had died. She couldn't explain why. She wanted him to be more at peace, too.

It was impossible to tell how much time had passed. All Luce knew was that it was dark and rank and her back ached and her throat was parched and she was exhausted—and she was better off than any of the men surrounding her.

She'd left the soldier on the bottom left-hand stretcher until last. He'd been hit badly in the neck, and Luce was worried that he would lose even more blood if she tried to re-dress the wound. She did the best she could, sitting on the side of his sling and sponging down his grimy face, washing some of the blood out of his blond hair. He was handsome under all the mud. Very handsome. But she was distracted by his neck, which was still bleeding through the gauze. Every time she even got near it, he cried out in pain.

"Don't worry," she whispered. "You're going to make it."

"I know." His whisper came so quietly, and sounded so impossibly sad, that Luce wasn't sure she'd heard him right. Until then, she'd thought he was unconscious, but something in her voice seemed to reach him.

His eyelids fluttered. Then, slowly, they opened.

They were violet.

The jug of water fell from her hands.

Daniel.

Her instinct was to crawl in next to him and cover his lips with kisses, to pretend he wasn't as badly wounded as he was.

At the sight of her, Daniel's eyes widened and he started to sit up. But then the blood began to flow from his neck again and his face drained of all its color. Luce had no choice but to restrain him.

"Shhh." She pressed his shoulders back against the stretcher, trying to get him to relax.

He squirmed under her grip. Every time he did, bright new blood bloomed through the bandage.

"Daniel, you have to stop fighting," she begged. "Please stop fighting. For me."

They locked eyes for a long, intense moment—and then the ambulance came to an abrupt stop. The back door swung open. A shocking breath of fresh air flowed in. The streets outside were quiet, but the place had the feel of a big city, even in the middle of the night.

Milan. That was where the soldier had said they were going when he assigned her to this ambulance. They must be at a hospital in Milan.

Two men in army uniforms appeared at the doors and began sliding the stretchers out with quick precision. Within minutes, the wounded were placed on rolling carts and wheeled off. The men pushed Luce out of the way so they could ease out Daniel's stretcher. His eyelids were fluttering again, and she thought he reached out his hand for her. She watched from the back of the ambulance until he disappeared from sight. Then she began to tremble.

"Are you all right?" A girl popped her head inside. She was fresh and pretty, with a small red mouth and long dark hair pulled into a low twist. Her nurse's dress was more fitted than the one Luce was wearing and so white and clean it made Luce aware of how bloody and muddy she was.

Luce hopped to her feet. She felt like she'd been caught doing something embarrassing.

"I'm fine," she said quickly. "I just—"

"You don't have to explain," the girl said. Her face fell as she looked around the inside of the ambulance. "I can tell, it was a bad one."

Luce stared as the girl heaved a bucket of water into the ambulance, then hoisted herself inside. She got to work immediately, scrubbing down the bloodied slings, mopping the floor, sending waves of red-tinged water out the back door. She replaced the soiled linens in the cabinet with clean ones and added more gas to the lantern. She couldn't have been older than thirteen.

Luce stood up to help, but the girl waved her off. "Sit down. Rest. You just got transferred here, didn't you?"

Hesitantly, Luce nodded.

"Were you all alone coming from the front?" The girl

stopped cleaning for a moment, and when she looked at Luce, her hazel eyes brimmed with compassion.

Luce started to reply, but her mouth was so dry she couldn't speak. How had it taken her this long to recognize that she was looking at herself?

"I was," she managed to whisper. "I was all alone."

The girl smiled. "Well, you're not anymore. There's a bunch of us here at the hospital. We've got all the nicest nurses. And the handsomest patients. You won't mind it, I don't think." She started to extend her hand but then looked down and realized how dirty it was. She giggled and picked up her mop again. "I'm Lucia."

I know, Luce stopped herself from saying. "I'm—"

Her mind went blank. She tried to think of one name, any name that would work. "I'm Doree— Doria," she finally said. Almost her mother's name. "Do you know—where do they take the soldiers who were in here?"

"Uh-oh. You're not already in love with one of them, are you?" Lucia teased. "New patients get taken to the east ward for vitals."

"The east ward," Luce repeated to herself.

"But you should go see Miss Fiero at the nurses' station. She does the registration and the scheduling"— Lucia giggled again and lowered her voice, leaning toward Luce—"and the doctor, on Tuesday afternoons!"

All Luce could do was stare at Lucia. Up close, her

past self was so *real*, so alive, so very much the kind of girl Luce would have befriended instantly if the circumstances had been any shade of normal. She wanted to reach out and hug Lucia, but she was overcome by an indescribable fear. She'd cleaned the wounds of seven half-dead soldiers—including the love of her life—but she was unsure what to do when it came to Lucia. The girl seemed too young to know any of the secrets Luce was searching for—about the curse, about the Outcasts. Luce feared she'd only frighten Lucia if she started talking about reincarnation and Heaven. There was something about Lucia's eyes, something about her innocence—Luce realized that Lucia knew even less than she did.

She stepped down from the ambulance and backed away.

"It was nice to meet you, Doria," Lucia called.

But Luce was already gone.

⁂

It took six wrong rooms, three startled soldiers, and one toppled-over medicine cabinet before Luce found him.

Daniel was sharing a room in the east ward with two other soldiers. One was a silent man whose entire face had been bandaged. The other was snoring loudly, a bottle of whiskey not very well hidden under his pillow, two broken legs raised in a sling.

The room itself was bare and sterile, but it had a window that looked out onto a broad city avenue lined with orange trees.

Standing over his bed, watching him sleep, Luce could see it. The way their love would have bloomed here. She could see Lucia coming in to bring Daniel his meals, him opening up to her slowly. The pair being inseparable by the time Daniel recovered. And it made her feel jealous and guilty and confused because she couldn't tell right now whether their love was a beautiful thing, or whether this was yet another instance of how very wrong it was.

If she was so young when they met, they must have had a long relationship in this life. She would have gotten to spend years with him before it happened. Before she died and was reincarnated into another life completely. She must have thought they'd spend forever together—and must not even have known how long *forever* meant.

But Daniel knew. He always knew.

Luce sank down at the side of his bed, careful not to wake him. Maybe he hadn't always been so closed off and hard to reach. She'd just seen him in their Moscow life whispering something to her at the critical moment before she died. Maybe if she could just talk to him in this life, he'd treat her differently than the Daniel she knew did. He might not hide so much from her. He might help her understand. Might tell her the truth, for a change.

Then she could go back to the present and there wouldn't have to be any more secrets. It was all she really wanted: for the two of them to love each other openly. And for her not to die.

She reached out and touched his cheek. She loved his cheek. He was beat-up and injured and probably concussed, but his cheek was warm and smooth and, mostly, it was Daniel's. He was as gorgeous as ever. His face was so peaceful in his sleep that Luce could have stared at him from every angle for hours without ever getting bored. He was perfect to her. His perfect lips were just the same. When she touched them with her finger, they were so soft she had to lean down for a kiss. He didn't stir.

She traced his jawline with her lips, kissed down the side of his neck that wasn't bruised and across his collarbone. At the top of his right shoulder, her lips paused over a small white scar.

It would have been almost indiscernible to anyone else, but Luce knew that this was the place from which Daniel's wings extended. She kissed the scar tissue. It was so hard to see him lying helpless on that hospital bed when she knew what he was capable of. With his wings wrapped around her, Luce always lost track of everything else. What she wouldn't give to see them unfurl now, into the vast white splendor that seemed to steal all the light from a room! She laid her head on his shoulder, the scar hot against her skin.

⚛

Her head shot up. She hadn't realized she'd drifted off until the stretcher wheeling squeakily down the uneven wood floor in the hallway startled her awake.

What time was it? Sunlight streamed through the window onto the white sheets on the beds. She rotated her shoulder, trying to loosen a crick. Daniel was still asleep.

The scar above his shoulder looked whiter in the morning light. Luce wanted to see the other side, the matching scar, but it was wrapped in gauze. At least, the wound seemed to have stopped bleeding.

The door opened and Luce jerked up.

Lucia was standing in the doorway, holding three covered trays stacked in her arms. "Oh! You're here." She sounded surprised. "So they've already had breakfast, then?"

Luce blushed and shook her head. "I—uh—"

"Ah." Lucia's eyes lit up. "I know that look. You've got it *bad* for someone." She put the breakfast trays on a cart and came to stand at Luce's side. "Don't worry, I won't tell—so long as I approve." She tilted her head to look at Daniel, and stared at him hard for a long time. She didn't move or breathe.

Sensing the girl's eyes widening at the sight of Daniel

⚛ 65 ⚛

for the first time, Luce didn't know what to feel. Empathy. Envy. Grief. All of it was there.

"He's *heavenly*." Lucia sounded as if she might cry. "What's his name?"

"His name is Daniel."

"Daniel," the younger girl repeated, making the word sound holy as it left her lips. "Someday, I'll meet a man like that. Someday, I'll drive all of them crazy. Just like you do, Doria."

"What do you mean?" Luce asked.

"There's that other soldier, two doors down?" Lucia addressed Luce without ever taking her eyes off Daniel. "You know, Giovanni?"

Luce shook her head. She didn't.

"The one who's about to go in for surgery—he keeps asking about you."

"Giovanni." The boy who'd been shot in the stomach. "He's okay?"

"Sure." Lucia smiled. "I won't tell him you have a boyfriend." She winked at Luce and pointed down at the breakfast trays. "I'll let you do the meals," she said on her way out. "Find me later? I want to hear everything about you and Daniel. The whole story, all right?"

"Sure," Luce lied, her heart sinking a little.

Alone with Daniel again, Luce was nervous. In her parents' backyard, after the battle with the Outcasts, Daniel had seemed so horrified when he saw her step through the Announcer. In Moscow, too. Who knew what this Daniel would do when he opened his eyes and found out where she'd come from?

If he ever opened his eyes.

She leaned down over his bed again. He had to open his eyes, didn't he? Angels couldn't *die*. Logically, she *thought* it was impossible, but what if—what if by coming back in time she'd messed something up? She'd seen the *Back to the Future* movies and she'd once passed a test in science class on quantum physics. What she was doing here was probably messing up the space-time continuum. And Steven Filmore, the demon who cotaught humanities at Shoreline, had said something about altering time.

She didn't really know what any of that meant, but she did know it could be *very* bad. Like erase-your-whole-existence bad. Or maybe kill-your-angel-boyfriend bad.

That was when Luce panicked. Grabbing hold of Daniel's shoulders, she began to shake. Lightly, gently—he'd been through a war, after all. But enough to let him know that she needed a sign. Right now.

"Daniel," she whispered. "Daniel?"

There. His eyelids began to flutter. She let out her breath. His eyes opened slowly, like they had last night. And like last night, when they registered the girl in front of them, they bulged. His lips parted. "You're . . . old."

Luce blushed. "I am not," she said, laughing. No one had ever called her old before.

"Yes, you are. You're really old." He looked almost disappointed. He rubbed his forehead. "I mean— How long have I been—?"

Then she remembered: Lucia was several years younger. But Daniel hadn't even met Lucia yet. How would he have known how old she was?

"Don't worry about that," she said. "I need to tell you something, Daniel. I'm—I'm not who you think I am. I mean, I am, I guess, I always am, but this time, I came from . . . uh . . ."

Daniel's face contorted. "Of course. You stepped through to get here."

She nodded. "I had to."

"I'd forgotten," he whispered, confusing Luce even more. "From how far away? No. Don't tell me." He waved her off, inching back in his bed as if she had some sort of disease. "How is that even possible? There were no loopholes in the curse. You shouldn't be able to be here."

"Loopholes?" Luce asked. "What kind of loopholes? I need to know—"

"I can't help you," he said, and coughed. "You have to learn on your own. Those are the rules."

"Doria." A woman Luce had never seen was standing in the doorway. She was older, blond and severe, with a starched Red Cross cap pinned so that it sat at an angle on her head. At first, Luce didn't realize that the woman was addressing her. "You are Doria, aren't you? The new transfer?"

"Yes," Luce said.

"We'll need to do your paperwork this morning," the woman said curtly. "I don't have any of your records. But first, you'll do me a favor."

Luce nodded. She could tell she was in trouble, but she had more important things to worry about than this woman and her paperwork.

"Private Bruno is going into surgery," the nurse said.

"Okay." Luce tried to focus on the nurse, but all she wanted was to go back to her conversation with Daniel. She had finally been getting somewhere, finally finding another piece in the puzzle of her lives!

"Private Giovanni Bruno? He's requested that the on-duty nurse be taken off his surgery. He says he's sweet on the nurse who saved his life. His *angel*?" The woman gave Luce a hard look. "The girls tell me that's you."

"No," Luce said. "I'm not—"

"Doesn't matter. It's what he believes." The nurse pointed toward the door. "Let's go."

Luce rose from Daniel's bed. He was looking away from her, out the window. She sighed. "I *have* to talk to you," she whispered, though he didn't meet her gaze. "I'll be right back."

The surgery wasn't as awful as it could have been. All Luce had to do was hold Giovanni's small, soft hand and whisper things, pass a few instruments to the doctor and try not to look when he reached into the dark red mass of Giovanni's exposed gut and extracted the bits of blood-sheathed shrapnel. If the doctor wondered about her evident lack of experience, he didn't say anything. She wasn't gone more than an hour.

Just long enough to come back to Daniel's bed and find it empty.

Lucia was changing the sheets. She rushed toward Luce, and Luce thought she was going to hug her. Instead she collapsed at her feet.

"What happened?" Luce asked. "Where did he go?"

"I don't know." The girl began to weep. "He left. He just left. I don't know where." She looked up at Luce, tears filling her hazel eyes. "He said to tell you good-bye."

"He can't be gone," Luce said under her breath. They hadn't even had a chance to talk—

Of course they hadn't. Daniel had known exactly what he was doing when he left. He didn't want to tell her the whole truth. He was hiding something. What were the *rules* he'd mentioned? And what loophole?

Lucia's face was flushed. Her speech was broken up by hiccups. "I know I shouldn't be crying, but I can't explain it. . . . I feel like someone has *died*."

Luce recognized the feeling. They had that in common: When Daniel left, both girls were inconsolable. Luce balled up her fists, feeling angry and despondent. "Don't be childish."

Luce blinked, thinking at first that the girl was speaking to her, but then she realized Lucia was chiding herself. Luce straightened, holding her trembling shoulders high again, as if she were trying to recover the calm poise the nurses had shown.

"Lucia." Luce reached for the girl, moving to embrace her.

But the girl inched away, turning from Luce to face Daniel's empty bed. "I'm fine." She went back to stripping the sheets. "The only thing we can control is the work we do. Nurse Fiero always says that. The rest is out of our hands."

No. Lucia was wrong, but Luce couldn't see how to correct her. Luce didn't understand much, but she understood *that*—her life didn't *have* to be out of her hands. She *could* shape her own destiny. Somehow. She didn't have it all figured out yet, but she could feel a solution drawing nearer. How else would she have found herself here in the first place? How else would she have known now that it was time to move on?

In the late-morning light, a shadow stretched out from the supply closet in the corner. It looked like one she could use, but she wasn't entirely confident of her abilities to summon. She focused on it for a moment and waited to see the place where it wobbled.

There. She watched it twitch. Fighting the disgust she still felt, she grabbed hold of it.

Across the room, Lucia's focus was on bundling the bedsheets, on trying hard not to show that she was still crying.

Luce worked fast, drawing the Announcer into a sphere, then working it out with her fingers more quickly than she ever had before.

She held her breath, made a wish, and disappeared.

FOUR

❧ ‡ ☙

TIME WOUNDS ALL HEELS

MILAN, ITALY · MAY 25, 1918

Daniel felt guarded and on edge as he pushed out of the Announcer.

He was unpracticed at how to quickly make sense of the new time and place, not knowing exactly where he was or what he should do. Knowing that at least one version of Luce was bound to be nearby, bound to need him.

The room was white. White sheets on the bed in front of him, white-framed window in the corner, bright white sunshine beating through the pane. For a moment, all was quiet. Then the chatter of memories rushed in.

Milan.

He was back in the hospital where she had been his nurse during the first of the mortal world wars. There, in the bed in the corner, was Traverti, his roommate from Salerno who'd stepped on a land mine on his way to the canteen. Both of Traverti's legs had been burned and broken, but he was so charming he had all the nurses sneaking him bottles of whiskey. He'd always had a joke for Daniel. And there, on the other side of the room, was Max Porter, the Brit with the burned face, who never made a peep until he screamed and fell to pieces when they took his bandage off.

Right now, both of Daniel's old roommates were far gone in morphine-induced afternoon naps.

In the middle of the room was the bed where he had lain after that bullet found his neck near the Piave River front. It was a stupid attack; they had walked right into it. But Daniel had only enlisted in the war because Lucia was a nurse, so it was just as well. He rubbed at the place where he'd been hit. He could feel the pain almost as if it had happened yesterday.

If Daniel had stuck around long enough to let the wound heal, the doctors would have been amazed by the absence of a scar. Today, his neck was smooth and flawless, as if he had never been shot.

Over the years, Daniel had been beaten, battered,

flung over balconies, shot in the neck and the gut and the leg, tortured over hot coals, and dragged through a dozen city streets. But a close study of every inch of his skin would reveal only two small scars: two fine white lines above his shoulder blades where his wings unfurled.

All of the fallen angels acquired these scars when they took their human bodies. In a way, the scars were all any of them had to show for themselves.

Most of the others reveled in their immunity to scarring. Well, except for Arriane, but the scar on her neck was another story. But Cam and even Roland would pick the most gruesome fights with just about anyone on Earth. Of course, they never lost to mortals, but they seemed to like getting a little bit shattered on the way. In a couple of days, they knew they'd look flawless again.

For Daniel, an existence without scars was just another indication that his destiny was out of his hands. Nothing he did ever made a dent. The weight of his own futility was crushing—especially when it came to Luce.

And he suddenly remembered seeing her here, back in 1918. Luce. And he remembered fleeing the hospital.

That was the one thing that *could* leave a scar on Daniel—on his soul.

He'd been confused by seeing her back then, just as he was confused now. At the time, he'd thought there was no way that the mortal Lucinda should be able to do this—to run pell-mell through time, visiting her old selves. No way she should be alive at all. Now, of course, Daniel knew that something had changed with the life of Lucinda Price, but what was it? It started with her lack of covenant with Heaven, but there was more—

Why couldn't he figure it out? He knew the rules and parameters of the curse as well as he knew anything, so how could the answer elude him—

Luce. *She* must have worked the change into her own past herself. The realization made his heart flutter. It must have happened during this very flight of hers through the Announcers. Of course, she must have shifted something to make all of this possible. But when? Where? *How?* Daniel could not interfere with any of it.

He had to find her, just as he'd always promised he would. But he also had to make sure she managed to do whatever it was she had to do, worked whatever change into her past she needed to work so that Lucinda Price— his Luce—could happen.

Maybe if he could catch up with her, he could help. He could steer her toward the moment when she changed the rules of the game for all of them. He'd just missed her in Moscow, but he would find her in this life. He just had to figure out why she had landed here. There was always a reason, something held inside, in deep folds of her memory—

Oh.

His wings burned and he felt ashamed. This life in

Italy had been a dark and ugly death for her. One of the worst. He would never stop blaming himself for the horrible way she had passed out of this life.

But that was years after where Daniel stood today. This was the hospital where they'd first met, when Lucia was so young and lovely, innocent and saucy in the same breath. Here she had loved him instantly and completely. Though she was too young for Daniel to show he loved her back, he had never discouraged her affection. She used to slip her hand inside his when they strolled under the orange trees on the Piazza della Repubblica, but when he squeezed her hand, she would blush. It always made him laugh, the way she could be so bold, then suddenly turn shy. She used to tell him that she wanted to marry him someday.

"You're back!"

Daniel spun around. He hadn't heard the door behind him opening. Lucia jumped when she saw him. She was beaming, showing a perfect row of tiny white teeth. Her beauty took his breath away.

What did she mean, he was back? Ah, this was when he'd hidden from Luce, frightened of killing her by accident. He was not allowed to reveal anything to her; she had to discover the details for herself. Were he even to hint broadly, she would simply combust. Had he stayed, she might have grilled him and perhaps forced the truth out of him. . . . He didn't dare.

So his earlier self had run away. He must be in Bologna by now.

"Are you feeling all right?" Lucia asked, walking toward him. "You really should lie back down. Your neck"—she reached out to touch the place where he'd been shot over ninety years ago. Her eyes widened and she drew back her hand. She shook her head. "I thought—I could have sworn—"

She began to fan her face with the stack of files she was holding. Daniel took her hand and led her to sit on the edge of the bed with him. "Please," he said, "can you tell me, was there a girl here—"

A girl just like you.

"Doria?" Lucia asked. "Your . . . friend? With pretty short hair and the funny shoes?"

"Yes." Daniel exhaled. "Can you show me where she is? It's very urgent."

Lucia shook her head. She couldn't stop staring at his neck.

"How long have I been here?" he asked.

"You just arrived last night," she said. "You don't remember?"

"Things are fuzzy," Daniel lied. "I must have taken a knock to the head."

"You were very badly wounded." She nodded. "Nurse Fiero didn't think you were going to make it until morning when the doctors came—"

"No." He remembered. "She didn't."

"But then you did, and we were all so glad. I think Doria stayed with you all night. Do you remember that?"

"Why would she do that?" Daniel said sharply, startling Lucia.

But of course Luce had stayed with him. Daniel would have done the same thing.

At his side, Lucia sniffed. He'd upset her, when it was really himself he had to be angry with. He put an arm around her shoulder, feeling almost dizzy. How easy it was to fall in love with every moment of her existence! He made himself lean back to focus.

"Do you know where she is now?"

"She went away." Lucia chewed on her lip nervously. "After you left, she was upset, and she took off somewhere. But I don't know where."

So she had run away again already. What a fool Daniel was, plodding through time while Luce was racing. He had to catch her, though; maybe he could help steer her toward that moment when she could make all the difference. Then he would never leave her side, never let any harm come to her, only be with her and love her always.

He leaped up from the bed. He was at the door when the young girl's hand tugged him back.

"Where are you going?"

"I have to go."

"After her?"

"Yes."

"But you should stay a little longer." Her palm was damp inside his. "The doctors, they all said you need some rest," she said softly. "I don't know what's come over me. I just can't bear it if you go."

Daniel felt horrible. He pressed her small hand to his heart. "We'll meet again."

"No." She shook her head. "My father said that, and my brother, and then they went to the war and they died. I don't have anyone left. Please don't go."

He couldn't bear to. But if he ever wanted to find her again, leaving now was his only chance.

"When the war is over, you and I will meet again. You'll go to Florence one summer, and when you're ready, you will find me at the Boboli Gardens—"

"I'll do *what*?"

"Right behind the Pitti Palace, at the end of Spider's Lane, where the hydrangeas bloom. Look for me."

"You must be feverish. This is crazy!"

He nodded. He knew it was. He loathed that there was no alternative to setting this beautiful, sweet girl on such an ugly course. She had to go to the gardens then, just as Daniel had to go after Lucinda now.

"I will be there, waiting for you. Trust in that."

When he kissed her forehead, her shoulders began to shake with quiet sobs. Against every instinct, Daniel turned away, darting off to find an Announcer that could take him back.

FIVE

OFF THE STRAIGHT PATH

HELSTON, ENGLAND · JUNE 18, 1854

Luce rocketed into the Announcer like a car speeding out of control.

She bounced and jostled against its shadowy sides, feeling as if she'd been thrown down a garbage chute. She didn't know where she was going or what she would find once she arrived, only that this Announcer seemed narrower and less pliable than the last one, and was filled by a wet, whipping wind that drove her ever deeper into the dark tunnel.

Her throat was dry and her body was weary from not having slept in the hospital. With every turn, she felt more lost and unsure.

What was she doing in this Announcer?

She closed her eyes and tried to fill her mind with thoughts of Daniel: the strong grasp of his hands, the burning intensity of his eyes, the way his whole face changed when she entered a room. The soft comfort of being wrapped in his wings, soaring high, the world and its worries far away.

How foolish she had been to run! That night in her backyard, stepping through the Announcer had seemed like the right thing to do—the only thing to do. But *why*? Why had she done it? What stupid idea had made that seem like a smart move? And now she was far away from Daniel, from everyone she cared about, from anyone at all. And it was all her fault.

"You're an idiot!" she cried into the dark.

"Hey, now," a voice called out. It was raspy and blunt and seemed to come from right beside her. "No need to be insulting!"

Luce went rigid. There couldn't be anyone inside the utter darkness of her Announcer. Right? She must be hearing things. She pushed forward, faster.

"Slow down, will ya?"

She caught her breath. Whoever it was didn't sound garbled or distant, like someone was speaking *through* the shadow. No, someone was *in* here. With her.

"Hello?" she called, swallowing hard.

No answer.

The whipping wind in the Announcer grew louder, howling in her ears. She stumbled forward in the dark, more and more afraid, until at last the noise of the air blowing past died out and was replaced by another sound—a staticky roar. Something like waves crashing in the distance.

No, the sound was too steady to be waves, Luce thought. A waterfall.

"I said *slow down*."

Luce flinched. The voice was back. Inches from her ear—and keeping pace with her as she ran. This time, it sounded annoyed.

"You're not going to learn *anything* if you keep zipping around like that."

"Who are you? What do you want?" she shouted. *"Oof!"*

Her cheek collided with something cold and hard. The rush of a waterfall filled her ears, close enough that she could feel cool drops of spray on her skin. "Where am I?"

"You're here. You're . . . on Pause. Ever heard of stopping to smell the peonies?"

"You mean roses." Luce felt around in the darkness, taking in a pungent mineral smell that wasn't unpleasant or unfamiliar, just confusing. She realized then that she hadn't yet stepped out of the Announcer and back into the middle of a life, which could only mean—

She was still inside.

It was very dark, but her eyes began to adjust. The Announcer had taken on the form of some sort of small cave. There was a wall behind her made of the same cool stone as the floor, with a depression cut into it where a stream of water trickled down. The waterfall she heard was somewhere above.

And below her? Ten feet or so of stone ledge—and then nothing. Beyond that was blackness.

"I had no idea you could do this," Luce whispered to herself.

"What?" the hoarse voice said.

"*Stop* inside an Announcer," she said. She hadn't been talking to him and she still couldn't see him, and the fact that she'd ended up stalled *wherever* she was with *whoever* he was—well, it was definitely cause for alarm. But still she couldn't help marveling at her surroundings. "I didn't know a place like this existed. An in-between place."

A phlegmy snort. "You could fill a book with all the things you don't know, girl. In fact—I think someone may have already written it. But that's neither here nor there." A rattling cough. "And I did mean peonies, by the way."

"Who *are* you?" Luce sat up and leaned back against the wall. She hoped whoever the voice belonged to couldn't see her legs trembling.

"Who? Me?" he asked. "I'm just . . . me. I'm here a lot."

"Okay. . . . Doing what?"

"Oh, you know, hanging out." He cleared his throat, and it sounded like someone gargling with rocks. "I like it here. Nice and calm. Some of these Announcers can be such zoos. But not yours, Luce. Not yet, anyway."

"I'm confused." More than confused, Luce was afraid. Should she even be talking to this stranger? How did he know her name?

"For the most part, I'm just your average casual observer, but sometimes I keep an ear out for travelers." His voice came closer, causing Luce to shiver. "Like yourself. See, I've been around awhile, and sometimes travelers, they need a smidge of advice. You been up by the waterfall yet? *Very* scenic. A-plus, as far as waterfalls go."

Luce shook her head. "But you said—this is *my* Announcer? A message of *my* past. So why would *you* be—"

"Well! Sor-reee!" The voice grew louder, indignant. "But may I just raise a question: If the channels to your past are so precious, why'd you leave your Announcers wide open for all the world to jump inside? Hmm? Why didn't you just lock them?"

"I didn't, um . . ." Luce had no idea she'd left anything wide open. And no idea Announcers could even be locked.

She heard a small *whoomp,* like clothes or shoes being thrown into a suitcase, but she still couldn't see a thing. "I see I've overstayed my welcome. I won't waste your time." The voice sounded suddenly choked up. And then more softly, from a distance: "Goodbye."

The voice vanished into the darkness. It was nearly silent inside the Announcer again. Just the soft cascade of the waterfall above. Just the desperate beat of Luce's heart.

For just a moment, she hadn't been alone. With that voice there, she'd been nervous, alarmed, on edge . . . but she hadn't been alone.

"Wait!" she called, pushing herself to her feet.

"Yes?" The voice was right back at her side.

"I didn't mean to kick you out," she said. For some reason, she wasn't ready for the voice to just disappear. There was something about him. He knew her. He had called her by name. "I just wanted to know who you were."

"Oh, hell," he said, a little giddy. "You can call me . . . Bill."

"Bill," she repeated, squinting to see more than the dim cave walls around her. "Are you invisible?"

"Sometimes. Not always. Certainly don't have to be. Why? You'd prefer to see me?"

"It might make things a little bit less weird."

"Doesn't that depend on what I look like?"

"Well—" Luce started to say.

"So"—his voice sounded as if he were smiling— "what do you want me to look like?"

"I don't know." Luce shifted her weight. Her left side was damp from the spray of the waterfall. "Is it really up to me? What do you look like when you're just being yourself?"

"I have a range. You'd probably want me to start with something cute. Am I right?"

"I guess. . . ."

"Okay," the voice muttered. *"Huminah huminah huminah hummm."*

"What are you doing?" Luce asked.

"Putting on my face."

There was a flash of light. A blast that would have sent Luce tumbling backward if the wall hadn't been right behind her. The flash died down into a tiny ball of cool white light. By its illumination she could see the rough expanse of a gray stone floor beneath her feet. A stone wall stretched up behind her, water trickling down its face. And something more:

There on the floor in front of her stood a small gargoyle.

"Ta-da!" he said.

He was about a foot tall, crouched low with his arms crossed and his elbows resting on his knees. His skin was the color of stone—he *was* stone—but when he waved at her, she could see he was limber enough to be made of flesh and muscle. He looked like the sort of statue you'd find capping the roof of a Catholic church. His fingernails and toenails were long and pointed, like little claws. His ears were pointed, too—and pierced with small stone hoops. He had two little hornlike nubs protruding from the top of a forehead that was fleshy and wrinkled. His large lips were pursed in a grimace that made him look like a very old baby.

"So you're Bill?"

"That's right," he said. "I'm Bill."

Bill was an odd-looking thing, but certainly not someone to be afraid of. Luce circled him and noticed the ridged vertebrae protruding from his spine. And the small pair of gray wings tucked behind his back so that the two tips were twined together.

"What do you think?" he asked.

"Great," she said flatly. One look at any other pair of wings—even Bill's—made her miss Daniel so much her stomach hurt.

Bill stood up; it was strange to see the arms and legs that were made of stone move like muscle.

"You don't like the way I look. I can do better," he said, disappearing in another flash of light. "Hold on."

Flash.

Daniel stood before her, cloaked in a shining aura of violet light. His unfurled wings were glorious and massive, beckoning her to step inside them. He held out a hand and she sucked in her breath. She knew something was strange about his being there, that she'd been in the middle of doing something else—only she couldn't recall what or with whom. Her mind felt hazy, her memory obscured. But none of that mattered. Daniel was here. She wanted to cry with happiness. She stepped toward him and put her hand in his.

"There," he said softly. "Now, that's the reaction I was after."

"What?" Luce whispered, confused. Something was rising to the forefront of her mind, telling her to pull away. But Daniel's eyes overrode that hesitation and she let herself be pulled in, forgetting everything but the taste of his lips.

"Kiss me." His voice was a raspy croak. *Bill's.*

Luce screamed and jumped back. Her mind felt jolted as if from a deep sleep. What had happened? How had she thought she'd seen Daniel in—

Bill. He'd tricked her. She jerked her hand away from his, or maybe he dropped hers during the flash when he changed into a large, warty toad. He croaked out two *ribbit*s, then hopped over to the spring of water dripping down the cave wall. His tongue shot out into the stream.

Luce was breathing hard and trying not to show how devastated she felt. "Stop it," she said sharply. "Just go back to the gargoyle. *Please.*"

"As you wish."

Flash.

Bill was back, crouched low with his arms crossed over his knees. Still as stone.

"I thought you'd come around," he said.

Luce looked away, embarrassed that he had gotten a rise out of her, angry that he seemed to have enjoyed it.

"Now that that's all settled," he said, scurrying around so he was standing where she could see him again, "what would you like to learn first?"

"From you? Nothing. I have no idea what you're even doing here."

"I've upset you," Bill said, snapping his stone fingers. "I'm sorry. I was just trying to learn your tastes. You know—likes: Daniel Grigori and cute little gargoyles." He listed on his fingers. "Dislikes: frogs. I think I've got it now. No more of that funny business from me." He spread his wings and flitted up to sit on her shoulder. He was heavy. "Just the tricks of the trade," he whispered.

"I don't need any tricks."

"Come now. You don't even know how to lock an Announcer to keep out the bad guys. Don't you want to at least know that?"

Luce raised an eyebrow at him. "Why would you help me?"

"You're not the first to skip around the past, you know, and everybody needs a guide. Lucky you, you chanced upon me. You could have gotten stuck with Virgil—"

"Virgil?" Luce asked, having a flashback to sophomore English. "As in the guy who led Dante through the nine circles of Hell?"

"That's the one. He's *so* by the book, it's a snooze. Anyway, you and I aren't sojourning through Hell right now," he explained with a shrug. "Tourist season."

Luce thought back to the moment she'd seen Luschka burst into flames in Moscow, to the raw pain she'd felt when Lucia had told her Daniel had disappeared from the hospital in Milan.

"Sometimes it feels like Hell," she said.

"That's only because it took us this long to be introduced." Bill extended his stony little hand toward hers.

Luce stalled. "So what, um, side are you on?"

Bill whistled. "Hasn't anyone told you it's more complicated than that? That the boundaries between 'good' and 'evil' have been blurred by millennia of free will?"

"I know all that, but—"

"Look, if it makes you feel any better, have you ever heard of the Scale?"

Luce shook her head.

"Sorta like hall monitors within Announcers who make sure travelers get where they're going. Members of the Scale are impartial, so there's no siding with Heaven or with Hell. Okay?"

"Okay." Luce nodded. "So you're in the Scale?"

Bill winked. "Now, we're almost there, so—"

"Almost where?"

"To the next life you're traveling to, the one that cast this shadow we're in."

Luce ran her hand through the water running down the wall. "This shadow—this Announcer—is different."

"If it is, it's only because that's what you want it to be. If you want a rest-stop–type cave inside an Announcer, it appears for you."

"I didn't want a rest stop."

"No, but you *needed* one. Announcers can pick up on that. Also, I was here helping out, wanting it on your behalf." The little gargoyle shrugged, and Luce heard a sound like boulders knocking against each other. "The inside of an Announcer isn't anyplace at all. It's a never-where, the dark echo cast by something in the past. Each one is different, adapting to the needs of its travelers, so long as they're inside."

There was something wild about the idea of this echo of Luce's past knowing what she wanted or needed better than she did. "So how long do people stay inside?" she asked. "Days? Weeks?"

"No time. Not the way you're thinking. Within Announcers, real time doesn't pass at all. But still, you don't want to hang around here *too* long. You could forget where you're going, get lost forever. Become a hoverer. And that's ugly business. These are portals, remember, not destinations."

Luce rested her head against the damp stone wall. She didn't know what to make of Bill. "This is your job. Serving as a guide to, uh, travelers like me?"

"Sure, exactly." Bill snapped his fingers, the friction sending up a spark. "You nailed it."

"How'd a gargoyle like you get stuck doing this?"

"Excuse me, I take pride in my work."

"I mean, who hired you?"

Bill thought for a moment, his marble eyes rolling back and forth in their sockets. "Think of it as a volunteer position. I'm good at Announcer travel, is all. No reason not to spread my expertise around." He turned to her with his palm cupping his stony chin. "When are we going to, anyway?"

"*When* are we . . . ?" Luce stared at him, confused.

"You have no idea, do you?" He slapped his forehead. "You're telling me that you dove out of the present without any fundamental knowledge about stepping through? That how you end up *when* you end up is a complete mystery to you?"

"How was I supposed to learn?" Luce said. "No one told me anything!"

Bill fluttered down from her shoulder and paced along the ledge. "You're right, you're right. We'll just go back to basics." He stopped in front of Luce, tiny hands on his thick hips. "So. Here we go: What is it that you want?"

"I want . . . to be with Daniel," she said slowly. There was more, but she wasn't sure how to explain it.

"Huh!" Bill looked even more dubious than his heavy brow, stone lips, and hooked nose made him look naturally. "The hole in your argument there, Counselor, is that Daniel was already right there beside you when you skipped out of your own time. Was he not?"

Luce slid down the wall and sat, feeling another strong rush of regret. "I had to leave. He wouldn't tell me anything about our past, so I had to go find out for myself."

She expected Bill to argue with her more, but he simply said, "So, you're telling me you're on a *quest*."

Luce felt a faint smile cross her lips. A quest. She liked the sound of that.

"So you *do* want something. See?" Bill clapped. "Okay, first thing you ought to know is that the Announcers are summoned to you based upon what's going on in here." He thumped his stony fist against his chest. "They're kind of like little sharks, drawn by your deepest desires."

"Right." Luce remembered the shadows at Shoreline, how it was almost as though the specific Announcers had chosen *her* and not the other way around.

"So when you step through, the Announcers that seem to quiver before you, begging you to pick them up? They funnel you to the place your soul longs to be."

"So the girl I was in Moscow, and in Milan—and all the other lives I glimpsed before I knew how to step through—I wanted to visit them?"

"Precisely," Bill said. "You just didn't know it. The Announcers knew it for you. You'll get better at this, too. Soon you should begin to feel yourself sharing their knowledge. As strange as it may feel, they're a part of you."

Each one of those cold, dark shadows, a part of her? It made sudden, unexpected sense. It explained how even from the beginning, even when it scared her, Luce hadn't been able to stop herself from stepping through them. Even when Roland warned her they were dangerous. Even when Daniel gaped at her like she'd committed some horrible crime. The Announcers always felt like a door opening. Was it possible that they really were?

Her past, once so unknowable, was out there, and all she had to do was step through into the right doorways? She could see who she'd been, what had drawn Daniel to her, why their love had been damned, how it had grown and changed over time. And, most importantly, what they could be in the future.

"We're already well on our way somewhere," Bill said, "but now that you know what you and your Announcers are capable of, the next time you go stepping through, you need to think about what you want. And don't think *place* or *time,* think overall *quest.*"

"Okay." Luce was working to tidy the jumble of emotions inside her into words that might make any sense out loud.

"Why not try it out now?" Bill said. "Just for practice.

Might give us a heads-up about what we're going to walk into. Think about what it is you're after."

"Understanding," she said slowly.

"Good," Bill said. "What else?"

A nervous energy was coursing through her, as if she was on the brink of something important. "I want to find out why Daniel and I were cursed. And I want to break that curse. I want to stop love from killing me so that we can finally be together—for real."

"Whoa, whoa, whoa." Bill started waving his hands like a man stranded on the side of a dark road. "Let's not get crazy. This is a very long-standing damnation you're up against here. You and Daniel, it's like . . . I don't know, you can't just snap your pretty little fingers and break out of that. You gotta start small."

"Right," Luce said. "Okay. Then I should start by getting to know one of my past selves. Get up close and see her relationship with Daniel unfold. See if she feels the same things I feel."

Bill was nodding, a wacky smile spreading across his full lips. He led her to the edge of the ledge. "I think you're ready. Let's go."

Let's go? The gargoyle was coming with her? Out of the Announcer and into another past? Yes, Luce could use some company, but she barely knew this guy.

"You're wondering why you should trust me, aren't you?" Bill asked.

"No, I—"

"I get it," he said, hovering in the air in front of her. "I'm an acquired taste. Especially compared to the company you're used to keeping. I'm certainly no angel." He snorted. "But I can help make this journey worth your while. We can make a deal, if you want. You get sick of me—just say so. I'll be on my way." He held out his long clawed hand.

Luce shuddered. Bill's hand was crusty with rocky cysts and scabs of lichen, like a ruined statue. The last thing she wanted to do was take it in her own hand. But if she didn't, if she sent him on his way right now . . .

She might be better off with him than without him.

She glanced down at her feet. The short wet ledge beneath them ended where she was standing, dropped off into nothing. Between her shoes, something caught her eye, a shimmer in the rock that made her blink. The ground was shifting . . . softening . . . swaying under her feet.

Luce looked behind her. The slab of rock was crumbling, all the way to the wall of the cave. She stumbled, teetering at the edge. The ledge jerked beneath her— harder—as the particles that held the rock together began to break apart. The ledge disappeared around her, faster and faster, until fresh air brushed the backs of her heels and she jumped—

And sank her right hand into Bill's extended claw. They shook in the air.

"How do we get out of here?" she cried, grasping tight to him now for fear of falling into the abyss she couldn't see.

"Follow your heart." Bill was beaming, calm. "It won't mislead you."

Luce closed her eyes and thought of Daniel. A feeling of weightlessness overcame her, and she caught her breath. When she opened her eyes, she was somehow soaring through static-filled darkness. The stone cave shifted and pulled in on itself into a small golden orb of light that shrank and was gone.

Luce glanced over, and Bill was right there with her.

"What was the first thing I ever told you?" he asked.

Luce recalled how his voice had seemed to reach all the way inside her.

"You said to slow down. That I'd never learn any-thing zipping around my past so quickly."

"And?"

"It was exactly what I wanted to do, I just didn't know I wanted it."

"Maybe that's why you found me when you did," Bill shouted over the wind, his gray wings bristling as they sped along. "And maybe that's why we've ended up . . . right . . . here."

The wind stopped. The static crackling smoothed to silence.

Luce's feet slammed onto the ground, a sensation like flying off a swing set and landing on a grassy lawn. She was out of the Announcer and somewhere else. The air was warm and a little humid. The light around her feet told her it was dusk.

They were sunk deep in a field of thick, soft, brilliant green grass, as high as her calves. Here and there the grass was dotted with tiny bright-red fruit—wild strawberries. Ahead, a thin row of silver birch trees marked the edge of the manicured lawn of an estate. Some distance beyond that stood an enormous house.

From here she could make out a white stone flight of stairs that led to the back entrance of the large, Tudor-style mansion. An acre of pruned yellow rosebushes bordered the lawn's north side, and a miniature hedge maze filled the area near the iron gate on the east. In the center lay a bountiful vegetable garden, beans climbing high along their poles. A pebble trail cut the yard in half and led to a large whitewashed gazebo.

Goose bumps rose on Luce's arms. This was the place. She had a visceral sense that she had been here before. This was no ordinary déjà vu. She was staring at a place that had meant something to her and Daniel. She half expected to see the two of them there right now, wrapped in each other's arms.

But the gazebo was empty, filled only with the orange light of the setting sun.

Someone whistled, making her jump.

Bill.

She'd forgotten he was with her. He hovered in the air so that their heads were on the same level. Outside the Announcer, he was somewhat more repulsive than he'd seemed at first. In the light, his flesh was dry and scaly, and he smelled pretty strongly of mildew. Flies buzzed around his head. Luce edged away from him a little, almost wishing he'd go back to being invisible.

"Sure beats a war zone," he said, eyeing the grounds.

"How did you know where I was before?"

"I'm . . . Bill." He shrugged. "I know things."

"Okay, then, where are we now?"

"Helston, England"—he pointed a claw tip toward his head and closed his eyes—"in what you'd call 1854." Then he clasped his stone claws together in front of his chest like a gnomey sort of schoolboy reciting a history report. "A sleepy southern town in the county of Cornwall, granted charter by King John himself. Corn's a few feet tall, so I'd say it's probably midsummer. Pity we missed the month of May—they have a Flora Day festival here like you wouldn't believe. Or maybe you would! Your past self was the belle of the ball the last two years in a row. Her father's very rich, see. Got in at the ground level of the copper trade—"

"Sounds terrific." Luce cut him off and started tramping across the grass. "I'm going in there. I want to talk to her."

"Hold up." Bill flew past her, then looped back, fluttering a few inches in front of her face. "Now, this? This won't do at all."

He waved a finger in a circle, and Luce realized he was talking about her clothes. She was still in the Italian nurse's uniform she'd worn during the First World War.

He grabbed the hem of her long white skirt and lifted it to her ankles. "What do you have on under there? Are those *Converse*? You've gotta be kidding me with those." He clucked his tongue. "How you ever survived those other lifetimes without me . . ."

"I got along fine, thank you."

"You'll need to do more than 'get along' if you want to spend some time here." Bill flew back up to eye level with Luce, then zipped around her three times. When she turned to look for him, he was gone.

But then, a second later, she heard his voice—though it sounded as if it was coming from a great distance. "Yes! Brilliant, Bill!"

A gray dot appeared in the air near the house, growing larger, then larger, until Bill's stone wrinkles became clear. He was flying toward her now, and carrying a dark bundle in his arms.

When he reached her, he simply plucked at her side, and the baggy white nurse's uniform split down its seam and slid right off her body. Luce flung her arms around her bare body modestly, but it seemed like only a second later that a series of petticoats was being tugged over her head.

Bill scrambled around her like a rabid seamstress, binding her waist into a tight corset, until sharp boning poked her skin in all sorts of uncomfortable places. There was so much taffeta in her petticoats that even standing still in a bit of a breeze, she rustled.

She thought she looked pretty good for the era—until she recognized the white apron tied around her waist, over her long black dress. Her hand went to her hair and yanked off a white servant's headpiece.

"I'm a *maid*?" she asked.

"Yes, Einstein, you're a maid."

Luce knew it was dumb, but she felt a little disappointed. The estate was so grand and the gardens so lovely and she knew she was on a quest and all that, but couldn't she have just strolled around the grounds here like a real Victorian lady?

"I thought you said my family was rich."

"Your *past* self's family was rich. Filthy rich. You'll see when you meet her. She goes by Lucinda and thinks your nickname is an *absolute abomination,* by the way." Bill pinched his nose and lifted it high in the air, giving a pretty laughable imitation of a snob. "*She's* rich, yes, but *you,* my dear, are a time-traveling intruder who knows not the ways of this high society. So unless you want to stick out like a Manchester seamstress and get shown the door before you even get to have a chat with Lucinda, you need to go undercover. You're a scullery maid. Serving girl. Chamber-pot changer. It's really up to you. Don't worry, I'll stay out of your way. I can disappear in the blink of an eye."

Luce groaned. "And I just go in and pretend like I work here?"

"No." Bill rolled his flinty eyes. "Go up and introduce yourself to the lady of the house, Mrs. Constance. Tell her your last placement moved to the Continent and you're looking for new employment. She's an evil old harridan and a stickler for references. Lucky for you, I'm one step ahead of her. You'll find yours inside your apron pocket."

Luce slipped her hand inside the pocket of her white linen apron and pulled out a thick envelope. The back was stamped shut with a red wax seal; when she turned it over, she read *Mrs. Melville Constance,* scrawled in black ink. "You're kind of a know-it-all, aren't you?"

"Thank you." Bill bowed graciously; then, when he realized Luce had already started toward the house, he flew ahead, beating his wings so rapidly they became two stone-colored blurs on either side of his body.

By then they had passed the silver birches and were crossing the manicured lawn. Luce was about to start up the pebble path to the house, but hung back when she noticed figures in the gazebo. A man and a woman, walking toward the house. Toward Luce.

"Get down," she whispered. She wasn't ready to be

seen by anyone in Helston, especially not with Bill buzzing around her like some oversized insect.

"*You* get down," he said. "Just because I made an invisibility exception for your benefit doesn't mean just any mere mortal can see me. I'm perfectly discreet where I am. Matter of fact, the *only* eyes I have to be watchful about are— Whoa, hey." Bill's stone eyebrows shot up suddenly, making a heavy dragging noise. "I'm out," he said, ducking down behind the tomato vines.

Angels, Luce filled in. They must be the only other souls who could see Bill in this form. She guessed this because she could finally make out the man and woman, the ones who'd prompted Bill to take cover. Gaping through the thick, prickly leaves of the tomato vine, Luce couldn't tear her eyes away from them.

Away from Daniel, really.

The rest of the garden grew very still. The birds' evening songs quieted, and all she could hear were two pairs of feet walking slowly up the gravel path. The last rays of the sun all seemed to fall upon Daniel, throwing a halo of gold around him. His head was tipped toward the woman and he was nodding as he walked. The woman who was not Luce.

She was older than Lucinda could have been—in her twenties, most likely, and very beautiful, with dark, silken curls under a broad straw hat. Her long muslin dress was the color of a dandelion and looked like it must have been very expensive.

"Have you come to like our little hamlet much at all, Mr. Grigori?" the woman was saying. Her voice was high and bright and full of natural confidence.

"Perhaps too much, Margaret." Luce's stomach tied up in a jealous knot as she watched Daniel smile at the woman. "It's hard to believe it's been a week since I arrived in Helston. I could stay on longer even than I'd planned." He paused. "Everyone here has been very kind."

Margaret blushed, and Luce seethed. Even Margaret's blushing was lovely. "We only hope that will come through in your work," she said. "Mother's thrilled, of course, to have an artist staying with us. Everyone is."

Luce crawled along after them as they walked. Past the vegetable garden, she crouched down behind the overgrown rosebushes, planting her hands on the ground and leaning forward to keep the couple in earshot.

Then Luce gasped. She'd pricked her thumb on a thorn. It was bleeding.

She sucked on the wound and shook her hand, trying not to get blood on her apron, but by the time the bleeding had stopped, she realized she'd missed part of the conversation. Margaret was looking up at Daniel expectantly.

"I asked you if you'll be at the solstice festivities later this week." Her tone was a bit pleading. "Mother always makes a big to-do."

Daniel murmured something like yes, he wouldn't

miss it, but he was clearly distracted. He kept looking away from the woman. His eyes darted around the lawn, as if he sensed Luce behind the roses.

When his gaze swept over the bushes where she crouched, they flashed the most intense shade of violet.

SIX

THE WOMAN IN WHITE

HELSTON, ENGLAND · JUNE 18, 1854

By the time Daniel got to Helston, he was angry.

He recognized the setting at once, as soon as the Announcer ejected him alone onto the shingle banks of the Loe. The lake was still, reflecting big tufts of pink cloud in the evening sky. Startled by his sudden appearance, a pair of kingfishers took off across the field of clover and came to rest in a crooked moorland tree beside the main road. The road led, he knew, into the small town where he'd spent a summer with Lucinda.

Standing again on this rich green earth touched a soft place inside him. As much as he worked to close every door to their past, as much as he strove to move beyond each one of her heartbreaking deaths—some mattered more than others. He was surprised at how clearly he still recalled their time in the South of England.

But Daniel wasn't here on holiday. He wasn't here to fall in love with the beautiful copper trader's daughter. He was here to stop a reckless girl from getting so lost in the dark moments of her past that it killed her. He was here to help her undo their curse, once and for all.

He started the long walk toward town.

It was a warm and lazy summer evening in Helston. Out on the streets, ladies in bonnets and lace-trimmed gowns spoke in low, polite voices to the linen-suited men whose arms they held. Couples paused in front of shop windows. They lingered to speak with their neighbors. They stopped on street corners and took ten minutes to say goodbye.

Everything about these people, from their attire to the pace of their strolling, was so infuriatingly slow. Daniel could not have felt more at odds with the passersby on the street.

His wings, hidden beneath his coat, burned with his impatience as he waded through the people. There was one fail-safe place where he knew he could find *Lucinda*—she visited the gazebo in his patron's back garden most evenings just after dusk. But where he might find *Luce*—the one hopping in and out of Announcers, the one he *needed* to find—that, there was no way of knowing.

The other two lives Luce had stumbled into made some sense to Daniel. In the grand scheme, they were . . . anomalies. Past moments when she had come close to unraveling the truth of their curse just before she died. But he couldn't figure out why her Announcer had brought her *here*.

Helston had been a mostly peaceful time for them. In this life, their love had grown slowly, naturally. Even her death had been private, between just the two of them. Once, Gabbe had used the word *respectable* to describe Lucinda's end in Helston. That death, at least, had been theirs alone to suffer.

No, nothing made sense about the accident of her re-visiting this life—which meant she could be anywhere in the hamlet.

"Why, Mr. Grigori," a trilling voice called out on the street. "What a wonderful surprise to find you here in town."

A blond woman in a long patterned blue dress stood before Daniel, taking him utterly by surprise. She held the hand of a pudgy, freckled eight-year-old boy, who looked miserable in a cream-colored jacket with a stain underneath the collar.

At last it dawned on Daniel: Mrs. Holcombe and her talentless son Edward, whom he'd given drawing lessons to for a few painful weeks while in Helston.

"Hello, Edward." Daniel leaned down to shake the little boy's hand, then bowed to his mother. "Mrs. Holcombe."

Until that moment, Daniel had given little thought to his wardrobe as he moved through time. He didn't care what someone on the street thought of his modern gray slacks or whether the cut of his white oxford shirt looked odd compared to any other man's in town. But if he was going to run into people he'd actually known nearly two hundred years ago wearing the clothes he'd worn two days ago to Luce's parents' Thanksgiving, word might begin to travel around.

Daniel didn't want to draw any attention to himself. Nothing could stand in the way of finding Luce. He would simply have to find something else to wear. Not that the Holcombes noticed. Luckily Daniel had returned to a time when he'd been known as an "eccentric" artist.

"Edward, show Mr. Grigori what Mama just bought you," Mrs. Holcombe said, smoothing her son's unruly hair.

The boy reluctantly produced a small paint kit from a satchel. Five glass pots of oil paint and a long red wooden-handled brush.

Daniel made the requisite compliments—about how

Edward was a very lucky little boy, one whose talent now had the proper tools—while trying not to be obvious about looking past the pair for the quickest way out of the conversation.

"Edward's such a gifted child," Mrs. Holcombe insisted, taking hold of Daniel's arm. "Trouble is, he finds your drawing lessons just a little less thrilling than a boy his age expects. It's why I thought a proper paint set might allow him to really come into his own. As an *artiste*. You understand, Mr. Grigori?"

"Yes, yes, of course." Daniel cut her off. "Give him whatever makes him want to paint. Brilliant plan—"

A coldness spread through him and froze his words in his throat.

Cam had just exited from a pub across the street.

For a moment, Daniel churned with anger. He'd been clear enough that he wanted no help from the others. His hands balled into fists, and he took a step toward Cam, but then—

Of course. This was Cam from the Helston era. And by the looks of it, Cam was having the time of his life in his fancy striped tapered slacks and Victorian smoking cap. His black hair was long, cascading just past his shoulders. He leaned against the pub's door, joking with three other men.

Cam slipped a gold-tipped cigar out of a square metal case. He hadn't seen Daniel yet. As soon as he did, he would quit laughing. From the beginning, Cam had traveled through the Announcers more than any of the fallen angels. He was an expert in ways Daniel never could be: That was a gift of those who'd thrown in with Lucifer—they had a talent for traveling through the shadows of the past.

One look at Daniel would tell this Victorian Cam that his rival was an Anachronism.

A man out of time.

Cam would realize that something big was going on. Then Daniel would never be able to shake him.

"You're so very generous, Mr. Grigori." Mrs. Holcombe was still nattering, still had Daniel gripped by his shirtsleeve.

Cam's head began to swivel in his direction.

"Think nothing of it." The words rushed out of Daniel. "Now, if you'll excuse me"—he pried her fingers loose—"I've just got to . . . buy some new clothes."

He made a speedy bow and rushed through the door of the nearest shop.

"Mr. Grigori—" Mrs. Holcombe was practically shouting his name.

Silently, Daniel cursed her, pretending he was out of earshot, which only made her call more loudly. "But that's a dressmaker's, Mr. Grigori!" she shouted, cupping her hands over her mouth.

Daniel was already inside. The glass door of the shop slammed behind him, the bell that was tied to the hinge ringing. He could hide here, at least for a few minutes, in the hopes that Cam hadn't seen him or heard Mrs. Holcombe's shrill voice.

The shop was quiet and smelled of lavender. Well-heeled shoes had worn down its wooden floors, and the shelves along the walls were stacked to the ceiling with bolts of colorful fabrics. Daniel lowered the lace curtain over the window so he'd be less visible from the street. When he turned, he caught a glimpse in the mirror of another person in the shop.

He swallowed a moan of surprised relief.

He'd found her.

Luce was trying on a long white muslin dress. Its high neck fastened with a yellow ribbon, bringing out the incredible hazel of her eyes. Her hair was tied back to one side, clipped with a beaded floral pin. She kept fidgeting with the way the sleeves fell on her shoulders as she stood, examining herself from as many angles as she could in the mirror. Daniel adored all of them.

He wanted to stand there, admiring her forever, but then he remembered himself. He strode toward her and grabbed her by the arm.

"This has gone on long enough." Even as he spoke, Daniel felt overcome by the delicious feel of her skin against his hand. The last time he'd touched her was the night he thought he'd lost her to the Outcasts. "Do you have any idea what a scare you gave me? You're not safe here on your own," he said.

Luce didn't start arguing with Daniel, as he'd

expected. Instead, she screamed and slapped him smartly across the face.

Because she wasn't Luce. She was Lucinda.

And, what was worse, they hadn't even met yet in this lifetime. She must have just come back from London with her family. She and Daniel must have been about to meet at the Constances' summer solstice party.

He could see all of that now as the shock registered on Lucinda's face.

"What day is this?" he asked desperately.

She would think he was insane. Across the room, he had been too love-struck to note the difference between the girl he'd already lost and the girl he had to save.

"I'm sorry," he whispered. This was exactly why he was so terrible as an Anachronism. He got completely lost in the smallest of things. One touch of her skin. One look into her deep hazel eyes. One whiff of the scented powder along her hairline. One shared breath in the cramped space of this tiny shop.

Lucinda winced as she looked at his cheek. In the mirror, it was bright red where she'd slapped him. Her eyes traveled to meet his—and his heart felt like it was caving in. Her pink lips parted and her head cocked slightly to the right. She was looking at him like a woman deep in love.

No.

There was a way it was supposed to happen. A way it

had to happen. They were not supposed to meet until the party. As much as Daniel cursed their fate, he would not disrupt the lives she'd lived before. They were what kept her coming back to him.

He tried to look as uninterested and scowly as possible. Crossing his arms over his chest, shifting his weight to create more space between them, keeping his eyes everywhere but where they wanted to be. On her.

"I'm sorry," Lucinda said, pressing her hands over her heart. "I don't know what came over me. I've *never* done anything like that. . . ."

Daniel wasn't going to argue with her now, though she'd slapped him so many times over the years that Arriane kept a tally in a little spiral notebook marked *You're Fresh*.

"My mistake," he said quickly. "I—I thought you were someone else." He'd already interfered with the past too much, first with Lucia in Milan, and now here. He began to back away.

"Wait." She reached for him. Her eyes were lovely hazel orbs of light pulling him back. "I feel almost as if we *do* know one another, though I can't quite remember—"

"I don't think so, I'm afraid."

He'd made it to the door by then, and was parting the curtain on the window to see if Cam was still outside. He was.

Cam's back was to the shop, and he was making

animated gestures, telling some fabricated story in which he was surely the hero. He could turn around at the slightest provocation. Then Daniel would be caught.

"Please, sir—stop." Lucinda hurried toward Daniel. "Who are you? I think I know you. Please. Wait."

He'd have to take his chances on the street. He could not stay here with Lucinda. Not when she was acting like this. Not when she was falling in love with the wrong version of himself. He'd lived this life before, and this was not how it had happened. So he had to flee.

It killed Daniel to ignore her, to go away from Lucinda when everything in his soul was telling him to turn around and fly right back to the sound of her voice, to the embrace of her arms and the warmth of her lips, to the spellbinding power of her love.

He yanked the shop door open and fled down the street, running at the sunset, running for all he was worth. He did not care at all what it looked like to anyone else in town. He was running out the fire in his wings.

SEVEN

SOLSTICE

HELSTON, ENGLAND · JUNE 21, 1854

Luce's hands were scalded and splotchy and tender to the bone.

Since she'd arrived at the Constances' estate in Helston three days before, she'd done little more than wash an endless pile of dishes. She worked from sunrise to sunset, scrubbing plates and bowls and gravy boats and whole armies of silverware, until, at the end of the day, her new boss, Miss McGovern, laid out supper for the kitchen staff: a sad platter of cold meat, dry hunks of cheese, and a few hard rolls. Each night, after dinner, Luce would fall into a dreamless, timeless sleep on the attic cot she shared with Henrietta, her fellow kitchen maid, a bucktoothed, straw-haired, bosomy girl who'd come to Helston from Penzance.

The sheer amount of work was astonishing.

How could one household dirty enough dishes to keep two girls working twelve hours straight? But the bins of food-caked plates kept arriving, and Miss Mc-Govern kept her beady eyes fixed on Luce's washbasin. By Wednesday, everyone at the estate was buzzing about the solstice party that evening, but to Luce, it only meant more dishes. She stared down at the tin tub of scuzzy water, full of loathing.

"This is *not* what I had in mind," she muttered to Bill, who was hovering, always, on the rim of the cupboard next to her washtub. She still wasn't used to being the only one in the kitchen who could see him. It made her nervous every time he hovered over other members of the staff, making dirty jokes that only Luce could hear and no one—besides Bill—ever laughed at.

"You children of the millennium have absolutely no work ethic," he said. "Keep your voice down, by the way."

Luce unclenched her jaw. "If scrubbing this disgusting soup tureen had anything to do with understanding my past, my *work ethic* would make your head spin. But this is pointless." She waved a cast iron skillet in Bill's face. Its handle was slick with pork grease. "Not to mention nauseating."

Luce knew her frustration didn't have anything to do with the dishes. She probably sounded like a brat. But she'd barely been above ground since she'd started working here. She hadn't seen Helston Daniel once since that first glimpse in the garden, and she had no idea where her past self was. She was lonely and listless and depressed in a way she hadn't been since those awful early days at Sword & Cross, before she'd had Daniel, before she'd had anyone she could truly count on.

She'd abandoned Daniel, Miles and Shelby, Arriane and Gabbe, Callie, and her parents—all for what? To be a scullery maid? No, to unravel this curse, something she didn't even know whether she was capable of doing. So Bill thought she was being whiny. She couldn't help it. She was inches away from a breakdown.

"I hate this job. I hate this place. I hate this stupid solstice party and this stupid pheasant soufflé—"

"Lucinda will be at the party tonight," Bill said suddenly. His voice was infuriatingly calm. "She happens to *adore* the Constances' pheasant soufflé." He flitted up to sit cross-legged on the countertop, his head twisting a creepy 360 degrees around his neck to make sure the two of them were alone.

"Lucinda will be there?" Luce dropped the skillet

and her scrub brush into the sudsy tub. "I'm going to talk to her. I'm getting out of this kitchen, and I'm going to talk to her."

Bill nodded, as if this had been the plan all along. "Just remember your position. If a future version of yourself had popped up at some boarding school party of yours and told you—"

"*I* would have wanted to know," Luce said. "Whatever it was, I would have insisted on knowing everything. I would have died to know."

"Mmm-hmm. Well." Bill shrugged. "Lucinda won't. I can guarantee you that."

"That's impossible." Luce shook her head. "She's . . . me."

"Nope. She's a version of you who has been reared by completely different parents in a very different world. You share a *soul*, but she's nothing like you. You'll see." He gave her a cryptic grin. "Just proceed with caution." Bill's eyes shot toward the door at the front of the large kitchen, which swung open abruptly. "Look lively, Luce!"

He plunked his feet into the washtub and let out a raspy, contented sigh just as Miss McGovern entered, pulling Henrietta by the elbow. The head maid was listing the courses for the evening meal.

"After the stewed prunes . . . ," she droned.

On the other side of the kitchen, Luce whispered to Bill. "We're not finished with this conversation."

His stony feet splashed suds onto her apron. "May I advise you to stop talking to your invisible friends while you're working? People are going to think you're crazy."

"I'm beginning to wonder about that myself." Luce sighed and stood straight, knowing that was all she was going to get out of Bill, at least until the others had left.

"I'll expect you and Myrtle to be in tip-top shape this evening," Miss McGovern said loudly to Henrietta, sending a quick glare back at Luce.

Myrtle. The name Bill had made up on her letters of reference.

"Yes, miss," Luce said flatly.

"Yes, miss!" There was no sarcasm in Henrietta's reply. Luce liked Henrietta well enough, if she overlooked how badly the girl needed a bath.

Once Miss McGovern had bustled out of the kitchen and the two girls were alone, Henrietta hopped up on the table next to Luce, swinging her black boots to and fro. She had no idea that Bill was sitting right beside her, mimicking her movements.

"Fancy a plum?" Henrietta asked, pulling two ruby-colored spheres from her apron pocket and holding one out to Luce.

What Luce liked most about the girl was that she never did a drop of work unless the boss was in the room. They each took a bite, grinning as the sweet juice trickled from the sides of their mouths.

"Thought I heard you talking to someone else in here before," Henrietta said. She raised an eyebrow. "Have you got yourself a fellow, Myrtle? Oh, please don't say it's Harry from the stables! He's a rotter, he is."

Just then, the kitchen door swung open again, making both girls jump, drop their fruit, and pretend to scrub the nearest dish.

Luce was expecting Miss McGovern, but she froze when she saw two girls in beautiful matching white silk dressing gowns, squealing with laughter as they tore through the filthy kitchen.

One of them was Arriane.

The other—it took Luce a moment to place her—was Annabelle. The hot-pink-headed girl Luce had met for just a moment at Parents' Day, all the way back at Sword & Cross. She'd introduced herself as Arriane's sister.

Some sister.

Henrietta kept her eyes down, as if this game of tag through the kitchen were a normal occurrence, as if she might get in trouble if she even pretended to see the two girls—who certainly didn't see either Luce or Henrietta. It was like the servants blended in with the filthy pots and pans.

Or else Arriane and Annabelle were just laughing too hard. As they squeezed past the pastry-making table, Arriane grabbed a fistful of flour from the marble slab and tossed it in Annabelle's face.

For half a second, Annabelle looked furious; then she started laughing even harder, grabbing a fistful herself and casting it at Arriane.

They were gasping for air by the time they barreled through the back door, out to the small garden, which led to the big garden, where the sun actually shone and where Daniel might be and where Luce was dying to follow.

Luce couldn't have pinned down what she was feeling if she'd tried—shock or embarrassment, wonder or frustration?

All of it must have shown on her face, because Henrietta eyed her knowingly and leaned in to whisper, "That lot arrived last night. Someone's cousins from London, in town for the party." She walked over to the pastry table. "They nearly wrecked the strawberry pie with their antics. Oh, it must be lovely, being rich. Maybe in our next lives, hey, Myrtle?"

"Ha." It was all Luce could manage.

"I'm off to set the table, sadly," Henrietta said, cradling a stack of china under her fleshy pink arm. "Why not have a handful of flour ready to toss, just in case those girls come back this way?" She winked at Luce and pushed the door open with her broad behind, then disappeared into the hallway.

Someone else appeared in her place: a boy, also in a servant's outfit, his face hidden behind a giant box of groceries. He set them down on the table across the kitchen from Luce.

She started at the sight of his face. At least, having just seen Arriane, she was a little more prepared.

"Roland!"

He twitched when he looked up, then collected himself. As he walked toward her, it was her clothes Roland couldn't stop staring at. He pointed at her apron. "Why are you dressed like that?"

Luce tugged at the tie on her apron, pulling it off. "I'm not who you think I am."

He stopped in front of her and stared, turning his head first slightly to the left, then to the right. "Well, you're the spitting image of another girl I know. Since when do the Biscoes go slumming in the scullery?"

"The Biscoes?"

Roland raised an eyebrow at her, amused. "Oh, I get it. You're playing at being someone else. What are you calling yourself?"

"Myrtle," Luce said miserably.

"And you are not the Lucinda Biscoe to whom I served that quince tart on the terrace two days ago?"

"No." Luce didn't know what to say, how to convince him. She turned to Bill for help, but he had disappeared even from her view. Of course. Roland, fallen angel that he was, would have been able to see Bill.

"What would Miss Biscoe's father say if he saw his daughter down here, up to her elbows in grease?" Roland smiled. "It's a fine prank to pull on him."

"Roland, it is not a—"

"What are you hiding from up there, anyhow?" Roland jerked his head toward the garden.

A tinny rumbling in the pantry at Luce's feet revealed where Bill had gone. He seemed to be sending her some kind of signal, only she had no idea what it was. Bill probably wanted her to keep her mouth shut, but what was he going to do, come out and stop her?

A sheen of sweat was visible on Roland's brow. "Are we alone, Lucinda?"

"Absolutely."

He cocked his head at her and waited. "I don't *feel* that we are."

The only other presence in the room was Bill. How could Roland sense him when Arriane had not?

"Look, I'm really not the girl you think I am," Luce said again. "I am *a* Lucinda, but I—I'm here from the future—it's hard to explain, actually." She took a deep breath. "I was born in Thunderbolt, Georgia . . . in 1992."

"*Oh.*" Roland swallowed. "Well, well." He closed his eyes and started speaking very slowly: "And the stars in the sky fell to the earth, like figs blown off a tree in a gale . . ."

The words were cryptic, but Roland recited them soulfully, almost like he was quoting a favorite line from an old blues song. The kind of song she'd heard him sing at a karaoke party back at Sword & Cross. In that moment, he seemed like the Roland she knew back home, as if he'd slipped out of this Victorian character for a little while.

Only, there was something else about his words. Luce recognized them from somewhere. "What is that? What does that mean?" she asked.

The cupboard rattled again. More loudly this time.

"Nothing." Roland's eyes opened and he was back to his Victorian self. His hands were tough and callused and his biceps were larger than she was used to seeing them. His clothes were soaked with sweat against his dark skin. He looked tired. A heavy sadness fell over Luce.

"You're a servant here?" she asked. "The others—Arriane—they get to run around and . . . But you have to work, don't you? Just because you're—"

"Black?" Roland said, holding her gaze until she looked away, uncomfortable. "Don't worry about me, Lucinda. I've suffered worse than mortal folly. Besides, I'll have my day."

"It gets better," she said, feeling that any reassurance she gave him would be trite and insubstantial, wondering if what she said was really true. "People can be awful."

"Well. We can't worry about them too much, can we?" Roland smiled. "What brought you back here, anyway, Lucinda? Does Daniel know? Does Cam?"

"Cam's here, too?" Luce shouldn't have been surprised, but she was.

"If my timing's right, he's probably just rolled into town."

Luce couldn't worry about that now. "Daniel doesn't know, not yet," she admitted. "But I need to find him, and Lucinda, too. I have to know—"

"Look," Roland said, backing away from Luce, his hands raised, almost as if she were radioactive. "You didn't see me here today. We didn't have this talk. But you can't just go up to Daniel—"

"I know," she said. "He'll freak out."

"Freak out?'" Roland tried out the strange-sounding phrase, almost making Luce laugh. "If you mean he might fall in love with *this* you"—he pointed at her— "then yes. It's really quite dangerous. You're a tourist here."

"Fine, then I'm a tourist. But I can at least talk to them."

"No, you can't. You don't inhabit this life."

"I don't want to inhabit anything. I just want to know *why*—"

"Your being here is dangerous—to you, to them, to everything. Do you understand?"

Luce didn't understand. How could she be dangerous? "I don't want to *stay* here, I just want to know why this keeps happening between me and Daniel—I mean, between this Lucinda and Daniel."

"That's precisely what I mean." Roland dragged his hand down his face, gave her a hard look. "Hear me: You can observe them from a distance. You can—I don't know—look through the windows. So long as you know nothing here is yours to take."

"But why can't I just *talk* to them?"

He went to the door and closed and bolted it. When he turned back, his face was serious. "Listen, it is *possible* that you might do something that changes your past, something that ripples down through time and rewrites it so that you—future Lucinda—will be changed."

"So I'll be careful—"

"There is no careful. You are a bull in the china shop of love. You'll have no way of knowing what you've broken or how precious it may be. Any change you enact is not going to be obvious. There will be no great sign reading IF YOU VEER RIGHT, YOU SHALL BE A PRINCESSS, VERSUS IF YOU VEER LEFT, YOU'LL REMAIN A SCULLERY MAID FOREVER."

"Come on, Roland, don't you think I have slightly loftier goals than ending up a princess?" Luce said sharply.

"I could venture a guess that there is a curse you want to put an end to?"

Luce blinked at him, feeling stupid.

"Right, then, best of luck!" Roland laughed brightly. "But even if you succeed, you won't know it, my dear.

The very *moment* you change your past? That event will be as it *has always been*. And everything that comes after it will be as it has always been. Time tidies up after itself. And you're part of it, so you will not know the difference."

"I'd have to know," she said, hoping that saying it aloud would make it true. "Surely I'd have some sense—"

Roland shook his head. "No. But most certainly, before you could do any good, you would distort the future by making the Daniel of this era fall in love with *you* instead of that pretentious twit Lucinda Biscoe."

"I need to meet her. I need to see why they love each other—"

Roland shook his head again. "It would be even *worse* to get involved with your past self, Lucinda. Daniel at least knows the dangers and can mind himself so as not to drastically alter time. But Lucinda Biscoe? She doesn't know *anything*."

"None of us ever do," Luce said around a sudden lump in her throat.

"This Lucinda, she doesn't have a lot of time left. Let her spend it with Daniel. Let her be happy. If you overstep into her world and anything changes for her, it could change for you, too. And that could be most unfortunate."

Roland sounded like a nicer, less sarcastic version of Bill. Luce didn't want to hear any more about all the things she couldn't do, shouldn't do. If she could just talk to her past self—

"What if Lucinda could have *more* time?" she asked. "What if—"

"It's impossible. If anything, you'll just hasten her end. You're not going to change anything by having a chat with Lucinda. You're just going to make a mess of your past lives along with your current one."

"My current life is not a mess. And I can fix things. I have to."

"I suppose that remains to be seen. Lucinda Biscoe's life is over, but your ending has yet to be written." Roland dusted off his hands on his trouser legs. "Maybe there *is* some change you can work into your life, into the grand story of you and Daniel. But you will not do that here."

As Luce felt her lips stiffen into a pout, Roland's face softened.

"Look," he said. "At least *I'm* glad you're here."

"You are?"

"No one else is going to tell you this, but we're all rooting for you. I don't know what brought you here or how the journey was even possible. But I have to think it's a good sign." He studied her until she felt ridiculous. "You're coming into yourself, aren't you?"

"I don't know," Luce said. "I think so. I'm just trying to understand."

"Good."

Voices in the hallway made Roland suddenly pull away from Luce, toward the door. "I'll see you tonight," he said, unbolting the door and quietly slipping out.

As soon as Roland was gone, the cupboard door swung open, banging the back of her leg. Bill popped out, gasping for air loudly as if he'd been holding his breath the whole time.

"I could wring your neck right now!" he said, his chest heaving.

"I don't know why you're all out of breath. It's not like you even breathe."

"It's for effect! All the trouble I go through to camouflage you here and you go and out yourself to the first guy who walks through the door."

Luce rolled her eyes. "Roland's not going to make a big deal out of seeing me here. He's cool."

"Oh, he's *so* cool," Bill said. "He's *so* smart. If he's so great, why didn't he tell you what I know about *not* keeping one's distance from one's past? About getting"— he paused dramatically, widening his stone eyes— *"inside?"*

Now she leaned down toward him. "What are you talking about?"

He crossed his arms over his chest and wagged his stone tongue. "I'm not telling."

"Bill!" Luce pleaded.

"Not yet, anyway. First let's see how you do tonight."

❋

Near dusk, Luce caught her first break in Helston. Right before supper, Miss McGovern announced to the entire kitchen that the front-of-house staff needed a few extra helping hands for the party. Luce and Henrietta, the two youngest scullery maids and the two most desperate to see the party up close, were the first to thrust up their hands to volunteer.

"Fine, fine." Miss McGovern jotted down the names of both girls, her eyes lingering on Henrietta's oily mop of hair. "On the condition that you bathe. Both of you. You stink of onions."

"Yes, miss," both girls chimed, though as soon as their boss had left the room, Henrietta turned to Luce. "Take a bath before this party? And risk getting me fingers all pruny? The miss is mad!"

Luce laughed but was secretly ecstatic as she filled the round tin tub behind the cellar. She could only carry enough boiling water to get the bath lukewarm, but still she luxuriated in the suds—and the idea that this night, finally, she would get to see Lucinda. Would she get to see Daniel, too? She donned a clean servant's dress of Henrietta's for the party. At eight o'clock that evening, the first guests began arriving through the wicket gate at the north entrance of the estate.

❋ 132 ❦

Watching from the window in the front hallway as the caravans of lamplit carriages pulled into the circular drive, Luce shivered. The foyer was warm with activity. Around her the other servants buzzed, but Luce stood still. She could feel it: a trembling in her chest that told her Daniel was nearby.

The house looked beautiful. Luce had been given one very brief tour by Miss McGovern the morning she started, but now, under the glow of so many chandeliers, she almost didn't recognize the place. It was as if she'd stepped into a Merchant-Ivory film. Tall pots of violet lilies lined the entryway, and the velvet-upholstered furniture had been pushed back against the floral wallpapered walls to make room for the guests.

They came through the front door in twos and threes, guests as old as white-haired Mrs. Constance and as young as Luce herself. Bright-eyed, and wrapped in white summer cloaks, the women curtseyed to the men in smart suits and waistcoats. Black-coated waiters whisked through the large open foyer, offering twinkling crystal goblets of champagne.

Luce found Henrietta near the doors to the main ballroom, which looked like a flower bed in bloom: Extravagant, brightly colored gowns of every color, in organza, tulle, and silk, with grosgrain sashes, filled the room. The younger ladies carried bright nosegays of flowers, making the whole house smell like summer.

Henrietta's task was to collect the ladies' shawls and

reticules as they entered. Luce had been told to distribute dance cards—small, expensive-looking booklets, with the Constances' jeweled family crest sewn into the front cover and the orchestra's set list written inside.

"Where are all the men?" Luce whispered to Henrietta.

Henrietta snorted. "That's my girl! In the smoking room, of course." She jerked her head left, where a hallway led into the shadows. "Where they'll be smart to stay until the meal is served, if you ask me. Who wants to hear all that jabbering on about some war all the way in Crimea? Not these ladies. Not I. Not you, Myrtle." Then Henrietta's thin eyebrows lifted and she pointed toward the French windows. "Oof, I spoke too soon. Seems one of 'em has escaped."

Luce turned. A single man was standing in the room full of women. His back was to them, showing nothing but a slick mane of jet-black hair and a long tailed jacket. He was talking to a blond woman in a soft rose-colored ball gown. Her diamond chandelier earrings sparkled when she turned her head—and locked eyes with Luce.

Gabbe.

The beautiful angel blinked a few times, as if trying to decide whether Luce was an apparition. Then she tilted her head ever so slightly at the man she was standing with, as if trying to send him a signal. Before he'd even turned all the way around, Luce recognized the clean, sharp profile.

Cam.

Luce gasped, dropping all the dance card booklets. She bent down and clumsily started scooping them up off the floor. Then she thrust them into Henrietta's hands and ducked out of the room.

"Myrtle!" Henrietta said.

"I'll be right back," Luce whispered, sprinting up the long, curved stairway before Henrietta could even reply.

Miss McGovern would send Luce packing as soon as she learned that Luce had abandoned her post—and the expensive dance cards—in the ballroom. But that was the least of Luce's problems. She was not prepared to deal with Gabbe, not when she needed to focus on finding Lucinda.

And she never wanted to be around Cam. In her own lifetime or any other one. She flinched, remembering the way he'd aimed that arrow straight at what he'd thought was her the night the Outcast tried to carry her reflection away into the sky.

If only Daniel were here . . .

But he wasn't. All Luce could do was hope that he'd be waiting for her—and not too angry—when she figured out what she was doing and came home to the present.

At the top of the stairs, Luce darted inside the first room she came to. She closed the door behind her and leaned against it to catch her breath.

She was alone in a vast parlor. It was a marvelous

room with a plush ivory-upholstered love seat and a pair of leather chairs set around a polished harpsichord. Deep-red curtains hugged the three large windows along the western wall. A fire crackled in the hearth.

Beside Luce was a wall of bookshelves, row after row of thick, leather-bound volumes, stretching from the floor to the ceiling, so high there was even one of those ladders that could be wheeled across the shelves.

An easel stood in the corner, and something about it beckoned to Luce. She'd never set foot upstairs in the Constance estate, and yet: One step onto the thick Persian carpet jogged some part of her memory and told her that she might have seen all of this before.

Daniel. Luce recalled the conversation he'd had with Margaret in the garden. They'd been talking about his painting. He was making his living as an artist. The easel in the corner—it must have been where he worked.

She moved toward it. She had to see what he'd been painting.

Just before she reached it, a trio of high voices made her jump.

They were right outside the door.

She froze, watching the door handle pivot as someone turned it from the outside. She had no choice but to slip behind the thick red-velvet curtain and hide.

There was a rustling of taffeta, the slamming of a door, and one gasp. Followed by a round of giggles. Luce cupped a hand over her mouth and leaned out slightly, just enough to peek around the curtain.

Helston Lucinda stood ten feet away. She was dressed in a fantastic white gown with a soft silk-crepe bodice and an exposed corset back. Her dark hair was pinned high on her head in an array of shiny, intricately placed curls. Her diamond necklace shone against her pale skin, giving her such a regal air it nearly took Luce's breath away.

Her past self was the most elegant creature Luce had ever seen.

"You're all aglow tonight, Lucinda," a soft voice said.

"Did Thomas call on you again?" another teased.

And the other two girls—Luce recognized one as Margaret, the elder Constance daughter, the one who'd walked with Daniel in the garden. The other, a fresher replica of Margaret, must have been the younger sister. She looked about Lucinda's age. She teased her like a good friend.

And she was right, too—Lucinda *was* glowing. It had to be because of Daniel.

Lucinda flopped on the ivory love seat and sighed in a way Luce would never sigh, a melodramatic sigh that begged for attention. Luce knew instantly that Bill was right: She and her past self were absolutely nothing alike.

"*Thomas?*" Lucinda wrinkled her small nose. "Thomas's father is a common logger—"

"Not so!" the younger daughter cried. "He's a very *uncommon* logger! He's *rich*."

"Still, Amelia," Lucinda said, spreading her skirt around her narrow ankles. "He's practically *working-class*."

Margaret perched on the edge of the love seat. "You didn't think so poorly of him last week when he brought you that bonnet from London."

"Well, things change. And I do love a sweet bonnet." Lucinda frowned. "But bonnets aside, I shall tell my father not to permit him to call on me again."

As soon as she'd finished speaking, Lucinda's frown eased into a dreamy smile and she began to hum. The other girls watched, incredulous, as she sang softly to herself, stroking the lace of her shawl and gazing out the window, only inches away from Luce's hiding place.

"What's gotten into her?" Amelia whispered loudly to her sister.

Margaret snorted. "*Who* is more like it."

Lucinda stood up and walked to the window, causing Luce to retreat behind the curtain. Luce's skin felt flushed, and she could hear the soft hum of Lucinda Biscoe's voice just inches away. Then footsteps as Lucinda turned away from the window and her strange song abruptly broke off.

Luce dared another peek from behind the curtain.

Lucinda had gone to the easel, where she stood, transfixed.

"What's this?" Lucinda held up the canvas to show her friends. Luce couldn't see it very clearly, but it looked ordinary enough. Just some kind of flower.

"That is Mr. Grigori's work," Margaret said. "His sketches showed so much promise when he first arrived, but I'm afraid something's come over him. It's been three whole days now of nothing but peonies." She gave a strained shrug. "Odd. Artists are so queer."

"Oh, but he's *handsome*, Lucinda." Amelia took Lucinda by the hand. "We must introduce you to Mr. Grigori tonight. He's got such lovely blond hair, and his eyes . . . Oh, his eyes could make you melt!"

"If Lucinda is too good for Thomas Kennington and all of his money, I doubt very much that a simple painter will measure up." Margaret spoke so sharply that it was clear to Luce that she must have had feelings for Daniel herself.

"I'd like very much to meet him," Lucinda said, drifting back into her soft hum.

Luce held her breath. So Lucinda hadn't even met him yet? How was that possible when she was so clearly in love?

"Let's go, then," Amelia said, tugging on Lucinda's hand. "We're missing half the party gossiping up here."

Luce had to do something. But from what Bill and

Roland had said, it was impossible to save her past life. Too dangerous to even try. Even if she managed it somehow, the cycle of Lucindas who lived after this one might be altered. Luce herself might be altered. Or worse.

Eliminated.

But maybe there was a way for Luce to at least warn Lucinda. So that she didn't walk into this relationship already blinded by love. So that she didn't die a pawn in an age-old punishment without even a speck of understanding. The girls were almost out the door when Luce got the courage to step from behind the curtain.

"Lucinda!"

Her past self whipped around; her eyes narrowed when they fell on Luce's servant's dress. "Have you been spying on us?"

No spark of recognition registered in her eyes. It was odd that Roland had mistaken Luce for Lucinda in the kitchen but Lucinda herself appeared to see no resemblance between them. What did Roland see that this girl couldn't? Luce took a deep breath and forced herself to go through with her flimsy plan. "N-not spying, no," she stammered. "I need to speak with you."

Lucinda chortled and glanced at her two friends. "I beg your pardon?"

"Aren't you the one handing out the dance cards?" Margaret asked Luce. "Mother won't be very happy to hear that you're neglecting your duties. What is your name?"

"Lucinda." Luce drew nearer and lowered her voice. "It's about the artist. Mr. Grigori."

Lucinda locked eyes with Luce, and something flickered between them. Lucinda seemed unable to pull away. "You go on without me," she said to her friends. "I'll be down in just a moment."

The two girls exchanged confused glances, but it was clear that Lucinda was the leader of the group. Her friends glided out the door without another word.

Inside the parlor, Luce closed the door.

"What is so important?" Lucinda asked, then gave herself away by smiling. "Did he ask about me?"

"Don't get involved with him," Luce said quickly. "If you meet him tonight, you're going to think he's very handsome. You're going to want to fall in love with him. Don't." Luce felt horrible speaking about Daniel in such harsh terms, but it was the only way to save the life of her past self.

Lucinda Biscoe huffed and turned to leave.

"I knew a girl from, um—Derbyshire," Luce went on, "who told all sorts of stories of his reputation. He's hurt a lot of other girls before. He's—he's destroyed them."

A shocked sound escaped Lucinda's pink lips. "How *dare* you address a lady like this! Just who do you think you are? Whether I fancy this artist or not is no concern of yours." She pointed a finger at Luce. "Are you in love with him yourself, you selfish little wench?"

"No!" Luce jerked back as if she'd been slapped.

Bill had warned her that Lucinda was very different, but this ugly side of Lucinda couldn't be all there was to her. Otherwise, why would Daniel love her? Otherwise, how could she be a part of Luce's soul?

Something deeper had to connect them.

But Lucinda was bent over the harpsichord, scrawling a note on a piece of paper. She straightened, folded it in two, and shoved it into Luce's hands.

"I won't report your impudence to Mrs. Constance," she said, eyeing Luce haughtily, "*if* you deliver this note to Mr. Grigori. Don't miss your chance to save your employment." A second later she was nothing but a white silhouette gliding down the hallway, down the stairs, back to the party.

Luce tore open the note.

Dear Mr. Grigori,

Since we happened upon each other in the dressmaker's the other day, I cannot get you out of my mind. Will you meet me in the gazebo this evening at nine o'clock? I'll be waiting.

Yours eternally,
Lucinda Biscoe

Luce ripped the letter into shreds and tossed them into the parlor fire. If she never gave Daniel the note,

Lucinda *would* be alone in the gazebo. Luce could go out there and wait for her and try to warn her again.

She raced into the hall and made a sharp turn toward the servants' stairs down to the kitchen. She ran past the cooks and the pastry makers and Henrietta.

"You got both of us in trouble, Myrtle!" the girl called out to Luce, but Luce was already out the door.

The evening air was cool and dry against her face as she ran. It was nearly nine o'clock, but the sun was still setting over the grove of trees on the western side of the property. She tore down the pink-hued path, past the overflowing garden and the heady, sweet scent of the roses, past the hedge maze.

Her eyes fell on the place where she'd first tumbled out of the Announcer into this life. Her feet pounded down the path toward the empty gazebo. She had stopped just short of it when someone caught her by the arm.

She turned around.

And ended up nose to nose with Daniel.

A light wind blew his blond hair across his forehead. In his formal black suit with the gold watch chain and a small white peony pinned to his lapel, Daniel was even more gorgeous than she remembered. His skin was clear and brilliant in the glow of the setting sun. His lips held the faintest smile. His eyes burned violet at the sight of her.

A soft sigh escaped her. She ached to lean a few short

inches closer to press her lips on his. To wrap her arms around him and feel the place on his broad shoulders where his wings unfurled. She wanted to forget what she had come here to do and just hold him, just let herself be held. There were no words for how much she had missed him.

No. This visit was about Lucinda.

Daniel, *her* Daniel, was far away right now. It was hard to imagine what he'd be doing or thinking right now. It was even harder to imagine their reunion at the end of all of this. But wasn't that what her quest was about? Finding out enough about her past so she could really be with Daniel in the present?

"You're not supposed to be here," she said to Helston Daniel. He couldn't have known that Helston Lucinda wanted to meet him here. But here he was. It was as if nothing could get in the way of their meeting—they were drawn toward each other, no matter what.

Daniel's laugh was precisely the same laugh Luce was used to, the one she'd heard for the first time at Sword & Cross, when Daniel kissed her; the laugh she loved. But *this* Daniel did not really know her. He didn't know who she was, where she was coming from, or what she was trying to do.

"You're not supposed to be here, either." He smiled. "First we're supposed to have a dance inside, and later, after we've gotten to know one another, I'm supposed to take you for a moonlit stroll. But the sun hasn't even set yet. Which means there's still a good deal of dancing to be done." He extended his hand. "My name is Daniel Grigori."

He hadn't even noticed that she was dressed in a maid's uniform instead of a ball gown, that she didn't act at all like a proper British girl. He'd only just laid eyes on her, but like Lucinda, Daniel was already blinded by love.

Seeing all of this from a new angle put a strange clarity on their relationship. It was wonderful, but it was tragically shortsighted. Was it even Lucinda whom Daniel loved and vice versa, or was it just a cycle they couldn't break free of?

"It isn't me," Luce told him sadly.

He took her hands. She melted a little.

"Of course it's you," he said. "It's always you."

"No," Luce said. "It isn't fair to her, you're not being fair. And besides, Daniel, she's *mean*."

"Who are you talking about?" He looked like he couldn't decide whether to take her seriously or laugh.

From the corner of her eye, Luce saw a figure in white walking toward them from the back of the house.

Lucinda.

Coming to meet Daniel. She was early. Her note said nine o'clock—at least it *had* said nine o'clock before Luce had tossed its fragments into the fire.

Luce's heart began to pound. She could not be caught here when Lucinda arrived. And yet, she couldn't leave Daniel so soon.

"Why do you love her?" Luce's words came out in a rush. "What makes you fall in love with her, Daniel?"

Daniel laid his hand on her shoulder—it felt wonderful. "Slow down," he said. "We've only just met, but I can promise you there isn't anyone I love except—"

"You there! Servant girl!" Lucinda had spotted them, and from the tone of her voice, she wasn't happy about it. She began to run toward the gazebo, cursing at her dress, at the muddiness of the grass, at Luce. "What have you done with my letter, girl?"

"Th-that girl, the one coming this way," Luce stammered, "is me, in a sense. I'm her. You love us, and I need to understand—"

Daniel turned to watch Lucinda, the one he had loved—would love in this era. He could see her face clearly now. He could see that there were two of them.

When he turned back to Luce, his hand on her shoulder began to tremble. "It's you, the other one. What have you done? How did you do this?"

"You! Girl!" Lucinda had registered Daniel's hand on Luce's shoulder. Her whole face puckered up. "I knew it!" she screeched, running even faster. "Get away from him, you trollop!"

Luce could feel panic washing over her. She had no choice now but to run. But first: She touched the side of

Daniel's face. "Is it love? Or is it just the curse that brings us together?"

"It's love," he gasped. "Don't you know that?"

She broke free of his grasp and fled, running fast and furiously across the lawn, back through the grove of silver birch trees, back to the overgrown grasses where she'd first arrived. Her feet became tangled and she tripped, landing flat on her face. Everything hurt. And she was mad. Fuming mad. At Lucinda for being so nasty. At Daniel for the way he just fell in love without thinking. At her own powerlessness to do anything that made a bit of difference. Lucinda would still die—Luce's having been here didn't matter at all. Beating her fists on the ground, she let out a groan of frustration.

"There, there." A tiny stone hand patted her back.

Luce flicked it away. "Leave me alone, Bill."

"Hey, it was a valiant effort. You really got out there in the trenches this time. But"—Bill shrugged—"now it's over."

Luce sat up and glared at him. His smug expression made her want to march right back there and tell Lucinda who she really was—tell her what things were like not so far down the road.

"No." Luce stood up. "It's not over."

Bill yanked her back down. He was shockingly strong for such a little creature. "Oh, it's over. Come on, get in the Announcer."

Luce turned where Bill was pointing. She hadn't

even noticed the thick black portal floating right in front of her. Its musty smell made her sick.

"No."

"*Yes,*" Bill said.

"You're the one who told me to slow down in the first place."

"Look, let me give you the CliffsNotes: You're a bitch in this life and Daniel doesn't care. Shocker! He courts you for a few weeks, there's some exchanging of flowers. A big kiss and then *kaboom.* Okay? Not much more to see."

"You don't understand."

"What? I don't understand that Victorians are as stuffy as an attic and as boring as watching wallpaper peel? Come on, if you're going to zigzag through your past, make it *count.* Let's hit some *highlights.*"

Luce didn't budge. "Is there a way to make you disappear?"

"Do I have to stuff you in this Announcer like a cat in a suitcase? Let's move!"

"I need to see that he loves *me,* not just some *idea* of me because of some curse that he's bound to. I need to feel like there's something stronger keeping us together. Something real."

Bill took a seat next to Luce on the grass. Then he seemed to think better of it and actually crawled onto her lap. At first, she wanted to swat him, and the flies buzzing around his head, but when he looked up at her, his eyes appeared sincere.

"Honey, Daniel loving the real you is the last thing you should be worried about. You're freaking *soul mates*. You two coined the phrase. You don't have to stick around here to see that. It's in every life."

"What?"

"You want to see true love?"

She nodded.

"Come on." He tugged her up. The Announcer hovered in front of them and began to morph into a new shape, until it almost resembled the flaps of a tent. Bill flew into the air, hooked his finger into an invisible latch, and tugged. The Announcer rearranged itself, lowering itself like a drawbridge until all Luce could see was a tunnel of darkness.

Luce glanced back toward Daniel and Lucinda, but she couldn't see them—only outlines of them, blurs of color pressing together.

Bill made a sweeping motion with his free hand into the belly of the Announcer. "Step right in."

And so she did.

EIGHT

WATCHING FROM THE WINGS

Helston, England · July 26, 1854

Daniel's clothes were sun-bleached and his cheek was caked with sand when he woke up on the desolate coast of Cornwall. It might have been a day, a week, a month that he'd been out there wandering alone. However much time had passed, he'd spent all of it punishing himself for his mistake.

Encountering Lucinda like that in the dressmaker's had been so grave an error that Daniel's soul burned every time he thought of it.

And he couldn't stop thinking of it.

Her full pink lips curling around the words: *I think I know you. Please. Wait.*

So lovely and so perilous.

Oh, why couldn't it have been something small? Some brief exchange well into their courtship? Then it might not have mattered so much. But a first sighting! Lucinda Biscoe's first sighting had been of *him,* the wrong Daniel. He could have jeopardized everything. He could have distorted the future so badly that his Luce could end up dead already, altered beyond recognition—

But no: If that were so, he wouldn't have his Luce in his memory. Time would have revised itself and he would have no regrets at all because his Luce would be different.

His past self must have responded to Lucinda Biscoe in a way that covered Daniel's mistake. He couldn't quite remember how things had begun, only how they'd ended. But no matter: He wouldn't get anywhere near his past self to warn him, for fear of running into Lucinda again and doing yet more damage. All he could do was back away and wait it out.

He was used to eternity, but this had been Hell.

Daniel lost track of time, let it drift into the sounds of the ocean washing up against the shore. For a little while, at least.

He could easily resume his quest by stepping into an

Announcer and chasing Luce to the next life she visited. But for some reason, he stuck around Helston, waiting until Lucinda Biscoe's life ended here.

Waking up that evening, the sky slashed by purple clouds, Daniel sensed it. Midsummer. The night she would die. He wiped the sand from his skin and felt the strange tenderness in his hidden wings. His heart throbbed with every beat.

It was time.

Lucinda's death would not happen until after nightfall.

Daniel's earlier self would be alone in the Constances' parlor. He would be drawing Lucinda Biscoe one last time. His bags would sit outside the door, empty as usual save for a leather-bound pencil case, a few sketchbooks, his book about the Watchers, an extra pair of shoes. He really had been planning to sail the next morning. What a lie.

In the moments leading up to her deaths, Daniel rarely was honest with himself. He always lost himself in his love. Every time, he fooled himself, got drunk on her presence, and lost track of what must be.

He remembered particularly well how it had ended in this Helston life: denying that she had to die right up until the instant he pressed her up against the ruby-velvet curtains and kissed her into oblivion.

He'd cursed his fate then; he had made an ugly

scene. He could still feel the agony, fresh as an iron's brand across his skin. And he remembered the visitation.

Waiting out the sunset, he stood alone on the shore and let the water kiss his bare feet. He closed his eyes and spread his arms and allowed his wings to burst out from the scars on his shoulders. They billowed behind him, bobbing in the wind and giving him a weightlessness that provided some momentary peace. He could see how bright they were in their reflection on the water, how huge and fierce they made him look.

Sometimes, when Daniel was at his most inconsolable, he refused to let his wings out. It was a punishment he could administer to himself. The deep relief, the palpable, incredible sense of freedom that unfurling his wings gave to his soul only felt false, like a drug. Tonight he allowed himself that rush.

He bent his knees to the sand and kicked off into the air.

A few feet above the surface of the water, he quickly rolled around so that his back was to the ocean, his wings spread beneath him like a magnificent shimmering raft.

He skimmed the surface, stretching out his muscles with each long beat of his wings, sliding along the waves until the water changed from turquoise to icy blue. Then he plunged down under the surface. His wings were warm where the ocean was cool, creating a small wake of violet to encircle him.

Daniel loved to swim. The chill of the water, the unpredictable beat of the current, the synchronicity of the ocean with the moon. It was one of a few earthly pleasures he truly understood. Most of all, he loved to swim with Lucinda.

With every stroke of his wings, Daniel imagined Lucinda there with him, sliding gracefully through the water as she had so many times before, basking in the warm shimmery glow.

When the moon was bright in the dark sky and Daniel was somewhere off the coast of Reykjavik, he shot out of the water. Straight up, beating his wings with a ferocity that shook off the cold.

The wind whipped at his sides, drying him in seconds as he sailed higher and higher into the air. He burst through thick gray banks of clouds, then turned back and began to coast under starry Heaven's expanse.

His wings beat freely, deeply, strong with love and terror and thoughts of her, rippling the water underneath him so that it shimmered like diamonds. He picked up tremendous speed as he flew back over the Faroe Islands and across the Irish Sea. He sailed down along St. George's Channel and, finally, back to Helston.

How against his nature to watch the girl he loved show up just to die!

But Daniel had to see beyond this moment and this pain. He had to look toward all the Lucindas who would come after this one sacrifice—and the one whom he pursued, the final Luce, who would end this cursed cycle.

Lucinda's death tonight was the only way the two of them could win, the only way they'd ever have a chance.

· By the time he reached the Constance estate, the house was dark and the air was hot and still.

He tucked his wings up close to his body, slowing his descent along the south side of the property. There was the white roof of the gazebo, an aerial view of the gardens. There was the moonlit pebbled path she should have walked along just moments ago, sneaking out of her father's house next door after everyone else was asleep. Her nightgown covered by a long black cloak, her modesty forgotten in her haste to find him.

And there—the light in the parlor, the single candelabra that had drawn her to him. The curtains were parted slightly. Enough for Daniel to look in without risk of being seen.

He reached the parlor window on the second floor of the great house and let his wings beat lightly, hovering outside like a spy.

Was she even there? He inhaled slowly, let his wings fill with air, and pressed his face against the glass.

Just Daniel sketching furiously on his pad in the corner. His past self looked exhausted and forlorn. He could remember the feeling exactly—watching the black tick of the clock on the wall, waiting every moment for her to burst through the door. He'd been so stunned when she sneaked up on him, silently, almost from behind the curtain.

He was stunned anew when she did so now.

Her beauty was beyond his most unrealistic expectations that night. Every night. Cheeks flushed with the love she felt but didn't understand. Her black hair falling from its long, lustrous braid. The wonderful sheerness of her nightgown, like gossamer floating over all that perfect skin.

Just then his past self rose and spun around. When he saw the gorgeous sight before him, the pain was obvious on his face.

If there had been something Daniel could have done to reach out and help his past self get through this, he would have done it. But all he could do was read his lips.

What are you doing here?

Luce drew closer and the color rose in her cheeks. The two of them moved together like magnets—pulled by a force greater than themselves one moment, then repelled with almost the same vigor the next.

Daniel hovered outside, in pain.

He couldn't watch. He had to watch.

The way they reached for each other was tentative right up until the moment his skin connected with hers. Then they became instantly, hungrily passionate. They weren't even kissing, just talking. When their lips were almost touching, their souls almost touching, a burning, pure, white-hot aura formed around them that neither was aware of.

It was something Daniel had never witnessed from the outside.

Was this what his Luce was after? Visual proof of how true their love was? For Daniel, their love was as much a part of him as his wings. But for Luce, it must be different. She didn't have access to the splendor of their love. Only its fiery end.

Every moment would be an utter revelation.

He laid his cheek against the glass, sighing. Inside, his past self was caving in, losing the resolve that had been a charade from the beginning, anyway. His bags were packed, but it was Lucinda who had to go.

Now his past self took her in his arms; even through the window, Daniel could smell the rich, sweet scent of her skin. He envied himself, kissing her neck, running his hands across her back. His desire was so intense it could have shattered that window if he hadn't willed himself to hold back.

Oh, draw it out, he willed his past self. Make it last a little longer. One more kiss. One more sweet touch before the room quakes and the Announcers begin to tremble in their shadows.

The glass warmed against his cheek. It was happening.

He wanted to close his eyes but could not. Lucinda writhed in his past self's arms. Her face contorted with pain. She looked up, and her eyes widened at the sight of the shadows dancing on the ceiling. The half-born realization of *something* was already too much for her.

She screamed.

And erupted into a glowing tower of flames.

Inside the room, Daniel's earlier self was blown back against the wall. He fell and lay huddled, like nothing more than the outline of a man. He buried his face in the carpet and shook.

Outside, Daniel watched with an awe he'd never managed before as the fire climbed the air and the walls. It hissed like a sauce simmering in a pan—and then it vanished, leaving no trace of her.

Miraculous. Every single inch of Daniel's body was tingling. If it hadn't wrecked his past self so completely, he might have found the spectacle of Lucinda's death almost beautiful.

His old self slowly got to his feet. His mouth gaped open and his wings burst out of his black dress coat, taking up most of the room. He raised his fists toward the sky and bellowed.

Outside, Daniel couldn't take it anymore. He rammed his wing through the window, sending shards of glass out into the night. Then he barreled through the jagged hole.

"What are you doing here?" his past self gasped, cheeks streaming with tears. With both pairs of wings fully extended, there almost wasn't room for them in the enormous parlor. They rolled back their shoulders as much as possible to draw away from each other. Both knew the danger of touching.

"I was watching," Daniel said.

"You—what? You come back to *watch*?" His past self flung out his arms and his wings. "Is this what you wanted to see?" The depths of his misery were achingly plain.

"This needed to happen, Daniel."

"Don't feed me those lies. Don't you dare. Have you gone back to taking advice from Cam again?"

"No!" Daniel almost shouted at his past self. "Listen: There is a time, not so very far from now, when we will have a chance to change this game. Something has shifted, and things are different. When we have an opportunity to stop doing this over and over. When Lucinda at last might—"

"Break the cycle?" his past self whispered.

"Yes." Daniel was beginning to feel light-headed. There was one too many of them in the room. It was time for him to go. "It will take some time," he instructed, turning back when he reached the window. "But maintain hope."

Then Daniel slipped through the broken window. His words—*maintain hope*—echoed in his mind as he took off across the sky, deep into the shadows of the night.

NINE

SO WE BEAT ON

Tahiti · December 11, 1775

Luce found herself balanced on a splintery wooden beam.

It creaked as it tilted slightly to the left, then creaked again as it eased very slowly to the right. The rocking was steady and ceaseless, as if the beam were attached to a very short pendulum.

A hot wind sent her hair lashing across her face and blew her servant's bonnet off her head. The beam beneath her swayed again, and her feet slipped. She fell against the beam and barely managed to hug it to herself before she went tumbling down—

Where was she? In front of her was the endless blue of open sky. A darker blue at what must have been the horizon. She looked down.

She was incredibly high up.

A waterlogged pole stretched a hundred feet beneath her, ending in a wooden deck. *Oh.* It was a mast. Luce was sitting on the top yard of a very large sailboat.

A very large *shipwrecked* sailboat, just off the coast of a black-shored island.

The bow had been smashed violently against a cluster of razor-sharp lava rocks that had left it a pulverized mess. The mainsail was shredded: tattered pieces of tawny canvas flapping loosely in the wind. The air smelled like the morning after a great storm, but this ship was so weathered, it looked like it had been there for years.

Every time the waves rushed up the black-sand shores, water sprayed dozens of feet up from the crevices in the rocks. The waves made the wreck—and the beam Luce clutched—sway so roughly she felt she might be sick.

How was she going to get down? How was she going to get to shore?

"Aha! Look who's landed like a bird on a perch." Bill's voice broke over the crashing waves. He appeared at the far tip of the ship's rotting yard, walking with his arms extended from his sides as if he were on a balance beam.

"Where are we?" Luce was too nervous to make any sudden movements.

Bill sucked in a big lungful of air. "Can't you taste it? The north coast of Tahiti!" He plopped down next to Luce, kicked out his stubby legs, stretched his short gray arms up, and clasped his hands behind his head. "Isn't it paradise?"

"I think I'm going to throw up."

"Nonsense. You just have to find your sea legs."

"How did we get—" Luce glanced around again for an Announcer. She didn't see a single shadow, just the endless blank blue of empty skies.

"I took care of the logistics for you. Think of me as your travel agent, and of yourself as on vacation!"

"We're not on vacation, Bill."

"We're not? I thought we were taking the Grand Tour of Love." He rubbed his forehead, and flinty flakes showered from his scalp. "Did I misunderstand?"

"Where are Lucinda and Daniel?"

"Hang on." He hovered in the air in front of Luce. "Don't you want a little history?"

Luce ignored him and scooted over toward the mast. She stretched an unsteady foot to the highest of the pegs that spiked out from the mast's sides.

"Don't you at least want a hand?"

She'd been holding her breath and trying not to look

down as her foot slid off the wooden peg a third time. Finally, she swallowed dryly and reached out to take the cold, rough claw Bill extended to her.

As she took Bill's hand, he pulled her forward, then off the mast entirely. She yelped as the wet wind battered her face, sending the skirt of her dress billowing around her waist. She shut her eyes and waited to plunge through the rotten decking below.

Only she didn't.

She heard a *throosh* and felt her body catch in the air. She opened her eyes. Bill's stubby wings had ballooned out and caught the wind. He was supporting her weight with just one hand, carrying her slowly to shore. It was miraculous how nimble he was, how light. Luce was surprised to find herself relaxing—somehow the sensation of flying was natural to her by now.

Daniel. As the air encircled her, the ache to be with him overtook her. To hear his voice and taste his lips—Luce could think of nothing else. What she wouldn't have given to be in his arms just then!

The Daniel she'd encountered in Helston, however happy he'd been to see her, had not really *known* her. Not the way her Daniel did. Where was he right now?

"Feeling better?" Bill asked.

"Why are we here?" Luce asked as they soared over the water. It was so clear she could see inky shadows moving underwater—giant schools of fish, swimming easily, following the shoreline.

"See that palm tree?" Bill pointed forward with his free claw. "The tallest one, third from the break in the sandbar?"

Luce nodded, squinting.

"That's where your father in this life built his hut. Nicest shack on the beach!" Bill coughed. "Actually, it's the only shack on the beach. The Brits haven't even discovered this side of the island yet. So when your pops is off fishing, you and Daniel have the place mostly to yourselves."

"Daniel and I . . . lived here . . . together?"

Hand in hand, Luce and Bill touched down on the shore with the soft elegance of two dancers in a *pas de deux*. Luce was grateful—and a little shocked—at how smoothly he'd been able to get her down from the mast of the ship, but as soon as she was firmly on the ground, she withdrew her hand from his grimy claw and wiped it on her apron.

It was starkly beautiful here. The crystal waters washed against the strange and lovely black-sand beaches. Groves of citrus and palm trees leaned over the coast, heavy with bright-orange fruit. Past the trees, low mountains rose up from the mists of the rain forest. Waterfalls cut into their sides. The wind down here wasn't as fierce; better still, it was thick with the scent of hibiscus. It was hard to imagine getting to spend a vacation here, let alone an entire life.

"*You* lived here." Bill started walking along the

curved shoreline, leaving little claw prints in the dark sand. "Your dad, and all ten of the other natives who lived within canoeing distance, called you—well, it sounded like *Lulu*."

Luce had been walking quickly to keep pace, balling up the layered skirts of her Helston servant's clothing to keep them from dragging in the sand. She stopped and made a face.

"What?" Bill said. "I think it's cute, Lulu. *Lulululu-lulu*."

"Stop it."

"Anyway, Daniel was a kind of rogue explorer. That boat back there? Your ace boyfriend stole it from George the Third's private slip." He glanced back at the ship-wreck. "But it'll take Captain Bligh and his mutinous crew another couple of years to track Daniel down here, and by then . . . you know."

Luce swallowed. Daniel would probably be long gone by then, because Lucinda would be long dead.

They'd reached a gap in the line of palm trees. A brackish river flowed in swirls between the ocean and a small inland freshwater pond. Luce edged along a few flat stones to cross the water. She was sweating through her petticoats and thought about stripping out of her stifling dress and diving straight into the ocean.

"How much time do I have with Lulu?" she asked. "Before it happens?"

Bill held up his hands. "I thought all you wanted to

see was proof that the love you share with Daniel is true."

"I do."

"For that, you won't need more than ten minutes."

They came upon a short orchid-lined path, which curved onto another pristine beach. A small thatch-roofed hut rose on stilts near the edge of the light-blue water. Behind the hut, a palm tree shuddered.

Bill perched above her shoulder, hovering in the air. "Check her out." His stone claw pointed toward the palm.

Luce watched in awe as a pair of feet emerged from the fronds high on the quaking tree trunk. Then a girl wearing little more than a woven skirt and an enormous floral lei tossed four shaggy brown coconuts to the beach before scampering down the knobby trunk to the ground.

Her hair was long and loose, catching in its dark strands diamonds of light from the sun. Luce knew the exact feel of it, the way it would tickle her arms as it swayed in waves past her waist. The sun had turned Lulu's skin a deep golden brown—darker than Luce had ever been, even when she spent a whole summer at her grandmother's beach house in Biloxi—and her face and arms were etched with dark geometric tattoos. She existed somewhere between utterly unrecognizable and absolutely Luce.

"Wow," Luce whispered as Bill yanked her behind

the shelter of a shrubby, purple-flowered tree. "Hey—Ow! What are you doing?"

"Escorting you to a safer vantage." Bill dragged her up again into the air, until they were rising through the canopy of leaves. Once they cleared the trees, he flew her to a high, sturdy branch and plunked her down, and she could see the whole beach.

"Lulu!"

The voice sank though Luce's skin and straight into her heart. Daniel's voice. He was calling to her. He wanted her. Needed her. Luce moved toward the sound. She hadn't even noticed that she'd started to rise from her seat on the high branch, as if she could just walk off the treetop and fly to him—until Bill gripped her elbow.

"Precisely why I had to drag your *popa'a* ass up here. He's not talking to you. He's talking to *her.*"

"Oh." Luce sank back down heavily. "Right."

On the black sand, the girl with the coconuts, Lulu, was running. And down the beach, sprinting toward her, was Daniel.

He was shirtless, gorgeously tanned and muscular, wearing only cropped navy-blue trousers that were fraying at the edges. His skin glittered with seawater, fresh from a dip in the ocean. His bare feet kicked up sand. Luce envied the water, envied the sand. Envied everything that got to touch Daniel when she was stuck up in this tree. She envied her past self the most.

Running toward Lulu, Daniel looked happier and more natural than Luce could ever remember seeing him. It made her want to cry.

They reached each other. Lulu threw her arms around him, and he swept her up, twirling her in the air. He set her back on her feet and showered her with kisses, kissing her fingertips and her forearms, all the way up to her shoulders, her neck, her mouth.

Bill reclined against Luce's shoulder. "Wake me up when they get to the good stuff," he said, yawning.

"Pervert!" She wanted to slug him, but she didn't want to touch him.

"I mean *the tattooing,* gutter-brain. I'm into tats, okay?"

When Luce looked back at the couple on the beach, Lulu was leading Daniel to a woven mat that was spread on the sand not far from the hut. Daniel pulled a short machete from the belt of his trousers and hacked at one of the coconuts. After a few slashes, he split off the top and handed the rest of it to Lulu. She drank deeply, milk dripping from the corners of her mouth. Daniel kissed them clean.

"There's no tattooing, they're just—" Luce broke off when her past self disappeared into the hut. Lulu reappeared a moment later carrying a small parcel bound in palm leaves. She unwrapped a tool that looked like a wooden comb. The bristles gleamed in the sun, as if they were needle-sharp. Daniel lay back on the mat, watching as Lulu dipped the comb into a large shallow seashell filled with a black powder.

Lulu gave him a quick kiss and then began.

Starting at his breastbone, she pressed the comb into his skin. She worked quickly, pressing hard and fast, and each time she moved the comb she left a smear of black pigment tattooed on his skin. Luce could begin to make out a design: a small checkerboard-patterned breastplate. It was going to span his entire chest. Luce's only trip to a tattoo parlor had been once in New Hampshire with Callie, who wanted a tiny pink heart on her hip. It had taken less than a minute and Callie had bellowed the whole time. Here, though, Daniel lay silently, never making a sound, never moving his eyes off Lulu. It took a long while, and Luce felt sweat trickle down the small of her back as she watched.

"Eh? How 'bout that?" Bill nudged her. "Did I promise to show you love or did I promise to show you love?"

"Sure, they seem like they're in love." Luce shrugged. "But—"

"But what? Do you have any idea how painful that is? Look at that guy. He makes getting inked look like being caressed by a soft breeze."

Luce squirmed on the branch. "Is that the lesson here? Pain equals love?"

"You tell me," Bill said. "It may surprise you to hear this, but the ladies aren't exactly banging down Bill's door."

"I mean, if I tattooed Daniel's name on my body would that mean I loved him more than I already do?"

"It's a symbol, Luce." Bill let out a raspy sigh. "You're being too literal. Think about it this way: Daniel is the first good-looking boy Lulu has ever seen. Until he washed ashore a few months ago, this girl's whole world was her father and a few fat natives."

"She's Miranda," Luce said, remembering the love story from *The Tempest,* which she'd read in her tenth-grade Shakespeare seminar.

"How very civilized of you!" Bill pursed his lips with approval. "They *are* like Ferdinand and Miranda: The handsome foreigner shipwrecks on her shores—"

"So, of course it was love at first sight for Lulu," Luce murmured. This was what she was afraid of: the same thoughtless, automatic love that had bothered her in Helston.

"Right," Bill said. "She didn't have a choice but to fall for him. But what's interesting here is Daniel. You see, he didn't *have* to teach her to craft a woven sail, or gain her father's trust by producing a season's worth of fish to cure, or exhibit C"—Bill pointed at the lovers on the beach—"agree to tattoo his whole body according to her local custom. It would have been enough if Daniel had just shown up. Lulu would have loved him anyway."

"He's doing it because—" Luce thought aloud. "Because he wants to earn her love. Because otherwise, he would just be taking advantage of their curse. Because no matter what kind of cycle they're bound to, his love for her is . . . true."

So then why wasn't Luce entirely convinced?

On the beach, Daniel sat up. He took hold of Lulu by the shoulders and began kissing her tenderly. His chest bled from the tattooing, but neither of them seemed to notice. Their lips barely parted, their eyes never left each other.

"I want to leave now," Luce said suddenly to Bill.

"Really?" Bill blinked, standing up on the tree branch as if she'd startled him.

"Yes, really. I've gotten what I came here for and I'm ready to move on. Right now." She tried to stand, too, but the branch swayed under her weight.

"Um, okay." Bill took her arm to steady her. "Where to?"

"I don't know, but let's hurry." The sun was sinking in the sky behind them, lengthening the lovers' shadows on the sand. "Please. I want to hold on to one good memory. I don't want to see her die."

Bill's face was pinched up and confused, but he didn't say anything.

Luce couldn't wait any longer. She closed her eyes and let her desire call to an Announcer. When she opened her eyes again, she could see a quiver in the shadow of a nearby passion fruit tree. She concentrated, summoning it with all her might until the Announcer began to tremble.

"Come on," she said, gritting her teeth.

At last, the Announcer freed itself, zipping off the tree and through the air, floating directly in front of her.

"Easy now," Bill said, hovering above the branch. "Desperation and Announcer-travel do not mix well. Like pickles and chocolate."

Luce stared at him.

"I mean: Don't get so desperate that you lose sight of what you want."

"I *want* to get out of here," Luce said, but she couldn't coax the shadow into a stable shape, no matter how hard she tried. She wasn't looking at the lovers on the beach, but nonetheless she could feel the darkness gathering in the sky over the beach. It wasn't rain clouds. "Help me, Bill?"

He sighed, reaching for the dark mass in the air, and drew it toward him. "This is your shadow, you realize. I'm manipulating it, but it's your Announcer and your past."

Luce nodded.

"Which means you have no idea where it's taking you, and I have no liability."

She nodded again.

"Okay, then." He rubbed at a part of the Announcer until it went darker; then he caught the dark spot with a claw and yanked on it. It worked like a sort of door-knob. The stink of mildew flooded out, making Luce cough.

"Yeah, I smell it, too," Bill said. "This is an old one." He gestured her forward. "Ladies first."

PRUSSIA · JANUARY 7, 1758

A snowflake kissed Luce's nose.

Then another, and another, and more, until a storm of flurries filled the air and the whole world turned white and cold. She exhaled a long cloud of breath into the frost.

Somehow, she'd known they would end up here, even though she wasn't exactly sure where *here* was. All she knew was that the afternoon skies were dark with a furious storm, and wet snow was seeping through her black leather boots, biting at her toes and chilling her to the bone.

She was walking into her own funeral.

She'd felt it in the instant passing through this last Announcer. An oncoming coldness, unforgiving as a sheet of ice. She found herself at the gates of a cemetery, everything blanketed by snow. Behind her was a tree-lined road, the bare branches clawing at the pewter sky. Before her was a low rise of snow-shrouded earth, tombstones and crosses jutting out of the white like jagged, dirty teeth.

A few feet behind her, someone whistled. "You sure you're ready for this?" Bill. He sounded out of breath, like he'd just caught up with her.

"Yes." Her lips were chattering. She didn't turn around until Bill swooped down near her shoulders.

"Here," he said, holding out a dark mink coat. "Thought you might be cold."

"Where did you—"

"I yoinked it off a broad coming home from the market back there. Don't worry, she had enough natural padding already."

"Bill!"

"Hey, you needed it!" He shrugged. "Wear it in good health."

He draped the thick coat over Luce's shoulders, and she pulled it closer. It was unbelievably soft and warm. A wave of gratitude rushed over her; she reached up and took his claw, not even caring that it was sticky and cold.

"Okay," Bill said, squeezing her hand. For a moment, Luce felt an odd warmth in her fingertips. But then it was gone, and Bill's stone fingers were stone cold. He took a deep, nervous breath. "Um. Uh. Prussia, mid-eighteenth century. You live in a small village on the banks of the river Handel. Very nice." He cleared his throat and hacked up a large wad of phlegm before he went on. "I should say, er, that you *lived*. You've actually, just—well—"

"Bill?" She craned her neck to look at him sitting hunched forward on her shoulder. "It's okay," she said softly. "You don't have to explain. Let me just, you know, feel it."

"That's probably best."

As Luce walked quietly through the cemetery gates, Bill hung back. He sat cross-legged on top of a lichen-swathed shrine, picking at the grit under his claws. Luce lowered her shawl over her head to obscure more of her face.

Up ahead were mourners, black-clad and somber, pressed so tightly together for warmth that they looked like a single mass of grief. Except for one person who stood behind the group and off to one side. He hung his bare blond head.

No one spoke to or even looked at Daniel. Luce couldn't tell whether he was bothered by being left out or whether he preferred it.

By the time she reached the back of the small crowd, the burial was drawing to a close. A name was carved into a flat gray tombstone: *Lucinda Müller*. A boy, no older than twelve, with dark hair and pale skin and tears streaming down his face, helped his father—her father from this other life?—shovel the first mound of dirt over the grave.

These men must have been related to her past self. They must have loved her. There were women and children crying behind them; Lucinda Müller must have meant something to them as well. Maybe she'd meant everything to them.

But Luce Price didn't know these people. She felt callous and strange to realize that they meant nothing to her, even as she saw the pain mar their faces. Daniel was the only one here who really mattered to her, the one she wanted to run to, the one she had to hold herself back from.

He wasn't crying. He wasn't even staring at the grave like everyone else. His hands were clasped in front of him and he was looking far away—not at the sky, but far into the distance. His eyes were violet one moment, gray the next.

When the family members had cast a few shovelfuls of dirt over the casket and the plot had been scattered with flowers, the funeral-goers split apart and walked shakily back to the main road. It was over.

Only Daniel remained. As immobile as the dead.

Luce hung back, too, dodging behind a squat mausoleum a few plots away, watching to see what he would do.

It was dusk. They had the graveyard to themselves. Daniel lowered himself to his knees next to Lucinda's grave. Snow thrummed down on the cemetery, coating

Luce's shoulders, fat flakes getting tangled in her eyelashes, wetting the tip of her nose. She edged around the corner of the mausoleum, her entire body tensed.

Would he lose it? Would he claw at the frozen dirt and pound on the gravestone and bawl until there were no more tears he could shed? He *couldn't* feel as calm as he looked. It was impossible, a front. But Daniel barely looked at the grave. He lay down on his side in the snow and closed his eyes.

Luce stared. He was so still and gorgeous. With his eyelids closed, he looked at absolute peace. She was half in love, half confused, and stayed that way for several minutes—until she was so frozen, she had to rub her arms and stamp her feet to warm up.

"What is he doing?" she finally whispered.

Bill appeared behind her and flitted around her shoulders. "Looks like he's sleeping."

"But why? I didn't even know angels needed to sleep—"

"*Need* isn't the right word. They can sleep if they feel like it. Daniel always sleeps for days after you die." Bill tossed his head, seeming to recall something unpleasant. "Okay, not always. Most of the time. Must be pretty taxing, to lose the one thing you love. Can you blame him?"

"S-sort of," Luce stammered. "I'm the one who bursts into flames."

"And he's the one who's left alone. The age-old question: Which is worse?"

"But he doesn't even look *sad*. He looked bored the entire funeral. If it were me, I'd . . . I'd . . ."

"You'd what?"

Luce moved toward the grave and stopped short at the loose earth where her plot began. A coffin lay beneath this.

Her coffin.

The thought sent shivers up her spine. She sank to her knees and put her palms down in the dirt. It was damp and dark and freezing cold. She buried her hands inside it, feeling frostbitten almost instantly and not caring, welcoming the burn. She'd wanted Daniel to do this, to feel for her body in the earth. To go mad with wanting her back—alive and in his arms.

But he was just *sleeping*, so dead asleep that he didn't even sense her kneeling right beside him. She wanted to touch him, to wake him, but she didn't even know what she'd say when he opened his eyes.

Instead, she pawed at the muddy earth, until the flowers laid so neatly on it were scattered and broken, until the beautiful mink coat was soiled and her arms and face were covered in mud. She dug and dug and tossed the earth aside, reaching deeper for her dead self. She ached for some connection.

At last her fingers hit something hard: the wooden

lid of the coffin. She closed her eyes and waited for the kind of flash she'd felt in Moscow, the bolt of memories that had flooded through her when she'd touched the abandoned church gate and *felt* Luschka's life.

Nothing.

Just emptiness. Loneliness. A howling white wind.

And Daniel, asleep and unreachable.

She sat back on her heels and sobbed. She didn't know a thing about the girl who had died. She felt she never would.

"Yoo-hoo," Bill said quietly from her shoulder. "You're not in there, you know?"

"What?"

"Think about it. You're not in there. You're a fleck of ash by now if you're anything. You didn't have a body to bury, Luce."

"Because of the fire. Oh. But then why . . . ?" she asked, then stopped herself. "My family wanted this."

"They're strict Lutherans." Bill nodded. "Every Müller for a hundred years has a tombstone in this cemetery. So your past self does, too. There's just nothing under it. Or not quite nothing. Your favorite dress. A childhood doll. Your copy of the Bible. That sort of thing."

Luce swallowed. No wonder she felt so empty inside. "So Daniel—that's why he wasn't looking at the grave."

"He's the only one who accepts that your soul is

someplace else. He stayed because this is the closest place he can go to hold on to your memory." Bill swooped down so close to Daniel that the buzz of his stony wings rustled Daniel's hair. Luce almost pushed Bill away. "He'll try to sleep until your soul is settled somewhere else. Until you've found your next incarnation."

"How long does that take?"

"Sometimes seconds, sometimes years. But he won't sleep for years. As much as he'd probably like to."

Daniel's movement on the ground made Luce jump.

He stirred in his blanket of snow. An agonized groan escaped his lips.

"What's happening?" Luce said, dropping to her knees and reaching for him.

"Don't wake him!" Bill said quickly. "His sleep is riddled with nightmares, but it's better for him than being awake. Until your soul is settled in a new life, Daniel's whole existence is a kind of torture."

Luce was torn between wanting to ease Daniel's pain and trying to understand that waking him up might only worsen it.

"Like I said, on occasion, he sort of has insomnia . . . and that's when it gets *really* interesting. But you wouldn't want to see that. Nah."

"I would," she said, sitting up. "What happens?"

Bill's fleshy cheeks twitched, as if he'd been caught at something. "Well, uh, a lot of times, the other fallen angels are around," he said, not meeting her eyes. "They get in and they, you know, try to console him."

"I saw them in Moscow. But that's not what you're talking about. There's something you're not telling me. What happens when—"

"You don't want to see those lives, Luce. It's a side of him—"

"It's a side of him that loves me, isn't it? Even if it's dark or bad or disturbing, I need to see it. Otherwise I still won't understand what he goes through."

Bill sighed. "You're looking at me like you need my permission. Your past belongs to you."

Luce was already on her feet. She glanced around the cemetery until her eyes fell on a small shadow stretching out from the back of her tombstone. *There. That's the one.* Luce was startled by her certainty. That had never happened before.

At first glance this shadow had looked like any of the other shadows she had clumsily summoned in the woods at Shoreline. But this time, Luce could see *something* in the shadow itself. It wasn't an image depicting any specific destination, but instead a strange silver glow that suggested that this Announcer would take her where her soul needed to go next.

It was calling to her.

She answered, reaching inside herself, drawing on that glow to guide the shadow up off the ground.

The shard of darkness peeled itself off the white

snow and took shape as it moved closer. It was deep black, colder than the snow falling all around her, and it swept toward Luce like a giant, dark sheet of paper. Her fingers were cracked and numb with cold as she expanded it into a larger, controlled shape. It emitted that familiar gust of foul-smelling wind from its core. The portal was wide and stable before Luce realized she was out of breath.

"You're getting good at this," Bill said. There was a strange edge to his voice that Luce didn't waste time analyzing.

She also didn't waste time feeling proud of herself—though somewhere she could recognize that if Miles or Shelby had been here, they'd have been doing cartwheels right now. It was by far the best summoning she'd ever done on her own.

But they weren't here. Luce was on her own, so all she could do was move on to the next life, observe more of Lucinda and Daniel, drink it all in until something began to make sense. She felt around the clammy edges for a latch or a knob, just some way in. Finally, the Announcer creaked open.

Luce took a deep breath. She looked back at Bill. "Are you coming or what?"

Gravely, he hopped onto her shoulder and grabbed hold of her lapel like the reins on a horse, and the two of them stepped through.

Luce gasped for breath.

She'd come out of the dark of the Announcer into a swirl of fast-moving fog. The air was thin and cold and every lungful stabbed at her chest. She couldn't seem to catch her breath. The fog's cool white vapor blew her hair back, rode along her open arms, soaked her garments with dew, and then was gone.

Luce saw that she was standing at the edge of the highest cliff she'd ever seen. She wobbled and staggered back, dizzy when she saw her feet dislodge a pebble. It rolled forward a few inches and over the edge, plummeting forever down.

She gasped again, this time from fear of heights.

"Breathe," Bill coached her. "More people pass out up here from panicking over not getting enough oxygen than from *actually* not getting enough oxygen."

Luce inhaled carefully. That was slightly better. She lowered the dirty mink on her shoulders and enjoyed the sun on her face. But she still couldn't get used to the view.

Stretching away from the cliff where she stood was a yawning valley spotted with what looked like farmland and flooded rice paddies. And to either side, rising into misty heights, were two towering mountains.

Far ahead, carved right into one of the steep mountainsides, was a formidable palace. Majestically white and capped by deep-red roofs, its outer walls were festooned with more staircases than she could count. The palace looked like something out of an ancient fairy tale.

"What is this place? Are we in China?" she asked.

"If we stood here long enough, we would be," Bill said. "But right now, it's Tibet, thanks to the Dalai Lama. That's his pad over there." He pointed at the monster palace. "Swanky, eh?"

But Luce wasn't following his finger. She'd heard a laugh from somewhere nearby and had turned to seek out its source.

Her laugh. The soft, happy laugh she hadn't known was hers until she'd met Daniel.

She finally spotted two figures a few hundred yards away along the cliff. She'd have to clamber across some boulders to get closer, but it wouldn't be that difficult. She hunched in her muddy coat and started carefully picking her way through the snow, toward the sound.

"Whoa there." Bill grabbed her by the collar of the coat. "Do you see any place for us to take cover?"

Luce looked around the bare landscape: all rocky drop-offs and open spaces. Nothing even to serve as shelter from the wind.

"We're above the tree line, pal. And you're small, but

you ain't invisible. You're going to have to hang back here."

"But I can't see a thing—"

"Coat pocket," Bill said. "You're welcome."

She felt around in the pocket of the coat—the same coat she'd been wearing at the funeral in Prussia—and pulled out a brand-new, very expensive-looking pair of opera glasses. She didn't bother asking Bill where or when he'd got them, she just held them up to her eyes and twisted the focus.

There.

The two of them stood facing each other, several feet apart. Her past self's black hair was knotted in a girlish bun, and her woven linen dress was the pink of an orchid. She looked young and innocent. She was smiling at Daniel, rocking back and forth on her feet like she was nervous, watching his every move with unbounded intensity. Daniel's eyes had a teasing look in them; a bunch of round white peonies were in his arms and he was doling them out to her one by one, making her laugh harder each time.

Watching closely through the opera glasses, Luce noticed that their fingers never touched. They kept a certain distance from each other. Why? It was almost startling.

In the other lives she'd spied upon, Luce had seen so much passion and hunger. But here, it was different.

Luce's body began to buzz, eager for just one moment of physical connection between them. If *she* couldn't touch Daniel, at least her old self could.

But they were just standing there, now walking in circles. Never getting any closer to each other or any farther apart.

Every once in a while, their laughter would carry over to Luce again.

"Well?" Bill kept trying to squish his little face next to Luce's so he could look through one of the lenses of the opera glasses. "What's the word?"

"They're just *talking*. They're flirting kind of like they're strangers, but at the same time they also seem to know each other really well. I don't get it."

"So they're taking it slow. What's wrong with that?" Bill asked. "Kids today, they just want things to go fast— boom boom BOOM."

"Nothing's wrong with taking it slow, I just—" Luce broke off.

Her past self fell to her knees. She began to rock back and forth, holding her head, then her heart. A horrified look crossed Daniel's face. He looked so stiff in his white pants and tunic, like a statue of himself. He shook his head, looking at the sky, his lips mouthing the words *No. No. No.*

The girl's hazel eyes had gone wild and fiery, like something had possessed her. A high-pitched scream echoed out across the mountains. Daniel fell to the ground and buried his face in his hands. He reached out for her, but his hand hung in the air without ever connecting with her skin. His body crumpled and quaked, and when it mattered most, he looked away.

Luce was the only one watching as the girl became, out of nowhere, a column of fire. So fast.

The acrid smoke swirled over Daniel. His eyes were closed. His face glistened—wet with tears. He looked as miserable as he had looked every other time she'd watched him watch her die. But this time, he also looked sick with shock. Something was different. Something was wrong.

When Daniel had first told her about his punishment, he'd said there had been some lives in which a single kiss had killed her. Worse, in which something short of a kiss had killed her. A single touch.

They had not touched. Luce had been watching the whole time. He'd been so careful not to come near her. Did he think he could have her longer by holding back the warmth of his embrace? Did he think he could outwit the curse by holding her always just out of reach?

"He didn't even touch her," she murmured.

"Bummer," Bill said.

Never touching her, not once the whole time they were in love. And now he'd have to wait it all out again, not knowing whether anything would even be different next time. How could hope live in the face of that kind of defeat? Nothing about this made sense.

"If he didn't touch her, then what triggered her death?" She turned to Bill, who tilted his head and looked up into the sky.

"Mountains," he said. "Pretty!"

"You know something," Luce said. "What is it?"

He shrugged. "I don't know anything," he said. "Or nothing I can tell you."

A horrible, desolate cry echoed across the valley. The sound of Daniel's agony resounded and returned, multiplied, as though a hundred Daniels were crying out together. Luce brought the opera glasses back up to her face and saw him dash the flowers in his hands to the ground.

"I have to go to him!" she said.

"Too late," Bill said. "Here it comes."

Daniel backed away from the cliff edge. Luce's heart pounded for fear of what he was about to do. He certainly wasn't going to sleep. He got a running start, picking up inhuman speed by the time he reached the cliff's edge, and then launched himself into the air.

Luce waited for his wings to unfurl. She waited for the soft thunder of their grand unfolding, opening wide and catching the air in awesome glory. She'd seen him take flight like this in the past, and every time, it struck her to her core: How desperately she loved him.

But Daniel's wings never shot out from his back. When he reached the edge of the cliff, he went over like any other boy.

And he fell like any other boy, too.

Luce screamed, a loud and long and terrified cry, until Bill clapped his dirty stone hand over her mouth. She threw him off, ran to the edge of the cliff, and crawled forward.

Daniel was still falling. It was a long way down. She watched his body grow smaller and smaller.

"He'll extend his wings, won't he?" she gasped. "He'll realize that he's going to fall and fall until . . ."

She couldn't even say it.

"No," Bill said.

"But—"

"He'll slam right into that ground a couple of thousand feet down, yes," Bill said. "He'll break every bone in his body. But don't worry, he can't kill himself. He only wishes he could." He turned to her and sighed. "Now do you believe his love?"

"Yes," Luce whispered, because all she wanted to do at that moment was plunge off the cliff after him. That was how much she loved him back.

But it wouldn't do any good.

"They were being so careful." Her voice was strained. "We both saw what happened, Bill: *nothing*. She was so innocent. So how could she have died?"

Bill sputtered a laugh. "You think you know everything about her just because you saw the last three minutes of her life from across a mountaintop?"

"You're the one who made me use binoculars . . . oh!" She froze. "Wait a minute!" Something haunted her about the way her past self's eyes had seemed to change, just for a moment, right at the end. And suddenly, Luce knew: "What killed her this time wasn't something I could have witnessed, anyway. . . ."

Bill rolled his claws, waiting for her to finish the thought.

"It was happening inside her."

He applauded slowly. "I think you might be ready now."

"Ready for what?"

"Remember what I mentioned to you in Helston? After you talked to Roland?"

"You disagreed with him . . . about me getting close to my past selves?"

"You still can't rewrite the story, Luce. You can't change the narratives. If you try to—"

"I know, it distorts the future. I don't want to change the past. I just need to know what happens—why I keep dying. I thought it was a kiss, or a touch, or something physical, but it seems more complicated than that."

Bill yanked the shadow out from behind Luce's feet like a bullfighter wielding a red cape. Its edges flickered with silver. "Are you ready to put your soul where your mouth is?" he asked. "Are you ready to go three-D?"

"I'm ready." Luce punched open the Announcer and braced herself against the briny wind inside. "Wait," she said, looking at Bill hovering at her side. "What's three-D?"

"Wave of the future, kid," he said.

Luce gave him a hard stare.

"Okay, there's an unsonorous technical term for it—*cleaving*—but to me, *three-D* sounds much more fun." Bill dove inside the dark tunnel and beckoned her with a crooked finger. "Trust me, you'll *love* it."

TEN

THE DEPTHS

LHASA, TIBET · APRIL 30, 1740

Daniel hit the ground running.

Wind ripped across his body. The sun felt close against his skin. He was running and running and had no idea where he was. He'd burst from the Announcer without knowing, and though it felt *right* in almost every way, something nagged at his memory. Something was wrong.

His wings.

They were *absent*. No—they were still there, of course, but he felt no urge to let them out, no burning itch for flight. Instead of the familiar yearning to soar into the sky, the pull he felt was *down*.

A memory was rising to the surface of his mind. He was nearing something painful, the edge of something dangerous. His eyes focused on the space in front of him—

And saw nothing but thin air.

He threw himself backward, arms flailing as his feet skidded along the rock. He hit the ground on his backside and came to a stop just before he plunged off an unfathomable cliff.

He caught his breath, then rolled his body carefully around so he could peer over the edge.

Below him: an abyss so eerily familiar. He got to his hands and knees and studied the vast darkness below. Was he down there still? Had the Announcer ejected him here before or after it had happened?

That was why his wings hadn't burst forth. They'd remembered this life's agony and stayed put.

Tibet. Where just his words had killed her. That life's Lucinda had been raised to be so chaste, she wouldn't even touch him. Though he'd ached for the feel of her skin on his, Daniel had respected her wishes. Secretly, he had hoped that her refusal might be a way to outsmart their curse at last. But he'd been a fool again. Of course, touch wasn't the trigger. The punishment ran far deeper than that.

And now he was back here, in the place where her

death had driven him into a despair so overwhelming that he'd tried to put an end to his pain.

As if that were possible.

The whole way down, he'd known he would fail. Suicide was a mortal luxury not afforded to angels.

His body trembled at the memory. It wasn't just the agony of all his shattered bones, or the way the fall had left his body black and blue. No, it was what came afterward. He'd lain there for weeks, his body wedged in the dark emptiness between two vast boulders. Occasionally he'd come to, but his mind was so awash in misery that he wasn't able to think about Lucinda. He wasn't able to think about anything at all.

Which had been the point.

But as was the way of angels, his body healed itself faster and more completely than his soul ever could.

His bones knit back together. His wounds sealed in neat scars and, over time, disappeared completely. His pulverized organs grew healthy. All too soon his heart was full again and strong and beating.

It was Gabbe who'd found him after more than a month, who'd helped him crawl out from the crevasse, who'd put splints on his wings and carried him away from this place. She'd made him vow to never do it again. She'd made him vow to always maintain hope.

And now here he was again. He got to his feet and, once more, teetered at the edge.

"No, please. Oh *God,* don't! I just couldn't bear it if you jumped."

It wasn't Gabbe speaking to him now on the mountain. This voice dripped with sarcasm. Daniel knew who it belonged to before he even spun around.

Cam lounged against a wall of tall black boulders. Over the colorless earth, he'd spread out an enormous prayer tapestry woven with rich strands of burgundy and ochre thread. He dangled a charred yak's leg in his hand and bit off a huge hunk of stringy meat.

"Oh, what the hell?" Cam shrugged, chewing. "Go ahead and jump. Any last words you want me to pass along to Luce?"

"Where is she?" Daniel started toward him, his hands balling into fists. Was the Cam reclining before him of this time period? Or was he an Anachronism, come back in time just as Daniel had?

Cam flung the yak bone off the cliff and stood up, wiping his greasy hands on his jeans. Anachronism, Daniel decided.

"You just missed her. Again. What took you so long?" Cam held out a small tin platter brimming with food. "Dumpling? They're divine."

Daniel knocked the plate to the ground. "Why didn't you stop her?" He had been to Tahiti, to Prussia, and now here to Tibet in less time that it would take a mortal to cross a street. Always he felt as if he were hot on

Luce's trail. And always she was just beyond reach. How did she continue to outpace him?

"You said you didn't need my help."

"But you saw her?" Daniel demanded.

Cam nodded.

"Did she see you?"

Cam shook his head.

"Good." Daniel scanned the bare mountaintop, trying to imagine Luce there. He cast a quick eye around, looking for traces of her. But there was nothing. Gray dirt, black rock, the cut of the wind, no life up here at all—it all seemed to him the loneliest place on earth.

"What happened?" he said, grilling Cam. "What did she do?"

Cam walked a casual circle around Daniel. "She, unlike the object of her affection, has an impeccable sense of timing. She arrived at just the right moment to see her own magnificent death—it is a good one, this time, looks quite grand against this stark landscape. Even *you* must be able to admit that. No?"

Daniel jerked his gaze away.

"Anyway, where was I? Hmm, her own magnificent death, already said that . . . Ah yes! She stayed just long enough to watch you throw yourself over the edge of the cliff and forget to use your wings."

Daniel hung his head.

"That didn't go over very well."

Daniel's hand snapped out and caught Cam by the

throat. "You expect me to believe you just watched? You didn't talk to her? Didn't find out where she was going next? Didn't try to stop her?"

Cam grunted and twisted out of Daniel's grip. "I was nowhere near her. By the time I reached this spot, she was gone. Again: You said you didn't need my help."

"I don't. Stay out of this. I'll handle it myself."

Cam chuckled and dropped back onto the tapestry rug, crossing his legs in front of him. "Thing is, Daniel," he said, drawing a handful of dried goji berries to his lips. "Even if I trusted that you *could* handle it yourself— which, based on your existing record, I don't"—he wagged a finger—"you're not alone in this. Everyone's looking for her."

"What do you mean, *everyone*?"

"When you took off after Luce the night we fought the Outcasts, do you think the rest of us just sat around and played canasta? Gabbe, Roland, Molly, Arriane, even those two idiot Nephilim kids—they're all some-where out there trying to find her."

"You *let* them do that?"

"I'm not anyone's keeper, brother."

"Don't call me that," Daniel snapped. "I can't be-lieve this. How could they? This is my responsibility—"

"Free will." Cam shrugged. "It's all the rage these days."

Daniel's wings burned against his back, useless. What could he do about half a dozen Anachronisms blundering about in the past? His fellow fallen angels would know how fragile the past was, would be careful. But Shelby and Miles? They were *kids*. They'd be reckless. They wouldn't know any better. They could destroy it all for Luce. They could destroy Luce herself.

No. Daniel wouldn't give any of them the chance to get to her before he did.

And yet—Cam had done it.

"How can I trust that you didn't interfere?" Daniel asked, trying not to show his desperation.

Cam rolled his eyes. "Because *you* know *I* know how dangerous interference is. Our end goals may be different, but we both need her to make it out of this alive."

"Listen to me, Cam. *Everything* is at stake here."

"Don't demean me. I know what's at stake. You're not the only one who's already struggled for too long."

"I'm—I'm afraid," Daniel admitted. "If she too deeply alters the past—"

"It could change who she is when she returns to the present?" Cam said. "Yeah, I'm scared, too."

Daniel closed his eyes. "It would mean that any chance she had of breaking free of this curse—"

"Would be squandered."

Daniel eyed Cam. The two of them hadn't spoken to each other like this—like brothers—in ages. "She was alone? You're sure none of the others had gotten to her, either?"

For a moment, Cam gazed past Daniel, at a space on the mountaintop beyond them. It looked as empty as Daniel felt. Cam's hesitation made the back of Daniel's neck itch.

"None of the others had reached her," Cam said finally.

"Are you certain?"

"I'm the one who saw her here. You're the one who never shows up on time. And besides, her being out here at all is no one's fault but yours."

"That's not true. I didn't show her how to use the Announcers."

Cam laughed bitterly. "I don't mean the Announcers, you moron. I mean that she thinks this is just about the two of you. A stupid lovers' quarrel."

"It *is* about the two of us." Daniel's voice was strained. He would have liked to pick up the boulder behind Cam's head and drop it over his skull.

"Liar." Cam leaped to his feet, hot fury flashing in his green eyes. "It's far bigger, and you know it is." He rolled back his shoulders and unleashed his giant marbled wings. They filled the air with golden glory, blocking the sun for a moment. When they curved toward Daniel, he stepped back, repulsed. "You'd better find her, before she—or someone else—steps in and rewrites our entire history. And makes you, me, all of this"— Cam snapped his fingers—"obsolete."

Daniel snarled, unfurling his own silvery-white wings, feeling them extend out and out and out at his sides, shuddering as they pulsed near Cam's. He felt warmer now, and capable of anything. "I'll handle it—" he started to say.

But Cam had already taken off, the kickback from his flight sending small tornadoes of dirt spiraling up from the ground. Daniel shielded his eyes from the sun and looked up as the golden wings beat across the sky, then, in an instant, were gone.

ELEVEN

COUP DE FOUDRE

VERSAILLES, FRANCE · FEBRUARY 14, 1723

Splash.

Luce came out of the Announcer underwater.

She opened her eyes, but the warm, cloudy water stung so sharply that she promptly clamped them shut again. Her soggy clothes dragged her down, so she wrestled off the mink coat. As it sank beneath her, she kicked hard for the surface, desperate for air.

It was only a few inches above her head.

She gasped; then her feet found bottom and she

stood. She wiped the water from her eyes. She was in a bathtub.

Granted, it was the largest bathtub she had ever seen, as big as a small swimming pool. It was kidney-shaped and made of the smoothest white porcelain and sat alone in the middle of a giant room that looked like a gallery in a museum. The high ceilings were covered by enormous frescoed portraits of a dark-haired family who looked royal. A chain of golden roses framed each bust, and fleshy cherubs hovered between, playing trumpets toward the sky. Against each of the walls—which were papered in elaborate swirls of turquoise, pink, and gold—was an oversized, lavishly carved wooden armoire.

Luce sank back into the tub. Where was she now? She used her hand to skim the surface, parting about five inches of frothy bubbles the consistency of Chantilly cream. A pillow-sized sponge bobbed up, and she realized she had not bathed since Helston. She was filthy. She used the sponge to scrub at her face, then set to work peeling off the rest of her clothes. She sloshed all the sopping garments over the side of the tub.

That was when Bill floated slowly up out of the bathwater to hover a foot above the surface. The portion of the tub from which he'd risen was dark and cloudy with gargoyle grit.

"Bill!" she cried. "Can't you tell I need a few minutes of privacy?"

He held a hand up to shield his eyes. "You done

thrashing around in here yet, Jaws?" With his other hand, he wiped some bubbles from his bald head.

"You could have warned me that I was about to take a plunge underwater!" Luce said.

"I did warn you!" He hopped up to the rim of the tub and tottered across it until he was in Luce's face. "Right as we were coming out of the Announcer. You just didn't hear me because you were underwater!"

"Very helpful, thank you."

"You needed a bath, anyway," he said. "This is a big night for you, toots."

"Why? What's happening?"

"What's happening, she asks!" Bill grabbed her shoulder. "Only the grandest ball since the Sun King popped off! And I say, so what if this *boum* is hosted by his greasy pubescent son? It's still going to be right downstairs in the largest, most spectacular ballroom in Versailles—and *everybody's* going to be there!"

Luce shrugged. A ball sounded fine, but it had nothing to do with her.

"I'll clarify," Bill said. "Everyone will be there including Lys Virgily. The Princess of Savoy? Ring a bell?" He bopped Luce on the nose. "That's you."

"Hmph," Luce said, sliding her head back to rest against the soapy wall of the tub. "Sounds like a big night for *her.* But what am I supposed to do while they're all at the ball?"

"See, remember when I told you—"

The knob on the door of the great bathroom was turning. Bill eyed it, groaning. "To be continued."

As the door swung open, he held his pointy nose and disappeared under the water. Luce writhed and kicked him to the other side of the tub. He resurfaced, glared at her, and started floating on his back through the suds.

Bill might have been invisible to the pretty girl with corn-colored curls who was standing in the doorway in a long cranberry-colored gown—but Luce wasn't. At the sight of someone in the tub, the girl reared back.

"Oh, Princess Lys! Forgive me!" she said in French. "I was told this chamber was empty. I—I'd run a bath for Princess Elizabeth"—she pointed to the tub where Luce was soaking—"and was just about to send her up along with her ladies."

"Well—" Luce racked her brain, desperate to come off as more regal than she felt. "You may not s-send her up. Nor her ladies. This is my chamber, where I intended to bathe in peace."

"I beg your pardon," the girl said, bowing, "a thousand times."

"It's all right," Luce said quickly when she saw the girl's honest despair. "There must just have been a misunderstanding."

The girl curtseyed and began to close the door. Bill peeked his horned head up above the surface of the water and whispered, "Clothes!" Luce used her bare foot to push him down.

"Wait!" Luce called after the girl, who slowly pushed the door open again. "I need your help. Dressing for the ball."

"What about your ladies-in-waiting, Princess Lys? There's Agatha or Eloise—"

"No, no. The girls and I had a spat," Luce hurried on, trying not to talk too much for fear of giving herself away completely. "They picked out the most, um, horrid gown for me to wear. So I sent them away. This is an important ball, you know."

"Yes, Princess."

"Could you find something for me?" Luce asked the girl, gesturing with her head at the armoire.

"Me? H-help you dress?"

"You're the only one here, aren't you?" Luce said, hoping that something in that armoire would fit her—and look halfway decent for a ball. "What's your name?"

"Anne-Marie, Princess."

"Great," Luce said, trying to channel Lucinda from Helston by simply acting self-important. And she threw in a bit of Shelby's know-it-all attitude for good measure. "Hop to it, Anne-Marie. I won't be late because of your sluggishness. Be a dear and fetch me a gown."

❄

Ten minutes later, Luce stood before an expansive three-way mirror, admiring the stitching on the bust of the first gown Anne-Marie had tugged from the armoire.

The gown was made of tiered black taffeta, tightly gathered at the waist, then swirling into a gloriously wide bell shape near the ground. Luce's hair had been swept up into a twist, then tucked under a dark, heavy wig of elaborate curls. Her face shimmered with a dusting of powder and rouge. She was wearing so many undergarments that it felt as though someone had draped a fifty-pound weight over her body. How did girls move in these things? Let alone dance?

As Anne-Marie drew the corset tighter around her torso, Luce gaped at her reflection. The wig made her look five years older. And she was sure she'd never had this much cleavage before. In any of her lives.

For the briefest moment, she allowed herself to forget her nerves about meeting her past princess self, and whether she'd find Daniel again before she made a huge mess out of their love—and simply felt what every other girl going to that ball that night must have felt: Breathing was overrated in a dress as amazing as this.

"You're ready, Princess," Anne-Marie whispered reverently. "I will leave you, if you'll allow me."

As soon as Anne-Marie shut the door behind her, Bill propelled himself out of the water, sending a cold spray of soapsuds across the room. He sailed over the armoire and came to rest on a small turquoise silk footstool. He pointed at Luce's gown, at her wig, then at her gown again. "Ooh la la. Hot stuff."

"You haven't even seen my shoes." She lifted the hem of her skirt to show off a pair of pointy-toed emerald-green heels inlaid with jade flowers. They matched the emerald-green lace that trimmed the bust of her dress and were easily the most amazing shoes she had ever seen, let alone slipped onto her feet.

"Oooh!" Bill squealed. "*Very* rococo."

"So, I'm really doing this? I'm just going to go down there and pretend—"

"No pretending." Bill shook his head. "*Own it*. Own that cleavage, girl, you know you want to."

"Okay, I am pretending you didn't say that." Luce laugh-winced. "So I go downstairs and 'own it' or what-ever. But what do I do when I find my past self? I don't know anything about her. Do I just—"

"Take her hand," Bill said cryptically. "She'll be very *touched* by the gesture, I'm sure."

Bill was hinting at something, clearly, but Luce didn't understand. Then she remembered his words right be-fore they dove through the last Announcer.

"Tell me about going three-D."

"Aha." Bill mimed leaning against an invisible wall in the air. His wings blurred as he fluttered in front of her. "You know how some things are just too out-of-this-world to be pinned down by dull old words? Like, for example, the way you swoon when Daniel comes in for a long kiss, or the feeling of heat that spreads through your body when his wings unfurl on a dark night—"

"Don't." Luce's hand went to her heart involuntarily. There *were* no words that could ever do justice to what Daniel made her feel. Bill was making fun of her, but that didn't mean she ached any less at being away from Daniel for so long.

"Same deal with three-D. You'll just have to live it to understand it."

As soon as Bill opened the door for Luce, the sounds of distant orchestra music and the polite murmuring of a large crowd flooded into the room. She felt something pulling her down there. Maybe it was Daniel. Maybe it was Lys.

Bill bowed in the air. "After you, Princess."

She followed the noise down two broad, winding flights of golden stairs, the music getting louder with each step. As she swept through empty gallery after empty gallery, she began to smell the mouthwatering aromas of roasted quail and stewed apples and potatoes *au gratin*. And perfume—so much she could hardly inhale without coughing.

"Now aren't you glad I made you take a bath?" Bill asked. "One less bottle of eau de reekette punching holes in l'ozone."

Luce didn't answer. She had entered a long hall of mirrors, and in front of her, a pair of women and a man were crossing toward the entrance of a main room. The women didn't walk, they glided. Their yellow and blue gowns practically swished across the floor. The man walked between them, his ruffled white shirt dapper under his long silver jacket and his heels nearly as high as the ones on Luce's shoes. All three of them wore wigs a full foot taller than the one on Luce's own head, which felt enormous and weighed a ton. Watching them, Luce felt clumsy, the way her skirts swung from side to side as she walked.

They turned to look at her and all three pairs of eyes narrowed, as if they could tell instantly that she had not been bred to attend high-society balls.

"Ignore them," Bill said. "There are snobs in every lifetime. In the end, they've got nothing on you."

Luce nodded, falling behind the trio, who passed through a set of mirrored doorways into the ballroom. The ultimate ballroom. The ballroom to end all ballrooms.

Luce couldn't help herself. She stopped in her tracks and whispered, "Wow."

It was majestic: A dozen chandeliers hung low from the faraway ceiling, glittering with bright white candles. Where the walls weren't made of mirrors, they were covered with gold. The parquet dance floor seemed to stretch on into the next city, and ringing the dance floor were long tables covered in white linen, laid with fine china place settings, platters of cakes and cookies, and great crystal goblets filled with ruby-colored wine. Thousands of white daffodils peeked out of hundreds of dark-red vases set upon the dozens of dining tables.

On the far side of the room, a line of exquisitely dressed young women was forming. There were about ten of them, standing together, whispering and laughing outside a great golden door.

Another crowd had gathered around an enormous crystal punch bowl near the orchestra. Luce helped herself to a glass.

"Excuse me?" she asked a pair of women next to her. Their artful gray curls formed twin towers on their heads. "What are those girls in line for?"

"Why, to please the king, of course." One woman chuckled. "Those *demoiselles* are here to see if they might please him into marriage."

Marriage? But they looked so young. All of a sudden Luce's skin began to feel hot and itchy. Then it hit her: *Lys is in that line.*

Luce gulped and studied each of the young women. There she was, third in line, magnificently wrapped in a long black gown only slightly different from the one that Luce herself was wearing. Her shoulders were covered with a black velvet capelet, and her eyes never rose from the floor. She wasn't laughing with the other girls. She looked as frustrated as Luce felt.

"Bill," Luce whispered.

But the gargoyle flew right in front of her face and shushed her with a finger to his fat stone lips. "Only crazies talk to their invisible gargoyles," he hissed, "and crazies don't get invited to many balls. Now, hush."

"But what about—"

"Hush."

What about going 3-D?

Luce took a deep breath. The last instruction he had given her was to take Lys by the hand. . . .

She strode over, crossing the dance floor and bypassing the servants with their trays of foie gras and Chambord. She nearly plowed right into the girl behind Lys, who was trying to cut ahead of Lys in line by pretending to whisper something to a friend.

"Excuse me," Luce said to Lys, whose eyes widened and whose lips parted and let a tiny confused sound escape her mouth.

But Luce couldn't wait for Lys to react. She reached down and grabbed her by the hand. It fit into her own like a puzzle piece. She squeezed.

Luce's stomach dropped as if she'd gone down the first hill of a roller coaster. Her skin began to vibrate, and a drowsy, gently rocking sensation came over her. She felt her eyelids flutter, but some instinct told her to keep holding fast to Lys's hand.

She blinked, and Lys blinked, and then they both

blinked at the same time—and on the other side of the blink, Luce could see herself in Lys's eyes . . . and then could see Lys from her own eyes . . . and then—

She could see no one in front of her at all.

"Oh!" she cried out, and her voice sounded just as it always had. She looked down at her hands, which looked just as they always had. She reached up and felt her face, her hair, her wig, all of which felt the same as they had before. But something . . . something had shifted.

She lifted the hem of her dress and peeked down at her shoes.

They were magenta. With diamond-shaped high heels, and tied at the ankle with an elegant silver bow.

What had she done?

Then she realized what Bill had meant by "going three-D."

She had literally stepped into Lys's body.

Luce glanced around her, terrified. To her horror, all the other girls in line were motionless. In fact, everyone Luce looked at was frozen stiff. It was if the entire party had been put on Pause.

"See?" Bill's voice came hotly in her ear. "No words for this, right?"

"What's happening, Bill?" Her voice was rising.

"Right now, not a whole lot. I had to put the brakes on the party, lest you freak out. Once we're straight on the three-D business, I'll start it back up again."

"So . . . no one can see this right now?" Luce asked,

waving her hand slowly in front of the face of the pretty brunette girl who'd been standing in front of Lys. The girl didn't flinch. She didn't blink. Her face was frozen in an unending openmouthed grin.

"Nope." Bill demonstrated by wiggling his tongue near the ear of an older man, who stood frozen with an *escargot* poised between his fingers, inches from his mouth. "Not until I snap me fingers."

Luce exhaled, once more strangely relieved at having Bill's help. She needed a few minutes to get used to the idea that she was—was she *really*—

"I'm inside my past self," she said.

"Yes."

"Then where did I go? Where's my body?"

"You're in there somewhere." He tapped at her collarbone. "You'll pop out again when— Well, when the time is right. But for now, you've slipped entirely inside your past. Like a cute little turtle in a borrowed shell. Except it's more than that. When you're in Lys's body, your very beings are entwined, so all sorts of good stuff comes with the package. Her memories, her passions, her manners— lucky for you. Of course, you also have to grapple with her shortcomings. This one, if I recall, puts her foot in her mouth with some regularity. So watch out."

"Amazing," Luce whispered. "So if I could just find Daniel, I'd be able to feel exactly what she feels toward him."

"Sure, I guess, but you do realize that once I snap my

fingers, Lys has obligations at this ball that don't include Daniel. This isn't really his scene, and by that I mean, no way the guards would let a poor stable boy in here."

Luce didn't care about any of that. Poor stable boy or not, she would find him. She couldn't wait. Inside Lys's body she could even hold him, maybe even kiss him. The anticipation of it was almost overwhelming.

"Hello?" Bill flicked a hard finger against her temple. "You ready yet? Get in there, see what you can see—then get out while the getting's good, if you know what I mean."

Luce nodded. She straightened Lys's black gown and held her head a little higher. "Snap to it."

"And . . . *go*." Bill snapped his fingers.

For a split second, the party snagged like a scratched record. Then every midconversation syllable, every whiff of perfume being carried through the air, every drop of punch sliding down every bejeweled throat, every note of music from every player in the orchestra, picked up, smoothed out, and carried on as if nothing in the world had happened.

Only Luce had changed. Her mind became assaulted by a thousand words and images. *A sprawling thatch-roofed country house in the foothills of the Alps. A chestnut-colored horse named Gauche. The smell of straw everywhere. A single long-stemmed white peony laid across her pillow. And Daniel. Daniel. Daniel. Com-*

ing back from the well with four heavy buckets of water balanced from a pole laid across his shoulders. Grooming Gauche first thing every morning so Lys could take him for a ride. When it came to small, lovely favors for Luce, there was nothing Daniel overlooked, even in the midst of all the labor he did for her father. His violet eyes finding her always. Daniel in her dreams, in her heart, in her arms. It was like the flashes of Luschka's memories that had come to her in Moscow when she'd touched the church gate—but stronger, more overwhelming, intrinsically a part of her.

Daniel was here. In the stables or the servants' quarters. He was here. And she would find him.

Something rustled near Luce's neck. She jumped.

"Just me." Bill flitted over the top of her capelet. "You're doing great."

The great golden doors at the head of the room were eased open by two footmen, who stood at attention on either side. The girls in line in front of Luce began to titter with excitement, and then a hush swept the room. Meanwhile, Luce was looking for the fastest way out of here and into Daniel's arms.

"Focus, Luce," Bill said, as if reading her mind. "You're about to be called into duty."

The strings of the orchestra began playing the baroque opening chords of the *Ballet de Jeunesse,* and the whole room shifted its attention. Luce followed everyone else's gaze and gasped: She *recognized* the man who stood there in the doorway, gazing out at the party with a patch over one eye.

It was the Duc de Bourbon, the cousin of the king.

He was tall and skinny, as wilted as a bean plant in a drought. His ill-fitting blue velvet suit was ornamented with a mauve sash to match the mauve stockings on his twig-thin legs. His ostentatious powdered wig and his milky-white face were both exceptionally ugly.

She didn't recognize the duke from some photograph in a history book. She knew far too much about him. She knew *everything*. Like how the royal ladies-in-waiting swapped bawdy jokes about the sad size of the duke's scepter. About how he'd lost that eye (hunting accident, on a trip he'd joined to appease the king). And about how right now, the duke was going to send in the girls whom he'd preselected as suitable marriage material for the twelve-year-old king waiting inside.

And Luce—no, Lys—was an early favorite of the duke's to fill the slot. That was the reason for the heavy, aching feeling in her chest: Lys couldn't marry the king, because she loved Daniel. She had loved him passionately for years. But in this life, Daniel was a servant, and the two of them were forced to hide their romance. Luce felt Lys's paralyzing fear—that if she took the king's fancy tonight, all hope of having a life with Daniel would disappear.

Bill had warned her that going 3-D would be intense,

but there was no way Luce could have prepared for the onslaught of so much emotion: Every fear and doubt that had ever crossed Lys's mind swamped Luce. Every hope and dream. It was too much.

She gasped and looked around her at the ball—anywhere but at the duke. And realized she knew everything there was to know about this time and place. She suddenly understood why the king was looking for a wife even though he was already engaged. She recognized half the faces moving around her in the ballroom, knew their stories, and knew which ones envied her. She knew how to stand in the corseted gown so that she could breathe comfortably. And she knew, judging from the skilled eye she cast on the dancers, that Lys had been trained in the art of ballroom dancing from childhood.

It was an eerie feeling, being in Lys's body, as if Luce were both the ghost and the one haunted.

The orchestra came to the end of the song, and a man near the door stepped forward to read from a scroll. "Princess Lys of Savoy."

Luce raised her head with more elegance and confidence than she'd expected, and accepted the hand of the young man in the pale-green waistcoat who had appeared to escort her into the king's receiving room.

Once inside the entirely pastel-blue room, Luce tried not to stare at the king. His towering gray wig looked silly poised over his small, drawn face. His pale-blue eyes leered at the line of duchesses and princesses—all beautiful, all dressed exquisitely—the way a man deprived of food might leer at a pig on a spit.

The pimply figure on the throne was little more than a child.

Louis XV had assumed the crown when he was only five years old. In compliance with his dying father's wishes, he'd been betrothed to the Spanish princess, the infanta. But she was still barely a toddler. It was a match made in Hell. The young king, who was frail and sickly, wasn't expected to live long enough to produce an heir with the Spanish princess, who herself might also die before reaching childbearing age. So the king had to find a consort to produce an heir. Which explained this extravagant party, and the ladies lined up on display.

Luce fidgeted with the lace on her gown, feeling ridiculous. The other girls all looked so patient. Maybe they truly *wanted* to marry the acne-ridden twelve-year-old King Louis, though Luce didn't see how that was possible. They were all so elegant and beautiful. From the Russian princess, Elizabeth, whose sapphire-velvet gown had a collar trimmed in rabbit's fur, to Maria, the princess from Poland, whose tiny button nose and full red mouth made her dizzyingly alluring, they all gazed at the boy king with wide, hopeful eyes.

But he was staring straight at Luce. With a satisfied smirk that made her stomach turn.

"That one." He pointed at her lazily. "Let me see her up close."

The duke appeared at Luce's side, gently shoving her shoulders forward with his long, icy fingers. "Present yourself, Princess," he said quietly. "This is a once-in-a-lifetime opportunity."

The Luce part of her groaned inwardly, but on the outside, Lys was in charge, and she practically floated forward to greet the king. She curtseyed with a perfectly proper bow of her head, extending her hand for his kiss. It was what her family expected of her.

"Will you get fat?" the king blurted out at Luce, eyeing her corset-squeezed waist. "I like the way she looks now," he said to the duke. "But I don't want her to get fat."

Had she been in her own body, Luce might have told the king exactly what she thought of his unappealing physique. But Lys had perfect composure, and Luce felt herself reply, "I should hope to always please the king, with my looks and with my temperament."

"Yes, of course," the duke purred, walking a tight circle around Luce. "I'm sure His Majesty could keep the princess on the diet of his choice."

"What about hunting?" the king asked.

"Your Majesty," the duke began to say, "that isn't befitting a queen. You have plenty of other hunting companions. I, for one—"

"My father is an excellent hunter," Luce said. Her brain was whirling, working toward something—anything—that might help her escape this scene.

"Should I bed down with your father, then?" the king sneered.

"Knowing Your Majesty likes guns," Luce said, straining to keep her tone polite, "I have brought you a gift—my father's most prized hunting rifle. He'd asked me to bring it to you this evening, but I wasn't sure when I'd have the pleasure of making your acquaintance."

She had the king's full attention. He was perched on the edge of his throne.

"What's it look like? Are there jewels in its butt?"

"The . . . the stock is hand-carved from cherry-wood," she said, feeding the king the details Bill called out from where he stood beside the king's chair. "The bore was milled by—by—"

"Oh, what would sound impressive? By a Russian metalworker who has since gone to work for the czar." Bill leaned over the king's pastries and sniffed hungrily. "These look good."

Luce repeated Bill's line and then added, "I could bring it to Your Majesty, if you'd just allow me to go and retrieve it from my chambers—"

"A servant can bring the gun down tomorrow, I'm sure," the duke said.

"I want to see it *now*." The king crossed his arms, looking even younger than he was.

"Please." Luce turned to the duke. "It would give me great pleasure to present the rifle to His Majesty myself."

"Go." The king snapped his fingers, dismissing Luce.

Luce wanted to spin on her heel, but Lys knew better—one never showed the king one's back—and she bowed and walked backward out of the room. She showed the most gracious restraint, gliding along as though she hadn't any feet at all—just until she got to the other side of the mirrored door.

Then she ran.

Through the ballroom, past the splendid dancing couples and the orchestra, whirring from one pastel-yellow room into another decorated all in deep chartreuse. She ran past gasping ladies and grunting gentlemen, over hardwood floors and thick, opulent Persian rugs, until the lights grew dimmer and the partygoers thinned out, and at last she found the mullioned doors that led outside. She thrust them open, gasping in her corset to draw the fresh air of freedom into her lungs. She strode onto an enormous balcony made of brilliant white marble that wrapped around the entire second story of the palace.

The night was bright with stars; all Luce wanted to do was to be in Daniel's arms and flying up toward those stars. If only he were by her side to take her far from all of this—

"What are you doing out here?"

She spun around. He'd come for her. He stood across the balcony in simple servant's clothes, looking confused and alarmed and tragically, hopelessly in love.

"Daniel." She dashed toward him. He moved toward her, too, his violet eyes lighting up; he threw open his arms, beaming. When they finally connected and Luce was wrapped up in his arms, she thought she might explode from happiness.

But she didn't.

She just stayed there, her head buried against his wonderful, broad chest. She was home. His arms were wrapped around her back, resting on her waist, and he pulled her as close to him as possible. She felt him breathe, and smelled the husky scent of straw on his neck. Luce kissed just below his left ear, then underneath his jaw. Soft, gentle kisses until she reached his lips, which parted against her own. Then the kisses became longer, filled with a love that seemed to pour out from the very depths of her soul.

After a moment, Luce broke away and stared into Daniel's eyes. "I've missed you so much."

Daniel chuckled. "I've missed you, too, these past . . . three hours. Are—are you all right?"

Luce ran her fingers through Daniel's silky blond hair. "I just needed to get some air, to find you." She squeezed him tightly.

Daniel narrowed his eyes. "I don't think we should be out here, Lys. They must be expecting you back in the receiving room."

"I don't care. I won't go back in there. And I would never marry that pig. I will never marry anyone but you."

"Shhh." Daniel winced, stroking her cheek. "Someone might hear you. They've cut off heads for less than that."

"*Someone* already did hear you," a voice called from the open doorway. The Duc de Bourbon stood with his arms crossed over his chest, smirking at the sight of Lys in the arms of a common servant. "I believe the king should hear of this." And then he was gone, disappearing inside the palace.

Luce's heart raced, driven by Lys's fear and her own: Had she altered history? Was Lys's life supposed to proceed differently?

But Luce couldn't know, could she? That was what Roland had told her: Whatever changes she made in time, they would immediately be part of what had happened. Yet Luce was still here, so if she'd changed history by ditching the king—well, it didn't seem to matter to Lucinda Price in the twenty-first century.

When she spoke to Daniel, her voice was steady. "I don't care if that vile duke kills me. I'd sooner die than give you up."

A wave of heat swept over her, causing her to sway where she stood. "Oh," she said, clasping a hand to her head. She recognized it distantly, like something she'd seen a thousand times before but had never paid attention to.

"Lys," he whispered. "Do you know what's coming?"

"Yes," she whispered.

"And you know that I'll be with you until the end?" Daniel's eyes bored into her, full of tenderness and worry. He wasn't lying to her. He'd never lied to her. He never would. She knew that now, could see it. He revealed just enough to keep her alive a few moments longer, to suggest everything Luce was already beginning to learn on her own.

"Yes." She closed her eyes. "But there's so much I still don't understand. I don't know how to stop this from happening. I don't know how to break this curse."

Daniel smiled, but there were tears brimming in his eyes.

Luce wasn't afraid. She felt free. Freer than she'd ever felt before.

A strange, deep understanding was unfurling in her memory. Something becoming visible in the fog of her head. One kiss from Daniel would open a door, releasing her from a loveless marriage to a bratty child, from the cage of this body. This body wasn't who she really was. It was just a shell, part of a punishment. And so this body's death wasn't a tragedy at all—it was simply the end of a chapter. A beautiful, necessary release.

Footsteps sounded on the stairs behind them. The duke returning with his men. Daniel gripped her shoulders.

"Lys, listen to me—"

"Kiss me," she begged. Daniel's face changed, as if he needed to hear nothing else. He lifted her off the ground and crushed her against his chest. Tingling heat coursed through her body as she kissed him harder and deeper, letting herself go completely. She arched her back and tilted her head toward the sky and kissed him until she was dizzy with bliss. Until dark traces of shadows swirled and blackened the stars overhead. An obsidian symphony. But behind it: There was light. For the first time, Luce could feel the light shining through.

It was absolutely glorious.

It was time for her to go.

Get out while the getting's good, Bill had warned her. While she was still alive.

But she couldn't leave yet. Not while everything was so warm and lovely. Not with Daniel still kissing her, wild with passion. She opened her eyes and the colors of his hair and his face and the night itself burned brighter and more beautiful, lit up by an intense radiance.

That radiance was coming from deep inside Luce herself.

With every kiss, her whole body edged closer to the light. This was the only true way back to Daniel. Out of one mundane life and into another. Luce would happily die a thousand times just as long as she could be with him again on the other side.

"Stay with me," Daniel pleaded even as she felt herself incandesce.

She moaned. Tears streamed down her face. The softest smile parted her lips.

"What is it?" Daniel asked. He would not stop kissing her. "Lys?"

"It's . . . so much *love*," she said, opening her eyes just as the fire bloomed through her chest. A great column of light exploded in the night, rocketing heat and flames high in the sky, knocking Daniel off his feet, knocking Luce clear out of Lys's death and into darkness, where she was ice-cold and could see nothing. A shuddering wave of vertigo overtook her.

Then: the smallest flash of light.

Bill's face came into view, hovering over Luce with a worried look. She was lying prone on a flat surface. She touched the smooth stone beneath her, heard the water trickling nearby, sniffed at the cool musty air. She'd come out inside an Announcer.

"You scared me," Bill said. "I didn't know . . . I mean, when she died, I didn't know how . . . didn't know whether maybe you might get stuck somehow. . . . But I wasn't sure." He shook his head as if to banish the thought.

She tried to stand, but her legs were wobbly and everything about her felt incredibly cold. She sat cross-legged against the stone wall. She was back in the black gown with the emerald-green trim. The emerald-green slippers stood side by side in the corner. Bill must have slipped them off her feet and laid her down after she'd . . . after Lys . . . Luce still could not believe it.

"I could *see* things, Bill. Things I never knew before."

"Like?"

"Like she was happy when she died. *I* was happy. *Ecstatic.* The whole thing was just so beautiful." Her mind raced. "Knowing he'd be there for me on the other side, knowing that all I was doing was escaping something wrong and oppressive. That the beauty of our love endures death, endures everything. It was incredible."

"Incredibly dangerous," Bill said shortly. "Let's not do that again, okay?"

"Don't you get it? Ever since I left Daniel in the present, this is the best thing that's happened to me. And—"

But Bill had disappeared into the darkness again. She heard the trickle of the waterfall. A moment later, the sound of water boiling. When Bill reappeared, he'd made tea. He carried the pot on a thin metal tray and handed Luce a steaming mug.

"Where did you get that?" she asked.

"I *said*, let's not do that again, okay?"

But Luce was too wrapped up in her own thoughts to really hear him. This was the closest she'd come to any kind of clarity. She would go 3-D—what had he called it? *cleaving*?—again. She would see her lives through to their ends, one after another until in one of those lives, she found out exactly why it happened.

And then she'd break this curse.

TWELVE

THE PRISONER

PARIS, FRANCE · DECEMBER 1, 1723

Daniel cursed.

The Announcer had dumped him out onto a bed of damp, dirty straw. He rolled and sat up, his back against a frozen stone wall. Something from the ceiling was dripping cold, oily drops onto his forehead, but there wasn't enough light to see what it was.

Opposite him was an open slot of a window, crudely cut into the stone and hardly wide enough to stick a fist through. It let in only a sliver of moonlight, but enough blustery night air to bring the temperature near freezing.

He couldn't see the rats scampering in the cell, but he could feel their slimy bodies writhing through the moldy straw beneath his legs. He could feel their ragged teeth sawing into the leather of his shoes. He could hardly breathe for the stink of their waste. He kicked out and there was a squeal. Then he gathered his feet beneath him and rose onto his haunches.

"You're late."

The voice next to Daniel made him jump. He had carelessly assumed he was alone. The voice was a parched and raspy whisper, but somehow still familiar.

Then came a scraping sound, like metal being dragged across stone. Daniel stiffened as a blacker piece of shadow detached itself from the darkness and leaned forward. The figure moved into the pale-gray light under the window, where at last the silhouette of a face grew dimly visible.

His own face.

He'd forgotten this cell, forgotten this punishment. So this was where he'd ended up.

In some ways, Daniel's earlier self looked just as he did now: the same nose and mouth, the same distance between the same gray eyes. His hair was scruffier and stiff with grease, but it was the same pale gold it was now. And yet, prisoner Daniel looked *so* different. His face was horribly gaunt and pale, his forehead creased with filth. His body looked emaciated, and his skin was beaded with sweat.

This was what her absence did to him. Yes, he wore the ball and chain of a prisoner—but the real jailer here was his own guilt.

He remembered it all now. And he remembered the visitation of his future self, and a frustrating, bitter interview. Paris. The Bastille. Where he'd been locked up by the Duc de Bourbon's guards after Lys disappeared from the palace. There had been other jails, crueler living conditions, and worse food in Daniel's existence, but the mercilessness of his own regret that year in the Bastille was one of the hardest trials he'd ever overcome.

Some, but not all of it, had to do with the injustice of being charged with her murder.

But—

If Daniel was already here, locked up in the Bastille, it meant that Lys was already dead. So Luce had already come . . . and gone.

His past self was right. He was too late.

"Wait," he said to the prisoner in the darkness, drawing closer, but not so close that they risked touching. "How did you know what I've come back for?"

The scrape of the ball being dragged across the stone meant his past self had leaned back against the wall. "You're not the only one who's come through here looking for her."

Daniel's wings burned, sending heat licking down his shoulder blades. "Cam."

"No, not Cam," his past self responded. "Two kids."

"Shelby?" Now Daniel pounded his fist into the stone floor. "And the other one . . . Miles. You're not serious? Those Nephilim? They were *here*?"

"About a month ago, I think." He pointed at the wall behind him, where some crooked tally marks were etched into the wall. "I tried to keep track of the day, but you know how it is. Time passes in funny ways. It gets away from you."

"I remember." Daniel shuddered. "But the Nephilim. You talked to them?" He racked his memory, and faint images came to mind from his imprisonment, images of a girl and boy. He'd always taken them for the phantoms of grief, just two more of the delusions that beset him when she'd gone and he was alone again.

"For a moment." The prisoner's voice sounded tired and far away. "They weren't all that interested in me."

"Good."

"Once they found out she was dead, they were in a great hurry to move on." His gray eyes were eerily penetrating. "Something you and I can understand."

"Where did they go?"

"Don't know." The prisoner cracked a smile too big for his thin face. "I don't think they did, either. You should have seen how long it took them to open an Announcer. Looked like couple of bumbling fools."

Daniel felt himself almost begin to laugh.

"It isn't funny," his past self said. "They care for her."

But Daniel felt no tenderness for the Nephilim. "They're a threat to all of us. The destruction they could cause . . ." He closed his eyes. "They have no idea what they're doing."

"Why can't you catch her, Daniel?" His past self laughed dryly. "We've seen each other before over the millennia—I remember you chasing her. And never catching her."

"I—I don't know." The words stuck in Daniel's throat, a long sob building behind them. Quivering, he stifled it. "I can't reach her. Somehow I am eternally arriving a heartbeat too late, as though someone or something is working behind the scenes to keep her from me."

"Your Announcers will always take you where you need to be."

"I need to be with her."

"Perhaps they know what you need better than you know yourself."

"What?"

"Maybe she shouldn't be stopped." The prisoner rattled his chain listlessly. "That she is able to travel at all means something fundamental was changed. Maybe you can't catch her until she works that change into the original curse."

"But—" He didn't know what to say. The sob rose in Daniel's chest, drowning his heart in a torrent of shame and sadness. "She needs me. Every second is a lost eternity. And if she makes a misstep, everything could be lost. She could change the past and . . . cease to exist."

"But that's the nature of risk, isn't it? You gamble everything on the slenderest of hopes." His past self began to reach out, almost touching Daniel's arm. Both of them wanted to feel a connection. At the last instant, Daniel jerked away.

His past self sighed. "What if it's *you,* Daniel? What if *you're* the one who has to alter the past? What if you can't catch her until you've rewritten the curse to include a loophole?"

"Impossible." Daniel snorted. "Look at me. Look at you. We're wretched without her. We're nothing when we're not with Lucinda. There is no reason why my soul wouldn't want to find her as quickly as possible."

Daniel wanted to fly away from here. But something was nagging at him.

"Why haven't you offered to accompany me?" he asked finally. "I would refuse you, of course, but some of the others—when I encountered myself in another life, he wanted to join in. Why don't you?"

A rat crawled along the prisoner's leg, stopping to sniff at the bloody chains around his ankles.

"I escaped once," he said slowly. "You remember?"

"Yes," Daniel said, "when you—when *we*—escaped, early on. We went straight back to Savoy." He looked up at the false hope offered by the light outside the window. "Why did we go there? We should have known we were walking right into a trap."

The prisoner leaned back and rattled his chains. "We had no other choice. It was the closest place to her." He drew in a ragged breath. "It's so hard when she's in between. I never feel I can go on. I was glad when the duke anticipated my escape, figured out where I'd go. He was waiting in Savoy, waiting at my patron's dinner table with his men. Waiting to drag me back here."

Daniel remembered. "The punishment felt like something I'd earned."

"Daniel." The prisoner's forlorn face looked like it had been given a jolt of electricity. He looked alive again, or at least, his eyes did. They glowed violet. "I think I've got it." The words rushed carelessly out. "Take a lesson from the duke."

Daniel licked his lips. "Excuse me?"

"All these lives you say that you've been trailing after her. Do as the duke did with us. *Anticipate* her. Don't just catch up. Get there first. Wait her out."

"But I don't know where her Announcers will take her."

"Of course you do," his past self insisted. "You must have faint memories of where she'll end up. Maybe not every step along the way, but eventually, it all has to end where it started."

A silent understanding passed between them. Running his hands along the wall near the window, Daniel summoned a shadow. It was invisible to him in the darkness, but he could feel it moving toward him, and he deftly worked it into shape. This Announcer seemed as despondent as he felt. "You're right," he said, jerking open the portal. "There is one place she's sure to go."

"Yes."

"And you. You should take your own advice and leave this place," Daniel said grimly. "You're rotting in here."

"At least this body's pain distracts me from the pain in my soul," his past self said. "No. I wish you luck, but I won't leave these walls now. Not until she's settled in her next incarnation."

Daniel's wings bristled at his neck. He tried to sort out time and lives and memories in his head, but he kept circling around the same irksome thought. "She—she should be settled now. In conception. Can't you feel it?"

"Oh," his imprisoned past self said softly. He closed his eyes. "I don't know that I can feel anything anymore." The prisoner sighed heavily. "Life's a nightmare."

"No, it's not. Not anymore. I'll find her. I'll redeem us both," Daniel shouted, desperate to get out of there, desperately taking another leap of faith through time.

THIRTEEN

❧ ✦ ❧

STAR-CROSSED

LONDON, ENGLAND · JUNE 29, 1613

Something crunched under Luce's feet.

She raised the hem of her black gown: A layer of discarded walnut shells on the ground was so thick the stringy brown bits rose up over the buckles of her emerald-green high-heeled slippers.

She was at the rear of a noisy crowd of people. Almost everyone around her was dressed in muted browns or grays, the women in long gowns with ruched bodices and wide cuffs at the ends of their bell sleeves. The men wore tapered pants, broad mantles draping their shoulders, and flat caps made of wool. She'd never stepped out of an Announcer into such a public place before, but here she was, in the middle of a packed amphitheater. It was startling—and riotously loud.

"Look out!" Bill grabbed the neck of her velvet capelet and yanked her backward, pinning her against the wooden rail of a staircase.

A heartbeat later, two grimy boys barreled past in a reckless game of tag that sent a trio of women in their path falling over one another. The women heaved themselves back up and shouted curses at the boys, who jeered back, barely slowing down.

"Next time," Bill shouted in her ear, cupping his stone claws around his mouth, "could you try directing your little stepping-through exercises into a more—I don't know—*serene* setting? How am I supposed to do your costuming in the middle of this mob?"

"Sure, Bill, I'll work on that." Luce edged back just as the boys playing tag zipped by again. "Where *are* we?"

"You've circled the globe to find yourself in the Globe, milady." Bill sketched a little bow.

"The Globe *Theatre*?" Luce ducked as the woman in front of her discarded a gnawed-on turkey leg by tossing it over her shoulder. "You mean, like, Shakespeare?"

"Well, he *claims* to be retired. You know those artist types. So moody." Bill swooped down near the ground, tugging at the hem of her dress and humming to himself.

"*Othello* happened here," Luce said, taking a moment

to let it all sink in. *"The Tempest. Romeo and Juliet.* We're practically standing in the center of all the greatest love stories ever written."

"Actually, you're standing in walnut shells."

"Why do you have to be so glib about everything? This is amazing!"

"Sorry, I didn't realize we'd need a moment of bardolatry." His words came out lisped because of the needle clipped between his jagged teeth. "Now stand still."

"Ouch!" Luce yelped as he jabbed sharply into her kneecap. "What are you doing?"

"Un-Anachronizing you. These folks'll pay good money for a freak show, but they're expecting it to stay *onstage*." Bill worked quickly, discreetly tucking the long, draped fabric of her black gown from Versailles into a series of folds and crimps so that it was gathered along the sides. He knocked away her black wig and pulled her hair into a frizzy pouf. Then he eyed the velvet capelet around her shoulders. He whipped off the soft fabric. At last, he hocked a giant loogie into one hand, rubbed his palms together, and welded the capelet into a high Jacobean collar.

"That is seriously disgusting, Bill."

"Be quiet," he snapped. "Next time give me more space to work. You think I like 'making do'? I don't." He jerked his head at the jeering throngs. "Luckily most of them are too drunk to notice the girl stepping out of the shadows at the back of the room."

Bill was right: No one was looking at them. Everyone was squabbling as they pressed closer to the stage. It was just a platform, raised about five feet off the ground, and, standing at the back of the rowdy crowd, Luce had trouble seeing it clearly.

"Come on, now!" a boy shouted from the back. "Don't make us wait all day!"

Above the crowd were three tiers of box seats, and then nothing: the O-shaped amphitheater opened on a midday sky the pale blue of a robin's egg. Luce looked around for her past self. For Daniel.

"We're at the opening of the Globe." She thought back to Daniel's words under the peach trees at Sword & Cross. "Daniel told me we were here."

"Sure, you *were* here," Bill said. "About fourteen years ago. Perched on your older brother's shoulder. You came with your family to see *Julius Caesar.*"

Bill hovered in the air a foot in front of her. It was unappetizing, but the high collar around her neck actually seemed to hold its shape. She almost resembled the sumptuously dressed women in the higher boxes.

"And Daniel?" she asked.

"Daniel was a player—"

"Hey!"

"That's what they call the *actors.*" Bill rolled his eyes. "He was just starting out then. To everyone else in the audience, his debut was utterly forgettable. But to little three-year-old Lucinda"—Bill shrugged—"it put the fire in you. You've been quote-unquote dying to get onstage ever since. Tonight's your night."

"I'm an actor?"

No. Her friend Callie was the actor, not her. During Luce's last semester at the Dover School, Callie had begged Luce to try out with her for *Our Town*. The two of them had rehearsed for weeks before the audition. Luce got one line, but Callie had brought the house down with her portrayal of Emily Webb. Luce had watched from the wings, proud of and awed by her friend. Callie would have sold off her life's possessions to stand in the old Globe Theatre for one minute, let alone to get up on the stage.

But then Luce remembered Callie's blood-drained face when she'd seen the angels battle the Outcasts. What had happened to Callie after Luce had left? Where were the Outcasts now? How would Luce ever explain to Callie, or her parents, what had happened—if, that is, Luce ever returned to her backyard and that life?

Because Luce knew now that she wouldn't go back to that life until she'd figured out how to stop it from ending. Until she'd unraveled this curse that forced her and Daniel to live out the same star-crossed lovers' tale again and again.

She must be here in this theater for a reason. Her soul had drawn her here; why?

She pushed through the crowd, moving along the

side of the amphitheater until she could see the stage. The wooden planks had been covered with a thick, hemplike matting made to look like rough grass. Two full-sized cannons stood like guards near either wing, and a row of potted orange trees lined the back wall. Not far from Luce, a rickety wooden ladder led to a curtained space: the tiring-room—she remembered from the acting class she'd taken with Callie—where the actors got into their costumes and prepared for their scenes.

"Wait!" Bill called as she hurried up the ladder.

Behind the curtain, the room was small and cramped and dimly lit. Luce passed stacks of manuscripts and open wardrobes full of costumes, ogling a massive lion's-head mask and rows of hanging gold and velvet cloaks. Then she froze: Several actors were standing around in various stages of undress—boys with half-buttoned gowns, men lacing up brown leather boots. Thankfully, the actors were busily powdering their faces and frantically rehearsing lines, so that the room was filled with short shouted-out fragments of the play.

Before any of the actors could look up and see her, Bill flew to Luce's side and pushed her into one of the wardrobes. Clothes closed around her.

"What are you doing?" she asked.

"Let me remind you that you're an *actor* in a time when there are no *actresses*." Bill frowned. "You don't belong back here as a woman. Not that that stopped you. Your past self took some pretty grand risks to get herself a role in *All Is True*."

"*All Is True?*" Luce repeated. She'd been hoping she would at least recognize the title. No such luck. She peeked out of the wardrobe into the room.

"You know it as *Henry the Eighth*," Bill said, yanking her back by the collar. "But pay attention: Would you like to venture a guess as to why your past self would lie and disguise herself to land a role—"

"Daniel."

He'd just come into the tiring-room. The door to the yard outside was still open behind him; the sun was at his back. Daniel walked alone, reading a handwritten script, hardly noticing the other players around him. He looked different than he had in any of her other lives. His blond hair was long and a bit wavy, gathered with a black band at the nape of his neck. He had a beard, neatly trimmed, just a bit darker in color than the hair on his head.

Luce felt an urge to touch it. To caress his face and run her fingers through his hair and trace the back of his neck and touch every part of him. His white shirt gaped open, showing the clean line of muscles on his chest. His black pants were baggy, gathered into knee-high black boots.

As he drew nearer, her heart began to pound. The

roar of the crowd in the pit fell away. The stink of dried sweat from the costumes in the wardrobe disappeared. There was just the sound of her breathing and his footsteps moving toward her. She stepped out of the wardrobe.

At the sight of her, Daniel's thunderstorm-gray eyes glowed violet. He smiled in surprise.

She couldn't hold it in any longer. She rushed toward him, forgetting Bill, forgetting the actors, forgetting the past self, who could be anywhere, steps away, the girl this Daniel really belonged to. She forgot everything but her need to be held by him.

He slid his arms easily around her waist, guiding her quickly to the other side of the bulky wardrobe, where they were hidden from the other actors. Her hands found the back of his neck. A warm rush rippled through her. She closed her eyes and felt his lips come down on hers, featherlight—almost *too* light. She waited to feel the hunger in his kiss. She waited. And waited.

Luce inched higher, arching her neck so that he would kiss her harder, more deeply. She needed his kiss to remind her why she was doing this, losing herself in the past and seeing herself dying again and again: because of him, because of the two of them together. Because of their love.

Touching him again reminded her of Versailles. She wanted to thank him for saving her from marrying the king. And to beg him never to hurt himself again as he'd done in Tibet. She wanted to ask what he'd dreamed about when he'd slept for days after she'd died in Prussia. She wanted to hear what he'd said to Luschka right before she died that awful night in Moscow. She wanted to pour out her love, and break down and cry, and let him know that every second of every lifetime she'd been through, she had missed him with all her heart.

But there was no way to communicate any of that to *this* Daniel. None of that had even happened yet to this Daniel. Besides, he took her for the Lucinda of this era, the girl who didn't know any of the things that Luce had come to know. There were no words to tell him.

Her kiss was the only way she could show him that she understood.

But Daniel wouldn't kiss her the way she wanted. The closer she pressed to him, the farther back he leaned.

Finally he pushed her away completely. He held on only to her hands, as if the rest of her were dangerous.

"Lady." He kissed the very tips of her fingers, making her shiver. "Would I be too bold to say your love makes you unmannerly?"

"Unmannerly?" Luce blushed.

Daniel took her back into his arms, slowly, a bit nervously. "Good Lucinda, you must not find yourself in this place dressed as you are." His eyes kept returning to her dress. "What clothes are these? Where is your costume?" He reached into a wardrobe and flicked through the clothes pegs.

Quickly, Daniel began to unlace his boots, tossing them on the floor with two thuds. Luce tried not to gape when he dropped his trousers. He wore short gray pantaloons underneath that left very little to the imagination.

Her cheeks burned as Daniel briskly unbuttoned his white shirt. He yanked it off, exposing the full beauty of his chest. Luce sucked in her breath. The only things missing were his unfurled wings. Daniel was so impeccably gorgeous—and he seemed to have no idea of the effect he was having on her by standing there in his underwear.

She gulped, fanning herself. "Is it hot in here?"

"Put these on until I can fetch your costume," he said, tossing the clothes at her. "Hurry, before someone sees you." He dashed to the wardrobe in the corner and rifled through it, pulling out a rich green-and-gold robe, another white shirt, and a pair of cropped green pants. He hurried into the new clothes—his costume, Luce guessed—as she picked up his discarded street clothes.

Luce remembered that it had taken the servant girl in Versailles a half hour to squeeze her into this dress. There were strings and ties and laces in all sorts of private places. There was no way she was going to be able to get out of it with any sort of dignity.

"There was, um, a costume change." Luce gripped the black fabric of her skirt. "I thought this would look nice for my character."

Luce heard footsteps behind her, but before she could turn, Daniel's hand pulled her deep into the wardrobe next to him. It was cramped and dark and wonderful to be so close. He pulled the door shut as far as it would go and stood before her, looking like a king with the green-and-gold robe wrapped around him.

He raised an eyebrow. "Where did you get this? Is our Anne Boleyn suddenly from Mars?" He chuckled. "I always thought she hailed from Wiltshire."

Luce's mind raced to catch up. She was playing Anne Boleyn? She'd never read this play, but Daniel's costume suggested he was playing the king, Henry VIII.

"Mr. Shakespeare—ah, Will—thought it would look good—"

"Oh, *Will* did?" Daniel smirked, not believing her at all but seeming not to care. It was strange to feel that she could do or say almost anything and Daniel would still find it charming. "You're a little bit mad, aren't you, Lucinda?"

"I—well—"

He brushed her cheek with the back of his finger. "I adore you."

"I adore you, too." The words tumbled from her mouth, feeling so real and so true after the last few stammering lies. It was like letting out a long-held breath.

"I've been thinking, thinking a lot, and I wanted to tell you that—that—"

"Yes?"

"The truth is that what I feel for you is . . . deeper than adoration." She pressed her hands over his heart. "I trust you. I trust your love. I know now how strong it is, and how beautiful." Luce knew that she couldn't come right out and say what she really meant—she was supposed to be a different version of herself, and the other times, when Daniel had figured out who she was, where she'd come from, he'd clammed up immediately and told her to leave. But maybe if she chose her words carefully, Daniel would understand. "It may seem like sometimes I—I forget what you mean to me and what I mean to you, but deep down . . . I know. I know because we are meant to be together. I love you, Daniel."

Daniel looked shocked. "You—you love me?"

"Of course." Luce almost laughed at how obvious it was—but then she remembered: She had no idea which moment from her past she'd walked into. Maybe in this lifetime they'd only exchanged coy glances.

Daniel's chest rose and fell violently and his lower lip began to quiver. "I want you to come away with me," he said quickly. There was a desperate edge to his voice.

Luce wanted to cry out *Yes!*, but something held her back. It was so easy to get lost in Daniel when his body was pressed so close to hers and she could feel the heat coming off his skin and the beating of his heart through his shirt. She felt she could tell him anything now—from how glorious it had felt to die in his arms in Versailles to how devastated she was now that she knew the scope of his suffering. But she held back: The girl he thought she was in this lifetime wouldn't talk about those things, wouldn't know about them. Neither would Daniel. So when she finally opened her mouth, her voice faltered.

Daniel put a finger over her lips. "Wait. Don't protest yet. Let me ask you properly. By and by, my love."

He peeked out the cracked wardrobe door, toward the curtain. A cheer came from the stage. The audience roared with laughter and applause. Luce hadn't even realized the play had begun.

"That's my entrance. I'll see you soon." He kissed her forehead, then dashed out and onto the stage.

Luce wanted to run after him, but two figures came and stood just beyond the wardrobe door.

The door squeaked open and Bill fluttered inside. "You're getting good at this," he said, flopping onto a sack of old wigs.

"Where have you been hiding?"

"Who, me? Nowhere. What would I have to hide from?" he asked. "That little costume-change sham was a wee stroke of genius," he said, raising his tiny hand for a high five.

It was always a bit of a buzz kill to be reminded that Bill was a fly on the wall during every interaction with Daniel.

"You're really going to leave me hanging like this?" Bill slowly withdrew his hand.

Luce ignored him. Something felt heavy and raw in her chest. She kept hearing the desperation in Daniel's voice when he'd asked her to run away with him. What had that meant?

"I'm dying tonight. Aren't I, Bill?"

"Well . . ." Bill cast his eyes down. "Yes."

Luce swallowed hard. "Where's Lucinda? I need to get inside her again so I can understand this lifetime." She pushed at the wardrobe door, but Bill took hold of the sash on her gown and pulled her back.

"Look kid, going three-D can't be your go-to move. Think of it as a special-occasion skill." He pursed his lips. "What is it you think you're going to learn here?"

"What she needs to escape *from,* of course," Luce said. "What is Daniel saving her from? Is she engaged to someone else? Living with a cruel uncle? Out of favor with the king?"

"Uh-oh." Bill scratched the top of his head. It made a grating sound, like nails on a chalkboard. "I must have made a pedagogical boo-boo somewhere. You think there's a reason for your death every time?"

"There's not?" She could feel her face fall.

"I mean, your deaths aren't *meaningless,* exactly. . . ."

"But when I died inside Lys, I felt everything—she believed that burning up freed her. She was happy because marrying that king would have meant her life was a lie. And Daniel could save her by killing her."

"Oh, honey, is that what you think? That your deaths are an out for bad marriages or something?"

She squeezed her eyes shut against the sting of sudden tears. "It has to be something like that. It has to be. Otherwise it's just pointless."

"It's *not* pointless," Bill said. "You *do* die for a reason. Just not so simple a reason. You can't expect to understand it all at once."

She grunted in frustration and banged her fist against the side of the wardrobe.

"I can see what you're all jacked up about," Bill said finally. "You went three-D and you think you unlocked the secret of your universe. But it's not always that neat and easy. Expect chaos. *Embrace* chaos. You should still try to learn as much as you can from every life you visit. Maybe in the end, it'll all add up to something. Maybe you'll end up with Daniel . . . or maybe you'll decide there's more to life than—"

A rustling startled them. Luce peeked around the wardrobe door.

A man, around fifty, with a salt-and-pepper goatee and a small potbelly, stood just behind an actor in a dress. They were whispering. When the girl turned her head a little, the stage lights lit up her profile. Luce froze at the sight: a delicate nose and small lips made up with pink powder. A dark brown wig with just a few strands of long black hair showing underneath. A gorgeous golden gown.

It was Lucinda, fully costumed as Anne Boleyn and about to go onstage.

Luce edged out of the wardrobe. She felt nervous and tongue-tied but also oddly empowered: If what Bill had told her was true, there wasn't a lot of time left.

"Bill?" she whispered. "I need you to do that thing where you press Pause so I can—"

"*Shhhh!*" Bill's hiss had a finality that said Luce was on her own. She would just have to wait until this man left so she could get Lucinda alone.

Unexpectedly, Lucinda moved toward the wardrobe where Luce was hiding. Lucinda reached inside. Her hand moved toward the golden cloak right next to Luce's shoulder. Luce held her breath, reached up, clasped her fingers with Lucinda's.

Lucinda gasped and threw the door wide, staring deep into Luce's eyes, teetering on the edge of some inexplicable understanding. The floor beneath them seemed to tilt. Luce grew dizzy, closing her eyes and feeling as if her soul had dropped out of her body. She saw herself from the outside: her strange dress that Bill had altered on the fly, the raw fear in her eyes. The hand in hers was soft, so soft she could barely feel it.

She blinked and Lucinda blinked and then Luce

didn't feel any hand at all. When she looked down, her hand was empty. She'd become the girl she'd been holding on to. Quickly, she grabbed the cloak and settled it over her shoulders.

The only other person in the tiring-room was the man who'd been whispering to Lucinda. Luce knew then that he was William Shakespeare. *William Shakespeare.* She *knew* him. They were, the three of them—Lucinda, Daniel, and Shakespeare—*friends.* There had been a summer afternoon when Daniel had taken Lucinda to visit Shakespeare at his home in Stratford. Toward sunset, they'd sat in the library, and while Daniel worked on his sketches at the window, Will had asked her question after question—all the while taking furious notes— about when she'd first met Daniel, how she felt about him, whether she thought she could one day fall in love.

Aside from Daniel, Shakespeare was the only one who knew the secret of Lucinda's identity—her gender—and the love the players shared offstage. In exchange for his discretion, Lucinda was keeping the secret that Shakespeare was present that night at the Globe. Everyone else in the company assumed that he was in Stratford, that he'd handed over the reins of the theater to Master Fletcher. Instead, Will appeared incognito to see the play's opening night.

When she returned to his side, Shakespeare gazed deep into Lucinda's eyes. "You've changed."

"I—no, I'm still"—she felt the soft brocade around her shoulders. "Yes, I found the cloak."

"The cloak, is it?" He smiled at her, winked. "It suits you."

Then Shakespeare put his hand on Lucinda's shoulder, the way he always did when he was giving directorial instructions: "Hear this: Everyone here already knows your story. They'll see you in this scene, and you won't say or do very much. But Anne Boleyn is a rising star in the court. Every one of them has a stake in your destiny." He swallowed. "As well: Don't forget to hit the mark at the end of your line. You need to be downstage left for the start of the dance."

Luce could feel her lines in the play run across her mind. The words would be there when she needed them, when she stepped onstage in front of all these people. She was ready.

The audience roared and applauded again. A rush of actors exited the stage and filled the space around her. Shakespeare had already slipped away. She could see Daniel on the opposite wing of the stage. He towered over the other actors, regal and impossibly gorgeous.

It was her cue to walk onstage. This was the start of the party scene at Lord Wolsey's estate, where the king—Daniel—would perform an elaborate masque before taking Anne Boleyn's hand for the first time. They were supposed to dance and fall heavily in love. It was supposed to be the very beginning of a romance that changed everything.

The beginning.

But for Daniel, it wasn't the beginning at all.

For Lucinda, however, and for the character she was playing—it was love at first sight. Laying eyes on Daniel had felt like the first real thing ever to happen to Lucinda, just as it had felt for Luce at Sword & Cross. Her whole world had suddenly meant something in a way it never had before.

Luce could not believe how many people were crowded into the Globe. They were practically on top of the actors, pressed so close to the stage in the pit that at least twenty spectators had their elbows propped up on the stage itself. She could smell them. She could hear them breathing.

And yet, somehow, Luce felt calm, even energized—as if instead of panicking under all this attention, Lucinda was coming to life.

It was a party scene. Luce was surrounded by Anne Boleyn's ladies-in-waiting; she almost laughed at how comical her "ladies" looked around her. These teen boys' Adam's apples bobbed obviously under the glare of the stage lanterns. Sweat formed rings under the arms of their padded dresses. Across the stage, Daniel and his court stood watching her unabashedly, his love plain on his face. She played her part effortlessly, sneaking just enough admiring glances at Daniel to pique both his and the audience's interest. She even improvised a move—pulling her hair away from her long, pale neck—that gave a foreboding hint of what everyone knew awaited the real Anne Boleyn.

Two players drew close, flanking Luce. They were the noblemen of the play, Lord Sands and Lord Wolsey.

"Ladies, you are not merry. Gentleman, whose fault is this?" Lord Wolsey's voice boomed. He was the host of the party—and the villain—and the actor playing him had incredible stage presence.

Then he turned and swept his gaze around to look at Luce. She froze.

Lord Wolsey was being played by Cam.

There was no space for Luce to shout, curse, or flee. She was a professional actor now, so she stayed collected, and turned to Wolsey's companion, Lord Sands, who delivered his lines with a laugh.

"The red wine first must rise in their fair cheeks, my lord," he said.

When it was Lucinda's turn to deliver her line, her body trembled, and she sneaked a peek at Daniel. His violet eyes smoothed over the roughness she felt. He believed in her.

"You are a merry gamester, my lord Sands," Luce felt herself say loudly, in a perfectly pitched teasing tone.

Then Daniel stepped forward and a trumpet sounded,

followed by a drum. The dance was beginning. He took her hand. When he spoke, he spoke to her, not to the audience, as the other players did.

"The fairest hand I ever touched," Daniel said. *"O Beauty, till now I never knew thee."* As if the lines had been written for the two of them.

They began to dance, and Daniel locked eyes with her the whole time. His eyes were crystal clear and violet, and the way they never strayed from hers chipped away at Luce's heart. She knew he'd loved her always, but until this moment, dancing with him on the stage in front of all these people, she had never really thought about what it meant.

It meant that when she saw him for the first time in every life, Daniel was already in love with her. Every time. And always had been. And every time, she had to fall in love with him from scratch. He could never pressure her or push her into loving him. He had to win her anew each time.

Daniel's love for her was one long, uninterrupted stream. It was the purest form of love there was, purer even than the love Luce returned. His love flowed without breaking, without stopping. Whereas Luce's love was wiped clean with every death, Daniel's grew over time, across all eternity. How powerfully strong must it be by now? Hundreds of lifetimes of love stacked one on top of the other? It was almost too massive for Luce to comprehend.

He loved her that much, and yet in every lifetime, over and over again, he had to wait for her to catch up.

All this time, they had been dancing with the rest of the troupe, bounding in and out of the wings at breaks in the music, coming back onstage for more gallantry, for longer sets with more ornate steps, until the whole company was dancing.

At the close of the scene, even though it wasn't in the script, even though Cam was standing right there watching, Luce held fast to Daniel's hand and pulled him to her, up against the potted orange trees. He looked at her like she was crazy and tried to tug her to the mark dictated by her stage directions. "What are you doing?" he murmured.

He had doubted her before, backstage when she'd tried to speak freely about her feelings. She *had* to make him believe her. Especially if Lucinda died tonight, understanding the depth of her love would mean everything to him. It would help him to carry on, to keep loving her for hundreds more years, through all the pain and hardship she'd witnessed, right up to the present.

Luce knew that it wasn't in the script, but she couldn't stop herself: She grabbed Daniel and she kissed him.

She expected him to stop her, but instead he swooped her into his arms and kissed her back. Hard and passionately, responding with such intensity that she felt the way she did when they were flying, though she knew her feet were planted on the ground.

For a moment, the audience was silent. Then they began to holler and jeer. Someone threw a shoe at Daniel, but he ignored it. His kisses told Luce that he believed her, that he understood the depth of her love, but she wanted to be absolutely sure.

"I will always love you, Daniel." Only, that didn't seem quite right—or not quite enough. She had to make him understand, and damn the consequences—if she changed history, so be it. "I'll always *choose* you." Yes, that was the word. "Every single lifetime, I'll choose you. Just as you have always chosen me. Forever."

His lips parted. Did he believe her? Did he already know? It *was* a choice, a long-standing, deep-seated choice that reached beyond anything else Luce was capable of. Something powerful was behind it. Something beautiful and—

Shadows began to swirl in the rigging overhead. Heat quaked through her body, making her convulse, desperate for the fiery release she knew was coming.

Daniel's eyes flashed with pain. "No," he whispered. "Please don't go yet."

Somehow, it always took both of them by surprise.

As her past self's body erupted into flames, there was a sound of cannon fire, but Luce couldn't be sure. Her eyes went blurry with brightness and she was cast far up and out of Lucinda's body, into the air, into darkness.

"No!" she cried as the walls of the Announcer closed around her. Too late.

"What's the problem now?" Bill asked.

"I wasn't ready. I *know* Lucinda had to die, but I—I was just—" She'd been on the brink of understanding something about the choice she'd made to love Daniel. And now everything about those last moments with Daniel had gone up in flames along with her past self.

"Well, there's not much more to see," Bill said. "Just the usual routine of a building catching fire—smoke, walls of flame, people screaming and stampeding toward the exits, trampling the less fortunate underfoot—you get the picture. The Globe burned to the ground."

"*What?*" she said, feeling sick. "I started the fire at the Globe?" Surely burning down the most famous theater in English history would have repercussions across time.

"Oh, don't get all self-important. It was going to happen anyway. If you hadn't burst into flames, the cannon onstage would have misfired and taken the whole place out."

"This is so much bigger than me and Daniel. All those people—"

"Look, Mother Teresa, no one died that night . . . besides you. No one else even got *hurt*. Remember that drunk leering at you from the third row? His pants catch on fire. That's the worst of it. Feel better?"

"Not really. Not at all."

"How about this: You're not here to add to your mountain of guilt. Or to change the past. There's a script, and you have your entrances and your exits."

"I wasn't ready for my exit."

"Why not? *Henry the Eighth* sucks, anyway."

"I wanted to give Daniel *hope.* I wanted him to know that I would always choose him, always love him. But Lucinda died before I could be sure he understood." She closed her eyes. "His half of our curse is so much worse than mine."

"That's good, Luce!"

"What do you mean? That's *horrible*!"

"I mean that little gem—that '*Wah, Daniel's agony is infinitely more horrible than mine*'—that's what you learned here. The more you understand, the closer you'll get to knowing the root of the curse, and the more likely it is that you'll eventually find your way out of it. Right?"

"I—I don't know."

"I *do*. Now come on, you've got bigger roles to play."

Daniel's side of the curse was worse. Luce could see that now very clearly. But what did it mean? She didn't feel any closer to being able to break it. The answer eluded her. But she knew Bill was right about one thing: She could do nothing more in this lifetime. All she could do was keep going back.

FOURTEEN

THE STEEP SLOPE

CENTRAL GREENLAND · WINTER, 1100

The sky was black when Daniel stepped through. Behind him, the portal billowed in the wind like a tattered curtain, snagging and tearing itself apart before falling to pieces on the night-blue snow.

A chill crept over his body. At first sight, there seemed to be nothing here at all. Nothing but arctic nights that seemed to go on forever, offering only the thinnest glimpse of day at the end.

He remembered now: These fjords were the place

where he and his fellow fallen angels held their meet-ings: all bleak dimness and harsh cold, a two days' trek north of the mortal settlement of Brattahlíõ. But he would not find her here. This land had never been a part of Lucinda's past, so there would be nothing in her An-nouncers to bring her here now.

Just Daniel. And the others.

He shivered and marched across the snow-swept fjord toward a warm glow on the horizon. Seven of them were gathered around the bright-orange fire. From a distance, the circle of their wings looked like a giant halo on the snow. Daniel didn't have to count their shin-ing outlines to know they were all there.

None of them noticed him crossing the snow toward their assembly. They always kept a single starshot on hand just in case, but the idea of an uninvited visitor happening upon their council was so implausible it was not even a real threat. Besides, they were too busy bick-ering among themselves to detect the Anachronism crouching behind a frozen boulder, eavesdropping.

"This was a waste of time." Gabbe's voice was the first one Daniel could make out. "We're not going to get anywhere."

Gabbe's patience could be a short-fused thing. At the start of the war, her rebellion had lasted a split second compared to Daniel's. Ever since then, her commitment to her side had run deep. She was back in the Graces of

Heaven, and Daniel's hesitation went against everything she believed in. As she paced the perimeter of the fire, the tips of her huge feathered white wings dragged in the snow behind her.

"You're the one who called this meeting," a low voice reminded her. "Now you want to adjourn?" Roland was seated on a short black log a few feet in front of where Daniel crouched behind a boulder. Roland's hair was long and unkempt. His dark profile and his marbled gold-black wings glittered like embers in the dusk of a fire.

It was all just as Daniel remembered.

"The meeting I called was for *them*." Gabbe stopped pacing and tossed her wing to point at the two angels sitting next to each other across the fire from Roland.

Arriane's slender iridescent wings were still for once, rising high above her shoulder blades. Their shimmer looked almost phosphorescent in the colorless night, but everything else about Arriane, from her short black bob to her pale, drawn lips, looked harrowingly somber and sedate.

The angel beside Arriane was quieter than usual, too. Annabelle stared blankly into the far reaches of the night. Her wings were dark silver, almost pewter-colored. They were broad and muscular, stretching around her and Arriane in a wide, protective arc. It had been a long time since Daniel had seen her.

Gabbe came to a stop behind Arriane and Annabelle and stood facing the other side: Roland, Molly, and Cam, who were sharing a coarse fur blanket. It was draped over their wings. Unlike the angels on the other side of the fire, the demons were shivering.

"We didn't expect your side tonight," Gabbe told them, "nor are we happy to see you."

"We have a stake in this, too," Molly said roughly.

"Not in the same way we do," Arriane said. "Daniel will never join you."

If Daniel hadn't recalled where he'd sat at this meeting over a thousand years before, he might have overlooked his earlier self entirely. That earlier self was sitting alone, in the center of the group, directly on the other side of the boulder. Behind the rock, Daniel shifted to get a better view.

His earlier self's wings bloomed out behind him, great white sails as still as the night. As the others talked about him as if he weren't there, Daniel behaved as if he were alone in the world. He tossed fistfuls of snow into the fire, watching the frozen clumps hiss and dissolve into steam.

"Oh, really?" Molly said. "Care to explain why he's inching closer to our side every lifetime? That little cursing-God bit he does whenever Luce explodes? I doubt it goes over so well upstairs."

"He's in *agony*!" Annabelle shouted at Molly. "You

wouldn't understand because you don't know how to love." She scooted nearer to Daniel, the tips of her wings dragging in the snow, and addressed him directly. "Those are just temporary blips. We all know your soul is pure. If you wanted to at last choose a side, to choose *us,* Daniel—if at any moment—"

"*No.*"

The clean finality of the word pushed Annabelle away as quickly as if Daniel had drawn a weapon. Daniel's earlier self would not look at any of them. And behind the boulder, watching them, Daniel remembered what had happened during this council, and shuddered at the forbidden horror of the memory.

"If you won't join *them,*" Roland said to Daniel, "why not join *us*? From what I can tell, there is no worse Hell than what you put yourself through every time you lose her."

"Oh, cheap shot, Roland!" Arriane said. "You don't even mean that. You can't believe—" She wrung her hands. "You're only saying that to provoke me."

Behind Arriane, Gabbe rested a hand on her shoulder. Their wing tips touched, flashing a bright burst of silver between them. "What Arriane means is that Hell is never a better alternative. No matter how terrible Daniel's pain may be. There is only one place for Daniel. There is only one place for all of us. You see how penitent the Outcasts are."

"Spare us the preaching, will ya?" Molly said. "There's a choir up there that might be interested in your brainwashing, but I'm not, and I don't think Daniel is, either."

The angels and demons all turned to stare at him together, as if they were still part of the host. Seven pairs of wings casting a glowing aura of silver-gold light. Seven souls he knew as well as his own.

Even behind his boulder, Daniel felt suffocated. He remembered this moment: They demanded so much of him. When he was so weakened by his broken heart. He felt the assault of Gabbe's plea for him to join with Heaven all over again. Roland's, too, to join with Hell. Daniel felt again the shape of the one word he had spoken at the meeting, like a strange ghost in his mouth: *No.*

Slowly, with a sick feeling creeping over him, Daniel remembered one more thing: That *no*? He hadn't meant it. In that moment, Daniel had been on the verge of saying *yes.*

This was the night he'd almost given up.

Now his shoulders burned. The sudden urge to let his wings out almost brought him to his knees. His insides roiled with shame-filled horror. It was rising in him, the temptation he'd fought so long to repress.

In the circle around the fire, Daniel's past self looked at Cam. "You're unusually quiet tonight."

Cam didn't answer right away. "What would you have me say?"

"You faced this problem once. You *know*—"

"And what would you have me say?"

Daniel sucked in his breath. "Something charming and persuasive."

Annabelle snorted. "Or something underhanded and absolutely evil."

Everyone waited. Daniel wanted to burst forth from behind the rock, to rip his past self away from here. But he couldn't. His Announcer had brought him here for a reason. He had to go through the whole thing again.

"You're trapped," Cam said at last. "You think because there was once a beginning, and because you're somewhere in the middle now, that there is going to be an end. But our world isn't rooted in teleology. It's chaos."

"*Our* world is not the same as yours—" Gabbe started to say.

"There's no way out of this cycle, Daniel," Cam went on. "She can't break it, and neither can you. Pick Heaven, pick Hell, I don't really care and you don't, either. It won't make any difference—"

"Enough." Gabbe's voice was breaking. "It *will* make a difference. If Daniel comes home to the place he belongs, then Lucinda . . . then Lucinda—"

But she couldn't go on. The words were blasphemy

to speak, and Gabbe wouldn't do it. She fell to her knees in the snow.

Behind the rock, Daniel watched his earlier self extend a hand to Gabbe and raise her from the ground. He watched it play out before his eyes now, just as he remembered:

He gazed into her soul and saw how brightly it burned. He glanced back and saw the others—Cam and Roland, Arriane and Annabelle, even Molly—and he thought about how long he'd dragged the whole lot of them through his epic tragedy.

And for what?

Lucinda. And the choice the two of them had made long ago—and over and over again: to put their love above everything else.

That night on the fjords, her soul was between incarnations, newly purged from her last body. What if he stopped seeking her out? Daniel was tired to his core. He didn't know if he had it in him anymore.

Watching his earlier struggle, sensing the imminent arrival of absolute breakdown, Daniel recalled what he had to do. It was dangerous. Forbidden. But it was absolutely necessary. Now, at least, he understood why his future self had taken him that long-ago night—to lend him strength, to keep him pure. He had weakened at this key moment in his past. And future Daniel could not let that weakness be magnified across the span of history, could not let it corrupt his and Lucinda's chances.

So he repeated what had happened to him nine hundred years before. He would make amends tonight by joining with—no, *overriding* his past.

Cleaving.

It was the only way.

He rolled back his shoulders, unleashed his trembling wings into the darkness. He could feel them catch the wind at his back. An aurora of light painted the sky a hundred feet above him. It was bright enough to blind a mortal, bright enough to catch the attention of seven squabbling angels.

Commotion from the other side of the boulder. Shouting and gasps and the beat of wings coming closer.

Daniel propelled himself off the ground, flying fast and hard so that he soared over the boulder just as Cam came around behind it. They missed each other by a wingspan, but Daniel kept moving, swooped down upon his past self as fast as his love for Luce could take him.

His past self drew back and held out his hands, warding Daniel off.

All the angels knew the risks of cleaving. Once joined, it was nearly impossible to free oneself from one's past self, to separate two lives that had been cloven together. But Daniel knew he'd been cloven in the past and had survived. So he had to do it.

He was doing it to help Luce.

He pressed his wings together and dove down at his past self, striking so hard he should have been crushed—

if he hadn't been absorbed. He shuddered, and his past self shuddered, and Daniel clamped his eyes shut and gritted his teeth to withstand the strange, sharp sickness that flooded his body. He felt as if he were tumbling down a hill: reckless and unstoppable. No way back up until he hit the bottom.

Then all at once, everything came to a stop.

Daniel opened his eyes and could hear only his breathing. He felt tired but alert. The others were staring at him. He couldn't be sure whether they had any idea what had just happened. They all looked afraid to come near him, even to speak to him.

He spread his wings and spun in a full circle, tilting his head toward the sky. "I choose my love for Lucinda," he called to Heaven and Earth, to the angels all around him and the ones who weren't there. To the soul of the one true thing he loved the most, wherever she was. "I now reaffirm my choice: I choose Lucinda over *everything*. And I will until the end. "

FIFTEEN

THE SACRIFICE

The Announcer spat Luce into the swelter of a summer day. Beneath her feet, the ground was parched, all cracked earth and tawny, dried-up blades of grass. The sky was barren blue, not a single cloud to promise rain. Even the wind seemed thirsty.

She stood in the center of a flat field bordered on three sides by a strange, high wall. From this distance, it looked a little like a mosaic made of giant beads. They were irregularly shaped, not spherical exactly, ranging in color from ivory to light brown. Here and there were tiny cracks between the beads, letting in light from the other side.

Besides a half dozen vultures cawing as they swooped in listless circles, no one else was around. The wind blew hotly through her hair and smelled like . . . she couldn't place the smell, but it tasted metallic, almost rusty.

The heavy gown she had been wearing since the ball at Versailles was soaked with sweat. It stank of smoke and ash and perspiration every time she breathed in. It had to go. She struggled to reach the laces and buttons. She could use a hand—even a tiny stone one.

Where *was* Bill, anyway? He was always disappearing. Sometimes Luce got the feeling the gargoyle had an agenda of his own, and that she was being shuffled forward according to *his* schedule.

She wrestled with the dress, tearing at the green lace around the collar, popping hooks as she walked. Thankfully, there was no one around to see. Finally she got down on her knees and shimmied free, pulling the skirts over her head.

As she sat back on her heels in her thin cotton shift, it hit Luce how exhausted she was. How long had it been since she'd slept? She stumbled toward the shade of the wall, her feet rustling through the brittle grass, thinking maybe she could lie down for a little while and close her eyes.

Her eyelids fluttered, so sleepy.

Then they shot open. And her skin began to crawl.

Heads.

Luce finally realized what the wall was made of. The bone-colored palisades—halfway innocent-looking from afar—were interlocking racks of impaled human *heads.*

She stifled a scream. Suddenly she could place the odor being carried in the wind—it was the stench of rot and spilled blood, of putrefying flesh.

Along the bottom of the palisades were sun-bleached, weathered skulls, whipped white and clean by the wind and the sun. Along the top, the skulls looked fresher. That is, they were still clearly people's *heads*—thick manes of black hair, skin mostly intact. But the skulls in the middle were someplace between mortal and monster: The frayed skin was peeling back, leaving dried brown blood on bone. The faces were stretched tight with what might have been terror or rage.

Luce staggered away, hoping for a breath of air that didn't stink of rot, but not finding it.

"It's not quite as gruesome as it looks."

She whirled around, terrified. But it was only Bill.

"Where were you? Where *are* we?"

"It's actually a great honor to get staked out like this," he said, marching right up to the next-to-lowest row. He looked one head in the eye. "All these innocent little lambs go straight to Heaven. Just what the faithful desire."

"Why did you leave me here with these—"

"Aw, come on. They won't bite." He eyed her side-long. "What have you done with your clothes?"

Luce shrugged. "It's hot."

He sighed lengthily, with a put-upon world-weariness. "*Now* ask me where I've been. And this time, try to keep the judgment out of your voice."

Her mouth twitched. There was something sketchy about Bill's occasional disappearances. But he was standing there now, with his little claws tucked neatly behind his back, giving her an innocent smile. She sighed. "Where have you been?"

"Shopping!" Bill gleefully extended both his wings, revealing a light-brown wraparound skirt hanging off one wing tip and a short matching tunic hanging off the other. "And the *coup de grâce*!" he said, withdrawing from behind his back a chunky white necklace. Bone.

She took the tunic and the skirt but waved off the necklace. She'd seen enough bone. "No, thanks."

"Do you want to blend in? Then you've got to wear the goods."

Swallowing her disgust, she slipped it over her head. The polished bone pieces had been strung along some kind of fiber. The necklace was long and heavy and, Luce had to admit, sort of pretty.

"And I think this"—he gave her a painted metal band—"goes in your hair."

"Where did you get all this stuff?" she asked.

"It's yours. I mean, it's not *yours*-Lucinda-Price, but it is *yours* in a larger cosmic sense. It belongs to the you that is part of this lifetime—Ix Cuat."

"Ix *who*?"

"Ix Cuat. Your name in this life meant 'Little Snake.' " Bill watched her face change. "It was a term of endearment in the Mayan culture. Sort of."

"The same way getting your head impaled on a stick was an honor?"

Bill rolled his stone eyes. "Stop being so ethnocentric. That means thinking your own culture is superior to other cultures."

"I know what it means," she said, working the band into her dirty hair. "But I'm not being superior. I just don't think having my head stuck on one of these racks would be so great." There was a faint thrumming in the air, like faraway drumbeats.

"That's exactly the sort of thing Ix Cuat would say! You always *were* a little bit backward!"

"What do you mean?"

"See, you—Ix Cuat—were born during the Wayeb', which are these five odd days at the end of the Mayan year that everyone gets real superstitious about because they don't fit into the calendar. Kind of like leap-year days. It's not exactly lucky to be born during Wayeb'. So no one was shocked when you grew up to be an old maid."

"Old maid?" Luce asked. "I thought I never live past seventeen . . . more or less."

"Seventeen here in Chichén Itzá is *ancient*," Bill said, floating from head to head, his wings humming as they fluttered. "But it's true, you never *used* to live much past seventeen or thereabouts. It's been kind of a mystery as to why in the lifetime of Lucinda Price you've managed to stick around so long."

"Daniel said it was because I wasn't baptized." Now Luce was sure she heard drums—and that they were drawing closer. "But how can that matter? I mean, I bet Ix Ca-whatever was baptized—"

Bill flapped his hand dismissively. "*Baptism* is just one word for a kind of sacrament or covenant, in which your soul is more or less claimed. Just about every faith has something similar. Christianity, Judaism, Islam, even the Mayan religion that is about to go marching past"— he nodded toward the drumming, which was now so loud that Luce wondered if they should hide—"they all feature sacraments of some kind in which one expresses one's devotion to one's god."

"So I'm alive in my current life in Thunderbolt because my parents didn't have me baptized?"

"No," Bill said, "you're able to be *killed* in your current life in Thunderbolt because your parents didn't have you baptized. You're *alive* in your current life because, well . . . no one really knows why."

There *must* have been a reason. Maybe it was the loophole Daniel had spoken about in the hospital in Milan. But even he didn't seem to understand how Luce was able to travel through the Announcers. With every life she visited, Luce could feel herself getting closer to fitting the pieces of her past together . . . but she wasn't there yet.

"Where's the village?" she asked. "Where are the people? Where's *Daniel*?" The drums grew so loud that she had to raise her voice.

"Oh," Bill said, "they're on the other side of the *tzompantlis*."

"The *what*?"

"This wall of heads. Come on—you've got to see this!"

Through the open spaces in the racks of skulls, flashes of color danced. Bill herded Luce to the edge of the skull wall and gestured for her to look.

Beyond the wall, a whole civilization paraded past. A long line of people danced and beat their feet against a broad packed-dirt road that wound through the boneyard. They had silky black hair and skin the color of chestnuts. They ranged in age from three to old enough to defy guessing. All of them were vibrant and beautiful and strange. Their clothes were sparse, weathered animal hides that barely covered their flesh, showing off tattoos and painted faces. It was the most remarkable body art—elaborate, colorful depictions of brightly feathered birds, suns, and geometric designs splayed across their backs and arms and chests.

In the distance, there were buildings—an orderly grid of bleached-stone structures and a cluster of smaller buildings with flat thatched roofs. Beyond that, there was jungle, but the leaves of its trees looked withered and brittle.

The crowd marched past, blind to Luce, caught up in the frenzy of their dance. "Come on!" Bill said, and shoved her out into the flow of people.

"What?" she shouted. "Go *in there*? With them?"

"It'll be fun!" Bill cackled, flying ahead. "You know how to dance, don't you?"

Cautiously at first, she and the little gargoyle joined the parade as they passed through what looked like a marketplace—a long, narrow strip of land packed with wooden casks and bowls full of goods for sale: dimply black avocados, deep red stalks of maize, dried herbs bundled with twine, and many other things Luce didn't recognize. She turned her head this way and that to see as much as possible as she passed, but there was no way to stop. The surge of the crowd pushed her inexorably forward.

The Mayans followed the road as it curved down onto a wide, shallow plain. The roar of their dance faded, and they gathered quietly, murmuring to one another. They numbered in the hundreds. At the repeated pressure of Bill's sharp claws on her shoulders, Luce lowered herself to her knees like the rest of them and followed the crowd's gaze upward.

Behind the marketplace, one building rose higher than all the others: a stepped pyramid of the whitest stone. The two sides visible to Luce each had steep staircases running up their centers that ended at a single-story structure painted blue and red. A shiver ran through Luce, part recognition and part inexplicable fear.

She'd seen this pyramid before. In history-book pictures, the Mayan temple had fallen to ruins. But it was far from ruins now. It was magnificent.

Four men holding drums made of wood and stretched hide stood in a row on the ledge around the pyramid's top. Their tanned faces were painted with strokes of red, yellow, and blue to look like masks. Their drums beat in unison, faster and faster until someone emerged from the doorway.

The man was taller than the drummers; beneath a towering red-and-white-feathered headdress, his entire face was painted with mazelike turquoise designs. His neck, wrists, ankles, and earlobes were adorned with the same kind of bone jewelry Bill had given Luce to wear. He was carrying something—a long stick decorated with painted feathers and shiny shards of white. At one end, something silver gleamed.

When he faced the people, the crowd fell silent, almost as if by magic.

"Who is that man?" Luce whispered to Bill. "What's he doing?"

"That's the tribal leader, Zotz. Pretty haggard, right? Times are tough when your people haven't seen rain for three hundred and sixty-four days. Not that they're counting on that stone calendar over there or anything." He pointed at a gray slab of rock marked with hundreds of sooty black lines.

Not one drop of water for almost an entire year? Luce could almost feel the thirst coming off the crowd. "They're dying," she said.

"They hope not. That's where you come in," Bill said. "You and a few other unfortunate wretches. Daniel, too—he's got a minor role. Chaat's *very* hungry by now, so it's really all hands on deck."

"Chaat?"

"The rain god. The Mayans have this absurd belief that a wrathful god's favorite food is blood. See where I'm going with this?"

"Human sacrifice," Luce said slowly.

"Yep. This is the beginning of a long day of 'em. More skulls to add to the racks. Exciting, isn't it?"

"Where's Lucinda? I mean, Ix Cuat?"

Bill pointed at the temple. "She's locked up in there, along with the other sacrificees, waiting for the ball game to be over."

"The ball game?"

"That's what this crowd is on their way to watch. See, the tribal leader likes to host a ball game before a big sacrifice." Bill coughed and brushed his wings back. "It's kind of a cross between basketball and soccer, if each team had only two players, and the ball weighed a ton, and the losers got their heads cut off and their blood fed to Chaat."

"To the court!" Zotz bellowed from the top step of the temple. The Mayan words sounded strangely guttural and yet were still comprehensible to Luce. She wondered how they made Ix Cuat feel, locked up in the room behind Zotz.

A great cheer erupted from the crowd. As a group, the Mayans rose and broke into a run toward what looked like a large stone amphitheater at the far side of the plain. It was oblong and low—a brown dirt playing field ringed by tiered stone bleachers.

"Ah—there's our boy!" Bill pointed at the head of the crowd as they neared the stadium.

A lean, muscular boy was running, faster than the others, his back to Luce. His hair was dark brown and shiny, his shoulders deeply tanned and painted with intersecting red-and-black bands. When he turned his head slightly to the left, Luce caught a quick glimpse of his profile. He was nothing like the Daniel she had left in her parents' backyard. And yet—

"Daniel!" Luce said. "He looks—"

"Different and also precisely the same?" Bill asked.

"Yes."

"That's his soul you recognize. Regardless of how you two may look on the outside, you'll always know each other's souls."

It hadn't occurred to Luce until now how remarkable it was that she recognized Daniel in every life. Her *soul* found his. "That's . . . beautiful."

Bill scratched at a scab on his arm with a gnarly claw. "If you say so."

"You said Daniel was involved in the sacrifice somehow. He's a ballplayer, isn't he?" Luce said, craning her neck toward the crowd just as Daniel disappeared inside the amphitheater.

"He is," Bill said. "There's a lovely little ceremony"—he raised a stone eyebrow—"in which the winners guide the sacrifices into their next life."

"The winners kill the prisoners?" Luce said quietly.

They watched the crowd as it funneled into the amphitheater. Drumbeats sounded from within. The game was about to begin.

"Not *kill*. They're not common murderers. *Sacrifice*. First they chop off the heads. Heads go back there." Bill nodded over his shoulder at the palisade of heads. "Bodies get tossed into a skuzzy—pardon me, *holy*—limestone sinkhole out in the jungle." He sniffed. "Me? I don't see how that's gonna bring rain, but who am I to judge?"

"Will Daniel win or lose?" Luce asked, knowing the answer before the words had even left her lips.

"I can see how the idea of Daniel decapitating you does not maybe scream out romance," Bill said, "but really, what's the difference between his killing you by fire and by the sword?"

"Daniel wouldn't do that."

Bill hovered in the air in front of Luce. "Wouldn't he?"

There came a great roar from inside the amphitheater. Luce felt that she should run onto the field, go up to Daniel, and take him in her arms; tell him what she'd left the Globe too soon to say: that she understood now everything he went through to be with her. That his sacrifices made her even more committed to their love. "I should go to him," she said.

But there was also Ix Cuat. Locked up in a room atop the pyramid waiting to be killed. A girl who might hold within her a valuable piece of information Luce needed to learn to break the curse.

Luce teetered in place—one foot toward the amphitheater, one toward the pyramid.

"What's it gonna be?" Bill taunted. His smile was too big.

She took off running, away from Bill and toward the pyramid.

"Good choice!" he called, flitting quickly around to keep pace at her side.

The pyramid towered over her. The painted temple at the top—where Bill had said Ix Cuat would be—felt as distant as a star. Luce was so thirsty. Her throat ached for water; the ground scorched the soles of her feet. It felt like the entire world was burning up.

"This place is very sacred," Bill murmured in her ear. "This temple was built on top of a previous temple, which was built on top of yet another temple, and so on, all of them oriented to mark the vernal and autumnal equinoxes. On those two days at sunset, the shadow of a serpent can be seen sliding up the steps of the northern stairs. Cool, huh?"

Luce just huffed and began climbing the stairs.

"The Mayans were geniuses. By this point in their civilization, they've already predicted the end of the world in 2012." He coughed theatrically. "But that remains to be seen. Time will tell."

As Luce neared the top, Bill swooped in close again.

"Now, listen," he said. "This time, if and when you go three-D—"

"Shhh," Luce said.

"No one can hear me but you!"

"Exactly. *Shhh!*" She took another step up the pyramid, quietly now, and stood on the ledge at the top. She pressed her body against the hot stone of the temple wall, inches away from the open doorway. Someone inside was singing.

"I'd do it now," Bill said, "while the guards are at the ball court."

Luce edged to the doorway and peered in.

The sunlight streaming through the open door lit up a large throne in the center of the temple. It was shaped like a jaguar and painted red, with spots of inlaid jade. To the left was a large statue of a figure reclining on its side with a hand over its stomach. Small burning lamps made of stone and filled with oil surrounded the statue and cast a flickering light. The only other things in the room were three girls bound together at the wrists by rope, huddled in the corner.

Luce gasped, and all three girls' heads shot up. They were all pretty, with dark hair in braids, and jade piercings through their ears. The one on the left had the darkest skin. The one on the right had deep-blue swirling lines painted up and down her arms. And the one in the middle . . . was Luce.

Ix Cuat was small and delicate. Her feet were dirty, and her lips were chapped. Of the three terrified girls, her dark eyes were the wildest.

"What are you waiting for?" Bill called out from his seat on the statue's head.

"Won't they see me?" Luce whispered through a clenched jaw. The other times she'd cleaved with her past selves, they'd either been alone or Bill had helped to shield her. What would it look like to these other girls if Luce went inside Ix Cuat's body?

"These girls have been half mad since they got selected to be sacrificed. If they cry out about any freaky business, guess how many people are going to care?" Bill made a show of counting on his fingers. "Right. *Zero.* No one's even going to hear them."

"Who are you?" one of the girls asked, her voice splintered with fear.

Luce couldn't answer. As she stepped forward, Ix Cuat's eyes ignited with what looked like terror. But then, to Luce's great shock, just as she reached down, her past self reached up with her bound hands and grabbed fast and hard to Luce's. Ix Cuat's hands were warm, and soft, and trembling.

She started to say something. Ix Cuat had started to say—

Fly me away.

Luce heard it in her mind as the ground beneath them shuddered and everything began to flicker. She saw Ix Cuat, the girl who'd been born unlucky, whose eyes told Luce she knew nothing about the Announcers, but who had seized hold of Luce as if Luce held her deliverance. And she saw herself, from outside herself, looking tired and hungry and ragged and rough. And older somehow. And stronger.

Then the world settled again.

Bill was gone from the statue's head, but Luce couldn't move to search for him. Her bound wrists were raw, and marked with black sacrificial tattoos. Her ankles, she realized, had been bound, too. Not that the bindings mattered much—fear bound her soul more tightly than any rope ever could. This wasn't like the other times Luce had gone inside her past. Ix Cuat knew exactly what was coming to her. Death. And she did not seem to welcome it as Lys had in Versailles.

On either side of Ix Cuat, her cocaptives had edged away from her, but they could move only a few inches. The girl on the left, with the dark skin—Hanhau—was crying; the other, with the painted blue body—Ghanan—was praying. They were all afraid to die.

"You are possessed!" Hanhau sobbed through her tears. "You will contaminate the offering!"

Ghanan was at a loss for words.

Luce ignored the girls and felt around Ix Cuat's own crippling fear. Something was running through her mind: a prayer. But not a prayer of sacrificial preparation. No, Ix Cuat was praying for Daniel.

Luce knew that the thought of him made Ix Cuat's skin flush and her heart beat faster. Ix Cuat had loved him her whole life—but only from afar. He'd grown up a few buildings away from her family's home. Sometimes he traded avocados to her mother at the market. Ix Cuat had been trying for years to get up the courage to talk to him. The knowledge that he was at the ball court now tormented her. Ix Cuat was praying, Luce realized, that he would lose. Her one prayer was that she did not want to die at his hand.

"Bill?" Luce whispered.

The little gargoyle swooped back inside the temple. "Game's over! The mob's heading over to the cenote now. That's the limestone pool where the sacrificing takes place. Zotz and the winning players are on their way up here to walk you gals over to the ceremony."

As the din of the mob faded, Luce trembled. There were footsteps on the stairs. Any moment now, Daniel would walk through that door.

Three shadows darkened the doorway. Zotz, the leader with the red-and-white-feathered headdress, stepped inside the temple. None of the girls moved; they were all staring in horror at the long decorative spear he held. A human head was spiked atop it. The eyes were open, crossed with strain; the neck was still dripping blood.

Luce looked away and her eyes fell on another, very muscular man entering the tomb. He was carrying another painted spear with another head impaled on its top. At least this one's eyes were closed. There was the faintest smile across the fat, dead lips.

"The losers," Bill said, zipping close to each of the heads to examine them. "Now aren't you glad Daniel's team won? Mostly thanks to this guy." He clapped the muscular man on the shoulder, though Daniel's teammate didn't seem to feel a thing. Then Bill was out the door again.

When Daniel walked into the temple at last, his head was hanging. His hands were empty and his chest was bare. His hair and skin were dark, and his posture was stiffer than Luce was used to. Everything from the way the muscles of his abdomen met the muscles of his chest to the way he held his hands lifelessly at his sides was different. He was still gorgeous, still the most gorgeous thing Luce had ever seen, though he looked nothing like the boy whom Luce had gotten used to.

But then he glanced up, and his eyes glowed exactly the same shade of violet that they always did.

"Oh," she said softly, thrashing against her bindings, desperate to escape the story they were stuck in during this lifetime—the skulls and the drought and the sacrifice—and hold on to him for all eternity.

Daniel shook his head slightly. His eyes pulsed at her, glowing. His gaze soothed her. Like he was telling her not to worry.

Zotz motioned with his free hand for the three girls to stand, then gave a swift nod, and everyone filed out through the northern door of the temple. Hanhau first, with Zotz at her side, Luce right behind her, and Ghanan bringing up the rear. The rope between them was just long enough for each girl to hold both wrists together at her side. Daniel came up and walked beside her, and the other victor walked beside Ghanan.

For the briefest instant, Daniel's fingertips grazed her bound wrists. Ix Cuat tingled at the touch.

Just outside the temple door, the four drummers were waiting on the ledge. They fell in line behind the processional and, as the party descended the pyramid's steep steps, played the same hectic beats Luce had heard when she'd first arrived in this life. Luce focused on walking, feeling as if she were riding a tide instead of choosing to put one foot in front of the other, down the pyramid, and then, at the base of the steps, along the wide, dusty path that led to her death.

The drums were all she could hear, until Daniel leaned in and whispered, "I'm going to save you."

Something deep inside Ix Cuat soared. This was the first time he had ever spoken to her in this life.

"How?" she whispered back, leaning toward him, aching for him to free her and fly her far, far away.

"Don't worry." His fingertips found hers again, brushing them softly. "I promise, I'll take care of you."

Tears stung her eyes. The ground was still searing the soles of her feet, and she was still marching to the place where Ix Cuat was supposed to die, but for the first time since arriving in this life, Luce was not afraid.

The path led through a line of trees and into the jungle. The drummers paused. Chanting filled her ears, the chants of the crowd deeper in the jungle, at the cenote. A song that Ix Cuat had grown up singing, a prayer for rain. The other two girls sang along softly, their voices quaking.

Luce thought of the words Ix Cuat had seemed to say as Luce entered her body: *Fly me away,* she'd shouted inside her head. *Fly me away.*

All at once, they stopped walking.

Deep in the dried-out, thirsty jungle, the path before them opened up. A huge water-filled crater in the limestone spanned a hundred feet in front of Luce. Around it were the bright, eager eyes of the Mayan people. Hundreds. They'd stopped chanting. The moment they'd been waiting for was here.

The cenote was a limestone pit, mossy and deep and filled with bright-green water. Ix Cuat had been there before—she'd seen twelve other human sacrifices just like this one. Below that still water were the decomposing remains of a hundred other bodies, a hundred souls who were supposed to have gone straight to Heaven—only, at that moment, Luce knew that Ix Cuat wasn't sure she believed in any of it.

Ix Cuat's family stood near the rim of the cenote. Her mother, her father, her two younger sisters, both holding babies in their arms. They believed—in the ritual, in the sacrifice that would take their daughter away and break their hearts. They loved her, but they thought she was unlucky. They thought this was the best way for her to redeem herself.

A gap-toothed man with long gold earrings guided Ix Cuat and the other two girls to stand before Zotz, who had taken a prominent place near the edge of the limestone pool. He gazed down into the deep water. Then he closed his eyes and began a new chant. The community and the drummers joined in.

Now the gap-toothed man stood between Luce and Ghanan and brought down his ax on the rope tying them together. Luce felt a jerk forward and the rope was severed. Her wrists were still bound, but she was now connected only to Hanhau on her right. Ghanan was on her own, marched forward directly in front of Zotz.

The girl rocked back and forth, chanting under her breath. Sweat trickled down the back of her neck.

When Zotz began to say words of prayer to the rain god, Daniel leaned toward Luce. "Don't look."

So Luce fastened her gaze on Daniel, and he on her. All around the cenote, the crowd drew in their breaths. Daniel's teammate grunted and brought the ax down heavily on the girl's neck. Luce heard the blade slice cleanly though, then the soft thump of Ghanan's head landing in the dirt.

The roar of the crowd rose up again: shouts of thanks to Ghanan, prayers for her soul in Heaven, vigorous wishes for rain.

How could people really think that killing an innocent girl would solve their problems? This was where Bill would usually pop in. But Luce didn't see him anywhere. He had a way of disappearing when Daniel came around.

Luce didn't want to see what had become of Ghanan's head. Then she heard a deep, reverberating splash and knew that the girl's body had reached its final resting place.

The gap-toothed man approached. This time he severed Ix Cuat's bond to Hanhau. Luce trembled as he marched her before the tribal leader. The rocks were sharp beneath her feet. She peered over the limestone rim into the cenote. She thought she might be sick, but then Daniel appeared at her side and she felt better. He nodded for her to look at Zotz.

The tribal leader beamed at her, showing two topazes set into his front teeth. He intoned a prayer that Chaat would accept her and bring the community many months of nourishing rainfall.

No, Luce thought. It was all wrong. *Fly me away!* she cried out to Daniel in her head. He turned toward her, almost as if he'd heard.

The gap-toothed man cleaned Ghanan's blood off the ax with a scrap of animal hide. With great pomp he handed the blade to Daniel, who turned to stand face to face with Luce. Daniel looked weary, as if dragged down by the weight of the ax. His lips were pursed and white, and his violet gaze never left hers.

The crowd was silent, holding their breaths. Hot wind rustled in the trees as the ax gleamed in the sun. Luce could feel that the end was coming, but why? Why had her soul dragged her here? What insight about her past, or the curse, could she possibly gain from having her head cut off?

Then Daniel dropped the ax to the ground.

"What are you doing?" Luce asked.

Daniel didn't answer. He rolled back his shoulders, turned his face toward the sky, and flung out his arms. Zotz stepped forward to interfere, but when he touched Daniel's shoulder, he screamed and recoiled as if he'd been burned.

And then—

Daniel's white wings unfurled from his shoulders. As they extended fully from his sides, huge and shockingly bright against the parched brown landscape, they sent twenty Mayans hurtling backward.

Shouts rang out around the cenote:

"What is he?"

"The boy is winged!"

"He is a god! Sent to us by Chaat!"

Luce thrashed against the ropes binding her wrists and her ankles. She needed to run to Daniel. She tried to move toward him, until—

Until she couldn't move anymore.

Daniel's wings were so bright they were almost unbearable. Only, now it wasn't just Daniel's wings that were glowing. It was . . . *all* of him. His entire body shone. As if he'd swallowed the sun.

Music filled the air. No, not music, but a single harmonious chord. Deafening and unending, glorious and frightening.

Luce had heard it before . . . somewhere. In the cemetery at Sword & Cross, the last night she'd been there, the night Daniel had fought Cam, and Luce hadn't been allowed to watch. The night Miss Sophia had dragged her away and Penn had died and nothing had ever been the same. It had begun with that very same chord, and it was coming out of Daniel. He was lit up so brightly, his body actually hummed.

She swayed where she stood, unable to take her eyes away. An intense wave of heat stroked her skin.

Behind Luce, someone cried out. The cry was followed by another, and then another, and then a whole chorus of voices crying out.

Something was burning. It was acrid and choking and turned her stomach instantly. Then, in the corner of her vision, there was an explosion of flame, right where Zotz had been standing a moment before. The boom knocked her backward, and she turned away from the burning brightness of Daniel, coughing on the black ash and bitter smoke.

Hanhau was gone, the ground where she'd stood

scorched black. The gap-toothed man was hiding his face, trying hard not to look at Daniel's radiance. But it was irresistible. Luce watched as the man peeked between his fingers and burst into a pillar of flame.

All around the cenote, the Mayans stared at Daniel. And one by one, his brilliance set them ablaze. Soon a bright ring of fire lit up the jungle, lit up everyone but Luce.

"Ix Cuat!" Daniel reached for her.

His glow made Luce scream out in pain, but even as she felt as if she were on the verge of asphyxiation, the words tumbled from her mouth. "You're *glorious.*"

"Don't look at me," he pleaded. "When a mortal sees an angel's true essence, then—you can see what happened to the others. I can't let you leave me again so soon. Always so soon—"

"I'm still here," Luce insisted.

"You're still—" He was crying. "Can you see me? The true me?"

"I can see you."

And for just a fraction of a second, she could. Her vision cleared. His glow was still radiant but not so blinding. She could see his *soul.* It was white-hot and immaculate, and it looked—there was no other way to say it—like *Daniel.* And it felt like coming home. A rush of unparalleled joy spread through Luce. Somewhere in the back of her mind, a bell of recognition chimed. She'd seen him like this before.

Hadn't she?

As her mind strained to draw upon the past she couldn't quite touch, the light of him began to overwhelm her.

"No!" she cried, feeling the fire sear her heart and her body shake free of something.

※

"Well?" Bill's scratchy voice grated on her eardrums.

She lay against a cold stone slab. Back in one of the Announcer caves, trapped in a frigid in-between place where it was hard to hold on to anything outside. Desperately, she tried to picture what Daniel had looked like out there—the glory of his undisguised soul—but she couldn't. It was already slipping away from her. Had it really even happened?

Luce closed her eyes, trying to remember exactly what he'd looked like. There were no words for it. It was just an incredible, joyous connection.

"I saw him."

"Who, Daniel? Yeah, I saw him, too. He was the guy who dropped the ax when it was his turn to do the chopping. Big mistake. Huge."

"No, I *really* saw him. As he truly is." Her voice shook. "He was so beautiful."

"Oh, *that*." Bill tossed his head, annoyed.

"I *recognized* him. I think I've seen him before."

"Doubt it." Bill coughed. "That was the first and *last*

time you'll be able to see him like that. You saw him, and then you died. That's what happens when mortal flesh looks upon an angel's unbridled glory. Instant death. Burned away by the angel's beauty."

"No, it wasn't like that."

"You saw what happened to everyone else. *Poof.* Gone." Bill plopped down beside her and patted her knee. "Why do you think the Mayans started doing sacrifices by fire after that? A neighboring tribe discovered the charred remains and had to explain it somehow."

"Yes, they burst into flames right away. But I lasted longer—"

"A couple of extra seconds? When you were turned away? Congratulations."

"You're wrong. And I know I've seen that before."

"You've seen his *wings* before, maybe. But Daniel shedding his human guise and showing you his true form as an angel? Kills you every time."

"No." Luce shook her head. "You're saying he can never show me who he really is?"

Bill shrugged. "Not without vaporizing you and everyone around you. Why do you think Daniel's so cautious about kissing you all the time? His glory shines pretty damn bright when you two get hot and heavy."

Luce felt like she could barely hold herself up. "That's why I sometimes die when we kiss?"

"How 'bout a round of applause for the girl, folks?" Bill said snarkily.

"But what about all those other times, when I die *before* we kiss, before—"

"Before you even have a chance to see how toxic your relationship might become?"

"Shut up."

"Honestly, how many times do you have to see the same story line before you realize *nothing* is ever going to change?"

"Something *has* changed," Luce said. "That's why I'm on this journey, that's why I'm still alive. If I could just see him again—all of him—I know I could handle it."

"You don't get it." Bill's voice was rising. "You're talking about this whole thing in very mortal terms." As he grew more agitated, spit flew from his lips. "This is the big time, and you clearly *cannot* handle it."

"Why are you so angry all of a sudden?"

"*Because!* Because." He paced the ledge, gnashing his teeth. "Listen to me: Daniel slipped up this once, he showed himself, but he never does that again. Never. He learned his lesson. Now you've learned one, too: Mortal flesh *cannot* gaze upon an angel's true form without dying."

Luce turned away from him, growing angrier herself. Maybe Daniel changed after this lifetime in Chichén

Itzá, maybe he'd become more cautious in the future. But what about the past?

She approached the limit of the ledge inside the Announcer, looking up into the vast, gaping blackness that tunneled above into her dark unknown.

Bill hovered over her, circling her head as if he were trying to get inside it. "I know what you're thinking, and you're only going to end up disappointed." He drew close to her ear and whispered. "Or worse."

There was nothing he could say to stop her. If there was an earlier Daniel who still dropped his guard, then Luce was going to find him.

SIXTEEN

⁜

BEST MAN

Daniel was not entirely himself.

He was still cloven to the body he had joined with on the dark fjords of Greenland. He tried to slow down as he left the Announcer, but his momentum was too great. Heavily off-balance, he spun out of the darkness and rolled across rocky earth until his head slammed into something hard. Then he was still.

Cleaving with his past self had been a vast mistake.

The simplest way to split apart two entwined incarnations of a soul was to kill the body. Freed from the cage of the flesh, the soul sorted itself out. But killing himself wasn't really an option for Daniel. Unless . . .

The starshot.

In Greenland, he had snatched it from where it lay nestled in the snow at the edge of the angels' fire. Gabbe had brought it along as symbolic protection, but she would never have expected Daniel to cleave and steal it.

Had he really thought he could just drag the dull silver tip across his chest and split apart his soul, casting his past self back into time?

Stupid.

No. He was too likely to slip up, to fail, and then instead of splitting his soul, he might accidentally kill it. Soulless, Daniel's earthly guise, this dull body, would wander the earth in perpetuity, searching for its soul but settling for the next best thing: Luce. It would haunt her until the day she died, and maybe after that.

What Daniel needed was a partner. What he needed was impossible.

He grunted and rolled over onto his back, squinting into the bright sun directly overhead.

"See?" a voice above him said. "I told you we were in the right place."

"I don't see why *this*"—another voice, a boy's this time—"is proof of us doing anything right."

"Oh, come on, Miles. Don't let your beef with

Daniel keep us from finding Luce. He obviously knows where she is."

The voices drew closer. Daniel opened his eyes in a squint and saw an arm slice the light of the sun, extending toward him.

"Hey there. Need a hand?"

Shelby. Luce's Nephilim friend from Shoreline.

And Miles. The one she'd kissed.

"What are you two doing here?" Daniel sat up sharply, rejecting Shelby's offered hand. He rubbed his forehead and glanced behind him—the thing he'd collided with was the gray trunk of an olive tree.

"What do you *think* we're doing here? We're looking for Luce." Shelby gaped down at Daniel and wrinkled her nose. "What's *wrong* with you?"

"Nothing." Daniel tried to stand up, but he was so dizzy he quickly lay down again. Cleaving—especially dragging his past body into another life—had made him sick. He fought his past from inside, slamming up against the edges, bruising his soul on bones and skin. He knew the Nephilim could sense that something unmentionable had happened to him. "Go home, trespassers. Whose Announcer did you use to get here? Do you know how much trouble you could get yourselves in?"

All of a sudden, something silver gleamed under his nose.

"Take us to Luce." Miles was pointing a starshot at

Daniel's neck. The brim of his baseball cap hid his eyes, but his mouth was screwed in a nervous grimace.

Daniel was dumbstruck. "You—you have a starshot."

"Miles!" Shelby whispered fiercely. *"What are you doing with that thing?"*

The dull tip of the arrow quaked. Miles was clearly nervous. "You left it in the yard after the Outcasts left," he said to Daniel. "Cam grabbed one, and in the chaos, no one noticed when I picked up this one. You took off after Luce. And we took off after you." He turned to Shelby. "I thought we might need it. Self-defense."

"Don't you dare kill him," Shelby said to Miles. "You're an idiot."

"No," Daniel said, very slowly sitting up. "It's okay."

His mind was spinning. What were the odds? He had only seen this done once before. Daniel was no expert at cleaving. But his past writhed inside him—he couldn't go on like this. There was only one solution. Miles was holding it in his hands.

But how could he get the boy to attack him without explaining everything? And could he trust the Nephilim?

Daniel edged backward until his shoulders were against the tree trunk. He slid up it, holding both empty hands wide, showing Miles there was nothing to be afraid of. "You took fencing?"

"What?" Miles looked bewildered.

"At Shoreline. Did you take a fencing class or not?"

"We all did. It was kind of pointless and I wasn't all that good, but—"

That was all Daniel needed to hear. *"En garde!"* he shouted, drawing out his concealed starshot like a sword.

Miles's eyes grew wide. In an instant he'd raised his arrow as well.

"Oh, crap," Shelby said, scurrying out of the way. "You guys, seriously. Stop!"

The starshots were shorter than fencing foils but a few inches longer than normal arrows. They were featherlight but as hard as diamonds, and if Daniel and Miles were very, very careful, the two of them might make it out of this alive. Somehow, with Miles's help, Daniel might cleave free of his past.

He sliced through the air with his starshot, advancing a few steps toward the Nephilim.

Miles responded, fighting off Daniel's blow, his arrow glancing hard toward the right. When the starshots clashed, they did not make the tinny clanks that fencing foils made. They made a deep, echoing *whooomp* that reverberated off the mountains and shook the ground under their feet.

"Your fencing lesson wasn't pointless," Daniel said as his arrow crisscrossed with Miles's in the air. "It was to prepare for a moment like this."

"A moment"—Miles grunted as he lunged forward,

sweeping his starshot up until it slid against Daniel's in the air—"like what?"

Their arms strained. The starshots made a frozen X in the air.

"I need you to release me from an earlier incarnation that I've cloven to my soul," Daniel said simply.

"What the . . . ," Shelby murmured from the sidelines.

Confusion flashed across Miles's face, and his arm faltered. His blade fell away, and his starshot clattered to the ground. He gasped and fumbled for it, looking back at Daniel, terrified.

"I'm not coming after you," Daniel said. "I need you to come after me." He managed a competitive smirk. "Come on. You know you want to. You've wanted to for a long time."

Miles charged, holding the starshot like an arrow instead of a sword. Daniel was ready for him, dipping to one side just in time and spinning around to clash his starshot against Miles's.

They were locked in each other's grip: Daniel with his starshot pointing past Miles's shoulder, using his strength to hold the Nephilim boy back, and Miles with his starshot inches away from Daniel's heart.

"Are you going to help me?" Daniel demanded.

"What's in it for us?" Miles asked.

Daniel had to think about this for a moment. "Luce's happiness," he said at last.

Miles didn't say yes. But he didn't say no.

"Now"—Daniel's voice faltered as he gave the instructions—"very carefully, drag your blade in a straight line down the center of my chest. Do not pierce the skin or you will kill me."

Miles was sweating. His face was white. He glanced over at Shelby.

"Do it, Miles," she whispered.

The starshot trembled. Everything was in this boy's hands. The blunt end of the starshot touched Daniel's skin and traveled down.

"Omigod." Shelby's lips curled up in horror. "He's *molting*."

Daniel could feel it, like a layer of skin was lifting off his bones. His past self's body was slowly cleaving from his own. The venom of separation coursed through him, threading deep into the fibers of his wings. The pain was so raw it was nauseating, roiling deep inside him with great tidal swells. His vision clouded; ringing filled his ears. The starshot in his hand tumbled to the ground. Then, all at once, he felt a great shove and a sharp, cold breath of air. There was a long grunt and two thuds, and then—

His vision cleared. The ringing ceased. He felt lightness, simplicity.

Free.

Miles lay on the ground below him, chest heaving.

The starshot in Daniel's hand had disappeared. Daniel spun around to find a specter of his past self standing behind him, his skin gray and his body wraithlike, his eyes and teeth coal-black, the starshot grasped in his hand. His profile wobbled in the hot wind, like the picture on a shorted-out television.

"I'm sorry," Daniel said, reaching forward and clutching his past self at the base of his wings. When Daniel lifted the shadow of himself off the ground, his body felt scant and insufficient. His fingers found the graying portal of the Announcer through which both Daniels had traveled just before it fell apart. "Your day will come," he said.

Then he pitched his past self back into the Announcer.

He watched the void fading in the hot sun. The body made a drawn-out whistling sound as it tumbled into time, as if it were falling off a cliff. The Announcer split into infinitesimal traces, and was gone.

"What the hell just happened?" Shelby asked, helping Miles to his feet.

The Nephilim was ghostly white, gaping down at his hands, flipping them over and examining them as if he'd never seen them before.

Daniel turned to Miles. "Thank you."

The Nephilim boy's blue eyes looked eager and terrified at the same time, as if he wanted to pump every detail out of Daniel about what had just happened but didn't want to show his excitement. Shelby was speech-less, which was an unprecedented event.

Daniel had despised Miles until then. He'd been an-noyed by Shelby, who'd practically led the Outcasts straight toward Luce. But at that moment, under the olive tree, he could see why Luce had befriended both of them. And he was glad.

A horn whined in the distance. Miles and Shelby jumped.

It was a shofar, a sacred ram's horn that made a long, nasal note—often used to announce religious services and festivals. Until then Daniel hadn't looked around enough to realize where they were.

The three of them stood under the mottled shade of the olive tree at the crest of a low hill. In front of them, the hill sloped down to a wide, flat valley, tawny with the tall native grasses that had never been cut by man. In the middle of the valley was a narrow strip of green, where wildflowers grew alongside a narrow river.

Just east of the riverbed, a small group of tents stood clustered together, facing a larger square structure made of white stones, with a latticed wooden roof. The blast of the shofar must have come from that temple.

A line of women in colorful cloaks that fell to their ankles moved in and out of the temple. They carried clay jugs and bronze trays of food, as if in preparation for a feast.

"Oh," Daniel said aloud, feeling a profound melancholy settle over him.

"Oh what?" Shelby asked.

Daniel gripped the hood of Shelby's camouflage sweatshirt. "If you're looking for Luce here, you won't find her. She's dead. She died a month ago."

Miles nearly choked.

"You mean the Luce from this lifetime," Shelby said. "Not our Luce. Right?"

"Our Luce—my Luce—isn't here, either. She never knew this place existed, so her Announcers wouldn't bring her here. Yours wouldn't have, either."

Shelby and Miles shared a glance. "You say you're looking for Luce," Shelby said, "but if you know she isn't here, why are you still hanging around?"

Daniel stared past them, at the valley below. "Unfinished business."

"*Who* is that?" Miles asked, pointing at a woman in a long white dress. She was tall and willowy, with red hair that shimmered in the sunlight. Her dress was cut low, showing off a lot of golden skin. She was singing something soft and lovely, a tease of a song they could barely hear.

"That's Lilith," Daniel said slowly. "She's supposed to be married today."

Miles took a few steps along a path leading down from the olive tree toward the valley where the temple stood, about a hundred feet below them, as if to get a better look.

"Miles, wait!" Shelby scrambled after him. "This isn't like when we were in Vegas. This is some freaking . . . other time or whatever. You can't just see a hot girl and go strolling in like you own the place." She turned to look at Daniel for help.

"Stay low," Daniel instructed them. "Keep under the grass line. And stop when I say stop."

Carefully, they wound down the path, stopping at last near the bank of the river, downstream from the temple. All the tents in the small community had been strewn with garlands of marigolds and cassis flowers. They were in earshot of the voices of Lilith and the girls who were helping prepare her for the wedding. The girls laughed and joined in Lilith's song as they braided her long red hair into a wreath around her head.

Shelby turned to Miles. "Doesn't she look kind of like Lilith from our class at Shoreline?"

"No," Miles said instantly. He studied the bride for a moment. "Okay, maybe a little bit. Weird."

"Luce probably never mentioned her," Shelby explained to Daniel. "She's a total bitch from Hell."

"It makes sense," Daniel said. "Your Lilith might come from the same long line of evil women. They're all descendants of the original mother Lilith. She was Adam's first wife."

"Adam had more than one wife?" Shelby gaped. "What about Eve?"

"Before Eve."

"*Pre-Eve?* No way."

Daniel nodded. "They weren't married very long when Lilith left him. It broke his heart. He waited for her a long time, but eventually, he met Eve. And Lilith never forgave Adam for getting over her. She spent the rest of her days wandering the earth and cursing the family Adam had with Eve. And her descendants—sometimes they start out all right, but eventually, well, the apple never really falls far from the tree."

"That's messed up," Miles said, despite seeming hypnotized by Lilith's beauty.

"You're telling me that Lilith Clout, the girl who set my hair on fire in ninth grade, could be *literally* a bitch from Hell? That all my voodoo toward her might have been justified?"

"I guess so." Daniel shrugged.

"I've never felt so vindicated." Shelby laughed. "Why wasn't this in any of our angelology books at Shoreline?"

"Shhh." Miles pointed toward the temple. Lilith had left her maidens to complete the decorations for the wedding—strewing yellow and white poppies near the entrance to the temple, weaving ribbons and small chimes made of silver into the low branches of the oak trees—and walked away from them, west, toward the river, toward where Daniel, Shelby, and Miles were hiding.

She carried a bouquet of white lilies. When she reached the riverbank, she plucked a few petals and scattered them over the water, still singing softly under her breath. Then she turned to walk north along the bank, toward a huge old carob tree with branches that drooped into the river.

A boy sat beneath it, staring into the current. His long legs were propped up close to his chest, with one arm draped over them. The other arm was skipping stones into the water. His green eyes sparkled against his tan skin. His jet-black hair was a little shaggy, and damp from a recent swim.

"Oh my god, that's—" Shelby's cry was cut off by Daniel's hand clamping over her mouth.

This was the moment he'd been afraid of. "Yes, it's Cam, but it's not the Cam you know. This is an earlier Cam. We are thousands of years in the past."

Miles narrowed his eyes. "But he's still evil."

"No," Daniel said. "He's not."

"Huh?" Shelby asked.

"There was a time when we were all part of one family. Cam was my brother. He was not evil, not yet. Maybe not even now."

Physically, the only difference between this Cam and the one Shelby and Miles knew was that his neck was bare of the sunburst tattoo he'd gotten from Satan when he'd thrown in his lot with Hell. Otherwise, Cam looked exactly as he did now.

Except that this long-ago Cam's face was stiff with worry. It was an expression Daniel hadn't seen on Cam in millennia. Probably not since this very moment.

Lilith stopped behind Cam and wrapped her arms around his neck so that her hands rested just over his heart. Without turning or saying a word, Cam reached up and cupped her hands in his. Both of them closed their eyes, content.

"This seems really private," Shelby said. "Should we be— I mean, I feel weird."

"Then leave," Daniel said slowly. "Don't make a scene on your way out—"

Daniel broke off. Someone was walking toward Cam and Lilith.

The young man was tall and tanned, dressed in a long white robe, and carrying a thick scroll of parchment. His blond head was down, but it was obviously Daniel.

"I'm not leaving." Miles's eyes locked on Daniel's past self.

"Wait, I thought we just sent that guy back into the Announcers," Shelby said, confused.

"That was a later early version of myself," Daniel said.

"*A later early version of myself,* he says!" Shelby snorted. "Exactly how many Daniels *are* there?"

"He came from two thousand years in the future

beyond the moment where we are right now, which is still one thousand years in the true past. That Daniel shouldn't have been here."

"We're three thousand years in the past right now?" Miles asked.

"Yes, and you really shouldn't be." Daniel stared Miles down. "But that past version of me"—he pointed at the boy who had stopped next to Cam and Lilith—"belongs here."

Across the river, Lilith smiled. "How are you, Dani?"

They watched as Dani knelt down next to the couple and unrolled the scroll of parchment. Daniel remembered: It was their marriage license. He'd inscribed the whole thing himself in Aramaic. He was supposed to perform the ceremony. Cam had asked him months before.

Lilith and Cam read over the document. They were good together, Daniel remembered. She wrote songs for him and spent hours picking wildflowers, weaving them into his clothes. He gave all of himself to her. He listened to her dreams and made her laugh when she was sad. Both of them had their volatile sides, and when they argued, the whole tribe heard about it—but neither one of them was yet the dark thing they would become after they split up.

"This part right here," Lilith said, pointing to a line in the text. "It says we will be married by the river. But you know I want to be married in the temple, Cam."

Cam and Daniel shared a look. Cam reached for Lilith's hand. "My love. I've already told you I cannot."

Something hot rose in Lilith's voice. "You refuse to marry me under the eyes of God? In the only place where my family will approve of our union! Why?"

"Whoa," Shelby whispered on the other side of the stream. "I see what's happening. Cam can't get married in the temple . . . he can't even set foot in the temple, because—"

Miles began to whisper, too: "If a fallen angel enters the sanctuary of God—"

"The whole thing bursts into flames," Shelby finished.

The Nephilim were right, of course, but Daniel was surprised by his own frustration. Cam loved Lilith, and Lilith loved Cam. They had a chance to make their love work, and as far as Daniel was concerned, to Hell with everything else. Why was Lilith so insistent on being married in the temple? Why couldn't Cam give her a good explanation for his refusal?

"I won't set foot in there." Cam pointed at the temple.

Lilith was close to tears. "Then you don't love me."

"I love you more than I ever thought possible, but it doesn't change a thing."

Lilith's thin body seemed to swell with rage. Could she sense that there was more to Cam's refusal than merely some wish to deny her? Daniel didn't think so. She clenched her fists and let out a long, shrill scream.

It seemed to shake the earth. Lilith grabbed Cam's wrists and pinned him against the tree. He didn't even struggle.

"My grandmother never liked you." Her arms trembled as she held him down. "She always said the most terrible things, and I always defended you. Now I see it. In your eyes and your soul." Her eyes bored into him. "Say it."

"Say what?" Cam asked, horrified.

"You're a bad man. You're a— I know what you are."

It was clear that Lilith didn't know. She was grasping at the rumors that flew around the community—that he was evil, a wizard, a member of the occult. All she wanted was to hear the truth from Cam.

Daniel knew that Cam *could* tell Lilith, but he wouldn't. He was afraid to.

"I am none of the bad things anyone says I am, Lilith," Cam said.

It was the truth and Daniel knew it, but it sounded so much like a lie. Cam was on the brink of the worst decision he would ever make. This was it: the moment that broke Cam's heart so that it rotted into something black.

"Lilith," Dani pleaded with her, pulling her hands away from Cam's throat. "He is not—"

"Dani," Cam warned. "Nothing you can say will fix this."

"That's right. It's broken." Lilith let go, and Cam fell backward into the dirt. She picked up their marriage contract and flung it into the river. It spun slowly in the current and sank. "I hope I live a thousand years and have a thousand daughters so there will always be a woman who can curse your name." She spat in his face, then turned and ran back to the temple, her white dress flowing behind her like a sail.

Cam's face turned as white as Lilith's wedding robe. He reached for Dani's hand to help himself up. "Do you have a starshot, Dani?"

"No." Dani's voice shook. "Don't talk like that. You'll get her back, or else—"

"I was naïve to think I could have gotten away with loving a mortal woman."

"If you'd only told her," Dani said.

"*Told her?* What happened to me—to all of us? The Fall and everything since?" Cam leaned closer to Dani. "Maybe she's right about me. You heard her: The whole village thinks I am a demon. Even if they won't use the word."

"They know nothing."

Cam turned away. "All this time I've been trying to deny it, but love is impossible, Dani."

"It is not."

"*It is.* For souls like ours. You'll see. You may hold out longer than I could, but you'll see. Both of us will eventually have to choose."

"*No.*"

"So quick to protest, brother." Cam squeezed Dani's shoulder. "It makes me wonder about you. Don't you ever think about it . . . crossing over?"

Dani shrugged away. "I think about her and only her. I count the seconds until she'll be with me again. I choose her, as she chooses me."

"How lonely."

"It's not lonely," Dani barked. "It's love. The love you want for yourself, too—"

"I meant: *I'm* lonely. And far less noble than you are. Any day. I fear a change is coming on."

"No." Now Dani moved toward Cam. "You wouldn't."

Cam reared away and spat. "Not all of us are lucky enough to be bound to our lover by a curse."

Daniel remembered this empty insult: It had made him furious. But still, he shouldn't have said what came next:

"Go, then. You won't be missed."

He regretted it instantly, but it was too late.

Cam rolled back his shoulders and threw out his arms. When his wings bloomed at his sides, they sent a burst of hot wind rippling across the grass where Daniel,

Shelby, and Miles were hiding. The three of them peered up. His wings were massive and glowing and—

"Wait a minute," Shelby whispered. "They're not gold!"

Miles blinked. "How can they not be gold?"

Of course the Nephilim would be confused. The division of wing color was as clear as night and day: gold for demons, silver or white for everyone else. And the Cam they knew was a demon. Daniel was in no mood to explain to Shelby why Cam's wings were pure, bright white, as radiant as diamonds, glistening like sun-kissed snow.

This long-ago Cam had not crossed over yet. He was merely on the brink.

That day Lilith lost Cam as a lover, and Daniel lost him as a brother. From this day on, they would be enemies. Could Daniel have stopped him? What if he hadn't spun away from Cam and unfurled his own wings like a shield—the way he watched Dani do now?

He should have. He burned to burst forth from the bushes and stop Cam now. How much could be different!

Cam's and Dani's wings did not yet have the tortured magnetic pull toward each other. All that repelled them in this moment was a stubborn difference of opinion, a philosophical sibling rivalry.

Both angels rose from the ground at the same time,

each facing a different direction. So when Dani soared east across the sky and Cam soared west, the three Anachronisms hiding in the grass were the only ones to see the gleam of gold bite into Cam's wings. Like a sparkling lightning bolt.

SEVENTEEN

❧ ✝ ❧

WRITTEN IN BONE

YIN, CHINA · QING MING
(APPROXIMATELY APRIL 4, 1046 BCE)

At the far end of the Announcer's tunnel was an engulfing brightness. It kissed her skin like a summer morning at her parents' house in Georgia.

Luce plunged toward it.

Unbridled glory. That was what Bill had called the burning light of Daniel's true soul. Merely looking upon Daniel's pure angelic self had made an entire community of people at the Mayan sacrifice spontaneously combust—including Ix Cuat, Luce's past self.

But there *had* been a moment.

A moment of pure wonder just before she died, when Luce had felt closer to Daniel than she ever had before. She didn't care what Bill said: She *recognized* the glow of Daniel's soul. She *had* to see it again. Maybe there was some way she could live through it. She had to at least try.

She burst out of the Announcer into the cold emptiness of a colossal bedroom.

The chamber was at least ten times bigger than any room Luce had ever seen, and everything about it was lavish. The floors were crafted of smoothest marble and covered by enormous rugs made of whole animal skins, one of which had an intact tiger's head. Four timber pillars held up a finely thatched gabled ceiling. The walls were made of woven bamboo. Near the open window was an enormous canopy bed with sheets of green-gold silk.

A tiny telescope rested on the window's ledge. Luce picked it up, parting the gold silk curtain to peer outside. The telescope was heavy and cold when she held it up to her eye.

She was in the center of a great walled city, looking down from a second story. A maze of stone roadways connected crammed, ancient-looking wattle-and-daub structures. The air was warm and smelled softly of cherry blossoms. A pair of orioles crossed the blue sky.

Luce turned to Bill. "Where are we?" This place

seemed as foreign as the world of the Mayans, and just as far back in time.

He shrugged and opened his mouth to speak, but then—

"Shhh," Luce whispered.

Sniffling.

Someone was crying soft, hushed tears. Luce turned toward the noise. There, through an archway on the far side of the room, she heard the sound again.

Luce moved toward the archway, sliding along the stone floor in her bare feet. The sobbing echoed, beckoning her. A narrow walkway opened up into another cavernous chamber. This one was windowless, with low ceilings, dimly lit by the glow of a dozen small bronze lamps.

She could make out a large stone basin, and a small lacquered table stocked with black pottery vials of aromatic oils that gave the whole room a warm and spicy smell. A gigantic carved jade wardrobe stood in the corner of the room. Thin green dragons etched into its face sneered at Luce, as if they knew everything she didn't.

And in the center of the chamber, a dead man lay sprawled on the floor.

Before Luce could see anything more, she was blinded by a bright light moving toward her. It was the same glow she'd sensed from the other side of the Announcer.

"What is that light?" she asked Bill.

"That . . . er, you see that?" Bill sounded surprised. "That's your soul. Yet another way for you to recognize your past lives when they appear physically different from you." He paused. "You've never noticed it before?"

"This is the first time, I think."

"Huh," Bill said. "That's a good sign. You're making progress."

Luce felt heavy and exhausted all of a sudden. "I thought it was going to be Daniel."

Bill cleared his throat like he was going to say something, but he didn't. The glow burned brightly for another heartbeat, then snapped out so suddenly she couldn't see for a moment, until her eyes adjusted.

"What are you doing here?" a voice asked roughly.

Where the light had been, in the center of the room, was a thin, pretty Chinese girl about seventeen—too young and too elegant to be standing over a dead man's body.

Dark hair hung to her waist, contrasting with her floor-length white silk robe. Dainty as she was, she seemed the kind of girl who didn't shy away from a fight.

"So, that's you," Bill's voice said in Luce's ear. "Your name is Lu Xin and you lived outside the capital city of Yin. We're at the close of the Shang dynasty, something like a thousand BCE, in case you want to make a note for your scrapbook."

Luce probably seemed crazy to Lu Xin, barging in

here wearing a singed animal hide and a necklace made out of bone, her hair a wild and tangled snarl. How long had it been since she'd looked in a mirror? Had a bath? Plus, she was talking to an invisible gargoyle.

But then again, Lu Xin was standing vigil over a dead guy, giving Luce don't-mess-with-me eyes, so she seemed a little crazy herself.

Oh boy. Luce hadn't noticed the jade knife with the turquoise-studded handle, or the small pond of blood in the middle of the marble floor.

"What do I—" she started to ask Bill.

"You." Lu Xin's voice was surprisingly strong. "Help me hide his body."

The dead man's hair was white around his temples; he looked about sixty years old, lean and muscular underneath many elaborate robes and embroidered cloaks.

"I—um, I don't really think—"

"As soon as they learn the king is dead, you and I will be dead, too."

"What?" Luce asked. "Me?"

"You, me, most of the people inside these walls. Where else will they find the thousand sacrificial bodies that must be buried with the despot?" The girl wiped her cheeks dry with slender, jade-ringed fingers. "Will you help me or not?"

At the girl's request, Luce moved to help pick up the king's feet. Lu Xin readied herself to lift him under his arms. "The king," Luce said, spouting out the old Shang words as if she'd spoken them forever. "Was he—"

"It is not as it appears." Lu Xin grunted under the weight of the body. The king was heavier than he looked. "I did not kill him. At least not"—she paused—"physically. He was dead when I walked into the room." She sniffed. "He stabbed himself in the heart. I used to say he did not have one, but he has proven me wrong."

Luce looked at the man's face. One of his eyes was open. His mouth was twisted. He looked as if he'd left this world in agony. "Was he your father?"

By then they'd reached the huge jade wardrobe. Lu Xin wedged its door open with her hip, took a step backward, and dropped her half of the body inside.

"He was to be my husband," she said coldly. "And a horrible one at that. The ancestors approved of our marriage, but I did not. Rich, powerful older men are nothing to be grateful for, if one enjoys romance." She studied Luce, who lowered the king's feet slowly to the floor of the wardrobe. "What part of the plains do you come from that word of the king's betrothal had not reached you?" Lu Xin had noticed Luce's Mayan clothing. She picked at the hem of the short brown skirt. "Did they hire you to perform at our wedding? Are you some sort of dancer? A clown?"

"Not exactly." Luce felt her cheeks flush as she tugged the skirt lower on her hips. "Look, we can't just leave his body here. Someone's going to find out. I mean, he's the king, right? And there's blood everywhere."

Lu Xin reached into the dragon wardrobe and pulled out a crimson silk robe. She dropped to her knees and tore a large strip of fabric from it. It was a beautiful soft silk garment, with small black blossoms embroidered around the neckline. But Lu Xin didn't think twice about using it to mop up the blood on the floor. She snatched a second, blue robe and tossed it to Luce to help with the mopping.

"Okay," Luce said, "well, there's still that knife." She pointed at the gleaming bronze dagger coated up to the hilt with the king's blood.

In a flash, Lu Xin slipped the knife inside a fold of her robe. She looked up at Luce, as if to say *Anything else?*

"What's that over there?" Luce pointed to what looked like the top of a small turtle's shell. She'd seen it fall out of the king's hand when they moved his body.

Lu Xin was on her knees. She tossed down the sopping bloodstained rag and cupped the shell between her hands. "The oracle bone," she said softly. "More important than any king."

"What is it?"

"This holds answers from the Deity Above."

Luce stepped closer, kneeling to see the object that

had had such an effect on the girl. The oracle bone was nothing more than a tortoiseshell, but it was small and polished and pristine. When Luce leaned closer, she saw that someone had painted something in soft black strokes on the smooth underside of the shell:

Is Lu Xin true to me or does she love another?

Fresh tears welled in Lu Xin's eyes, a crack in the cool resolve she'd shown to Luce. "He asked the ancestors," she whispered, closing her eyes. "They must have told him of my deceit. I—I could not help myself."

Daniel. She must be talking about Daniel. A secret love she'd hidden from the king. But she hadn't been able to hide it well enough.

Luce's heart went out to Lu Xin. She understood with every fiber of her soul precisely what the girl was feeling. They shared a love that no king could take away, that nobody could extinguish. A love more powerful than nature.

She swept Lu Xin into a deep embrace.

And felt the floor drop away beneath them.

She hadn't meant to do this! But her stomach was already pitching, and her vision shifted uncontrollably, and she saw herself from outside, looking alien and wild and holding on for dear life to her past. Then the room stopped spinning and Luce was alone, clutching the oracle bone in her hand. It was done. She'd become Lu Xin.

"I disappear for three minutes and you go three-D?"

Bill said, reappearing in a huff. "Can't a gargoyle enjoy a nice cup of jasmine tea without coming back to find that his charge has dug her own grave? Have you even thought about what's going to happen when the guards knock on that door?"

A knock sounded sharply on the great bamboo door in the main chamber.

Luce jumped.

Bill folded his arms over his chest. "Speak of the devil," he said. Then, in a high, affected shriek, he cried out, "Oh, Bill! Help me, Bill, what do I do now? I didn't think to ask you any questions *before* I put myself into a *very stupid situation, Bill!*"

But Luce didn't have to ask Bill any questions. Knowledge was rising to the front of Lu Xin's mind: She knew that this day would be marked not just by the suicide of one crappy king, but by something even bigger, even darker, even bloodier: a huge clash between armies. That knock on the door? It was the king's council waiting to escort him to war. He was to lead the troops in battle.

But the king was dead and stuffed in a wardrobe.

And Luce was in Lu Xin's body, holed up in his private chambers. If they found her here alone . . .

"King Shang." Heavy knocks echoed throughout the room. "We await your orders."

Luce stood very still, freezing in Lu Xin's silk robe. There was no King Shang. His suicide had left the dynasty without a king, the temples without a high priest, and the army without a general, right before a battle to maintain the dynasty.

"Talk about an ill-timed regicide," Bill said.

"What do I do?" Luce spun back to the dragon wardrobe, wincing when she peered in at the king. His neck was bent at an unnatural angle, and the blood on his chest was drying a rusty brown. Lu Xin had hated the king when he'd been alive. Luce knew now that the tears she'd cried weren't tears of sadness, but of fear for what would become of her love, De.

Until three weeks before, Lu Xin had lived on her family's millet farm on the banks of the Huan River. Passing through her river valley on his shining chariot one afternoon, the king had glimpsed Lu Xin tending the crops. He had decided that he fancied her. The next day, two militiamen had arrived at her door. She'd had to leave her family and her home. She'd had to leave De, the handsome young fisherman from the next village.

Before the king's summons, De had shown Lu Xin how to fish using his pair of pet cormorants, by tying a bit of rope loosely around their necks so that they could catch several fish in their mouths but not swallow them. Watching De gently coax the fish from the depths of the funny birds' beaks, Lu Xin had fallen in love with him. The very next morning, she'd had to say goodbye to him. Forever.

Or so she'd thought.

It had been nineteen sunsets since Lu Xin had seen De, seven sunsets since she'd received a scroll from home with bad news: De and some other boys from the neighboring farms had run away to join the rebel army, and no sooner had he left than the king's men had ransacked the village, looking for the deserters.

With the king dead, the Shang men would show no mercy to Lu Xin, and she would never find De, never reunite with Daniel.

Unless the king's council didn't find out that their king was dead.

The wardrobe was jammed with colorful, exotic garments, but one object caught her eye: a large curved helmet. It was heavy, made mostly of thick leather straps stitched together with tight seams. At the front was a smooth bronze plate with an ornate fire-breathing dragon carved into the metal. The dragon was the zodiac animal of the king's birth year.

Bill floated toward her. "What are you doing with the king's helmet?"

Luce slid the helmet onto her head, tucking her black hair inside it. Then she opened the other side of the wardrobe, thrilled and nervous about what she had found.

"The same thing I'm doing with the king's armor," she said, gathering a heavy tangle of goods into her arms. She donned a pair of wide leather pants, a thick leather tunic, a pair of chain-mail gloves, leather slippers that were certainly too big but that she'd have to make work, and a bronze chest guard made of overlapping metal plates. The same black, fire-breathing dragon on the helmet was embroidered on the front of the tunic. It was hard to believe that anyone could fight a war under the weight of these clothes, but Lu Xin knew that the king didn't really fight—he only led battles from the seat of his war chariot.

"This is not the time to play dress-up!" Bill jabbed a claw at her. "You can't go out there like that."

"Why not? It fits. Almost." She folded over the top of the pants so that she could belt them tightly.

Near the water basin, she found a crude mirror of polished tin inside a bamboo frame. In the reflection, Lu Xin's face was disguised by the thick bronze plate of the helmet. Her body looked bulky and strong under the leather armor.

Luce started to walk out of the dressing chamber, back into the bedroom.

"Wait!" Bill shouted. "What are you going to say about the king?"

Luce turned to Bill and raised the heavy leather helmet so that he could see her eyes. "*I'm* the king now."

Bill blinked, and for once made no attempt at a comeback.

A bolt of strength surged through Luce. Disguising herself as the head of the army was, she realized, exactly what Lu Xin would have done. As a common soldier, of course De would be on the front lines in this battle. And she was going to find him.

The pounding on the door again. "King Shang, the Zhou army is advancing. We must request your presence!"

"I believe there's someone talking to you, *King Shang*." Bill's voice had changed. It was deep and scratchy and echoed around the room so violently that Luce flinched, but she didn't turn to look at him. She unbolted the heavy bronze handle and opened the thick bamboo door.

Three men in flamboyant red-and-yellow martial robes greeted her anxiously. Instantly, Luce recognized the king's three closest councilors: Hu, with the tiny teeth and narrowed, yellowed eyes. Cui, the tallest one, with broad shoulders and wide-set eyes. Huang, the youngest and kindest on the council.

"The king is already dressed for war," Huang said, peering past Luce into the empty chamber quizzically. "The king looks . . . different."

Luce froze. What to say? She'd never heard the dead king's voice, and she was exceptionally bad at impersonations.

"Yes." Hu agreed with Huang. "Well rested."

After a deep, relieved sigh, Luce nodded stiffly, careful not to send the helmet tumbling from her head.

The three men gestured for the king—for Luce—to walk down the marble hall. Huang and Hu flanked her, and murmured in low voices about the sad state of morale among the soldiers. Cui walked directly behind Luce, making her uncomfortable.

The palace went on forever—high gabled ceilings, all gleaming white, the same jade and onyx statues at every turn, the same bamboo-framed mirrors on every wall. When finally they crossed the last threshold and stepped into the gray morning, Luce spotted the red wooden chariot in the distance, and her knees nearly buckled under her.

She had to find Daniel in this lifetime, but going into battle terrified her.

At the chariot, the king's council members bowed and kissed her gauntlet. She was grateful for the armored gloves but still pulled back quickly, afraid her grip might give her away. Huang handed her a long spear with a wooden handle and a curved spike a few inches below the spearhead. "Your halberd, Majesty."

She nearly dropped the heavy thing.

"They will take you to the overlook above the front lines," he said. "We will follow behind and meet you there with the cavalry."

Luce turned to the chariot. It was basically a wooden

platform atop a long axle connecting two great wooden wheels, drawn by two immense black horses. The carriage was made of shiny lacquered red wood and had space enough for about three people to sit or stand. A leather awning and curtains could be removed during battle, but for now, they hung down, giving the passenger some privacy.

Luce climbed up, passed through the curtains, and took a seat. It was padded with tiger skins. A driver with a thin mustache took the reins, and another soldier with drooping eyes and a battle-ax climbed up to stand at his side. At the crack of a whip, the horses broke into a gallop and she felt the wheels beneath her begin to turn.

As they rolled past the high, austere gates of the palace, sun streamed through pockets of fog onto a great expanse of green farmland to the west. The land was beautiful, but Luce was too nervous to appreciate it.

"Bill," she whispered. "Help?"

No answer.

"Bill?"

She peeked outside the curtains, but that only attracted the attention of the droopy-eyed soldier who was supposed to be the king's bodyguard during the journey. "Your Majesty, please, for your safety, I must insist." He gestured for Luce to withdraw.

Luce groaned and leaned back against the padded chariot seat. The paved streets of the city must have ended, for the ride became incredibly bumpy. Luce was flung against the seat, feeling like she was on a wooden roller coaster. Her fingers gripped the plush fur of the tiger skin.

Bill hadn't wanted her to do this. Was he teaching her a lesson by bailing now when she most needed his help?

Her knees rattled with each jolt in the road. She had absolutely no idea how she'd find De. If the king's guards wouldn't even let her look out past a curtain, how were they going to let her near the front lines?

But then:

Once, thousands of years ago, her past self had sat alone in this chariot, disguised as the deceased king. Luce could feel it—even if she hadn't joined with her past body, Lu Xin would have been here right now.

Without the aid of some weird ornery gargoyle. And, more importantly, without all the knowledge that Luce had amassed so far on her quest. She had seen Daniel's unbridled glory in Chichén Itzá. She had witnessed and finally understood the depths of his curse in London. She'd seen him go from suicidal in Tibet to saving her from a rotten life in Versailles. She'd watched him sleep through the pain of her death in Prussia as if he were under a spell. She'd seen him fall for her even when she was snotty and immature in Helston. She'd touched the scars of his wings in Milan and understood how much he'd given up in Heaven just for her. She'd seen the tortured look in his eyes when he lost her in Moscow, the same misery over and over again.

Luce owed it to him to find a way to break this curse.

The chariot jolted to a stop, and Luce was nearly flung off her seat. Outside, there was a thunderous pounding of horses' hooves—which was strange because the king's chariot was standing still.

Someone else was out there.

Luce heard a clash of metal and a long, pained grunt. The chariot was jostled roughly. Something heavy thumped to the ground.

There was more clashing, more grunting, a harsh cry, and another thump on the ground. Her hands trembling, Luce parted the leather curtains the tiniest bit and saw the droopy-eyed solder lying in a pool of blood on the ground beneath.

The king's chariot had been ambushed.

The curtains before her were thrust apart by one of the insurgents. The foreign fighter raised his sword.

Luce couldn't help herself: She screamed.

The sword faltered in the air—and then, the warmest feeling washed over Luce, flooding her veins, calming her nerves, and slowing the pounding of her heart.

The fighter on the chariot was De.

His leather helmet covered his black, shoulder-length hair, but it left his face wonderfully unobstructed. His violet eyes stood out against his clear olive skin. He looked baffled and hopeful at the same time. His sword was drawn, but he held it as if he sensed he shouldn't strike. Quickly, Luce lifted her helmet over her head and flung it onto the seat.

Her dark hair cascaded down, her locks tumbling all the way to the bottom of her bronze breastplate. Her vision blurred as her eyes filled with tears.

"Lu Xin?" De gathered her tightly into his arms. His nose grazed hers and she rested her cheek on his, feeling warm and safe. He seemed unable to stop smiling. She lifted her head and kissed the beautiful curve of his lips. He answered her kiss hungrily, and Luce soaked up every wonderful moment, feeling the weight of his body against hers, wishing there weren't so much heavy armor between them.

"You're the last person I expected to see," De said softly.

"I could say the same for you," she said. "What are you doing here?"

"When I joined forces with the Zhou rebels, I vowed to kill the king and get you back."

"The king is— Oh, none of that matters anymore," Luce whispered, kissing his cheeks and his eyelids, holding tight around his neck.

"Nothing matters," De said. "Except that I'm with you."

Luce thought back to his luminous glow back in Chichén Itzá. Seeing him in these other lives, in places and times that were so far from home—each one confirmed how much she loved him. The bond between them was unbreakable—it was clear from the way they looked at each other, the way they could read each other's thoughts, the way one made the other feel whole.

But how could she forget the curse they had been suffering through for eternity? And the quest she was on to break it? She had come too far to forget that there were obstacles still in the way of her truly being with Daniel.

Every life had taught her something so far. Surely this life must hold its own key. If only she knew what to search for.

"We had word the king would arrive here to direct the troops down below," De said. "The rebels had planned an ambush of the king's cavalry."

"They're on their way," Luce said, remembering Huang's instructions. "They'll be here any moment."

Daniel nodded. "And when they get here, the rebels will expect me to fight."

Luce winced. She'd been with Daniel twice already when he was gearing up for battle, and both times it had led to something she'd never wanted to see again. "What should I do while you're—"

"I'm not going into battle, Lu Xin."

"What?"

"This isn't our war. It never was. We can stay and fight other people's battles or we can do as we have *al-*

ways done and choose each other over everything else. Do you understand what I mean?"

"Yes," she whispered. Lu Xin did not know the deeper meaning of De's words, but Luce was nearly sure that she understood—that Daniel loved her, that she loved him, and that they were choosing to be together.

"They will not let us go easily. The rebels will kill me for deserting." He replaced her helmet on her head. "You will have to fight your way out of this, too."

"What?" she whispered. "I can't fight. I can barely lift this thing"—she gestured at the halberd. "I can't—"

"Yes," he said, imparting profound meaning with the single word. "You can."

The carriage filled with light. For a moment Luce thought that this was it, the moment when her world would ignite, when Lu Xin would die, when her soul would be exiled to the shadows.

But that didn't happen. The glow shone out of De's chest. It was the glow of Daniel's soul. It wasn't as strong or as radiant as it had been at the Mayan sacrifice, but it was just as breathtaking. It reminded Luce of the glow of her own soul when she'd first seen Lu Xin. Maybe she was learning to truly *see* the world as it was. Maybe, at last, illusion was falling away.

"Okay," she said, stuffing her long hair back inside the helmet. "Let's go."

They parted the curtains and stood on the platform of the chariot. Before them, a rebel force of twenty men on horseback waited near a hill's edge maybe fifty feet ahead of where the king's chariot had been overtaken. They were dressed in simple peasants' clothing, brown trousers and coarse, filthy shirts. Their shields bore the sign of the rat, the symbol of the Zhou army. They were all looking to De for orders.

From the valley below came the rumbling of hundreds of horses. Luce understood that the entire Shang army was down there, thirsty for blood. She could hear them chanting an old war song Lu Xin had known since she could speak.

And somewhere behind them, Luce knew that Huang and the rest of the king's private soldiers were on their way to what they thought would be a rendezvous at the overlook. They were riding into a bloodbath, an ambush, and Luce and Daniel had to get away before they arrived.

"Follow my lead," De murmured. "We will head for the hills to the west, as far from this battle as our horses can take us."

He freed one of the horses from the chariot and guided it to Luce. The horse was stunning, black as coal, with a diamond-shaped white patch on its chest. De helped Luce into the saddle and held up the king's halberd in one hand and a crossbow in the other. Luce had never fired or even touched a crossbow in her life, and Lu Xin had only used one once, to scare a lynx away from her baby sister's crib. But the weapon felt light in Luce's hands, and she knew that if it came down to it, she could fire it.

De smiled at her choice and whistled for his horse. A beautiful brindle mare trotted over. He hopped onto its back.

"De! What are you doing?" an alarmed voice called from the line of horses. "You were to kill the king! Not mount him on one of our horses!"

"Yes! Kill the king!" a chorus of angry voices called.

"The king is dead!" Luce shouted, silencing the soldiers. The feminine voice behind the helmet brought gasps from all of them. They stood frozen, uncertain whether to raise their weapons.

De drew his horse close to Luce's. He took her hands in his. They were warmer and stronger and more reassuring than anything she'd ever felt.

"Whatever happens, I love you. Our love is worth everything to me."

"And to me," Luce whispered back.

De let out a battle cry, and their horses took off at a breakneck pace. The crossbow nearly slipped out of Luce's grasp as she lurched forward to clutch the reins.

Then the rebel soldiers began to shout. "Traitors!"

"Lu Xin!" De's voice rose above the shrillest cry, the heaviest horse's hoof. *"Go!"* He raised his arm high, pointing toward the hills.

Her horse galloped so fast it was hard to see anything clearly. The world whizzed by in one terrifying whoosh. A tangle of rebel soldiers fell in behind them, their horses' hoofbeats as loud as an earthquake that went on forever.

Until the rebel came at Daniel with his halberd, Luce had forgotten about the crossbow in her hands. Now she raised it effortlessly, still unsure how to use it, knowing only that she would slaughter anyone who tried to hurt Daniel.

Now.

She released her arrow. To her shock, it stopped the rebel dead, knocking him off his horse. He collapsed in a cloud of dust. She gazed back in horror at the dead man with the arrow through his chest lying on the ground.

"Keep going!" De called out.

She swallowed hard, letting her horse guide her. Something was happening. She began to feel lighter in her saddle, as if gravity suddenly had less power over her, as if De's faith in her was propelling her through it all. She could do this. She could escape with him. She slipped another bolt onto the crossbow, fired, and fired again. She didn't aim at anyone except in self-defense, but there were so many soldiers coming at her that she was soon nearly out of arrows. Just two left.

"De!" she cried.

He was almost fully out of his saddle, using an ax to beat down hard on a Shang soldier. De's wings weren't extended, but they might as well have been—he seemed lighter than air, yet deadly skillful. Daniel killed his foes so cleanly, their deaths were instantaneous, as close to painless as possible.

"De!" she shouted, more loudly.

At the sound of her voice, his head shot up. Luce leaned over her saddle to show him her nearly empty quiver. He tossed her a hooked sword.

She caught it by the hilt. It felt strangely natural in her hand. Then she remembered—the fencing lesson she'd taken at Shoreline. In her very first match, she'd destroyed Lilith, a prissy, cruel classmate who'd been fencing all her life.

Certainly she could do it again.

Just then, a warrior leaped from his horse onto hers. The sudden weight of him made her mount stumble and made Luce scream, but a moment later, his throat was slit and his body shoved to the ground and the blade of her sword shone with fresh blood.

There was a warm flush across her chest. Her entire body buzzed. She charged ahead, spurring her horse to full speed, faster and faster until—

The world went white.

Then slammed into black.

Finally it flared through a blaze of brilliant colors.

She raised her hand to block the light, but it wasn't coming from outside her. Her horse still galloped beneath her. Her dagger was still gripped in her fist, still slashing right and left, into throats, into chests. Enemies still fell at her feet.

But somehow Luce wasn't quite there anymore. A riot of visions assaulted her mind, visions that must have belonged to Lu Xin—and then some visions that couldn't possibly have belonged to Lu Xin.

She saw Daniel hovering over her in his simple peasant's clothes . . . but then, a moment later, he was barechested, with long blond hair . . . and suddenly he wore a knight's helmet, whose visor he lifted to kiss her lips . . . but before he did, he shifted into his present self, the Daniel she'd left in her parents' backyard in Thunderbolt when she stepped through into time.

This was the Daniel, she realized, she'd been looking for all along. She reached for him, she called his name, but then he changed again. And again. She saw more Daniels than she'd ever thought possible, each one more gorgeous than the last. They folded into each other like a vast accordion, each image of him tilting and altering in the light of the sky behind him. The cut of his nose, the line of his jawbone, the tone of his skin, the shape of his lips, all whirled in and out of focus, morphing all the time. Everything changed except his eyes.

His violet eyes always stayed the same. They haunted her, hiding something terrible, something she didn't understand. Something she didn't want to understand.

Fear?

In the visions, the terror in Daniel's eyes was so intense Luce actually wanted to look away from their beauty. What could someone as powerful as Daniel fear?

There was only one thing: Luce's dying.

She was experiencing a montage of her death over and over and over again. This was what Daniel's eyes looked like, throughout time, just before her life went up in flames. She had seen this fear in him before. She hated it because it always meant their time was over. She saw it now in every one of his faces. The fear flashed from infinite times and places. Suddenly, she knew there was more:

He wasn't afraid *for* her, not because she was walking into the darkness of another death. He didn't fear that it might cause her pain.

Daniel was afraid *of* her.

"Lu Xin!" his voice cried out to her from the battlefield. She could see him through the haze of visions. He was the only thing coming in clearly—because everything else around her was lit up startlingly white. Everything *inside* her was, too. Was her love of Daniel burning her up? Was it her own passion, not his, that destroyed her every time?

"No!" His hand reached out for hers. But it was too late.

⚜

Her head hurt. She didn't want to open her eyes.

Bill was back, the floor was cool, and Luce was in a

347

welcome pocket of darkness. A waterfall sprayed somewhere in the background, drizzling on her hot cheeks.

"You did okay out there after all," he said.

"Don't sound so disappointed," Luce said. "How about explaining where you disappeared to?"

"Can't." Bill sucked in his fat lips to show that they were sealed.

"Why not?"

"Personal."

"Is it Daniel?" she asked. "He'd be able to see you, wouldn't he? And there's some reason you don't want him to know that you're helping me."

Bill snorted. "My business isn't always about *you*, Luce. I have other things stewing in the pot. Besides, you seem pretty independent of late. Maybe it's time to end our little arrangement, bust off your training wheels. What the hell do you need me for anymore?"

Luce was too exhausted to pander to him, and too stunned by what she'd just seen. "It's hopeless."

All the rage left Bill like air being let out of a balloon. "How do you mean?"

"When I die, it's not because of anything that Daniel *does*. It's something that happens inside me. Maybe his love brings it out, but—it's my fault. That has to be part of the curse, only I have no idea what it means. All I know is, I saw a look in his eyes right before I died—it's always the same."

He tilted his head. "So far."

"I make him miserable more than I make him happy," she said. "If he hasn't given up on me, he should. I can't do this to him anymore."

She dropped her head into her hands.

"Luce?" Bill sat on her knee. There was the strange tenderness he'd shown when she first met him. "Do you want to put this endless charade to rest? For Daniel's sake?"

Luce looked up and wiped her eyes. "You mean, so he won't have to go through this again? There's something I can do?"

"When you assume one of your past self's bodies, there is one moment in each one of your lives, just before you die, where your soul and the two bodies—past and present—split apart. It only happens for a fraction of an instant."

Luce squinted. "I think I've felt that. At the moment when I realize I'm going to die, right before I actually do?"

"Exactly. It has to do with how your lives cleave together. In that fraction of a moment, there is a way to cleave your cursed soul *from* your present body. Kind of like carving out your soul. It would, effectively, extinguish that pesky reincarnation element of your curse."

"But I thought I was already at the end of my cycle of

reincarnations, that I wasn't coming back anymore. Because of the baptism thing. Because I never—"

"That doesn't matter. You're still bound to see the cycle to its end. As soon as you go back to the present, you could still die at any moment because of—"

"My love of Daniel."

"Sure, something like that," Bill said. "Ahem. That is, unless you break the bond with your past."

"So I'd cleave from my past and she would still die as she always did—"

"And you would still be cast out just as you've been before, only you'd leave your soul behind to die, too. And the body you would return to"—he poked her in the shoulder—"this one—would be free to live outside the curse that's been hanging over you since the dawn of time."

"No more dying?"

"Not unless you jump off a building or get into a car with a murderer or take a whole lot of Unisom or—"

"I get it," she cut him off. "But it's not like"—she struggled to steady her voice—"it's not like Daniel would kiss me and I'd . . . or—"

"It's not like Daniel would *do* anything." Bill stared at her purposefully. "You wouldn't be drawn to him anymore. You'd move on. Probably marry some dull sweetheart and have twelve kids of your own."

"No."

"You and Daniel would be free of the curse you so despise. *Free.* Hear that? He could move on and be happy, too. Don't you want Daniel to be happy?"

"But Daniel and I—"

"Daniel and you would be nothing. It's a hard reality, okay, fine. But think about it: You wouldn't have to *hurt* him anymore. Grow up, Luce. There's more to life than teenage passion."

Luce opened her mouth but didn't want to hear her voice break. A life without Daniel was unimaginable. But so was going back to her current life and trying to be with Daniel and having it kill her for good. She had tried so hard to find a way to break this curse, but the answer still eluded her. Maybe this was the way. It sounded awful now, but if she went back to her life and didn't even know Daniel, she wouldn't miss him. And he wouldn't miss her. Maybe that would be better. For both of them.

But no. They were soul mates. And Daniel brought more into her life than just his love. Arriane, Roland, and Gabbe. Even Cam. It was because of all of them that she'd learned about herself—what she wanted, what she didn't, how to stand up for herself. She'd grown up and become a better person. Without Daniel, she would never have gone to Shoreline, never have found the true friends she'd made of Shelby and Miles. Would she even have gone to Sword & Cross? Where on earth would she be? *Who* would she be?

Could she be happy one day without him? Fall in love with someone else? She couldn't bear to think about that. Life without Daniel sounded colorless and grim—except for one bright spot that Luce kept circling back to:

What if she never had to hurt him again?

"Say I did want to consider this." Luce could barely muster a whisper. "Just to think it over. How does it even work?"

Bill reached behind him and slowly unsheathed something long and silver from a tiny black strap on his back. She'd never noticed it before. He held out a dull, flat-tipped silver arrow that she immediately recognized.

Then he smiled. "Have you ever seen a starshot?"

EIGHTEEN

BAD DIRECTIONS

JERUSALEM, ISRAEL · 27 NISSAN 2760

"So, you're not actually that bad of a guy?" Shelby said to Daniel.

They were sitting on the lush bank of the old Jerusalem riverbed, watching the horizon where the two fallen angels had just parted ways. The lightest breath of gold-hued light hung in the sky where Cam had been, and the air was beginning to smell a bit like rotten eggs.

"Of course I'm not." Daniel dipped his hand in the cool water. His wings and his soul still felt hot from watching Cam make his choice. How simple it had seemed for him. How easy and how swift.

And all because of a broken heart.

"It's just that when Luce found out you and Cam struck up that truce, she was devastated. None of us could understand it." Shelby looked to Miles for affirmation. "Could we?"

"We thought you were hiding something from her." Miles took off his baseball cap and rubbed his head. "All we knew of Cam was that he was supposed to be pure evil."

Shelby made claws with her fingers. "All *hiss!* and *rawr!* and like that."

"Few souls are pure anything," Daniel said, "in Heaven, in Hell, or on Earth." He turned away, looking high in the eastern sky for a hint of the silver dust Dani would have left when he unfurled his wings and flew away. There was nothing.

"Sorry," Shelby said, "but it's so weird to think of you as brothers."

"We were all a family at one point."

"Yeah, but, like, *forever* ago."

"You think just because something's been one way for a few thousand years, that it's fixed across eternity." Daniel shook his head. "Everything is in flux. I was with Cam at the Dawn of Time, and I'll see him through the End Times."

Shelby's eyebrows shot up in disbelief. "You think Cam's going to come back around? Like, see the light side again?"

Daniel started to stand. "Nothing stays the same forever."

"What about your love with Luce?" Miles asked.

That stopped Daniel cold. "That's changing, too. She'll be different, after this experience. I just hope . . ." He looked down at Miles, who was still seated on the bank, and Daniel realized he didn't hate Miles. In their recklessly idiotic way, the Nephilim had been trying to help.

For the first time, Daniel could say truthfully that he didn't need help anymore; he'd gotten all the help he needed along the way from each of his past selves. Now, finally, he was ready to catch up with Luce.

Why was he still standing here?

"It's time for you two to go home," he said, helping Shelby, then Miles to their feet.

"No," Shelby said, reaching for Miles, who gave her hand a squeeze. "We made a pact. We're not going back until we know she's—"

"It won't be long," Daniel said. "I think I know where to find her, and it's no place you two can go."

"Come on, Shel." Miles was already peeling away the shadow cast by the olive tree near the riverbank. It pooled and swirled in his hands and looked unwieldy for a moment, like potter's clay about to spin off the wheel. But then Miles reined it in, spinning it into an impressively large black portal. He pressed open the Announcer lightly, gesturing for Shelby to step through first.

"You're getting good at that." Daniel had drawn up his own Announcer, summoning it from the shadow of his own body. It trembled before him.

Because the Nephilim were not here through their own past experiences, they would have to leapfrog from Announcer to Announcer to get back to their own time. It would be difficult, and Daniel did not envy them their journey, but he did envy them because they were going home.

"Daniel." Shelby's head popped out of the Announcer. Her body looked warped and dim through the shadows. "Good luck."

She waved, and Miles waved, and the two of them stepped through. The shadow closed in on itself, collapsing into a dot just before it vanished.

Daniel didn't see that happen. He was already gone.

❄

Cold wind gnawed into him.

He sped through, faster than he'd ever traveled before, back to a place, and a time, to which he'd never thought he would return.

"Hey," a voice called out. It was raspy and blunt and seemed to come from right beside Daniel. "Slow down, will ya?"

Daniel jerked away from the sound. "Who are you?" he shouted into the invisible darkness. "Make yourself known."

When nothing appeared before him, Daniel unfurled his rippling white wings—as much to challenge the intruder inside his Announcer as to help slow him down. They lit up the Announcer with their glow, and Daniel felt the tension inside him ease a little.

Fully extended, his wings spanned the width of the tunnel. Their narrow tips were the most sensitive to touch; when they brushed against the dank walls of the Announcer, it gave Daniel a queasy, claustrophobic feeling.

In the darkness before him, a figure slowly filtered into view.

First, the wings: undersized and gossamer-thin. Then the body deepened in color just enough for Daniel to see a small, pale angel sharing his Announcer. Daniel did not know him. The angel's features were soft and innocent-looking, like a baby's. In the cramped tunnel, his fine blond hair blew across his silver eyes in the wind that Daniel's wings sent back each time they pulsed. He looked so young, but of course, he was just as old as any of them.

"Who are you?" Daniel asked again. "How did you get in here? Are you Scale?"

"Yes." Despite his innocent, infantile appearance, the angel's voice was gravel-deep. He reached behind his back for a moment, and Daniel thought perhaps he was hiding something there—perhaps one of his kind's trapping devices—but the angel simply turned around to reveal the scar on the back of his neck. The seven-pointed gold insignia of the Scale. "I'm Scale." His deep voice was rough and clotted. "I'd like to speak with you."

Daniel gnashed his teeth. The Scale must have known he had no respect for them or their meddlesome duties. But it didn't matter how much he loathed their high-flown manners, always seeking to nudge the fallen to one side: He still had to honor their requests. Something seemed odd about this one, but who other than a member of the Scale could have found a way into his Announcer?

"I'm in a hurry."

The angel nodded, as if he already knew this. "You search for Lucinda?"

"Yes," Daniel blurted out. "I—I don't need help."

"You do." The angel nodded. "You missed your exit"—he pointed down, toward the place in the vertical tunnel where Daniel had just come from. "Right back there."

"No—"

"Yes." The angel smiled, showing a row of tiny, jagged teeth. "We wait and watch. We see who travels by Announcer and where they go."

"I didn't know that policing the Announcers fell under the Scale's jurisdiction."

"There is much you don't know. Our monitor caught a trace of her passing through. She'll be well on her way by now. You must go after her."

Daniel stiffened. The Scale were the only angels granted vision between Announcers. It was possible a Scale member would have seen Luce's travels.

"Why would you want to help me find her?"

"Oh, Daniel." The angel frowned. "Lucinda is a part of your destiny. We want you to find her. We want you to be true to your nature—"

"And then to side with Heaven," Daniel snarled.

"One step at a time." The angel tucked his wings to his sides and plummeted through the tunnel. "If you want to catch her," his deep voice rumbled, "I'm here to show you the way. I know where the connection points are. I can open up a portal between the tissue of past times." Then, faintly: "No strings attached."

Daniel was lost. The Scale had been a nuisance to him ever since the War in Heaven, but at least their motives were transparent. They wanted him to side with Heaven. That was it. He guessed it would behoove them to lead him to Luce if they could.

Maybe the angel was right. One step at a time. All he cared about was Luce.

He tucked his wings in at his sides as the angel had done and felt his body moving through the darkness. When he caught up to the angel, he stopped.

The angel pointed. "Lucinda stepped through there."

The shadow-way was narrow and perpendicular to the path Daniel had been on. It didn't look any more right or wrong than where Daniel had been headed before.

"If this works," he said, "I'll owe you. If not, I'll hunt you down."

The angel said nothing.

So Daniel leaped before he looked, feeling a wind lick wetly at his wings, a current picking up again and speeding him along, and hearing—somewhere far behind him—the faintest peal of laughter.

NINETEEN

THE MORTAL COIL

MEMPHIS, EGYPT · PERET—"THE SEASON OF SOWING"
(AUTUMN, APPROXIMATELY 3100 BCE)

"You there," a voice bellowed as Luce crossed the threshold of the Announcer. "I should like my wine. On a platter. And bring in my dogs. No—my lions. No—both."

She'd stepped through into a vast white room with alabaster walls and thick columns holding up a lofty ceiling. A faint scent of roasting meat was in the air.

The room was empty except for a tall platform at the far end, which had been dressed with antelope hide.

Atop it sat a colossal throne, carved from marble, padded with plush emerald-green pillows, and adorned along the back with a decorative crest of interlocking ivory tusks.

The man on the throne—with his kohl-rimmed eyes, bare muscular chest, gold-capped teeth, bejeweled fingers, and tower of ebony hair—was talking to her. He had turned away from a thin-lipped, blue-robed scribe holding a papyrus-reed script, and now both men stared at Luce.

She cleared her throat.

"Yes, Pharaoh," Bill hissed into her ear. "Just say Yes, Pharaoh."

"Yes, Pharaoh!" Luce shouted across the endless chamber.

"Good," Bill said. "Now scram!"

Ducking backward through a shadowed doorway, Luce found herself in an interior courtyard surrounding a still pond. The air was cool, but the sun was fierce, scorching the rows of potted lotus flowers that lined the walkway. The courtyard was huge, but, eerily, Luce and Bill had the whole thing to themselves.

"There's something strange about this place, isn't there?" Luce stayed close to the walls. "The pharaoh didn't even seem alarmed by seeing me step out of nowhere."

"He's too important to be bothered with actually

noticing people. He saw movement in his peripheral vision and deduced that someone was there for him to boss around. That's all. It explains why he also didn't seem fazed by the fact that you're wearing Chinese battle garb from two thousand years in the future," Bill said, snapping his stone fingers. He pointed to a shadowed niche in the corner of the courtyard. "Hang tight right there and I'll be back with something a little more *à la mode* for you to wear."

Before Luce could strip off the Shang king's cumbersome armor, Bill was back with a simple white Egyptian shift dress. He helped tug off her leather gear and slipped the dress over her head. It draped over one shoulder, tied around the waist, and tapered into a narrow skirt ending a few inches above her ankles.

"Forgetting anything?" Bill said with a strange intensity.

"Oh." Luce reached back into the Shang armor for the dull-tipped starshot tucked inside. When she pulled it out, it felt so much heavier than she knew it really was.

"Don't touch the point!" Bill said quickly, wrapping the tip in fabric and tying it off. "Not yet."

"I thought it could only harm angels." She tilted her head, remembering the battle against the Outcasts, remembering the arrow glancing off Callie's arm without a scratch, remembering Daniel telling her to stay far out of the arrow's range.

"Whoever told you that didn't tell you the whole truth," Bill said. "It only affects *immortals.* You have a part of you that is immortal—the cursed part, your soul. That's the part you're going to kill here, remember? So that your mortal self, Lucinda Price, can go on and live a normal life."

"*If* I kill my soul," Luce said, securing the starshot under her new dress. Even through the coarse cloth, it was warm to the touch. "I still haven't decided—"

"I thought we were agreed." Bill swallowed. "Starshots are very valuable. I would not have given it to you unless—"

"Let's just find Layla."

It wasn't just the eerie silence of the palace that was unsettling—something seemed strange between Luce and Bill. Ever since he'd given her the silver arrow, they were edgy around each other.

Bill took a deep, raspy breath. "Okay. Ancient Egypt. This is the early dynastic period in the capital city of Memphis. We're pretty far back now, about five thousand years before Luce Price graces the world with her magnificent presence."

Luce rolled her eyes. "Where's my past self?"

"Why do I even bother with the history lessons?" Bill said to a pretend audience. "All she ever wants to know is where her past self is. So self-centered it's disgusting."

Luce crossed her arms. "If you were going to *kill*

your soul, I think you'd want to get it over with before you had a chance to change your mind."

"So, you've decided now?" Bill sounded a little breathless. "Oh, come on, Luce. This is our last gig together. I figured you'd want to know the details, for old times' sake? Your life here was really one of the most romantic of all." He hunkered down on her shoulder, in storytelling mode. "You're a slave named Layla. Sheltered, lonely—never been beyond the palace walls. Until, one day, in walks the handsome new commander of the army—guess who?"

Bill hovered at her side as Luce left the armor piled in the alcove and walked slowly along the pool's edge.

"You and the dashing Donkor—let's just call him Don—fall in love, and all is rosy except for one cruel reality: Don is betrothed to the pharaoh's bitchy daughter, Auset. Now, how dramatic is that?"

Luce sighed. There was always some complication. One more reason to put an end to all this. Daniel shouldn't be shackled to some earthly body, getting caught up in useless mortal drama just so he could be with Luce. It wasn't fair to him. Daniel had been suffering for too long. Maybe she really *would* end it. She could find Layla and join with her body. Then Bill would tell her how to kill her cursed soul, and she would give Daniel his freedom.

She'd been pacing the oblong courtyard, brooding.

When she rounded the portion of the path nearest the pond, fingers clasped her wrist.

"Caught you!" The girl who'd seized Luce was lean and muscular, with sultry, dramatic features under layers of makeup. Her ears were pierced by at least ten gold hoops, and a heavy gold pendant hung from her neck, ornamented with a pound of precious jewels.

The pharaoh's daughter.

"I—" Luce started to say.

"Don't you dare say a word!" Auset barked. "The sound of your pathetic voice is like pumice on my eardrums. Guard!"

An enormous man appeared. He had a long black ponytail and forearms thicker than Luce's legs. He carried a long wooden spear topped with a sharp copper blade.

"Arrest her," Auset said.

"Yes, Highness," the guard barked. "On what grounds, Highness?"

The question lit an angry fire inside the pharaoh's daughter. "Theft. Of my personal property."

"I will imprison her until the council rules on the matter."

"We did that once before," Auset said. "And yet here she is, like an asp, able to slither free of any bonds. We need to lock her away someplace she can never escape."

"I will assign a continuous watch—"

"No, that won't be good enough." Something dark crossed Auset's face. "I never want to see this girl again. Throw her into my grandfather's tomb."

"But, Your Highness, no one but the high priest is allowed—"

"Precisely, Kafele," Auset said, smiling. "Throw her down the entryway stairs and bolt the door behind you. When the high priest goes to perform the tomb-sealing ceremony this evening, he will discover this tomb raider and will punish her as he sees fit." She drew near Luce and scoffed. "You'll find out what happens to those who try to steal from the royal family."

Don. She meant that Layla was trying to steal Don.

Luce didn't care if they locked her up and threw away the key as long as she got a chance to cleave with Layla first. Otherwise how could she set Daniel free? Bill paced the air, scheming, claws tapping against his stone lip.

The guard produced a pair of shackles from the satchel at his waist and fastened the iron chains over Luce's wrists.

"I'll see to it myself," Kafele said, yanking her after him by a length of chain.

"Bill!" Luce whispered. "You have to help me!"

"We'll think of something," Bill whispered as Luce was dragged across the courtyard. They turned a corner into a dark hallway, where a larger-than-life stone sculpture of Auset stood, looking grimly beautiful.

When Kafele turned to squint at Luce because she was talking to herself, his long black hair swished across his face and gave Luce an idea.

He never saw it coming. She wrestled her shackled hands up and tugged down hard on his hair, clawing at his head with her fingernails. He yelped and stumbled backward, bleeding from a long scratch on his scalp. Then Luce elbowed him hard in the gut.

He grunted and doubled over. The spear slipped from his hands.

"Can you get these shackles off?" Luce hissed at Bill.

The gargoyle wagged his eyebrows. A short black bolt shot into the shackles, and they fizzled into nothingness. Luce's skin felt hot where they had been, but she was free.

"Huh," she said, glancing briefly down at her bare wrists. She grabbed the spear from the ground. She spun around to draw the blade to Kafele's neck.

"One step ahead of you, Luce," Bill called. When she turned, Kafele was sprawled flat on his back with his wrists shackled around the stone ankle of Auset's likeness.

Bill dusted off his hands. "Teamwork." He glanced down at the white-faced guard. "We'd better hurry. He'll find his vocal cords again soon enough. Come with me."

Bill led Luce quickly down the dark hallway, up a short flight of sandstone stairs, and across another hall lit by small tin lamps and lined with clay figures of hawks and hippopotamuses. A pair of guards turned into the hallway, but before they could see Luce, Bill pushed her through a doorway covered by a reed curtain.

She found herself in a bedroom. Stone columns carved to look like bundled papyrus stems rose to a low ceiling. A wooden sedan chair inlaid with ebony sat by an open window opposite a narrow bed, which was carved of wood and painted with so much gold leaf that it gleamed.

"What do I do now?" Luce pressed against the wall in case anyone walking by peered in. "Where are we?"

"This is the commander's chamber."

Before Luce could piece together that Bill meant Daniel, a woman parted the reed curtain and stepped into the room.

Luce shivered.

Layla wore a white dress with the same narrow cut as the one Luce had on. Her hair was thick and straight and glossy. She had a white peony tucked behind one ear.

With a heavy feeling of sadness, Luce watched Layla glide to the wooden vanity and pour fresh oil into the lamp from a canister she carried on a black resin tray. This was the last life Luce would visit, the body where she would part ways with her soul so that all of this could end.

When Layla turned to refill the lamps beside the bed, she noticed Luce.

"Hello," she said in a soft, husky voice. "Are you

looking for someone?" The kohl rimming her eyes looked much more natural than Auset's makeup.

"Yes, I am." Luce wasted no time. Just as she reached forward to grab the girl's wrist, Layla looked past her toward the doorway, and her face stiffened with alarm. "Who is *that*?"

Luce turned and saw only Bill. His eyes were wide.

"You can"—she gaped at Layla—"you can see him?"

"No!" Bill said. "She's talking about the footsteps she hears running down the corridor outside. Better hurry, Luce."

Luce swiveled back and took her past self's warm hand, knocking the canister of oil to the ground. Layla gasped and tried to jerk away, but then it happened.

The feeling of the sinkhole opening in Luce's stomach was almost familiar. The room swirled, and the only thing in focus was the girl standing before her. Her inky-black hair and gold-flecked eyes, the flush of love fresh on her cheeks. Foggily, Luce blinked, and Layla blinked, and on the other side of the blink—

The ground settled. Luce looked down at her hands. Layla's hands. They were trembling.

Bill was gone. But he'd been right: There were footsteps in the hallway.

She dipped to pick up the canister and turned away from the door to start pouring oil into the lamp. Best not to be seen by anyone who passed doing anything but her job.

The footsteps behind her stopped. A warm brush of fingertips traveled up her arms as a firm chest pressed against her back. Daniel. She could sense his glow without even turning. She closed her eyes. His arms wrapped around her waist and his soft lips swept across her neck, stopping just below her ear.

"I found you," he whispered.

She turned slowly in his arms. The sight of him took her breath away. He was still her Daniel, of course, but his skin was the color of rich hot chocolate, and his wavy black hair was cropped very short. He wore only a short linen loincloth, leather sandals, and a silver choker around his neck. His deep-set violet eyes swept over her, happy.

He and Layla were deeply in love.

She rested her cheek on his chest and counted the beats of his heart. Would this be the last time she did this, the last time he held her against his heart? She was about to do the right thing—the *good* thing for Daniel. But still it pained her to think about it. She loved him! If this journey had taught her anything, it was how much she truly loved Daniel Grigori. It hardly seemed fair that she was forced to make this decision.

Yet here she was.

In ancient Egypt.

With Daniel. For the very last time. She was about to set him free.

Her eyes blurred with tears as he kissed the part in the center of her hair.

"I wasn't sure we'd have a chance to say goodbye," he said. "I leave this afternoon for the war in Nubia."

When Luce lifted her head, Daniel cupped her damp cheeks in his hands. "Layla, I'll return before the harvest. Please don't cry. In no time you'll be sneaking back into my bedchamber in the dark of night with platters of pomegranates just like always. I promise."

Luce took a deep, shuddering breath. "Goodbye."

"Goodbye *for now*." His face grew serious. "Say it: *Goodbye for now.*"

She shook her head. "Goodbye, my love. Goodbye."

The reed curtain parted. Layla and Don broke from their embrace as a cluster of guards with their spears drawn barreled into the room. Kafele led them, his face dark with rage. "Get the girl," he said, pointing at Luce.

"What's going on?" Daniel shouted as the guards surrounded Luce and reshackled her hands. "I order you to stop. Unhand her."

"Sorry, Commander," Kafele said. "Pharaoh's orders. You should know by now—when Pharaoh's daughter is not happy, Pharaoh is not happy."

They marched Luce away as Daniel shouted, "I'll come for you, Layla! I'll find you!"

Luce knew he would. Wasn't that how it always played out? They met, she got into trouble, and he showed up and saved the day—year in and year out across eternity, the angel swooping in at the last minute to rescue her. It was tiring to think about.

But this time when he got there, she would have the starshot waiting. The thought sent a raw pain through her gut. A well of tears rose up inside her again, but she swallowed them. At least she had gotten to say goodbye.

The guards ushered her down an endless series of hallways and outside into the blistering sun. They marched her down streets made of uneven slabs of rock, through a monumental arched gate, and past small sandstone houses and shimmering silty farmland on the way out of the city. They were dragging her toward an enormous golden hill.

Only as they drew near did Luce realize it was a man-made structure. The necropolis, she realized at the same time that Layla's mind became jumbled with fear. Every Egyptian knew this was the tomb of the last pharaoh, Meni. No one except a few of the holiest priests—and the dead—dared approach the place where the royal bodies were interred. It was locked with spells and incantations, some to guide the dead in their journey toward the next life, and some to ward off any living being who dared approach. Even the guards dragging her there seemed to grow nervous as they approached.

Soon they were entering a pyramid-shaped tomb made of baked mud bricks. All but two of the burliest guards remained outside the entrance. Kafele shoved

Luce through a darkened doorway and down a darker flight of stairs. The other guard followed them, carrying a flaming torch to light their path.

The torchlight flickered on the stone walls. They were painted with hieroglyphics, and now and then Layla's eyes caught bits of prayers to Tait, the goddess of weaving, asking for help to keep the pharaoh's soul in one piece during his journey to the afterlife.

Every few steps they passed false doors—deep stone recesses in the walls. Some of them, Luce realized, had once been entryways leading to the final resting places of members of the royal family. They were now sealed off with stone and gravel so that no mortal could pass.

Their way grew cooler; it grew darker. The air became heavy with the faded must of death. When they neared the one open doorway at the end of the hallway, the guard with the torch would go no farther—"I will not be cursed by the gods for this girl's insolence"—so Kafele did it himself. He wrestled aside the stone bolt that pinned the door, and a harsh, vinegary smell flooded out, poisoning the air.

"Think you have any hope of escape now?" he asked, releasing her wrists from the shackles and shoving her inside.

"Yes," Luce whispered to herself as the heavy stone door shut behind her and the bolt thudded back into place. "Only one."

She was alone in utter darkness, and the cold clawed at her skin.

Then something snapped—stone on stone, so recognizable—and a small golden light bloomed in the center of the room. It was cupped between the two stone hands of Bill.

"Hello, hello." He floated to the side of the room and poured the ball of fire out of his hands and into an opulently painted purple-and-green stone lamp. "We meet again."

As Luce's eyes adjusted, the first thing she saw was the writing on the walls: They were painted with the same hieroglyphics as in the hallway, only this time they were prayers to the pharaoh—"*Do not decay. Do not rot. Stride into the Imperishable Stars.*" There were chests that wouldn't close because they overflowed with gold coins and sparkling orange gems. An enormous collection of obelisks spread out before her. At least ten embalmed dogs and cats seemed to eye her.

The chamber was huge. She circled a set of bedroom furniture, complete with a vanity stacked with cosmetics. There was a votive palette with a two-headed serpent chiseled on its face. The interlocking necks formed a recess in the black stone, which held a circle of bright blue eye shadow.

Bill watched Luce pick it up. "Gotta look one's best in the afterlife."

He was sitting atop the head of a startlingly lifelike sculpture of the former pharaoh. Layla's mind told Luce that this sculpture represented the pharaoh's *ka,* his soul, and it would watch over the tomb—the real pharaoh lay mummified behind it. Inside the limestone sarcophagus would be nested wooden coffins; inside the smallest one of them: the embalmed pharaoh.

"Watch out," Bill said. Luce hadn't even realized she was resting her hands on a small wooden chest. "That contains the pharaoh's entrails."

Luce jerked away and slid the starshot out from her dress. When she picked it up, its shaft warmed her fingers. "Is this really going to work?"

"If you pay attention and do as I say," Bill said. "Now, the soul resides directly in the center of your being. To reach it, you must draw the blade precisely down the middle of your chest, right at the critical moment, right when Daniel kisses you and you feel yourself start to cook. Then you, Lucinda Price, will be flung out of your past self, as usual, but your cursed soul will be trapped in Layla's body, where it will burn up and be gone."

"I'm—I'm afraid."

"Don't be. It's like having your appendix out. You're better off without it." Bill looked at his empty gray wrist. "By my watch, Don will be here any moment."

Luce held the silver arrow so that its blade pointed at

her breast. The swirling etched designs tingled under her fingers. Her hands quaked with nerves.

"Steady now." Bill's earnest call sounded far away.

Luce was trying to pay attention, but her heart was pounding in her ears. She had to do this. She had to. For Daniel. To free him from a punishment he'd taken on only because of her.

"You'll have to do it a lot faster than that during the real thing or Daniel will surely stop you. One quick slit on your soul. You will feel something loosen, a breath of coldness, and then—*bam!*"

"*Layla!*" Don bounded into her sight. The door behind her was still bolted. Where had he come from?

The starshot tumbled from her hands and clattered to the floor. She snatched it up and slipped it back inside her dress. Bill was gone. But Don was—Daniel was right where she wanted him to be.

"What are you doing here?" Her voice broke with the force of having to act surprised to see him.

He didn't seem to hear it. He rushed toward her and wrapped her in his arms. "Saving your life."

"How did you get in?"

"Don't worry about that. No mortal man, no slab of stone can obstruct a love as true as ours. I will always find you."

In his bare, bronzed arms, it was Luce's instinct to feel comforted. But she couldn't right then. Her heart felt ragged and cold. This easy happiness, these feelings of complete trust, every one of the lovely emotions Daniel had shown her how to feel in every life—they were torture to her now.

"Fear not," he whispered. "Let me tell you, love, what happens after this life. You come back, you rise again. Your rebirth is beautiful and real. You come back to me, again and again—"

The light from the lamp flickered and made his violet eyes sparkle. His body was so warm against hers.

"But I die again and again."

"What?" He tilted his head. Even when his physique looked exotic to her, she knew his expressions so well—that bemused adoration when she expressed something he hadn't expected her to understand. "How do you— Never mind. It doesn't matter. What matters is that we will again be together. We will always find each other, always love each other, no matter what. I will never leave you."

Luce fell to her knees on the stone steps. She hid her face in her hands. "I don't know how you can stand it. Over and over again, the same sadness—"

He lifted her up. "The same ecstasy—"

"The same fire that kills everything—"

"The same passion that ignites it all again. You don't know. You can't remember how wonderful—"

"I've seen it. I do know."

Now she had his attention. He didn't seem sure whether or not to believe her, but at least he was listening.

"What if there's no hope of anything ever changing?" she asked.

"There is *only* hope. One day, you will live through it. That absolute truth is the only thing that keeps me going. I will never give up on you. Even if it takes forever." He wiped away her tears with his thumb. "I'll love you with all my heart, in every life, through every death. I will not be bound by anything but my love for you."

"But it's so hard. Isn't it hard for you? Haven't you ever thought, what if . . ."

"One day, our love will conquer this dark cycle. That's worth everything to me."

Luce looked up and saw the love glowing in his eyes. He believed what he was saying. He didn't care if he suffered again and again; he'd forge on, losing her over and over, buoyed by the hope that one day this wouldn't be their end. He knew it was doomed, but he tried over and over again anyway, and he always would.

His commitment to her, to them, touched a part of her that she'd thought she'd given up on.

She still wanted to argue: This Daniel didn't know the challenges coming their way, the tears they would shed over the ages. He didn't know that she'd seen him in his moments of deepest desperation. What the pain of her deaths would do to him.

But then—

Luce knew. And that made all the difference in the world.

Daniel's lowest moments had terrified her, but things had changed. All along, she'd felt bound to their love, but now she knew how to protect it. Now she had seen their love from so many different angles. She understood it in a way she'd never thought she would. If Daniel ever faltered, *she* could raise *him* up.

She had learned how to do it from the best: from Daniel. Here she was, about to *kill her soul,* about to take away their love permanently, and five minutes alone with him brought her back to life.

Some people spent their entire lives looking for love like this.

Luce had had it all along.

The future held no starshot for her. Only Daniel. Her Daniel, the one she'd left in her parents' backyard in Thunderbolt. She had to go.

"Kiss me," she whispered.

He was seated on the steps with his knees parted just enough to let her body slide between them. She sank to her knees and faced him. Their foreheads were touching. The tips of their noses.

Daniel took her hands. He seemed to want to tell her something, but he could not find the words.

"Please," she begged, her lips edging toward his. "Kiss me and set me free."

Daniel lunged for her, swooping her up and laying her sideways across his lap to cradle her in his arms. His lips found hers. They were as sweet as nectar. She moaned as a deep current of joy flowed through her, every inch of her. Layla's death was near, she knew that, but she never felt safer or more alive than she did when Daniel held her.

Her hands locked around the back of his neck, feeling the firm sinews of his shoulders, feeling the tiny raised scars protecting his wings. His hands roved up her back, through her long, thick hair. Every touch was rapture, every kiss so wonderful and pure it left her dizzy.

"Stay with me," he pleaded. The muscles in his face had grown tense, and his kisses had become hungrier, more desperate.

He must have sensed Luce's body warming. The heat rising in her core, spreading through her chest and flushing her cheeks. Tears filled her eyes. She kissed him harder. She'd been through this so many times before, but for some reason this felt different.

With a loud *whoosh* he stretched his wings out, and then deftly wrapped them tight around her, a cradle of soft white holding the two of them fast.

"You really believe it?" she whispered. "That someday I'll live through this?"

"With all my heart and soul," he said, cupping her face in his hands, pulling his wings tighter around them both. "I will wait for you as long as it takes. I will love you every moment across time."

By then, Luce was broiling hot. She cried out from the pain, thrashing in Daniel's arms as the heat overwhelmed her. She was burning his skin, but he never let her go.

The moment had come. The starshot was tucked inside her dress, and this—right now—was when she would have used it. But she was never going to give up. Not on Daniel. Not when she knew, no matter how hard it got, that he would never give up on her.

Her skin began to blister. The heat was so brutal, she could do nothing but shiver.

And then she could only scream.

Layla combusted, and as the flames engulfed her body, Luce felt her own body and the soul they were sharing untwine, seeking the fastest escape from the unforgiving heat. The column of fire grew taller and wider until it filled the room and the world, until it was everything, and Layla was nothing at all.

※

Luce expected darkness and found light.

Where was the Announcer? Could she still be inside Layla?

The fire blazed on. It did not extinguish. It spread. The flames consumed more and more of the darkness, reaching into the sky as if the great night itself were flammable, until the hot blaze of red and gold was all that Luce could see.

Every other time one of her past selves had died, Luce's release from the flames and into the Announcer had been simultaneous. Something was different, something that was making her see things that couldn't possibly be real.

Wings on fire.

"Daniel!" she cried out. What looked like Daniel's wings soared through waves of flames, catching fire but not smoldering, as if they were *made* of fire. All she could make out were white wings and violet eyes. "Daniel?"

The fire rolled across the darkness like a giant wave across an ocean. It crashed onto an invisible shore and washed furiously over Luce, rushing up her body, over her head, and far behind her.

Then, as if someone had pinched out a candle, there was a quick hiss and everything went black.

A cold wind crept up behind her. Goose bumps spread across her skin. She hugged her body closer, drawing up her knees and realizing with a jolt of surprise that no ground held up her feet. She wasn't flying exactly, just hovering, directionless. This darkness was not an Announcer. She had not used the starshot, but had she somehow . . . died?

She was afraid. She didn't know where she was, only that she was alone.

No. There was someone else. A scraping sound. A dim gray light.

"Bill!" Luce shouted at the sight of him, so relieved she began to laugh. "Oh, thank God. I thought I was lost—I thought— Oh, never mind." She took a deep breath. "I couldn't do it. I couldn't kill my soul. I'll find another way to break the curse. Daniel and I—we won't give up on each other."

Bill was far away, but floating toward her, making loops in the air. The nearer he got, the larger he appeared, swelling until he was two, then three, then ten times the size of the small stone gargoyle she had traveled with. Then the real metamorphosis began:

Behind his shoulders, a pair of thicker, fuller, jet-black wings burst forth, shattering his familiar small stone wings into a chaos of broken bits. The wrinkles on his forehead deepened and expanded across his entire body until he looked horrifically shriveled and old. The claws on his feet and hands grew longer, sharper, yellower.

They glinted in the darkness, razor-sharp. His chest swelled, sprouting thick, curly black hairs as he grew infinitely larger than he had been before.

Luce strained to suppress the wail climbing in her throat. And she managed—right up until Bill's stony gray eyes, their irises dulled beneath layers of cataracts, glowed as red as fire.

Then she screamed.

"You always *did* make the wrong choice." Bill's voice had turned monstrous, deep and phlegm-filled and grating, not just on Luce's ears but on her very soul. His breath punched her, reeking of death.

"You're—" Luce could not finish her sentence. There was only one word for the evil creature before her, and the idea of saying it aloud was frightening.

"The bad guy?" Bill cackled. "Surprise!" He held out the *I* sound of the word so long that Luce was sure he would double over and cough, but he didn't.

"But—you taught me so much. You helped me figure out— Why would you— How— The *whole* time?"

"I was deceiving you. It's what I *do*, Lucinda."

She had cared for Bill, roguish and disgusting as he was. She'd confided in him, listened to him, had almost killed her soul because he'd told her to. The thought cut her. She had almost lost Daniel because of Bill. She might lose Daniel still because of Bill. But he wasn't Bill—

He was no mere demon, not like Steven, or even Cam at his worst.

He was Evil incarnate.

And he had been with Luce, breathing down her neck the whole time.

She tried to turn away from him, but his darkness was everywhere. It looked as if she were floating in a night sky, but all the stars were impossibly far away; there was no sign of Earth. Close by were patches of darker blackness, swirling abysses. And every now and then a shaft of light appeared, a beacon of hope, illumination. Then the light would vanish.

"Where are we?" she asked.

Satan sneered at the pointlessness of her question. "Neverwhere," he said. His voice no longer had the familiar tone of her traveling companion. "The dark heart of nothing at the center of everything. Neither Heaven, nor Earth, nor Hell. A place of the darkest transits. Nothing your mind at this stage can fathom, so it probably just looks"—his red eyes bulged—"*scary* to you."

"What about those flashes of light?" Luce asked, trying not to let on just how frightening the place did look to her. She'd seen at least four flashes of light already, brilliant conflagrations igniting out of nowhere, vanishing fast into darker regions in the sky.

"Oh, those." Bill watched one as it blazed and disappeared over Luce's shoulder. "Angel travel. Demon travel. Busy night, isn't it? Everyone seems to be going somewhere."

"Yes." Luce had been waiting for another burst of light in the sky. When it came, it cast a shadow across her, and she clawed at it, desperate to shake out an Announcer before the light disappeared. "Including me."

The Announcer expanded rapidly in her hands, so

heavy and urgent and lithe that, for a moment, she thought she might make it.

Instead she felt a scabrous grip around her sides. Bill had her entire body nestled in his grimy claw. "I'm just not ready to say goodbye yet," he whispered in a voice that made her shiver. "See, I've grown so fond of you. No, wait, that's not it. I have *always* been . . . fond of you."

Luce let the shadow in her fingers wisp away into nothing.

"And like all beloveds, I need you in my presence, especially now, so you don't corrupt my designs. Again."

"At least now you've given me a goal," Luce said, straining against his grasp. It was no use. He gripped her tighter, squeezing her bones.

"You always did have an inner fire. I love that about you." He smiled, and it was a terrible thing. "If only your spark *stayed* inside, hmm? Some people are just unlucky in love."

"Don't talk to me about love," Luce spat. "I can't believe I ever listened to a word that came out of your mouth. You don't know a thing about love."

"I've heard *that* one before. And I happen to know one important thing about love: You think yours is bigger than Heaven and Hell and the fate of all that rests between. But you're wrong. Your love for Daniel Grigori is less than insignificant. It is *nothing!*"

His shout was like a shock wave that blew back Luce's hair. She gasped and struggled for air. "Say whatever you want. I love Daniel. I always will. And it has nothing to do with you."

Satan held her up to his red eyes, pinching her skin with his sharpest pointer claw. "I know you love him. You're a *fool* for him. Just tell me why."

"Why?"

"Why. Why *him*? Put it into words. Really make me *feel* it. I want to be moved."

"A million reasons. I just do."

His snaggletoothed smile deepened, and a sound like a thousand growling dogs came from deep inside him. "That was a test. You failed, but it isn't your fault. Not really. That is an unfortunate side effect of the curse you bear. You don't get to make choices anymore."

"That's not true. If you remember, I just made a big choice *not* to kill my soul."

That angered him—she could see it in the way his nostrils flared, the way he reached up and balled his claw into a fist and made a patch of the starry sky go out like a light switch had been flicked somewhere. But he said nothing for the longest time. Just stared away into the night.

A horrible thought struck Luce. "Were you even telling the truth? What would really have happened if I'd used the starshot to—" She shuddered, sickened that she'd come so close. "What's in all this for you? You want me out of the picture or something so you can get to Daniel? Is that why you would never show yourself in front of him? Because he would have gone after you and—"

Satan chuckled. His laughter dimmed the stars. "You think *I'm* scared of Daniel Grigori? You *do* think very highly of him. Tell me, what kind of wild lies has he been filling your head with about his grandiose place in Heaven?"

"You're the liar," Luce said. "You've done nothing but lie from the moment I met you. No wonder the whole universe despises you."

"Fears. Not *despises*. There's a difference. Fear has envy in it somewhere. You may not believe it, but there are many who wish to wield the power that I wield. Who . . . adore me."

"You're right. I don't believe you."

"You just don't know enough. About anything. I've taken you on a tour of your past—shown you the futility of this existence, hoping to awaken you to the truth, and all I get from you is 'Daniel! I want Daniel!' "

He flung her down and she fell into blackness, coming to a stop only when he glared at her, as if he could fix her in place. He moved in a tight circle around her, his hands behind his back, his wings drawn tight, his head tilted toward the sky. "Everything you see here is everything there is to see. From far away, yes, but it's all there—all the lives and worlds and more, far beyond the weak conception of mortals. Look at it."

She did, and it looked different than it had before. The veldt of stars was endless, the dark of night folded again and again over so many bright spots that the sky was more light than black. "It's beautiful."

"It's about to be a tabula rasa." His lips curled into a twisted smile. "I've grown tired of this game."

"This is all a game to you?"

"It's a game to *him*." He swept his hand across the sky and left a dark swath of night in his wake. "And I refuse to concede it to that Other simply because of a cosmic scale. Simply because our sides are in balance."

"Balance. You mean, the scale between the fallen angels who allied themselves with you, and those who allied themselves with—"

"Don't say it. But yes, that *other*. Right now there is a balance, and—"

"And one more angel has to side," Luce said, remembering the long talk Arriane had given her at the diner in Las Vegas.

"Mmm-hmm. Except this time, I won't leave it to chance. It was a shortsighted goal of mine, the whole starshot bit, but I've seen the error of my ways. I've been plotting. I've been planning. Often while you and some past iteration of Grigori were preoccupied with your

B-grade heavy petting. So, you see, no one will be able to sabotage what I have planned next.

"I'm going to wipe the slate clean. Start over. I can skip the millennia that led up to you and your loophole of a life, *Lucinda Price*"—he snorted—"and begin again. And this time, I will play more wisely. This time I will win."

"What does that mean, 'wipe the slate clean'?"

"All of time is like a grand slate, Lucinda. Nothing is written that can't be erased by one clever sort. It's a drastic move, yes, and it means that I'll be throwing away thousands of years. A big setback for everyone concerned—but hey, what's a handful of lost millennia in the yawning concept of eternity?"

"How can you do that?" she said, knowing he could feel her tremble in his grasp. "What does it mean?"

"It means I'm going back to the beginning. To the Fall. To all of us being cast out of Heaven because we dared to exercise free will. I'm talking about the first great injustice."

"Reliving your greatest hits?" she said, but he wasn't listening, lost in the details of his scheme.

"You and the tiresome Daniel Grigori will make the trip with me. In fact, your soul mate is on his way there now."

"Why would Daniel—"

"I showed him the way, of course. Now all I have to

do is get there in time to see the angels cast out and begin their fall to Earth. What a beautiful moment that will be."

"When they *begin* their fall? How long did it take?"

"Nine days by some accounts," he murmured, "but it seemed an eternity to those of us cast out. You never asked your friends about it? Cam. Roland. Arriane. Your precious Daniel? All of us were there."

"So you see it happen again. So what?"

"So then I do something unexpected. And do you know what that is? " He snickered, and his red eyes gleamed.

"I don't know," she said softly. "Kill Daniel?"

"Not kill. *Catch.* I'm going to catch every last one of us. I'll open up an Announcer like a great net, casting it to the forward edge of time. Then I'll cleave to my old self and spirit the full host of angels into the present with me. Even the ugly ones."

"So what?"

"*So what?* We will be once more starting at the beginning. Because the Fall *is* the beginning. It isn't a part of history; it is when history *begins*. And all that has come before? It will no longer have happened."

"No longer have hap— You mean, like that life in Egypt?"

"Never happened."

"China? Versailles? Las Vegas?"

"Never, never, never. But it's more than just you and your boyfriend, selfish child. It's the Roman empire and the so-called Son of that Other. It is the long sad festering of humanity rising from the primordial murk of the earth and turning its world into a cesspool. It is everything that has ever taken place, taken away by a tiny little skip across time, like a stone skipping across water."

"But you can't just . . . erase all of the past!"

"Sure I can. Like shortening a skirt's waistband. Just remove the excess fabric and draw the two parts together and it's like that middle part never existed. We start fresh. The whole cycle will repeat itself, and I'll have another shot at luring in the important souls. Souls like—"

"You will never get him. He will never join your side."

Daniel hadn't given in once across the five thousand years she'd witnessed. No matter that they killed her again and again and denied him his one true love, he would not give in and choose a side. And even if he did somehow lose his resolve, she would be there to support him: She knew now that she was strong enough to carry Daniel if he faltered. Just as he'd carried her.

"No matter how many times you wipe the slate clean," she said, "it won't change a thing."

"Oh." He laughed as if he were embarrassed for Luce—a thick, scary guffaw. "Of course it will. It will change *everything*. Shall I count the ways?" He stuck out a spiky, yellowed claw. "First of all, Daniel and Cam will be brothers again, just as they were in the early days after the Fall. Won't that be fun for you? Worse still: no Nephilim. No time will have passed for angels to walk the earth and copulate with the mortals, so say goodbye to your little friends from school."

"No—"

He snapped his claws. "Oh, one more thing I forgot to mention: Your history with Daniel? That gets erased. So everything you've discovered on your little quest, all those things you so earnestly told me you'd learned in between our jaunts in the past? You can kiss them goodbye."

"No! You can't do this!"

He swept her into his cold grasp once more. "Oh, darling—it's practically done." He cackled, and his laughter sounded like an avalanche as time and space folded around the two of them. Luce shuddered and cringed and fought to loosen his grip, but he had her tucked too tightly, too deeply under his vile wing. She could see nothing, could only feel a rush of wind rip into them and a burst of heat, and then an unshakable chill settling over her soul.

TWENTY

JOURNEY'S END

HEAVEN'S GATE · THE FALL

Of course, there had only ever been one place to find her.

The first one. The beginning.

Daniel tumbled toward the first life, ready to wait there for as long as it would take Luce to make her way there, too. He would take her in his arms, whisper in her ear, *At last. I found you. I will never let you go.*

He stepped from the shadows and froze in blinding brightness.

No. This was not his destination.

This ambrosial air and opalescent sky. This cosmic gulf of adamantine light. His soul constricted at the sight of the waves of white clouds brushing against the black Announcer. There it was, in the distance: the unmistakable three-note hum playing softly, endlessly. The music the Throne of the Ethereal Monarch made purely by radiating light.

No. No! *No!*

He was not supposed to be here. He meant to meet Lucinda in her first incarnation on Earth. How had he landed *here,* of all places?

His wings had instinctively unfurled. The unfolding felt different than it did on Earth—not the vast release of finally letting himself go, but an occurrence as commonplace as breathing was to mortals. He knew that he was glowing, but not in the way he sometimes shone under mortal moonlight. His glory was nothing to hide here, and nothing to show, either. It just was.

It had been so long since Daniel had been home.

It drew him in. It drew them all in, the way the scent of a childhood home—pine trees or homemade cookies, sweet summer rain or the musk of a father's cigar—could do for any mortal. It held a mighty power. This was why Daniel had stayed away these last six thousand years.

He was back now—and not of his own volition.

That cherub!

The pale, wispy angel in his Announcer—he had tricked Daniel.

The pinions of Daniel's wings stood on end. There had been something not quite right about that angel. His Scale brand was too fresh. Still raised and red on the back of his neck, as if it had been freshly carved . . .

Daniel had flown into some sort of trap. He had to leave, no matter what.

Aloft. You were always aloft up here. Always gliding through the purest air. He spread his wings and felt the white mist ripple over him. He soared across the pearly forests, swooping above the Orchard of Knowledge, curving around the Grove of Life. He passed satin-white lakes and the foothills of the shining silver Celeste Mountains.

He'd spent so many happy epochs here.

No.

All that must remain in the recesses of his soul. This was no time for nostalgia.

He slowed and approached the Meadow of the Throne. It was just as he remembered it: the flat plain of brilliant white cloudsoil leading up toward the center of everything. The Throne itself, dazzlingly bright, radiating the warmth of pure goodness, so luminous that, even for an angel, it was impossible to look directly at it. One could not even get close to *seeing* the Creator, who sat upon the Throne clothed in brightness, so the customary synecdoche—calling the whole entity the Throne—was apt.

Daniel's gaze drifted to the arc of rippled silver ledges circling the Throne. Each one was marked with the rank of a different Archangel. This used to be their headquarters, a place to worship, to attend, to call on and deliver messages for the Throne.

There was the lustrous altar that had been his seat, near the top right corner of the Throne. It had been there for as long as the Throne had been in existence.

But there were only seven altars now. Once there had been eight.

Wait—

Daniel winced. He knew he'd come through the Gates of Heaven, but he hadn't thought about precisely *when*. It mattered. The Throne had only been imbalanced like that for a very short period: the sliver of time right after Lucifer stated his plans to defect but before the rest of them had been called upon to choose sides.

He arrived in that blink of a moment after Lucifer's betrayal but before the Fall.

The great rift was coming during which some would side with Heaven and some would side with Hell, when Lucifer would turn into Satan before their eyes, and the Great Arm of the Throne would sweep legions of them off the surface of Heaven and send them plummeting.

He drew nearer to the Meadow. The harmonious note grew louder, as did the choral buzz of angels. The Meadow was glowing with the gathering of all the brightest souls. His past self would be down there; all of them were. It was so bright Daniel couldn't see clearly, but his memory told him that Lucifer had been permitted to hold court from his repositioned silver altar at the far end of the Meadow, in direct opposition to—though not nearly as high as—the Throne. The other angels were assembled before the Throne, in the middle of the Meadow.

This was the roll call, the last moment of unity before Heaven lost half its souls. At the time Daniel had wondered why the Throne ever permitted the roll call to occur. Did he who had dominion over everything think Lucifer's appeal to the angels would end in sheer humiliation? How could the Throne have been so wrong?

Gabbe still spoke of the roll call with startling clarity. Daniel could remember little of it—other than the soft brush of a single wing reaching out to him in solidarity. The brush that told him: *You are not alone.*

Could he dare to look upon that wing now?

Perhaps there was a way to go about the roll call differently, so that the curse that befell them afterward did not strike so hard. With a shiver that reached his very core, Daniel realized that he could turn this trap into an opportunity.

Of course! *Someone* had reworked the curse so that there was a way out for Lucinda. The whole time he'd been racing after her, Daniel had assumed it must have been Lucinda herself. That somewhere in her heedless flight backward through time, she'd opened up a loop-hole. But maybe . . . maybe it had been Daniel all along.

He was here now. He could do it. In some sense, he must already have done it. Yes, he'd been chasing its implications through the millennia he'd traveled to get here. What he did here, now, at the very beginning, would ripple forward into every one of her lives. Finally, things were beginning to make sense.

He would be the one to soften the curse, to allow Lucinda to live and travel into her past—it had to have begun here. And it had to have begun with Daniel.

He descended to the plain of cloudsoil, edging along the glowing border. There were hundreds of angels there, thousands, filling it up with lustrous anxiety. The light was astonishing as he slipped in among the crowd. No one perceived his Anachronism; the tension and fear among the angels were too bright.

"The time has come, Lucifer," his Voice called from the Throne. This voice had given Daniel immortality, and all that came with it. "This is truly what you desire?"

"Not just for us, but for our fellow angels," Lucifer was saying. "Free will is deserved by everyone, not just the mortal men and women whom we watch from above." Lucifer appealed now to the angels, burning brighter than the morning star. "The line has been drawn in the cloudsoil of the Meadow. Now you are all free to choose."

The first heavenly scribe stood at the base of the Throne in shimmery incandescence and began to call out the names. It started with the lowest-ranking angel, the seven thousand eight hundred and twelfth son of Heaven:

"Geliel," the scribe called, "last of the twenty-eight angels who govern the mansions of the moon."

That was how it began.

The scribe kept a running tally in the opalescent sky as Chabril, the angel of the second hour of the night, chose Lucifer, and Tiel, the angel of the north wind, chose Heaven, along with Padiel, one of the guardians of childbeds, and Gadal, an angel involved with magical rites for the ill. Some of the angels made lengthy appeals, some of them scarcely said a word; Daniel kept little track of the tally. He was on a quest to find himself, and besides, he already knew how this ended.

He waded through the field of angels, grateful for the time it took to call out all the choices. He had to recognize his own self before he rose up out of the masses and said the naïve words he'd been paying for ever since.

There was commotion in the Meadow—whispering and flashing lights, a grumble of low thunder. Daniel hadn't heard the name called, had not seen the angel float up to declare his choice. He shoved through the souls in front of him to get a better view.

Roland. He bowed before the Throne. "With respect, I am not ready to choose." He looked at the Throne but gestured at Lucifer. "You are losing a son today, and all of us are losing a brother. Many more, it seems, will follow. Please, do not enter lightly into this dark decision. Do not force our family to splinter apart."

Daniel teared up at the sight of Roland's soul—the angel of poetry and music, Daniel's brother and his *friend*—pleading in the white sky.

"You are wrong, Roland," the Throne boomed. "And in defying me, you *have* made your choice. Welcome him to your side, Lucifer."

"No!" Arriane shrieked, and flew up out of the center of brightness to hover beside Roland. "Please, only give him time to understand what his decision means!"

"The decision has been made" was all the Throne said in reply. "I can tell what is in his soul, despite his words—he has already chosen."

A soul brushed up against Daniel's. Hot and stunning, instantly recognizable.

Cam.

"What are you?" Cam whispered. He sensed innately that something was different about Daniel, but there was no way to explain who Daniel really was to an angel who'd never left Heaven, who had no conception of what was to come.

"Brother, do not fret," Daniel pleaded. "It is me."

Cam grasped his arm. "I perceive that, though I see you're also not you." He grimly shook his head. "I trust you are here for a reason. Please. Can you stop this from happening?"

"Daniel." The scribe was calling his name. "Angel of the silent watchers, the Grigori."

No. Not yet. He had not worked out what to say, what to do. Daniel tore through the blinding light of souls around him, but it was too late. His earlier self rose slowly, gazing neither at the Throne nor at Lucifer.

Instead, he was looking into the hazy distance. Looking, Daniel remembered, at her.

"With respect, I will not do this. I will not choose Lucifer's side, and I will not choose the side of Heaven."

A roar went up from the camps of angels, from Lucifer, and from the Throne.

"Instead, I choose love—the thing you have all forgotten. I choose love and leave you to your war. You're wrong to bring this upon us," Daniel said evenly to Lucifer. Then, turning, he addressed the Throne. "All that is good in Heaven and on Earth is born of love. This war is not just. This war is not good. Love is the only thing worth fighting for."

"My child," the rich, steady voice boomed from the Throne. "You misunderstand. I *am* standing firm on my ruling out of love—love for all of my creations."

"No," Daniel said softly. "This war is about pride. Cast me out, if you must. If that is my destiny, I surrender to it, but not to you."

Lucifer's laughter was a foul belch. "You've got the courage of a god, but the mind of a mortal adolescent.

And your punishment shall be that of an adolescent." Lucifer swept his hand to one side. "Hell will not have him."

"And he has already made plain his choice to forsake Heaven," came the disappointed voice from the Throne. "As with all my children, I see what is in your soul. But I do not know now what will become of you, Daniel, nor your love."

"He will not have his *love*!" Lucifer shouted.

"Then you have something to propose, Lucifer?" asked the Throne.

"An example must be made." Lucifer seethed. "Can you not see? The love he speaks of is destructive!" Lucifer grinned as the seeds of his most evil act began to sprout. "So let it destroy the lovers and not the rest of us! She will die!"

Gasps from the angels. It was impossible, the very last thing anyone expected.

"She will die always and forevermore," Lucifer continued, his voice thick with venom. "She will never pass out of adolescence—will die again and again and again at precisely the moment when she remembers your *choice*. So that you will never truly be together. That will be her punishment. And as for you, Daniel—"

"That is sufficient," the Throne said. "Should Daniel choose to stand by his decision, what you propose, Lucifer, will be punishment enough." There was a long, strained pause. "Understand: I do not wish this upon any of my children, but Lucifer is right: An example must be made."

This was the moment when it had to happen, Daniel's chance to open a loophole in the curse. Boldly, he flew upward in the Meadow to hover side by side with his earlier self. Now was the time to change things, to alter the past.

"What is this twinning?" Lucifer seethed. His newly red eyes narrowed at the two Daniels.

The host of angels below Daniel flickered in confusion. His earlier self looked on in wonder. "Why are you here?" he whispered.

Daniel did not wait for anyone to question him further, did not even wait for Lucifer to sit down or for the Throne to recover from this surprise.

"I have come from our future, from millennia of your punishment—"

The sudden bewilderment of the angels was palpable in the heat sent out of their souls. Of course, this was beyond anything any of them could fathom. Daniel could not see the Throne clearly enough to tell what effect his return had on *him,* but Lucifer's soul glowed red-hot with rage. Daniel forced himself to go on:

"I come here to beg clemency. If we must be punished—and my Master, I do not question your decision—please at least remember that one of the great features of your power is your mercy, which is mysterious and large and humbles us all."

"*Mercy?*" Lucifer cried. "After the size of your betrayals? And does your future self regret his choice?"

Daniel shook his head. "My soul is old, but my heart is young," he said, looking at his earlier self, who seemed stunned. Then he gazed at his beloved's soul, beautiful and burning bright. "I cannot be other than what I am, and I am the choices of all my days. I stand by them."

"The choice is made," the Daniels said in unison.

"Then we stand by the punishment meted out," the Throne boomed.

The great light shuddered, and in the long moment of utter silence, Daniel wondered whether he had been right to come forward at all.

Then, at last: "But we will grant your request for mercy."

"No!" Lucifer cried. "Heaven is not the only party wronged!"

"*Quiet!*" The Throne's voice grew louder as he spoke. He sounded tired, and pained, and less certain than Daniel had ever imagined possible. "If one day her soul comes into being without the weight of sacrament having chosen a side for her, then she shall be free to grow and choose for herself, to reenact this moment. To escape the ordained punishment. And in so doing, to put the final test to this love that you claim supersedes the rights of Heaven and family; her choice then will be your redemption or the final seal on your punishment. That is all that can be done."

Daniel bowed down, and his past self bowed down beside him.

"I cannot abide this!" Lucifer bellowed. "They must never! *Never*—"

"It is done," the Voice thundered, as if he had reached his capacity for mercy. "I will not tolerate those who would argue with me on this or any other matter. Begone, all of those who have chosen ill or not chosen at all. The Gates of Heaven are closed to you!"

Something flickered. The brightest light of all suddenly *went out*.

Heaven grew dark and deadly cold.

The angels gasped and shivered, huddling closer together.

Then: silence.

No one moved and no one spoke.

What happened next was unimaginable, even to Daniel, who had already witnessed the whole thing once before.

The sky beneath them shuddered and the white lake brimmed over, sending a fiery surge of steamy white water flooding over everything. The Orchard of Knowledge and the Grove of Life fell into each other, and all of Heaven shook as they shuddered to their deaths.

A silver lightning bolt cracked forth from the Throne and struck the west end of the Meadow. The cloud-soil boiled into blackness, and a pit of the darkest despair opened up like a sinkhole right under Lucifer. With all his impotent rage, he and the angels closest to him—vanished.

As for the angels who had yet to choose, they, too, lost their purchase on Heaven's plains and slid into the abyss. Gabbe was one of them; Arriane and Cam, too, as well as the others dearest to his heart—collateral damage from Daniel's choice. Even his past self, eyes wide, was swept toward the black hole in Heaven and vanished within.

Once again, Daniel could do nothing to stop it from happening.

He knew that a nine-day fugue of tumbling ever downward stood between the fallen and the moment they would reach Earth. Nine days he couldn't afford to spend not finding her. He plunged toward the abyss.

At the edge of nothingness, Daniel looked down and saw a spot of brightness, farther away than the farthest thing imaginable. It was not an angel, but a beast with vast black wings darker than the night. And it was flying toward him, moving *upward*. How?

Daniel had just seen Lucifer at the Judgment up above. He'd fallen *first* and should be far below. Still, it could be no one else. Daniel's vision focused sharply and his wings burned from shoot to tip when he realized that the beast was carrying someone tucked under his wing.

"Lucinda!" he shouted, but the beast had already dropped her.

His whole world stopped.

Daniel did not see where Lucifer went after that because he was diving across the sky toward Luce. The burning of her soul was so bright and so familiar. He shot forward, his wings clasped close to his body so that he fell faster than seemed possible, so fast that the world around him blurred. He reached out and—

She landed in his arms.

Immediately, his wings pulled forward, making a protective shield around her. She seemed startled at first, as if she'd just awakened from a terrible dream, and gazed deeply into his eyes, letting out all the air in her lungs. She touched his cheek, ran her fingers across the tingling ridges of his wings.

"At last." He breathed into her, finding her lips.

"You found me," she whispered.

"Always."

Just below them, the mass of fallen angels lit up the sky like a thousand brilliant stars. They all seemed drawn together by the pull of some unseen force, clinging to one another during the long plunge from Heaven. It was tragic and awe-inspiring. For a moment, they all seemed to hum and burn with a beautiful perfection. As he and Luce watched, a bolt of black lightning darted across the sky and seemed to encircle the bright mass of the falling.

Then everything but Luce and Daniel grew absolutely dark. As if all of the angels, all at once, had tumbled through a pocket in the sky.

EPILOGUE

NO MORE BUT THIS

SAVANNAH, GEORGIA · NOVEMBER 27, 2009

It was the last Announcer Luce wanted to step through for a very long time. When Daniel stretched open the shadow cast by the inexplicable brightening of the stars in that strange, neverwhere sky, Luce did not look back. She held fast to his hand, overcome with relief. She was with Daniel now. Wherever they went would be home.

"Wait," he said before she plunged inside the shadow.

"What is it?"

His lips traced her collarbone. She arched her back

and grabbed the back of his neck and pulled him closer. Their teeth clicked and his tongue found hers and as long as she could stay there like that, she didn't need to breathe.

They left the distant past locked in the kiss—one so long awaited and so passionate it made everything else around Luce go fuzzy. It was a kiss most people dreamed of all their lives. Here was the soul Luce had been searching for ever since she left him in her parents' backyard. And they were still together when Daniel swooped them out of the Announcer under the peaceful drifting of a silver cloud.

"More," she said when at last he pulled away. They were so high up, Luce could see little of the ground below. A swath of moonlit ocean. Tiny white waves crashing against a darkened shore.

Daniel laughed and drew her close again. He couldn't seem to stop smiling. His body felt so good against hers and his skin looked so spectacular under the light of the stars. The more they kissed, the more certain Luce was she'd never get enough. There was little difference—and yet all the difference in the world— between the Daniels she'd met when she visited her other lifetimes and the Daniel pressing his lips to hers now. Finally, Luce could return his kiss without doubting herself, or their love. She felt unbounded happiness. And to think, she had almost given this up.

Reality began to set in. She had failed in her quest to break her and Daniel's curse. She had been tricked, deceived . . . by Satan.

Though she hated to stop kissing, Luce held Daniel's warm face in her hands. She gazed into his violet eyes, trying to draw strength.

"I'm sorry," she said. "For running off like I did."

"Don't be," he said, slowly and with absolute sincerity. "You had to go. It was preordained; it had to happen." He smiled again. "We did what we needed to do, Lucinda."

A jet of warmth shot through her, making her dizzy. "I was starting to think I'd never see you again."

"How many times have I told you that I will always find you?" Then Daniel turned her around so that her back was pressed against his chest. He kissed the nape of her neck and looped his arms around her torso—their flying position—and they were off.

Flying with Daniel was something Luce would never tire of. His white wings extended into the air, beating against the midnight sky as they moved with an unbelievable grace. Moisture from the clouds dotted her forehead and her nose while Daniel's strong arms stayed wrapped around her, making her feel safer and more secure than she'd felt in a long time.

"Look," Daniel said, extending his neck slightly. "The moon."

The orb seemed close enough and large enough for Luce to touch.

They whipped through the air, barely making any noise at all. Luce took a deep breath and widened her eyes in surprise. She knew this air! It was the particular briny ocean breeze of coastal Georgia. She was . . . home. Tears stung her eyes as she thought about her mother and father and her dog, Andrew. How long had she been gone from them? What would it be like when she came back?

"Are we going to my house?" she asked.

"Sleep first," Daniel said. "You've only been gone a few hours as far as your parents are concerned. It's nearly midnight there. We'll swing by first thing in the morning, once you're rested."

Daniel was right: She should rest now and see them in the morning. But if he wasn't taking her to her house, where were they going?

They neared the tree line. The narrow tops of the pines wobbled in the wind, and the empty sandy shores sparkled as they flew over. They were drawing near a small island not far off the coast. Tybee. She'd been there a dozen times as a kid—

And once, more recently . . . a small log cabin with a gabled roof and smoke coming out of its chimney. The red door with the pane of salt-stained glass. The window looking into the small loft. It looked familiar, but Luce was so tired and had been so many places recently that it wasn't until her feet touched down on the soft, silty ground that she recognized the cabin she'd stayed at right after she'd left Sword & Cross.

After Daniel had first told her of their past lives together, after the ugly battle in the cemetery, after Miss Sophia had morphed into something evil and Penn had been killed and all the angels had told Luce that her life was suddenly in danger, she had slept here, alone, for three delirious days.

"We can rest here," Daniel said. "It's a safe haven for the fallen. We have a few dozen of these places scattered around the world."

She should have been thrilled by the prospect of a full night's rest—with Daniel at her side!—but something was nagging at her.

"I need to tell you something." She faced him on the path. An owl hooted from the pine tree and the water lapped along the shore, but otherwise the dark island was quiet.

"I know."

"You know?"

"I saw." Daniel's eyes went stormy gray. "He tricked you, didn't he?"

"Yes!" Luce cried, burning with the shame of it.

"How long was he with you?" Daniel fidgeted, almost as if he were trying to suppress jealousy.

"A long time." Luce winced. "But it gets worse—he's planning something terrible."

"He is always planning something terrible," Daniel muttered.

"No, this was big." She stepped into Daniel's arms and pressed her hands to his chest. "He told me—he said he wanted to wipe the slate clean."

Daniel's grip tightened around her waist. "He said *what*?"

"I didn't understand everything. He said he was going back to the Fall to open up an Announcer and take all the angels with him from that moment straight into the present. He said he was going to—"

"Wipe clean the time between. Wipe clean our existence," Daniel said hoarsely.

"Yes."

"*No.*" He grabbed her hand and pulled her toward the cabin. "They could be spying on us. Sophia. The Outcasts. Anyone. Come inside where it's safe. You must tell me everything he said, Luce, everything."

Daniel practically ripped open the red wooden door of the cabin, bolting it behind them. An instant later, before they could do anything else, a pair of arms engulfed both Luce and Daniel in a giant hug.

"You're safe." The voice broke with relief.

Cam. Luce turned her head to see the demon dressed all in black, like the "uniform" they'd worn at Sword &

Cross. His massive golden wings were pulled back behind his shoulders. They sent sparkles of light reflecting off the walls. His skin was pale and he looked gaunt; his eyes stood out like emeralds.

"We're back," Daniel said warily, clapping Cam on the shoulder. "I'm not sure I would say safe."

Cam's gaze swept carefully over Luce. Why was he here? Why did Daniel seem happy to see him?

Daniel led Luce to the worn wicker rocking chair near the crackling hearth and gestured for her to sit. She collapsed into the chair, and he sat on the arm, resting his hand on her back.

The cabin was as she remembered it: warm and dry and smelling like cinnamon. The narrow canvas cot in the corner where she had slept was neatly made. There was the narrow wooden ladder leading up to the small loft that overlooked the main room. The green lamp still hung from a rafter.

"How did you know to come here?" Daniel asked Cam.

"Roland read something in the Announcers this morning. He thought you might be coming back—and that something else might be developing." Cam eyed Daniel. "Something that affects us all."

"If what Luce says is true, this is not something any of us can take on alone."

Cam tilted his head at Luce. "I know. The others are on their way. I took the liberty of spreading the word."

Just then, in the loft, a window shattered. Daniel and Cam shot to their feet.

"Just us!" Arriane's voice sang down. "We've got Nephilim in tow, so we travel with the grace of a college hockey team."

A great burst of light—gold and silver—from above made the walls of the cabin shudder. Luce jumped to her feet just in time to see Arriane, Roland, Gabbe, Molly, and Annabelle—the girl Luce had realized in Helston was an angel—slowly floating down from the rafters, all with their wings extended. Together they were a myriad of colors: black and gold, white and silver. The colors stood for different sides, but here they were. Together.

A moment later, Shelby and Miles thundered down the wooden ladder. They were still dressed in the clothes—Shelby's green sweater and Miles's jeans and baseball cap—that they'd worn to Thanksgiving dinner, which seemed like an eternity ago.

Luce felt like she was dreaming. It was so wonderful to see these familiar faces right now—faces that she'd truly wondered if she would ever see again. The only people missing were her parents, of course, and Callie, but she would see them soon enough.

Starting with Arriane, the angels and Nephilim all circled Luce and Daniel in another massive hug. Even Annabelle, whom Luce barely knew. Even Molly.

Suddenly, everyone was shouting over everyone else—
Annabelle, batting shimmering pink eyelids: "When

did you get back? We have *so* much to catch up on!"
And Gabbe, kissing Luce on the cheek: "I hope you were
careful . . . and I hope you saw what you needed to see."
And Arriane: "Did you bring us back anything good?"
And Shelby, out of breath: "We were searching for you
for, like, ever. Weren't we, Miles?" And Roland: "Pretty
cool to see you made it home in one piece, kid." And
Daniel, silencing them all with the gravity of his tone:
"Who brought the Nephilim?"

"I did." Molly draped an arm around Shelby and
Miles. "You got something to say about it?"

Daniel cast his eyes over Luce's Shoreline friends.
Before she had a chance to stick up for them, the corners
of his lips pulled upward into a smile, and he said,
"Good. We're going to need all the help we can get.
Everyone sit down."

⽸⽶

"Lucifer can't mean it," Cam said, shaking his
head, stunned. "This is just a desperate last resort. He
wouldn't— He was probably just trying to get Luce to—"

"He would," Roland said.

They were spread out in a circle near the fire, facing
Luce and Daniel on the rocking chair. Gabbe had found
hot dogs and marshmallows and packets of powdered
hot chocolate in the kitchen cupboard and had set up a
little cook station in front of the fire.

"He would rather start again than to lose his pride,"

Molly added. "Besides, he has nothing to lose by erasing the past."

Miles dropped his hot dog and the plate clattered on the hardwood floor. "Wouldn't that mean Shelby and I—wouldn't exist anymore? And what about Luce, where would she be?"

No one answered. Luce felt embarrassingly aware of her nonangelic status. A hot flush spread across the tops of her shoulders.

"How are we still here if time has been rewritten?" Shelby asked.

"Because they haven't finished their fall yet," Daniel said. "When they do, the act is done and can't be stopped."

"So we have—" Arriane counted under her breath. "Nine days."

"Daniel?" Gabbe looked up at him. "Tell us what we can do."

"There is only one thing to do," Daniel said. All the glowing wings in the cabin pulled toward him in expectation. "We must draw everyone to the place where the angels first fell."

"Which is where?" Miles asked.

No one spoke for a very long time.

"It's hard to say," Daniel finally answered. "It happened long ago, and we were all new to Earth. But"—he glanced at Cam—"we do have means of figuring it out."

Cam whistled lowly. Was he afraid?

"Nine days isn't a lot of time to locate the site of the Fall," Gabbe said. "Let alone figure out how to stop Lucifer if and when we do arrive."

"We have to try." Luce answered without thinking, surprised by her own certainty.

Daniel scanned the gathering of angels, the so-called demons, and the Nephilim. His gaze encompassed them all, his family. "We're in this together, then? All of us?" At last, his eyes rested on Luce.

And though she couldn't imagine tomorrow, Luce stepped into Daniel's arms and said, "Always."

RAPTURE

THE FINAL BOOK IN THE FALLEN SERIES

SPRING 2012

WWW.FALLENBOOKS.COM

DELACORTE PRESS

LAUREN KATE is the internationally bestselling author of *The Betrayal of Natalie Hargrove* and the FALLEN novels: *Fallen, Torment, Passion,* and the forthcoming *Rapture.* Her books have been translated into more than thirty languages. She lives in Los Angeles with her husband. You can visit her online at:

laurenkatebooks.net